"THIS FUTURE SUCKS!"
-RANMA

IMAGE COMICS, INC. • **Robert Kirkman:** Chief Operating Officer • **Erik Larsen:** Chief Financial Officer • **Todd McFarlane:** President • **Marc Silvestri:** Chief Executive Officer • **Jim Valentino:** Vice President • **Eric Stephenson:** Publisher / Chief Creative Officer • **Jeff Boison:** Director of Publishing Planning & Book Trade Sales • **Chris Ross:** Director of Digital Sales • **Jeff Stang:** Director of Direct Market Sales • **Kat Salazar:** Director of PR & Marketing • **Drew Gill:** Cover Editor • **Heather Doornink:** Production Director • **Nicole Lapalme:** Controller • IMAGECOMICS.COM

• **Deanna Phelps:** Production Artist for CROWDED •

CROWDED, VOL. 1, Second printing. November 2019. Published by Image Comics, Inc. Office of publication: 2701 NW Vaughn St., Suite 780, Portland, OR 97210. Copyright © 2019 Christopher Sebela, Ro Stein, Ted Brandt, Triona Farrell, Cardinal Rae & Juliette Capra. All rights reserved. Contains material originally published in single magazine form as CROWDED #1-6. "Crowded," its logos, and the likenesses of all characters herein are trademarks of Christopher Sebela, Ro Stein, Ted Brandt, Triona Farrell, Cardinal Rae & Juliette Capra, unless otherwise noted. "Image" and the Image Comics logos are registered trademarks of Image Comics, Inc. No part of this publication may be reproduced or transmitted, in any form or by any means (except for short excerpts for journalistic or review purposes), without the express written permission of Christopher Sebela, Ro Stein, Ted Brandt, Triona Farrell, Cardinal Rae & Juliette Capra, or Image Comics, Inc. All names, characters, events, and locales in this publication are entirely fictional. Any resemblance to actual persons (living or dead), events, or places, without satirical intent, is coincidental. Printed in the USA. For information regarding the CPSIA on this printed material call: 203-595-3636. For international rights, contact: foreignlicensing@imagecomics.com. ISBN: 978-1-5343-1054-4.

VOLUME ONE
SOFT APOCALYPSE

CHRISTOPHER SEBELA
::.SCRIPT + DESIGN.::

RO STEIN + TED BRANDT
::.LINE ART.::

TRIONA FARRELL
::.COLORS.::

CARDINAL RAE
::.LETTERS.::

JULIETTE CAPRA
::.EDITS.::

DYLAN TODD
::.LOGO.::

KATIE O'MEARA
HOLLEY MCKEND
ALBERTO HERNANDEZ
::.COLOR FLATTING.::

::.CR̶̶̶̶̶̶̶̶̶̶̶̶̶̶̶̶̶̶̶̶̶̶L, RAE & CAPRA.::

CHAPTER ONE

WELCOME TO THE WORKING WEEK

YOU ARE NOW CONNECTED WITH YOUR NEXT POTENTIAL DFENDER. ALL CONTRACTS MADE OUTSIDE DFEND™ ARE NOT COVERED UNDER TERMS OF SERVICE AND UNINSURED FOR LIABILITY. PLEASE PROCEED WITH CAUTION.
hello?????
hi hi hey are you free like right now?
No. But I can be in 30. That work for your schedule?
if im still alive in 30 ducking minutes
ducking
DUCKING
FUCKING!!
Be at the AutoMac on Ivar in 30 minutes. Do not be late.
...
Dfender for 2 yrs. Licensed & Bonded.
18 minutes [2.3 mi away]
ViS
CONTACT
RESERVE
Select DFEND package
• Pay by-the-hour (subject to surge rate)
• Half-day block (fixed price)
• 1 day package (fixed price)
DFENDER DETAILS

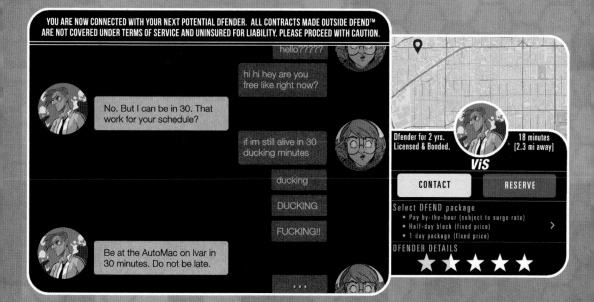

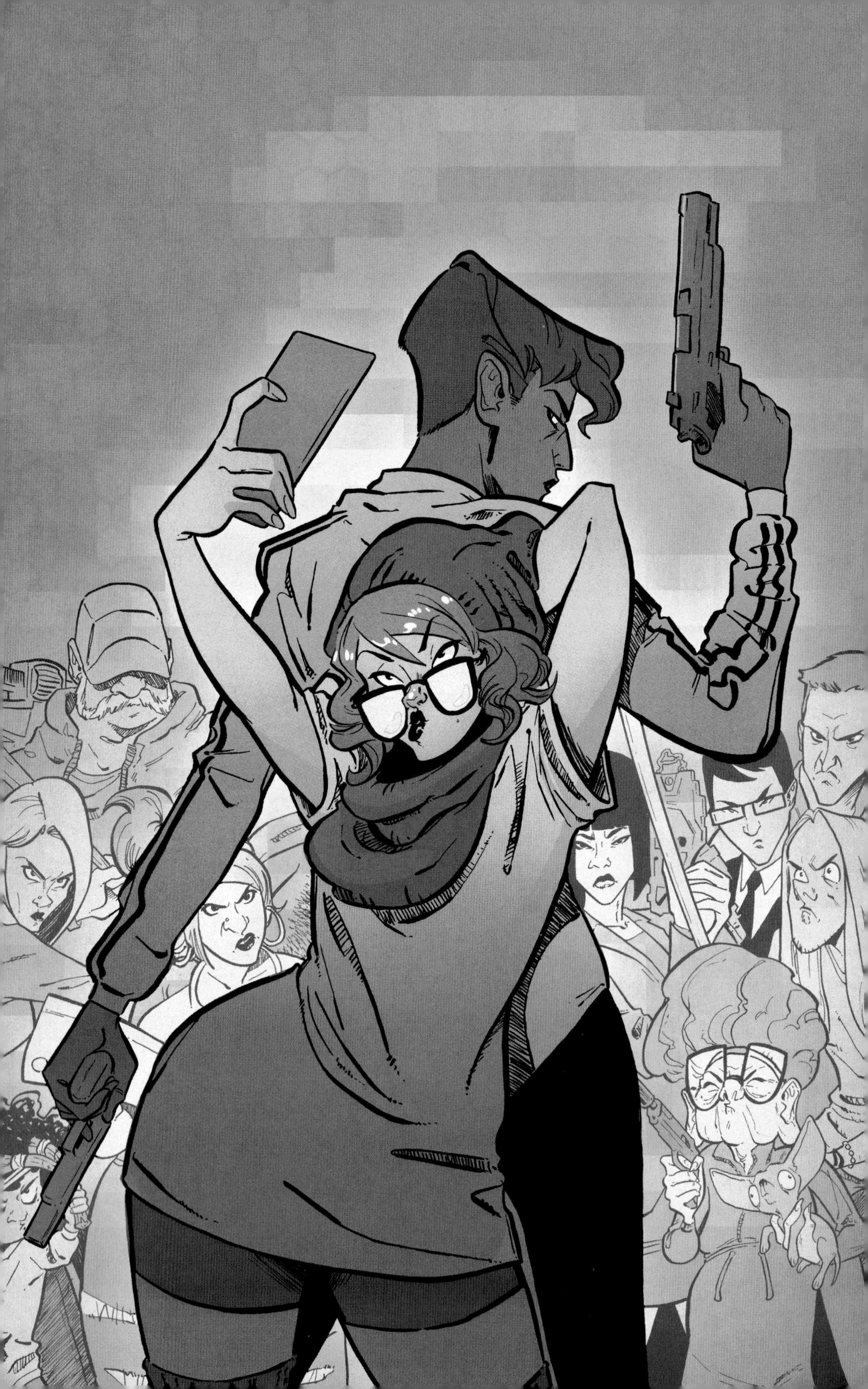

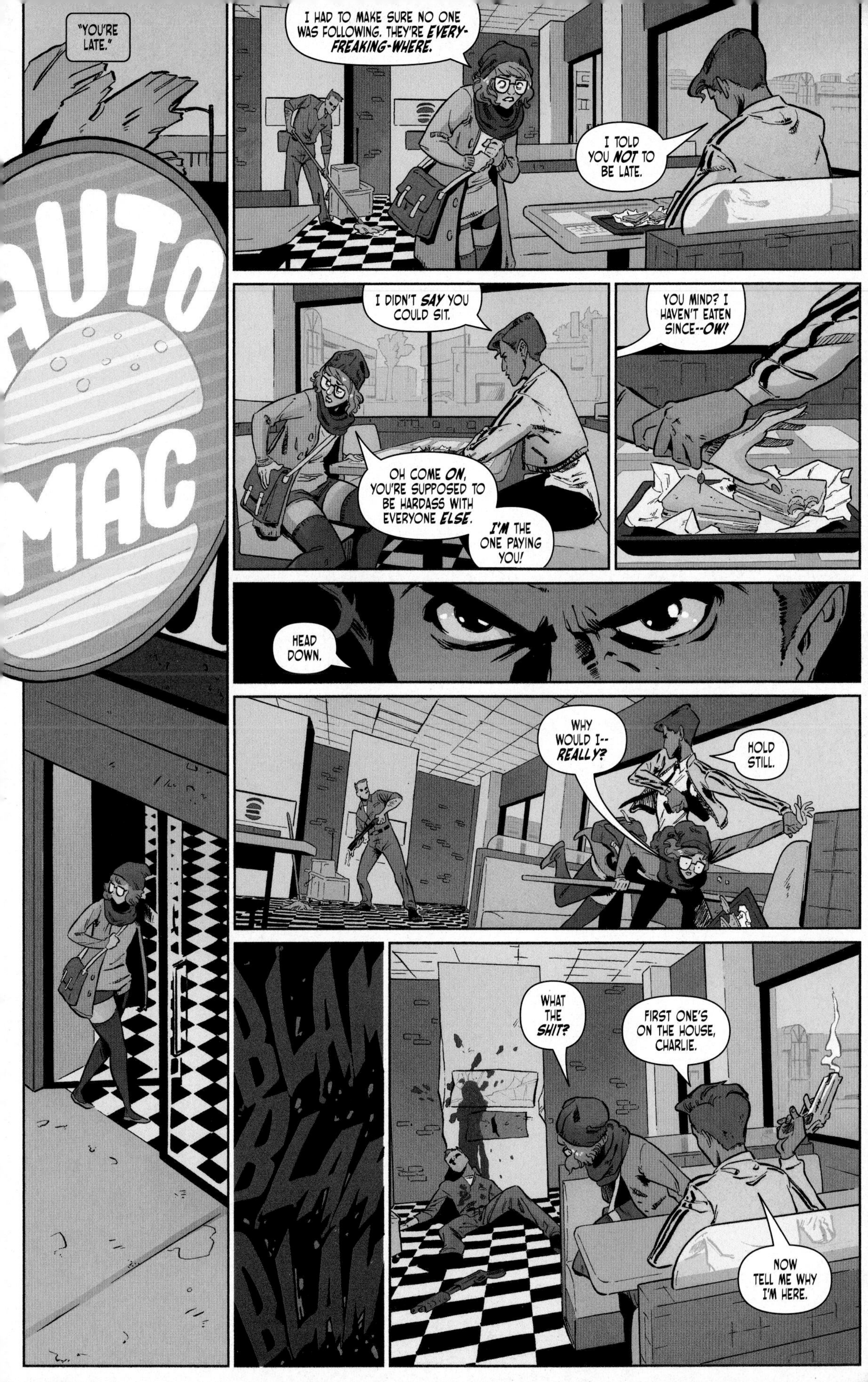
"YOU'RE LATE."
AUTO MAC
I HAD TO MAKE SURE NO ONE WAS FOLLOWING. THEY'RE EVERY-FREAKING-WHERE.
I TOLD YOU NOT TO BE LATE.
I DIDN'T SAY YOU COULD SIT.
OH COME ON, YOU'RE SUPPOSED TO BE HARDASS WITH EVERYONE ELSE.
I'M THE ONE PAYING YOU!
YOU MIND? I HAVEN'T EATEN SINCE--OW!
HEAD DOWN.
WHY WOULD I-- REALLY?
HOLD STILL.
BLAM BLAM BLAM
WHAT THE SHIT?
FIRST ONE'S ON THE HOUSE, CHARLIE.
NOW TELL ME WHY I'M HERE.

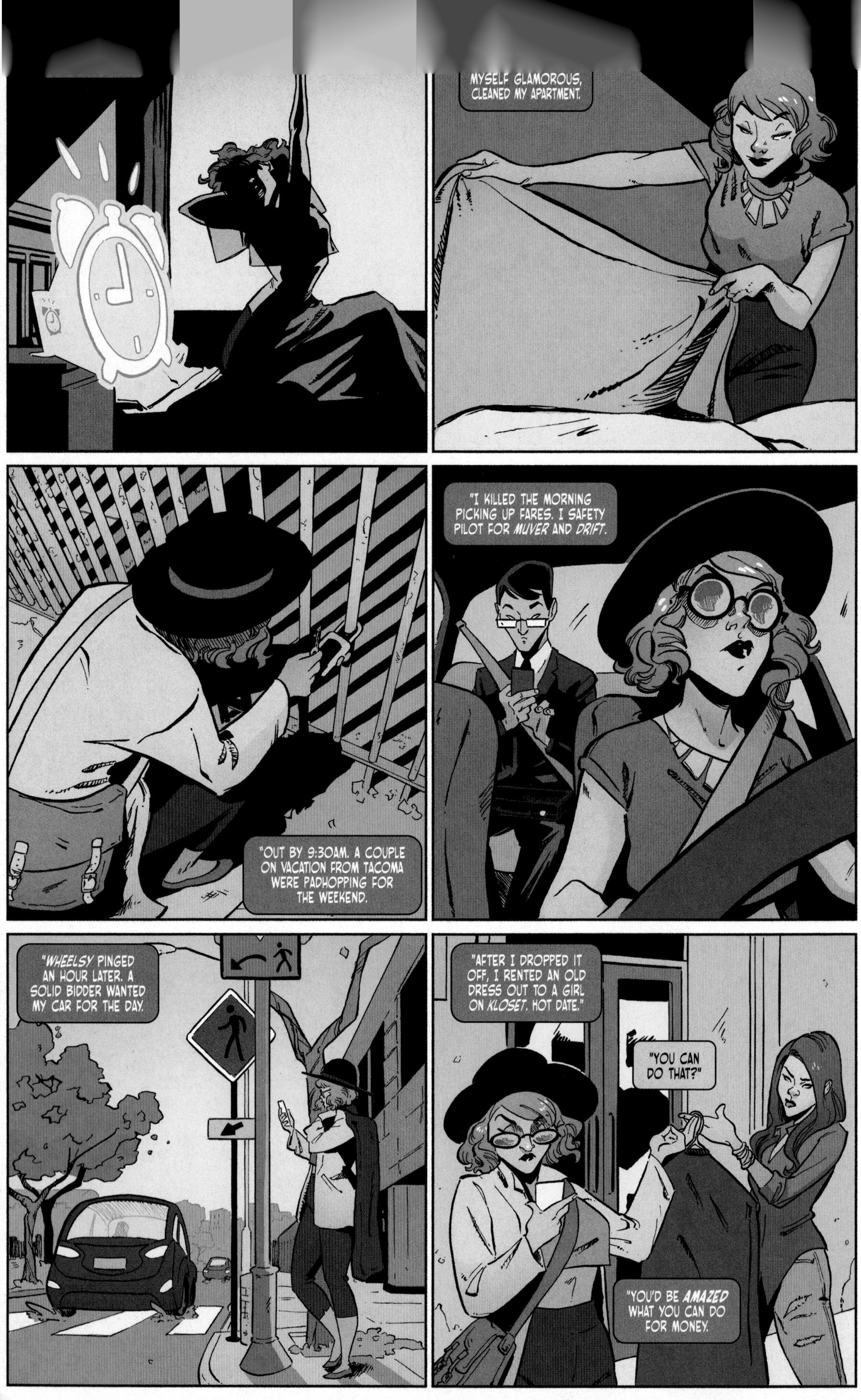
MYSELF GLAMOROUS, CLEANED MY APARTMENT.
"OUT BY 9:30AM. A COUPLE ON VACATION FROM TACOMA WERE PADHOPPING FOR THE WEEKEND.
"I KILLED THE MORNING PICKING UP FARES. I SAFETY PILOT FOR *MUVER* AND *DRIFT*.
"*WHEELSY* PINGED AN HOUR LATER. A SOLID BIDDER WANTED MY CAR FOR THE DAY.
"AFTER I DROPPED IT OFF, I RENTED AN OLD DRESS OUT TO A GIRL ON *KLOSET*. HOT DATE."
"YOU CAN DO THAT?"
"YOU'D BE ***AMAZED*** WHAT YOU CAN DO FOR MONEY.

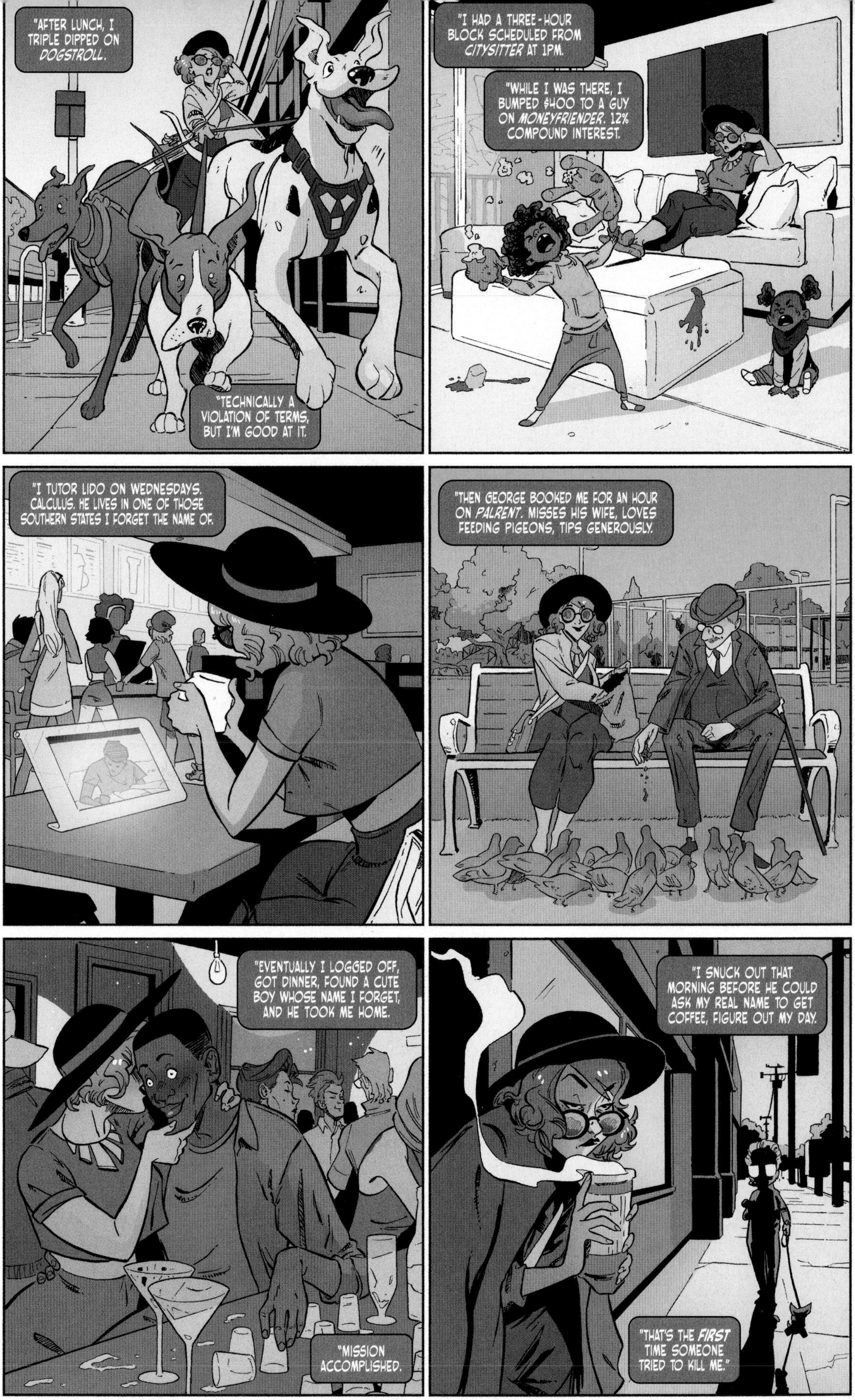

"AFTER LUNCH, I TRIPLE DIPPED ON DOGSTROLL.
"TECHNICALLY A VIOLATION OF TERMS, BUT I'M GOOD AT IT.
"I HAD A THREE-HOUR BLOCK SCHEDULED FROM CITYSITTER AT 1PM.
"WHILE I WAS THERE, I BUMPED $400 TO A GUY ON MONEYFRIENDER. 12% COMPOUND INTEREST.
"I TUTOR LIDO ON WEDNESDAYS. CALCULUS. HE LIVES IN ONE OF THOSE SOUTHERN STATES I FORGET THE NAME OF.
"THEN GEORGE BOOKED ME FOR AN HOUR ON PALRENT. MISSES HIS WIFE, LOVES FEEDING PIGEONS, TIPS GENEROUSLY.
"EVENTUALLY I LOGGED OFF, GOT DINNER, FOUND A CUTE BOY WHOSE NAME I FORGET, AND HE TOOK ME HOME.
"MISSION ACCOMPLISHED.
"I SNUCK OUT THAT MORNING BEFORE HE COULD ASK MY REAL NAME TO GET COFFEE, FIGURE OUT MY DAY.
"THAT'S THE FIRST TIME SOMEONE TRIED TO KILL ME."

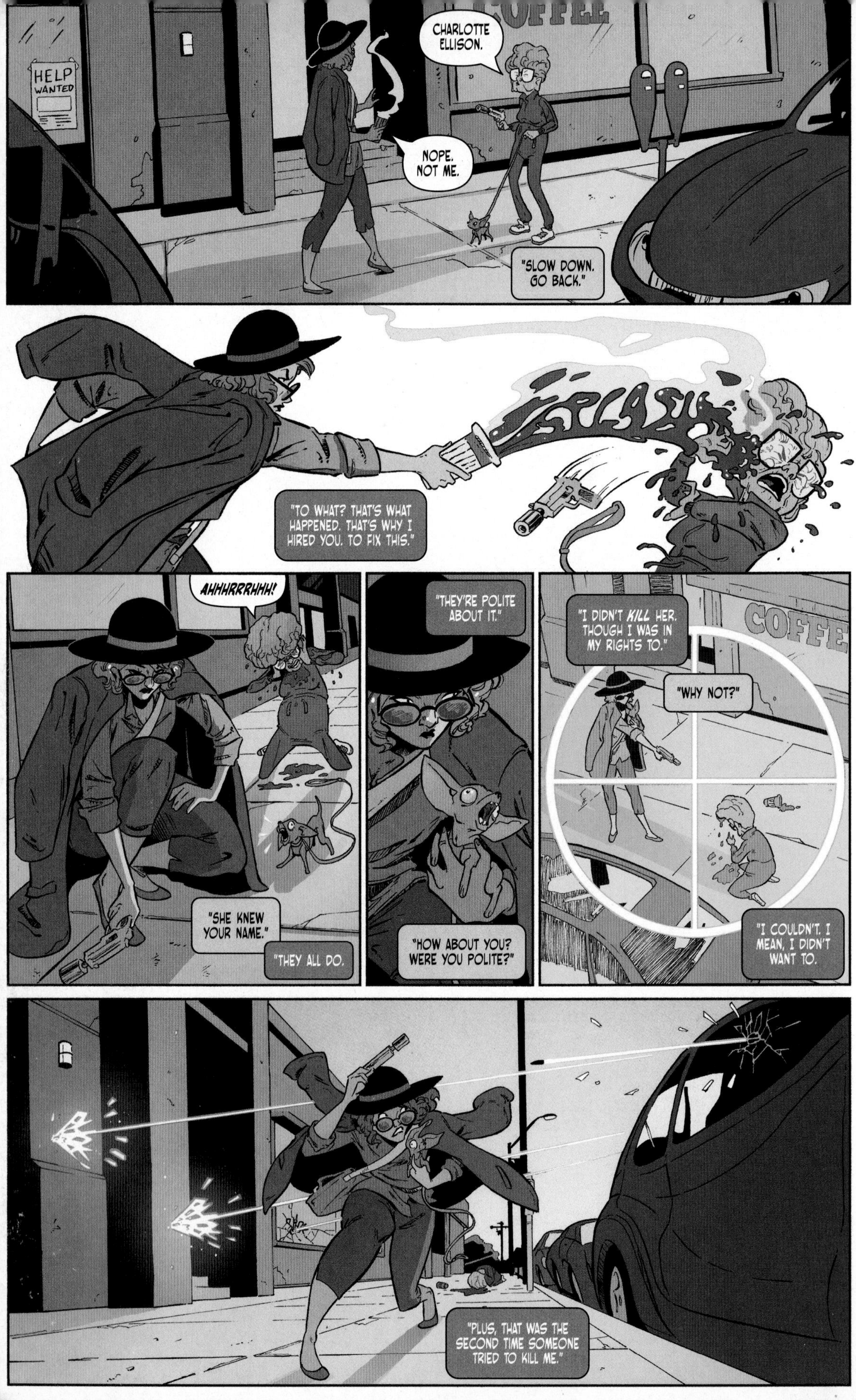
COFFEE
HELP WANTED
CHARLOTTE ELLISON.
NOPE. NOT ME.
"SLOW DOWN. GO BACK."
SPLASH
"TO WHAT? THAT'S WHAT HAPPENED. THAT'S WHY I HIRED YOU. TO FIX THIS."
AHHHRRRHHH!
"SHE KNEW YOUR NAME."
"THEY ALL DO.
"THEY'RE POLITE ABOUT IT."
"HOW ABOUT YOU? WERE YOU POLITE?"
COFFE
"I DIDN'T KILL HER. THOUGH I WAS IN MY RIGHTS TO."
"WHY NOT?"
"I COULDN'T. I MEAN, I DIDN'T WANT TO.
"PLUS, THAT WAS THE SECOND TIME SOMEONE TRIED TO KILL ME."

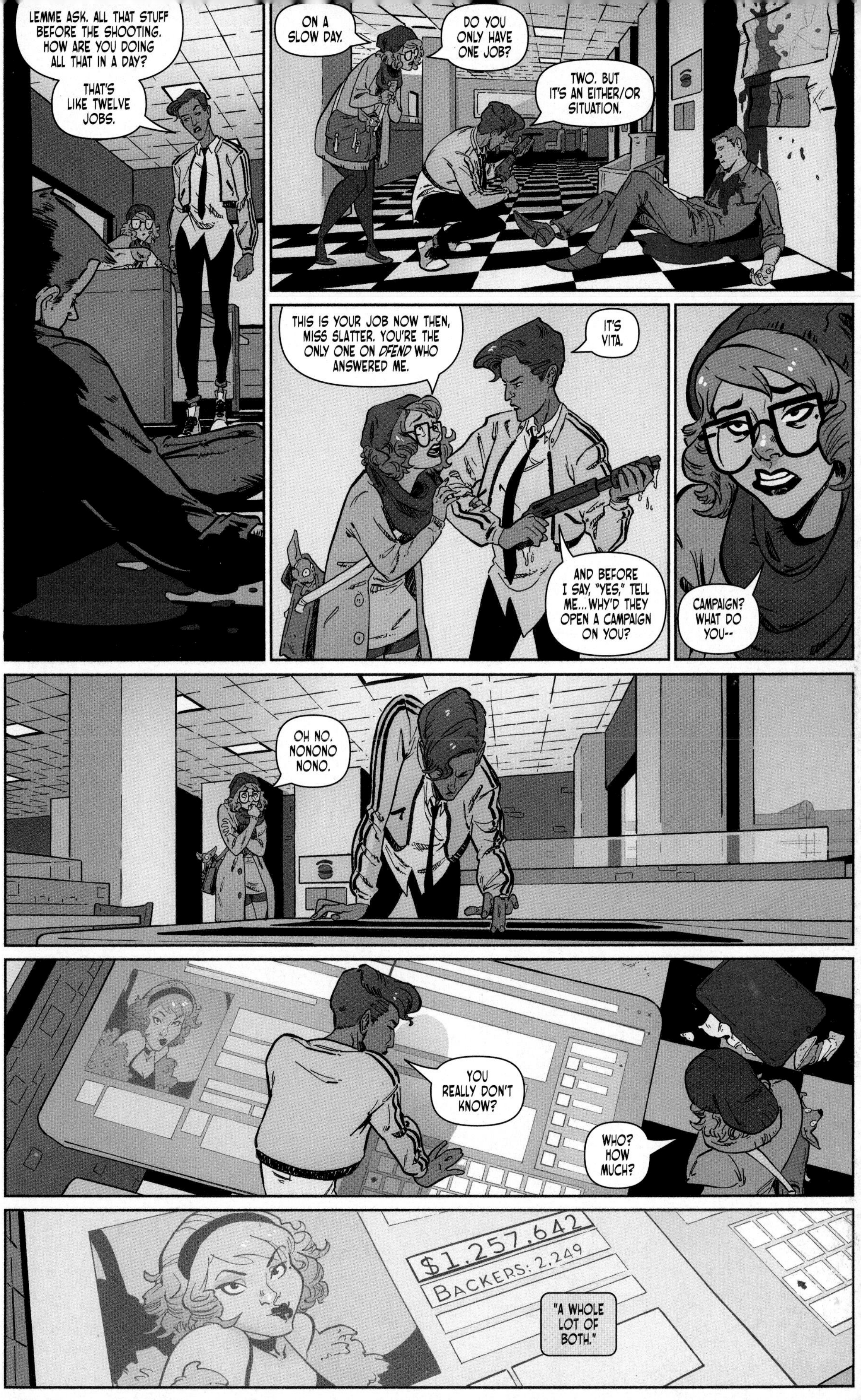
LEMME ASK. ALL THAT STUFF BEFORE THE SHOOTING. HOW ARE YOU DOING ALL THAT IN A DAY?
THAT'S LIKE TWELVE JOBS.
ON A SLOW DAY.
DO YOU ONLY HAVE ONE JOB?
TWO. BUT IT'S AN EITHER/OR SITUATION.
THIS IS YOUR JOB NOW THEN, MISS SLATTER. YOU'RE THE ONLY ONE ON *DFEND* WHO ANSWERED ME.
IT'S VITA.
AND BEFORE I SAY, "YES," TELL ME...WHY'D THEY OPEN A CAMPAIGN ON YOU?
CAMPAIGN? WHAT DO YOU--
OH NO. NONONO NONO.
YOU REALLY DON'T KNOW?
WHO? HOW MUCH?
$1,257,642
BACKERS: 2,249
"A WHOLE LOT OF BOTH."

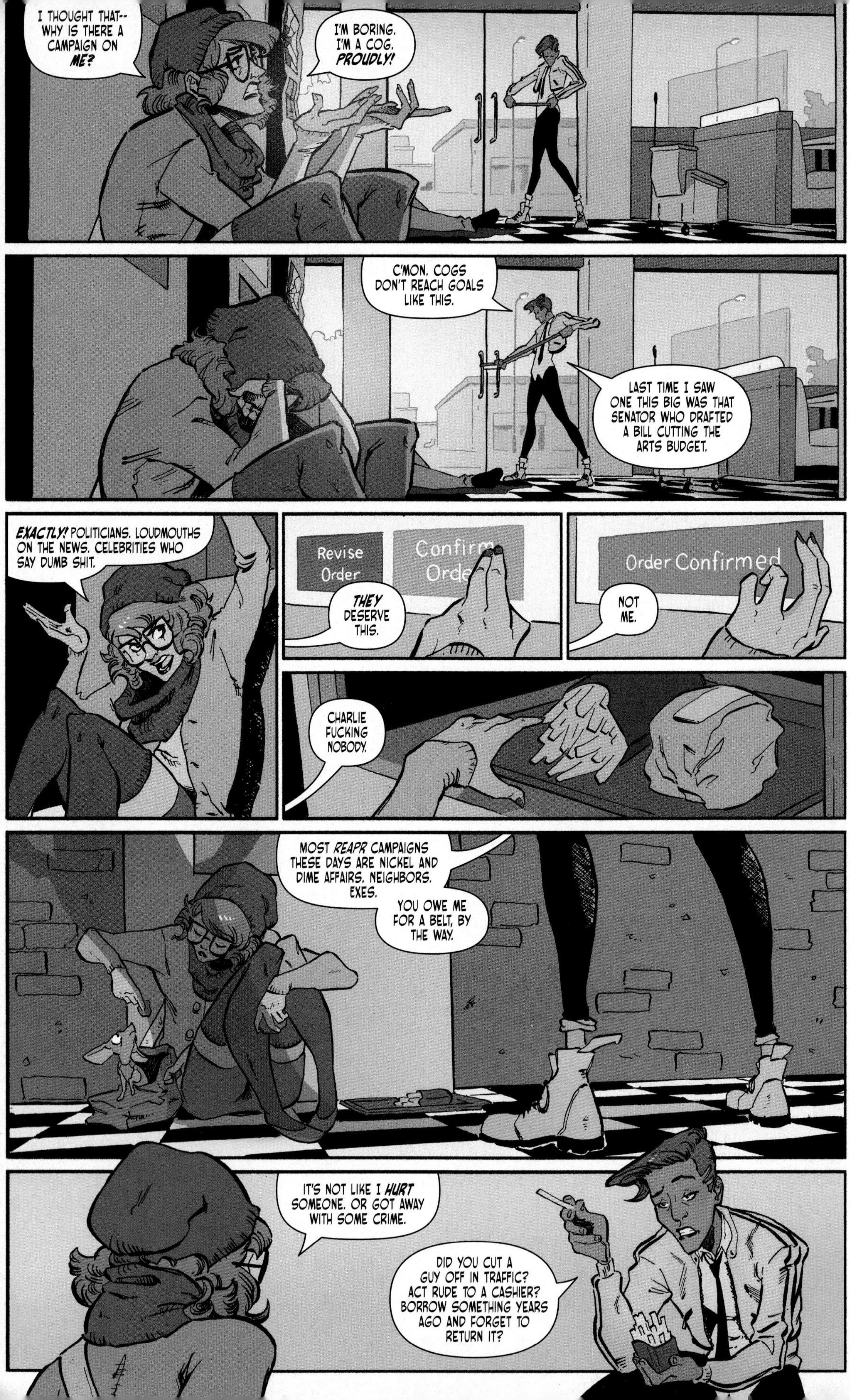
I THOUGHT THAT-- WHY IS THERE A CAMPAIGN ON *ME?*
I'M BORING. I'M A COG. *PROUDLY!*
C'MON. COGS DON'T REACH GOALS LIKE THIS.
LAST TIME I SAW ONE THIS BIG WAS THAT SENATOR WHO DRAFTED A BILL CUTTING THE ARTS BUDGET.
EXACTLY! POLITICIANS. LOUDMOUTHS ON THE NEWS. CELEBRITIES WHO SAY DUMB SHIT.
Revise Order
Confirm Order
THEY DESERVE THIS.
Order Confirmed
NOT ME.
CHARLIE FUCKING NOBODY.
MOST *REAPR* CAMPAIGNS THESE DAYS ARE NICKEL AND DIME AFFAIRS. NEIGHBORS. EXES.
YOU OWE ME FOR A BELT, BY THE WAY.
IT'S NOT LIKE I *HURT* SOMEONE. OR GOT AWAY WITH SOME CRIME.
DID YOU CUT A GUY OFF IN TRAFFIC? ACT RUDE TO A CASHIER? BORROW SOMETHING YEARS AGO AND FORGET TO RETURN IT?

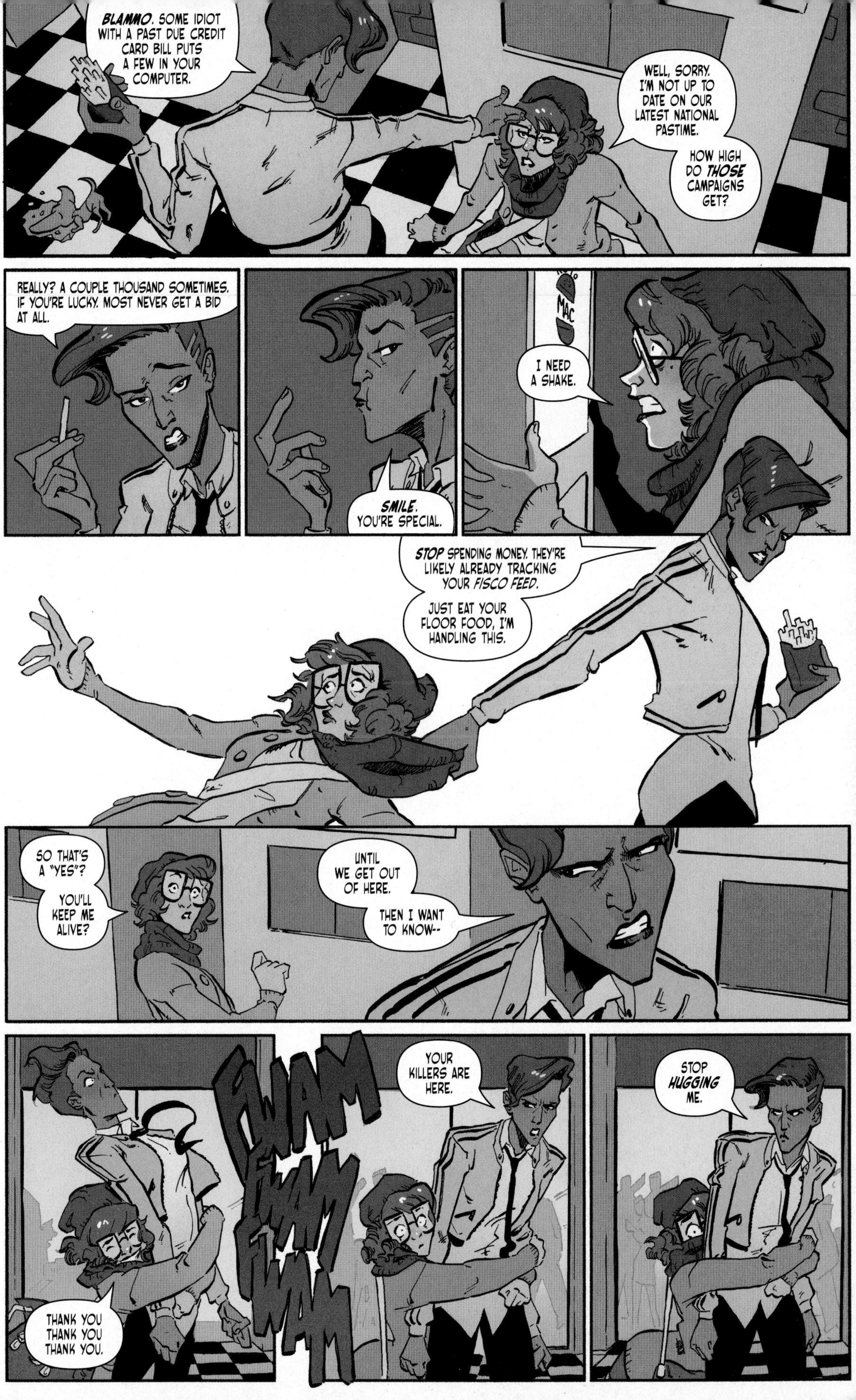
BLAMMO. SOME IDIOT WITH A PAST DUE CREDIT CARD BILL PUTS A FEW IN YOUR COMPUTER.
WELL, SORRY. I'M NOT UP TO DATE ON OUR LATEST NATIONAL PASTIME.
HOW HIGH DO THOSE CAMPAIGNS GET?
REALLY? A COUPLE THOUSAND SOMETIMES. IF YOU'RE LUCKY. MOST NEVER GET A BID AT ALL.
SMILE. YOU'RE SPECIAL.
MAC
I NEED A SHAKE.
STOP SPENDING MONEY. THEY'RE LIKELY ALREADY TRACKING YOUR FISCO FEED.
JUST EAT YOUR FLOOR FOOD, I'M HANDLING THIS.
SO THAT'S A "YES"?
YOU'LL KEEP ME ALIVE?
UNTIL WE GET OUT OF HERE.
THEN I WANT TO KNOW--
THANK YOU THANK YOU THANK YOU.
FWAM FWAM FWAM FWAM
YOUR KILLERS ARE HERE.
STOP HUGGING ME.

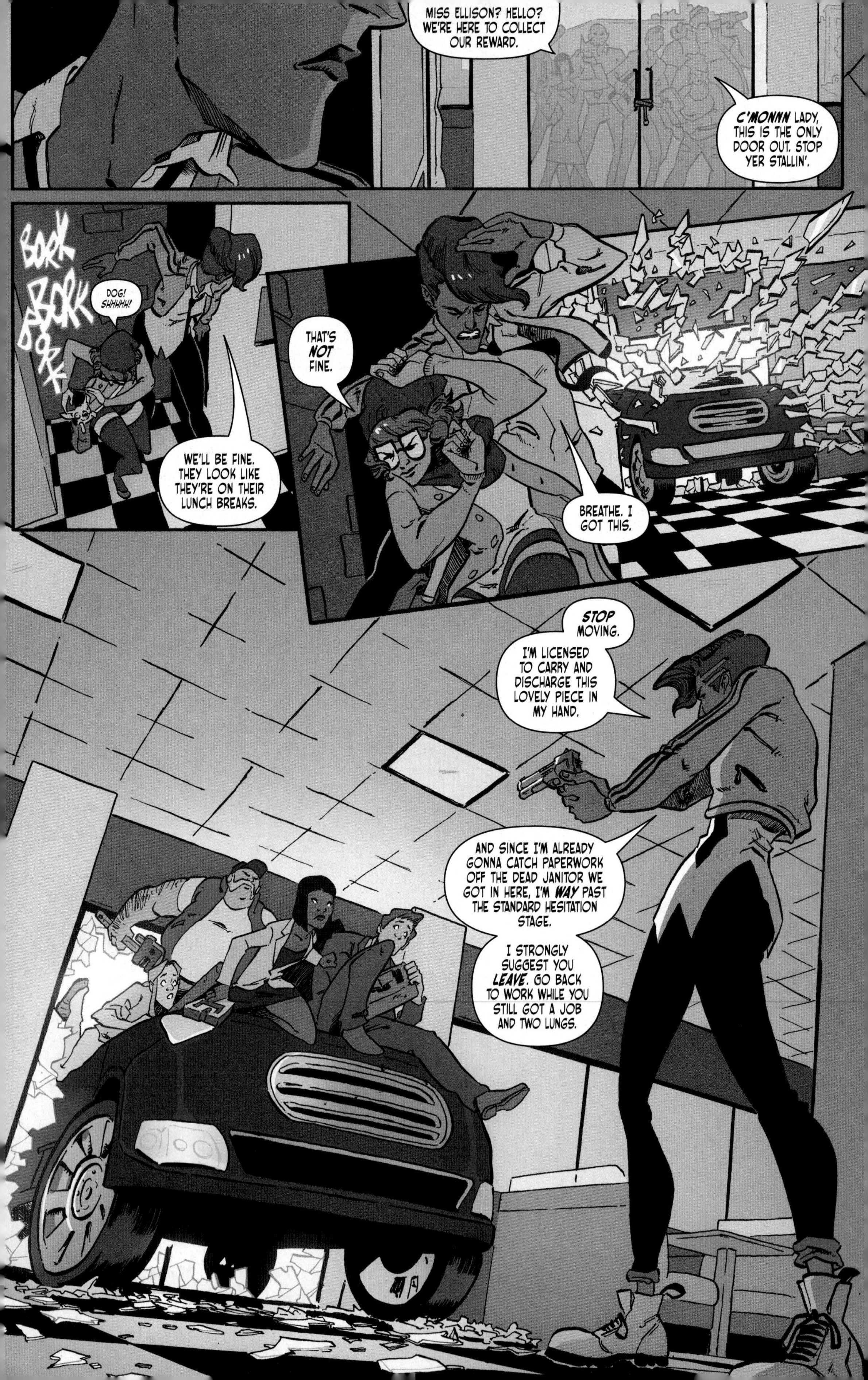
MISS ELLISON? HELLO? WE'RE HERE TO COLLECT OUR REWARD.
C'MONNN LADY, THIS IS THE ONLY DOOR OUT. STOP YER STALLIN'.
BORK BORK BORK
DOG! SHHHHH!
WE'LL BE FINE. THEY LOOK LIKE THEY'RE ON THEIR LUNCH BREAKS.
THAT'S NOT FINE.
BREATHE. I GOT THIS.
STOP MOVING.
I'M LICENSED TO CARRY AND DISCHARGE THIS LOVELY PIECE IN MY HAND.
AND SINCE I'M ALREADY GONNA CATCH PAPERWORK OFF THE DEAD JANITOR WE GOT IN HERE, I'M WAY PAST THE STANDARD HESITATION STAGE.
I STRONGLY SUGGEST YOU LEAVE. GO BACK TO WORK WHILE YOU STILL GOT A JOB AND TWO LUNGS.

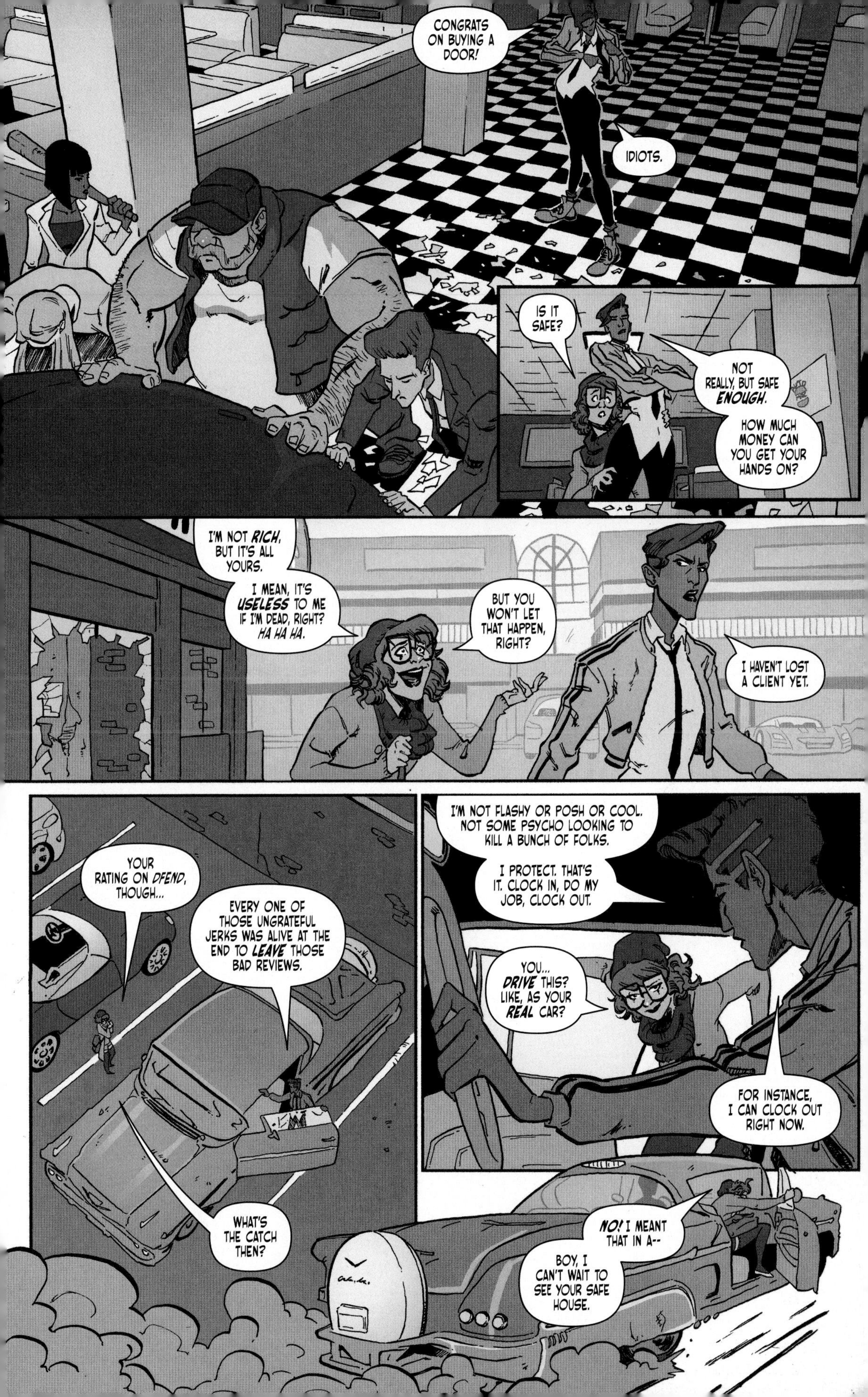
CONGRATS ON BUYING A DOOR!
IDIOTS.
IS IT SAFE?
NOT REALLY, BUT SAFE *ENOUGH*.
HOW MUCH MONEY CAN YOU GET YOUR HANDS ON?
I'M NOT *RICH*, BUT IT'S ALL YOURS.
I MEAN, IT'S *USELESS* TO ME IF I'M DEAD, RIGHT? *HA HA HA*.
BUT YOU WON'T LET THAT HAPPEN, RIGHT?
I HAVEN'T LOST A CLIENT YET.
YOUR RATING ON *DFEND*, THOUGH...
EVERY ONE OF THOSE UNGRATEFUL JERKS WAS ALIVE AT THE END TO *LEAVE* THOSE BAD REVIEWS.
I'M NOT FLASHY OR POSH OR COOL. NOT SOME PSYCHO LOOKING TO KILL A BUNCH OF FOLKS.
I PROTECT. THAT'S IT. CLOCK IN, DO MY JOB, CLOCK OUT.
YOU... *DRIVE* THIS? LIKE, AS YOUR *REAL* CAR?
FOR INSTANCE, I CAN CLOCK OUT RIGHT NOW.
WHAT'S THE CATCH THEN?
NO! I MEANT THAT IN A--
BOY, I CAN'T WAIT TO SEE YOUR SAFE HOUSE.

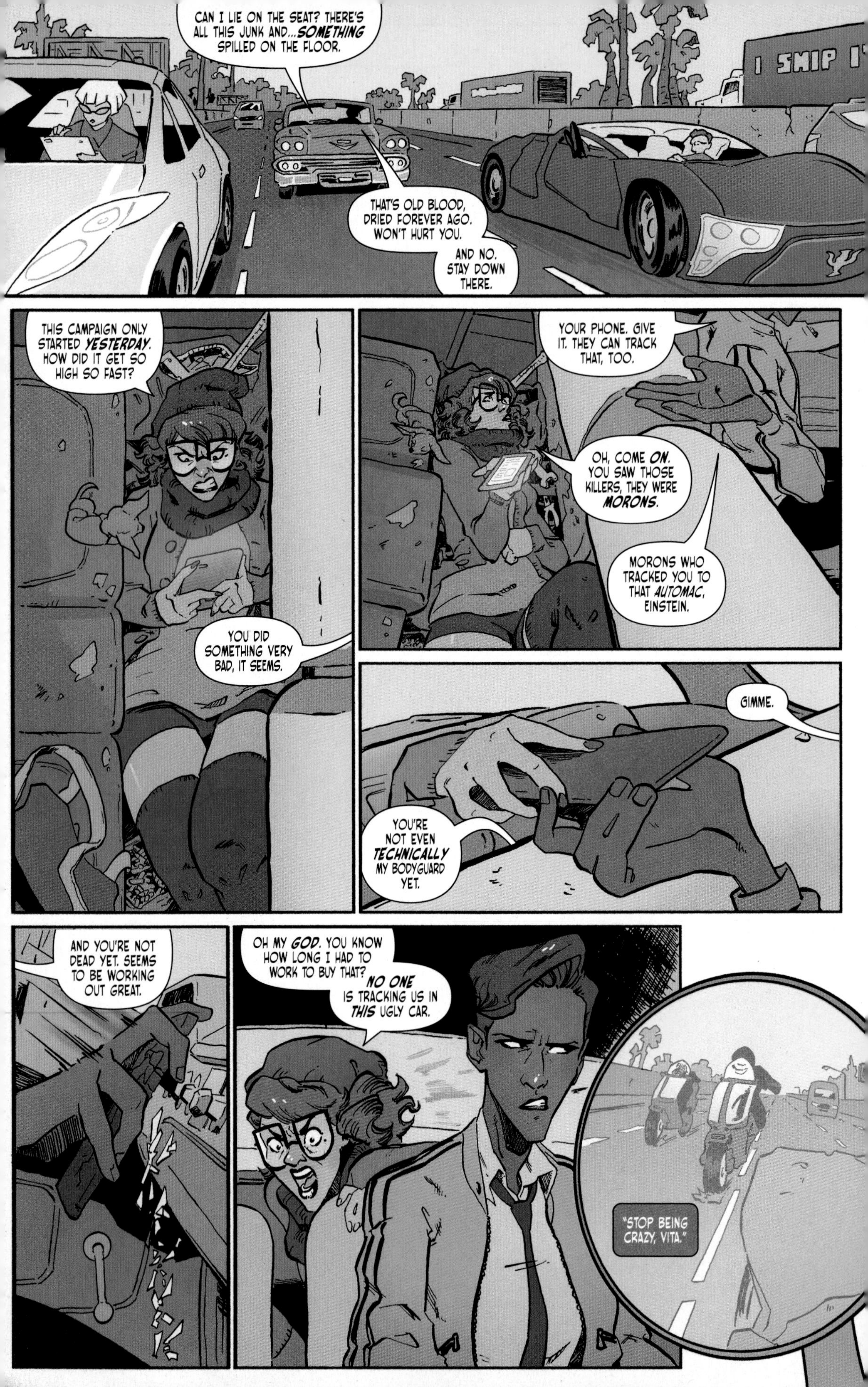
CAN I LIE ON THE SEAT? THERE'S ALL THIS JUNK AND...SOMETHING SPILLED ON THE FLOOR.
I SHIP I
THAT'S OLD BLOOD, DRIED FOREVER AGO. WON'T HURT YOU.
AND NO. STAY DOWN THERE.
THIS CAMPAIGN ONLY STARTED YESTERDAY. HOW DID IT GET SO HIGH SO FAST?
YOU DID SOMETHING VERY BAD, IT SEEMS.
YOUR PHONE. GIVE IT. THEY CAN TRACK THAT, TOO.
OH, COME ON. YOU SAW THOSE KILLERS, THEY WERE MORONS.
MORONS WHO TRACKED YOU TO THAT AUTOMAC, EINSTEIN.
GIMME.
YOU'RE NOT EVEN TECHNICALLY MY BODYGUARD YET.
AND YOU'RE NOT DEAD YET. SEEMS TO BE WORKING OUT GREAT.
OH MY GOD. YOU KNOW HOW LONG I HAD TO WORK TO BUY THAT? NO ONE IS TRACKING US IN THIS UGLY CAR.
"STOP BEING CRAZY, VITA."

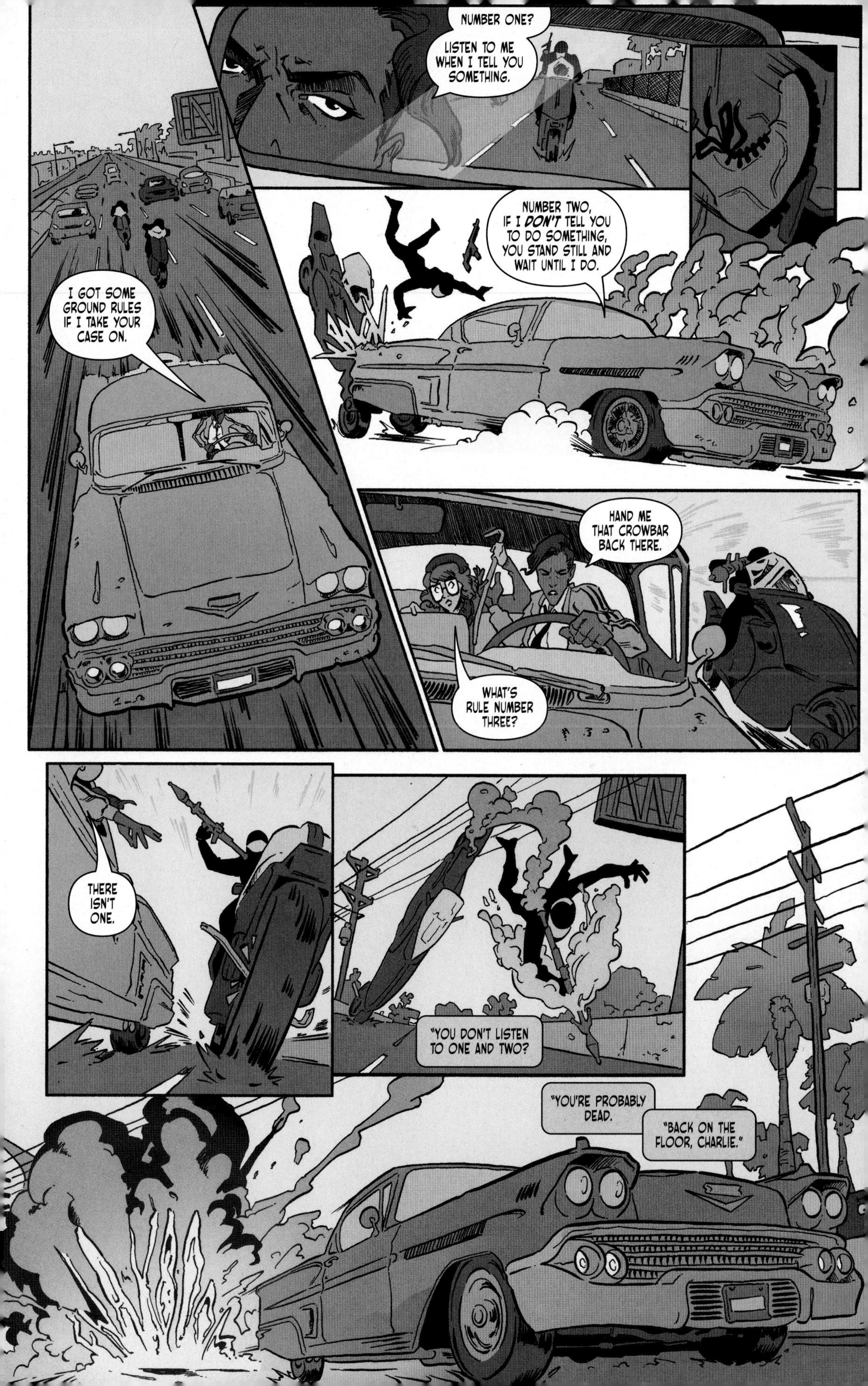
NUMBER ONE?
LISTEN TO ME WHEN I TELL YOU SOMETHING.
I GOT SOME GROUND RULES IF I TAKE YOUR CASE ON.
NUMBER TWO, IF I *DON'T* TELL YOU TO DO SOMETHING, YOU STAND STILL AND WAIT UNTIL I DO.
HAND ME THAT CROWBAR BACK THERE.
WHAT'S RULE NUMBER THREE?
THERE ISN'T ONE.
"YOU DON'T LISTEN TO ONE AND TWO?
"YOU'RE PROBABLY DEAD.
"BACK ON THE FLOOR, CHARLIE."

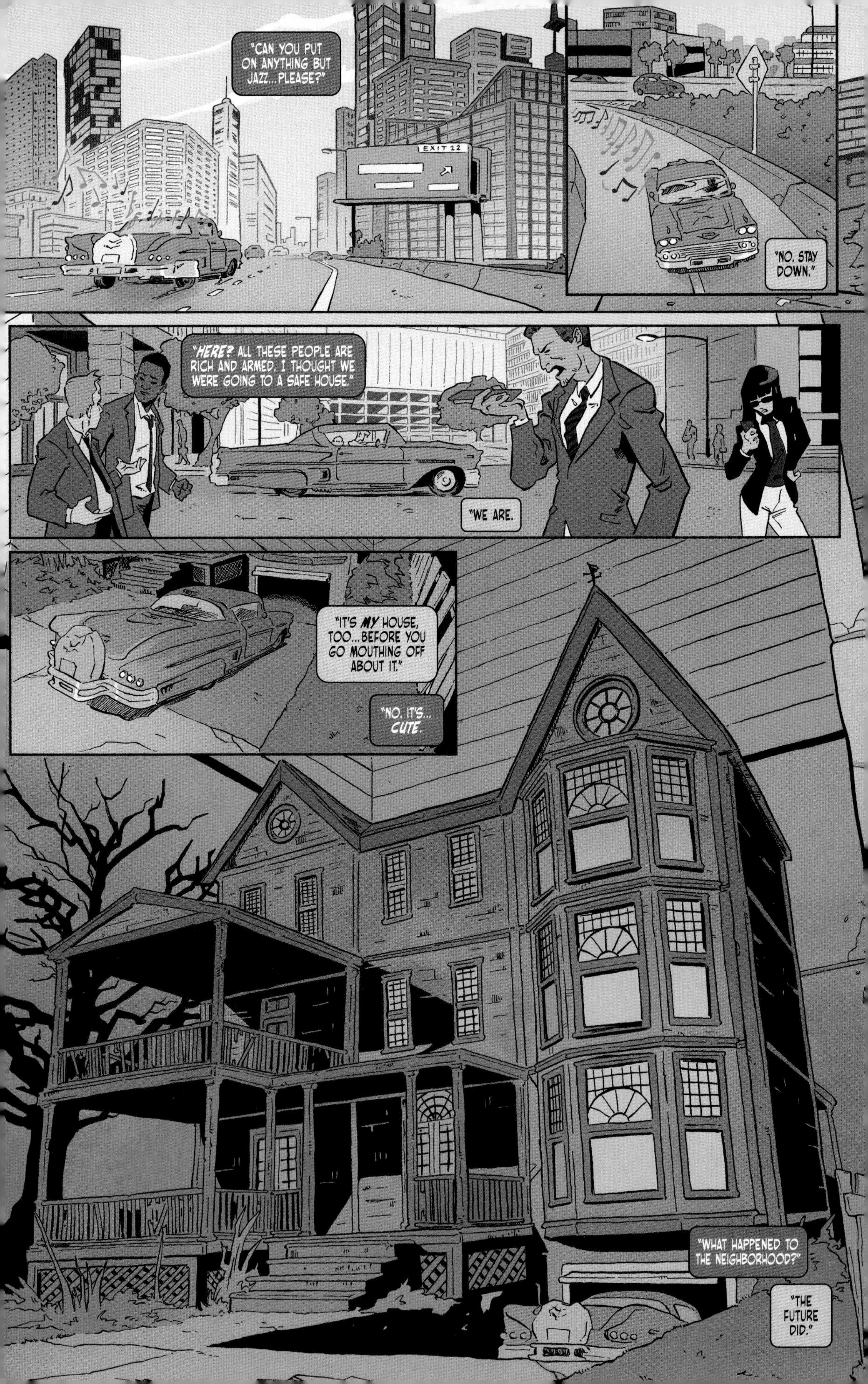
"CAN YOU PUT ON ANYTHING BUT JAZZ...PLEASE?"
EXIT 22
"NO. STAY DOWN."
"HERE? ALL THESE PEOPLE ARE RICH AND ARMED. I THOUGHT WE WERE GOING TO A SAFE HOUSE."
"WE ARE.
"IT'S MY HOUSE, TOO...BEFORE YOU GO MOUTHING OFF ABOUT IT."
"NO. IT'S... CUTE.
"WHAT HAPPENED TO THE NEIGHBORHOOD?"
"THE FUTURE DID."

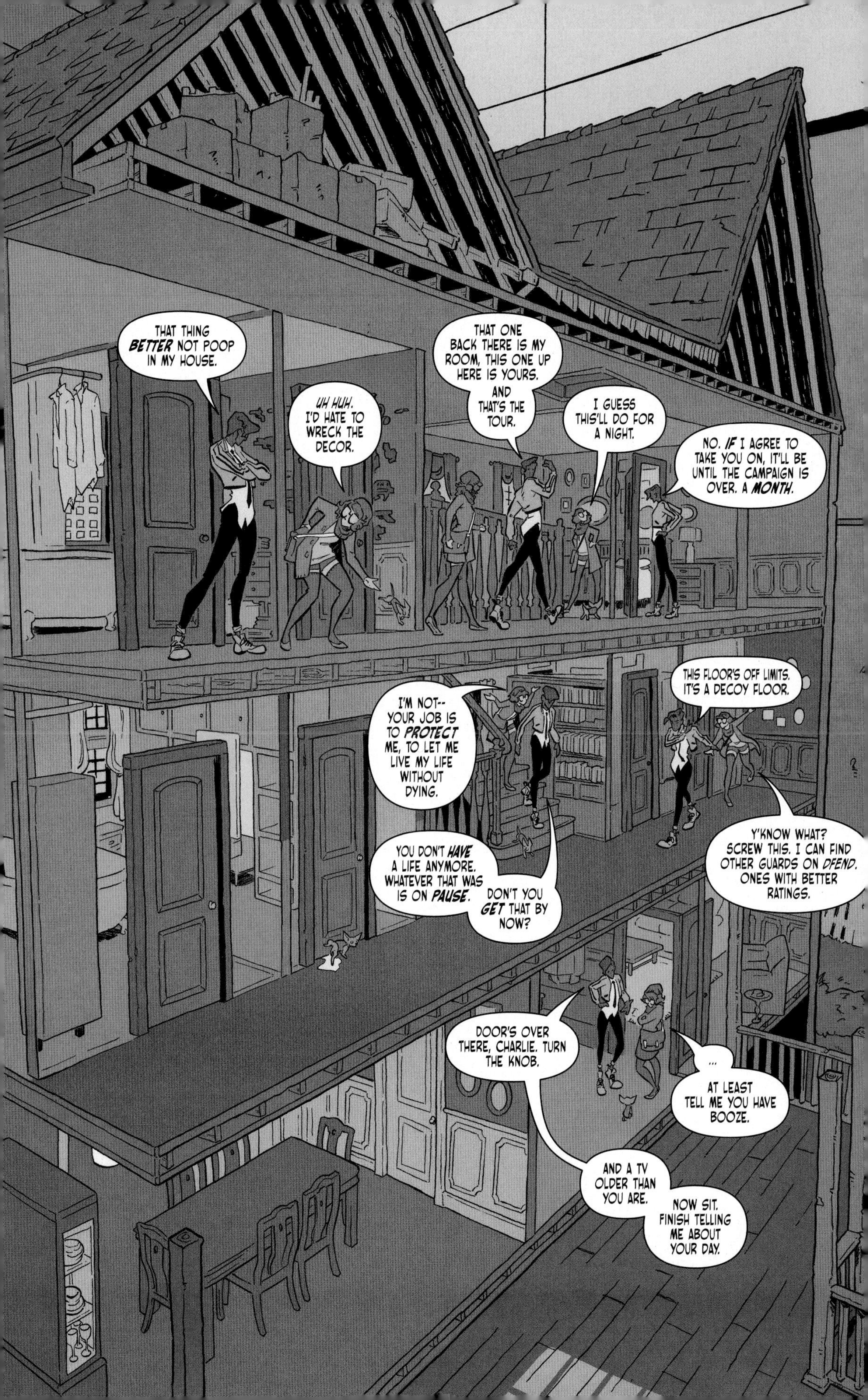
THAT THING BETTER NOT POOP IN MY HOUSE.
UH HUH. I'D HATE TO WRECK THE DECOR.
THAT ONE BACK THERE IS MY ROOM, THIS ONE UP HERE IS YOURS.
AND THAT'S THE TOUR.
I GUESS THIS'LL DO FOR A NIGHT.
NO. IF I AGREE TO TAKE YOU ON, IT'LL BE UNTIL THE CAMPAIGN IS OVER. A MONTH.
THIS FLOOR'S OFF LIMITS. IT'S A DECOY FLOOR.
I'M NOT-- YOUR JOB IS TO PROTECT ME, TO LET ME LIVE MY LIFE WITHOUT DYING.
YOU DON'T HAVE A LIFE ANYMORE. WHATEVER THAT WAS IS ON PAUSE.
DON'T YOU GET THAT BY NOW?
Y'KNOW WHAT? SCREW THIS. I CAN FIND OTHER GUARDS ON DFEND. ONES WITH BETTER RATINGS.
DOOR'S OVER THERE, CHARLIE. TURN THE KNOB.
...
AT LEAST TELL ME YOU HAVE BOOZE.
AND A TV OLDER THAN YOU ARE.
NOW SIT. FINISH TELLING ME ABOUT YOUR DAY.

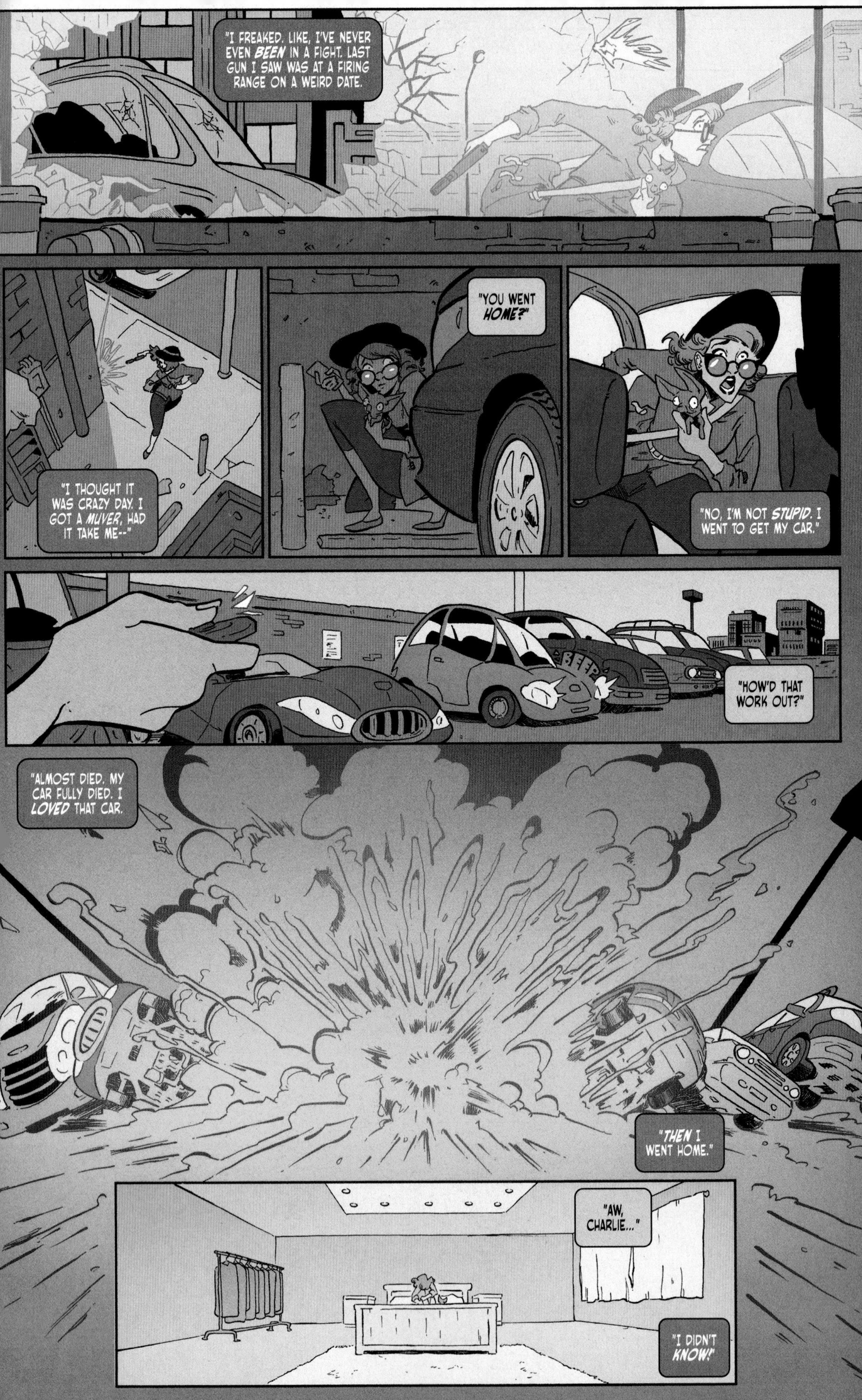
"I FREAKED. LIKE, I'VE NEVER EVEN *BEEN* IN A FIGHT. LAST GUN I SAW WAS AT A FIRING RANGE ON A WEIRD DATE.
"I THOUGHT IT WAS CRAZY DAY. I GOT A *MUVER*, HAD IT TAKE ME--"
"YOU WENT *HOME?*"
"NO, I'M NOT *STUPID*. I WENT TO GET MY CAR."
BEEP
"HOW'D THAT WORK OUT?"
"ALMOST DIED. MY CAR FULLY DIED. I *LOVED* THAT CAR.
"*THEN* I WENT HOME."
"AW, CHARLIE..."
"I DIDN'T *KNOW!*"

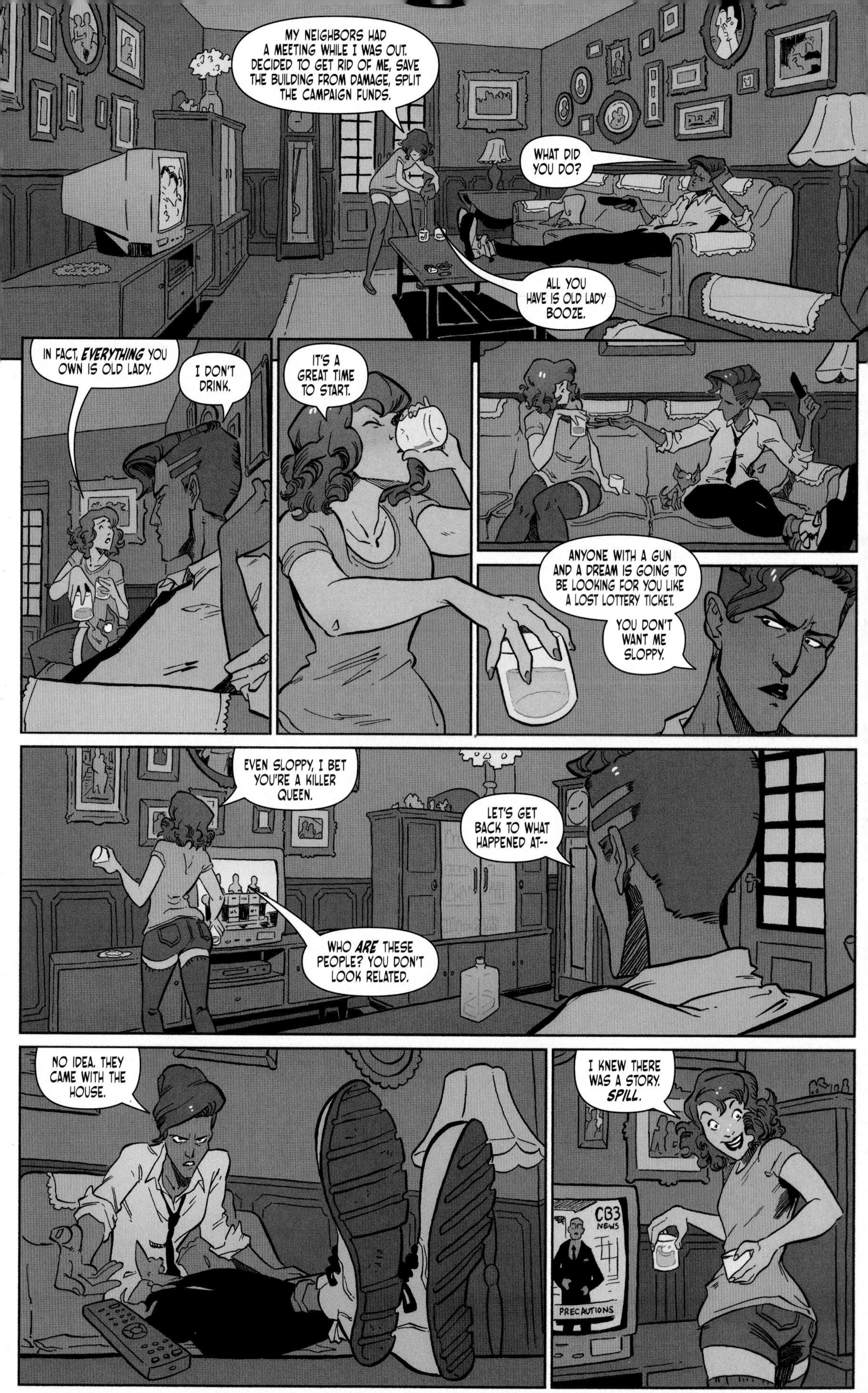
MY NEIGHBORS HAD A MEETING WHILE I WAS OUT. DECIDED TO GET RID OF ME, SAVE THE BUILDING FROM DAMAGE, SPLIT THE CAMPAIGN FUNDS.
WHAT DID YOU DO?
ALL YOU HAVE IS OLD LADY BOOZE.
IN FACT, **EVERYTHING** YOU OWN IS OLD LADY.
I DON'T DRINK.
IT'S A GREAT TIME TO START.
ANYONE WITH A GUN AND A DREAM IS GOING TO BE LOOKING FOR YOU LIKE A LOST LOTTERY TICKET.
YOU DON'T WANT ME SLOPPY.
EVEN SLOPPY, I BET YOU'RE A KILLER QUEEN.
LET'S GET BACK TO WHAT HAPPENED AT--
WHO **ARE** THESE PEOPLE? YOU DON'T LOOK RELATED.
NO IDEA. THEY CAME WITH THE HOUSE.
I KNEW THERE WAS A STORY. **SPILL.**
CB3 NEWS
PRECAUTIONS

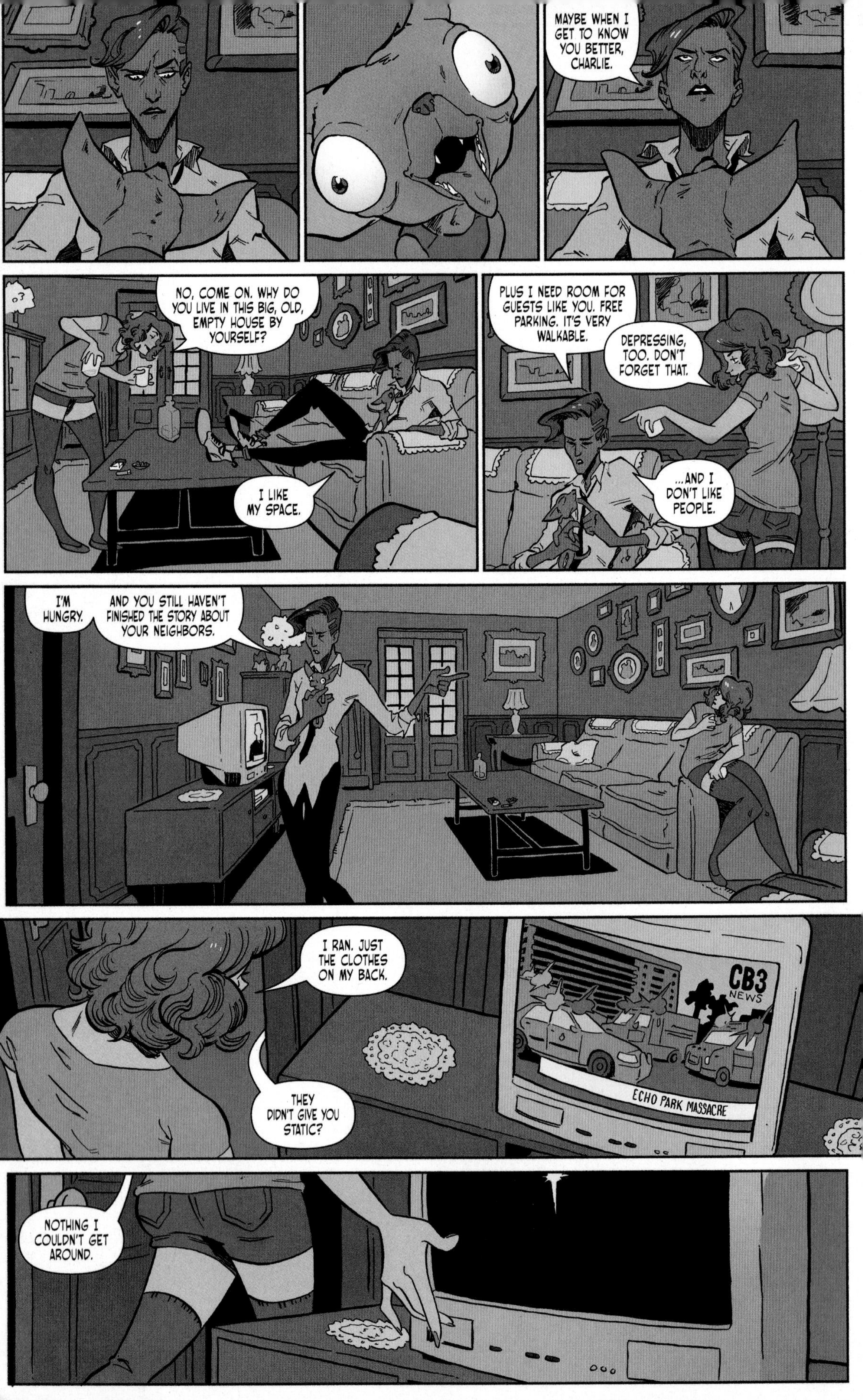
MAYBE WHEN I GET TO KNOW YOU BETTER, CHARLIE.
NO, COME ON. WHY DO YOU LIVE IN THIS BIG, OLD, EMPTY HOUSE BY YOURSELF?
I LIKE MY SPACE.
PLUS I NEED ROOM FOR GUESTS LIKE YOU. FREE PARKING. IT'S VERY WALKABLE.
DEPRESSING, TOO. DON'T FORGET THAT.
...AND I DON'T LIKE PEOPLE.
I'M HUNGRY.
AND YOU STILL HAVEN'T FINISHED THE STORY ABOUT YOUR NEIGHBORS.
I RAN. JUST THE CLOTHES ON MY BACK.
CB3 NEWS
ECHO PARK MASSACRE
THEY DIDN'T GIVE YOU STATIC?
NOTHING I COULDN'T GET AROUND.

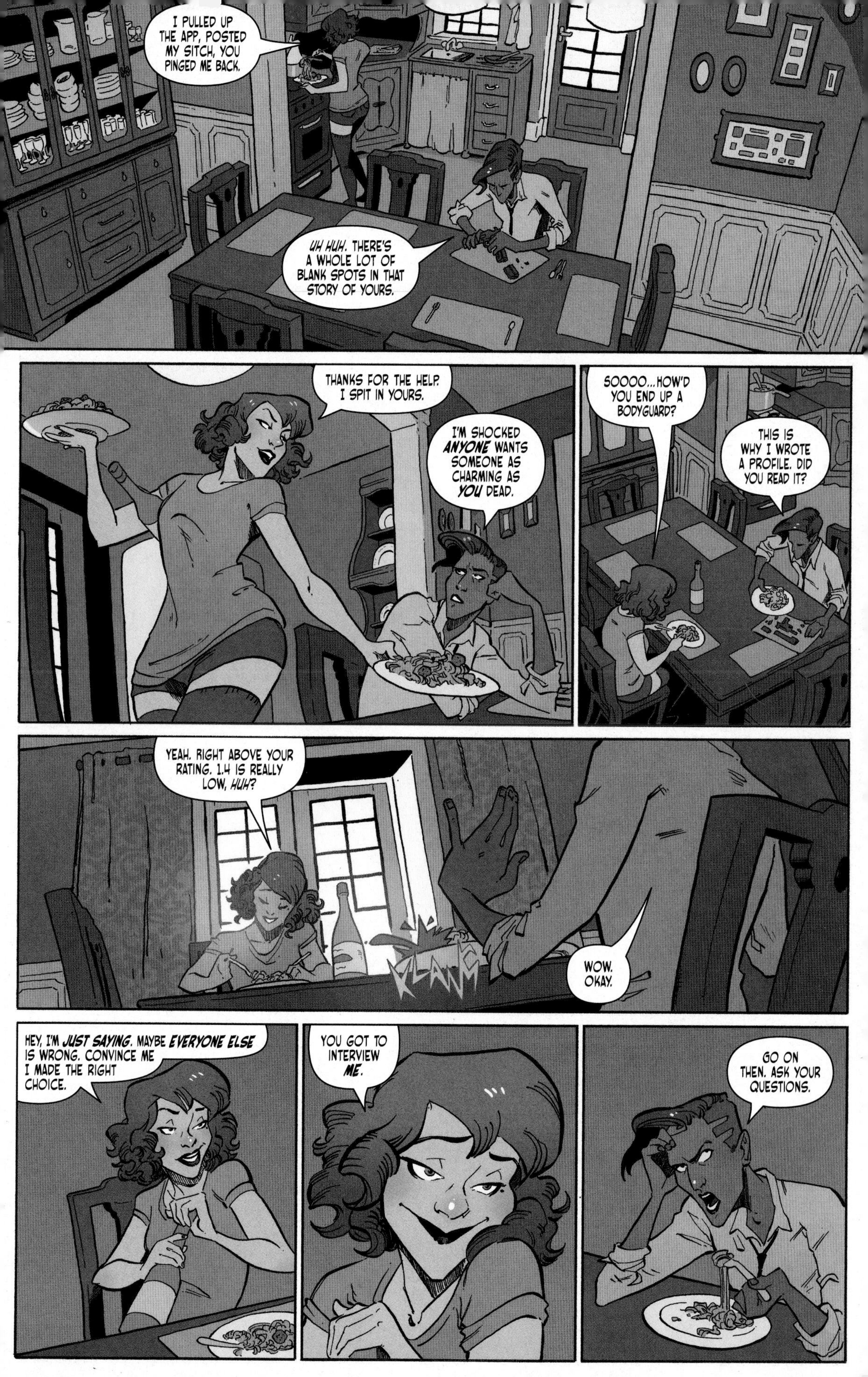
I PULLED UP THE APP, POSTED MY SITCH, YOU PINGED ME BACK.
UH HUH. THERE'S A WHOLE LOT OF BLANK SPOTS IN THAT STORY OF YOURS.
THANKS FOR THE HELP. I SPIT IN YOURS.
I'M SHOCKED ANYONE WANTS SOMEONE AS CHARMING AS YOU DEAD.
SOOOO...HOW'D YOU END UP A BODYGUARD?
THIS IS WHY I WROTE A PROFILE. DID YOU READ IT?
YEAH. RIGHT ABOVE YOUR RATING. 1.4 IS REALLY LOW, HUH?
KLANG
WOW. OKAY.
HEY, I'M JUST SAYING. MAYBE EVERYONE ELSE IS WRONG. CONVINCE ME I MADE THE RIGHT CHOICE.
YOU GOT TO INTERVIEW ME.
GO ON THEN. ASK YOUR QUESTIONS.

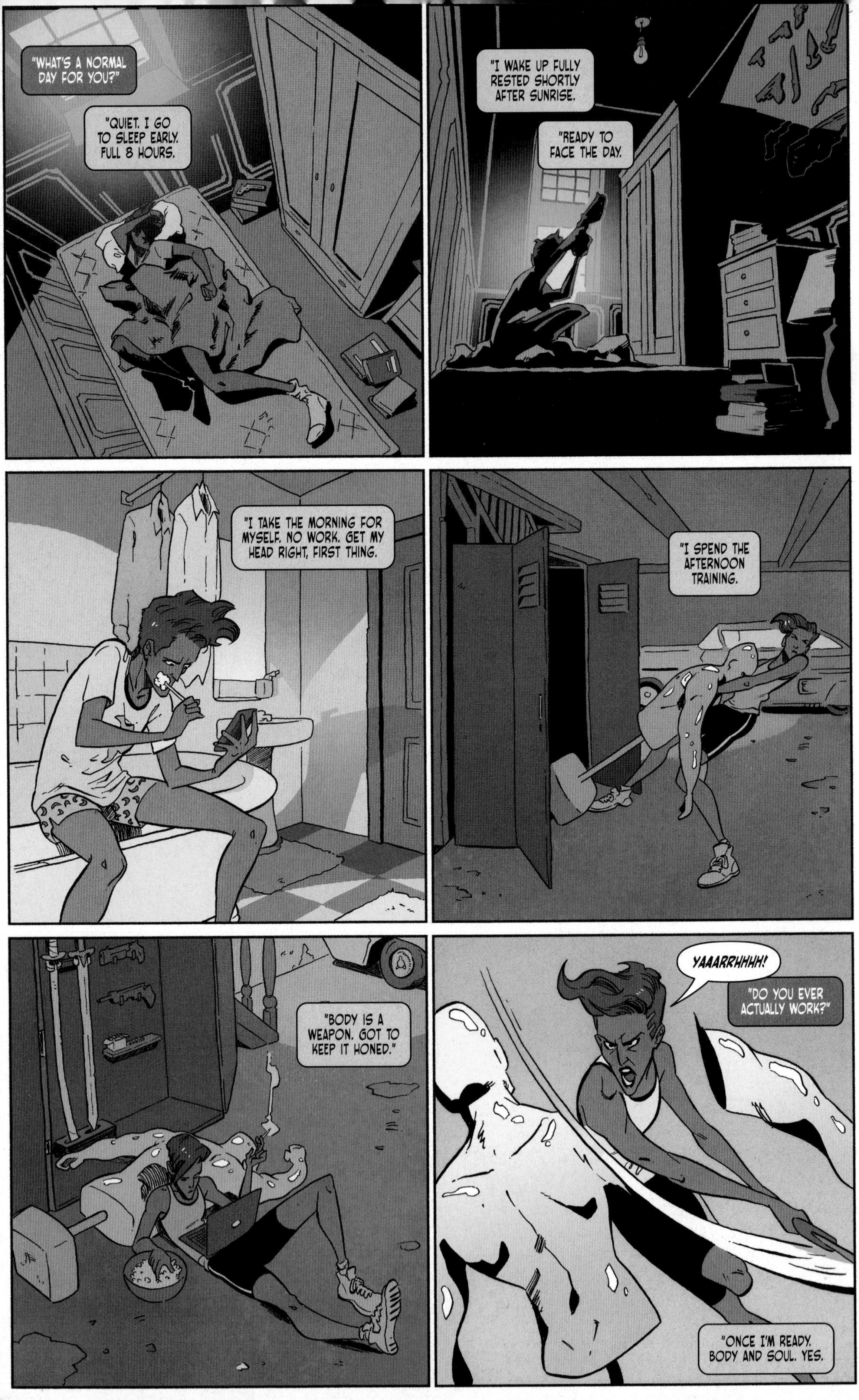
"WHAT'S A NORMAL DAY FOR YOU?"
"QUIET. I GO TO SLEEP EARLY. FULL 8 HOURS.
"I WAKE UP FULLY RESTED SHORTLY AFTER SUNRISE.
"READY TO FACE THE DAY.
"I TAKE THE MORNING FOR MYSELF. NO WORK. GET MY HEAD RIGHT, FIRST THING.
"I SPEND THE AFTERNOON TRAINING.
"BODY IS A WEAPON. GOT TO KEEP IT HONED."
YAAARRHHHH!
"DO YOU EVER ACTUALLY WORK?"
"ONCE I'M READY. BODY AND SOUL. YES.

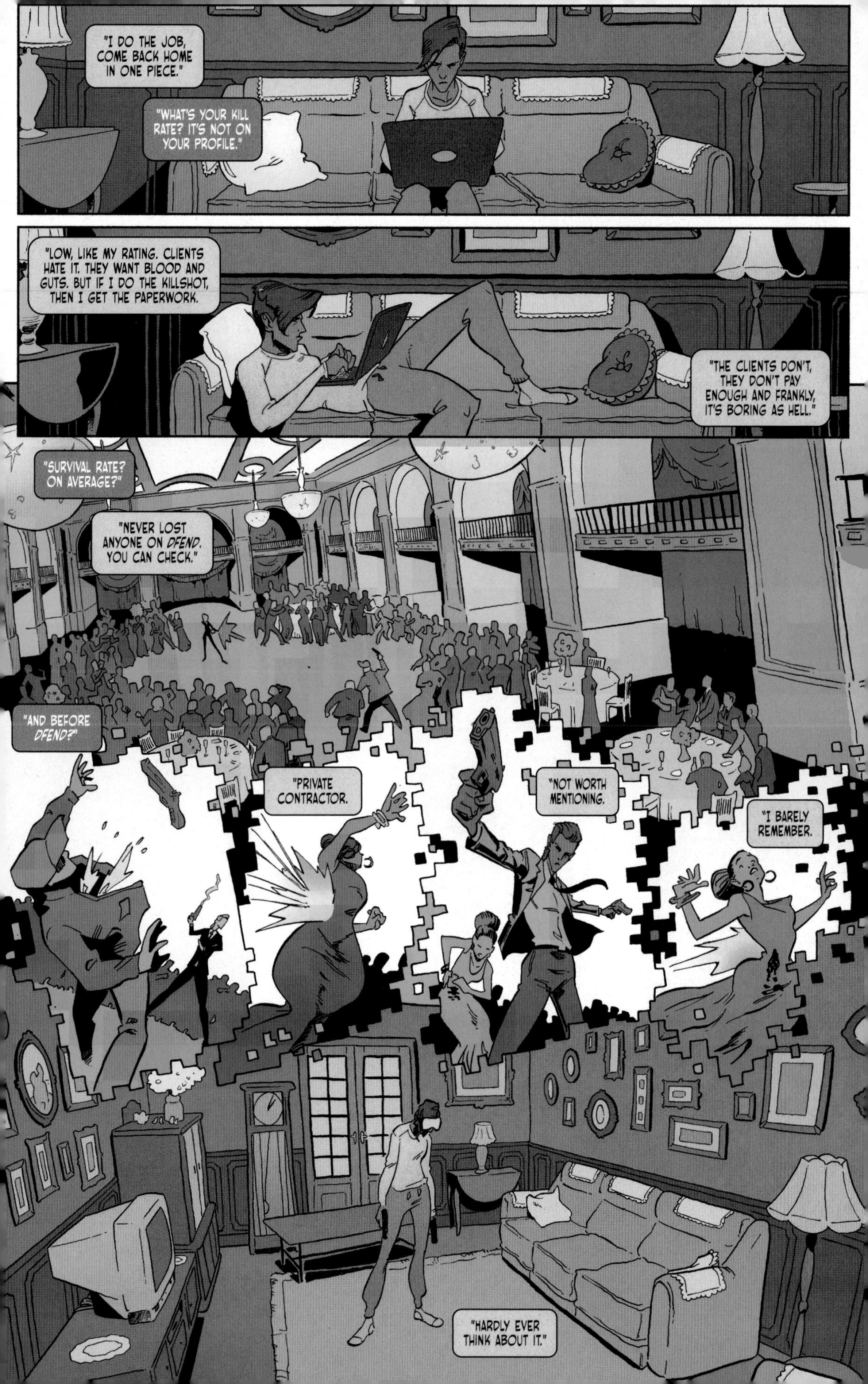
"I DO THE JOB, COME BACK HOME IN ONE PIECE."
"WHAT'S YOUR KILL RATE? IT'S NOT ON YOUR PROFILE."
"LOW, LIKE MY RATING. CLIENTS HATE IT. THEY WANT BLOOD AND GUTS. BUT IF I DO THE KILLSHOT, THEN I GET THE PAPERWORK.
"THE CLIENTS DON'T, THEY DON'T PAY ENOUGH AND FRANKLY, IT'S BORING AS HELL."
"SURVIVAL RATE? ON AVERAGE?"
"NEVER LOST ANYONE ON *DFEND*. YOU CAN CHECK."
"AND BEFORE *DFEND*?"
"PRIVATE CONTRACTOR.
"NOT WORTH MENTIONING.
"I BARELY REMEMBER.
"HARDLY EVER THINK ABOUT IT."

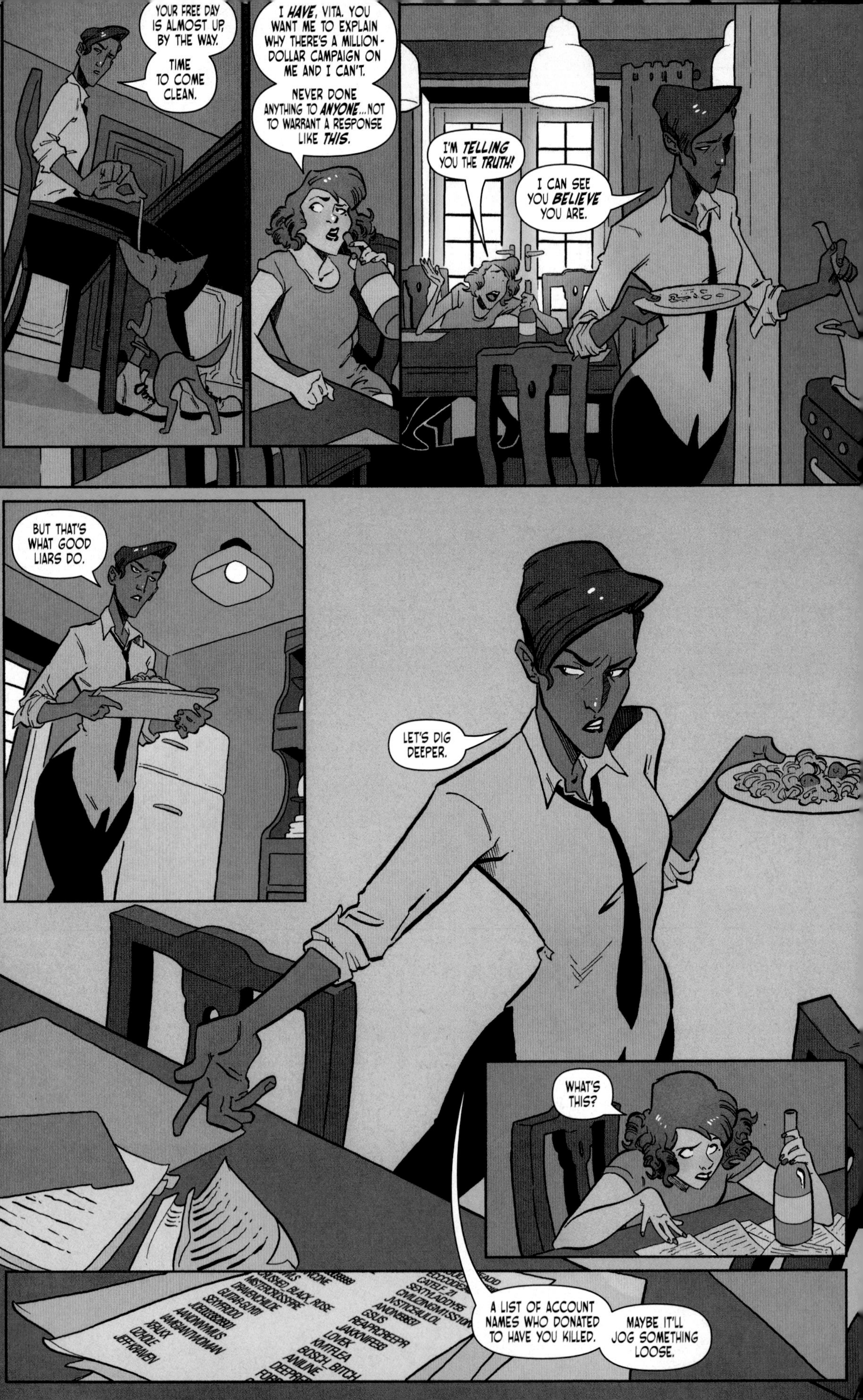
YOUR FREE DAY IS ALMOST UP, BY THE WAY.
TIME TO COME CLEAN.
I HAVE, VITA. YOU WANT ME TO EXPLAIN WHY THERE'S A MILLION-DOLLAR CAMPAIGN ON ME AND I CAN'T.
NEVER DONE ANYTHING TO ANYONE...NOT TO WARRANT A RESPONSE LIKE THIS.
I'M TELLING YOU THE TRUTH!
I CAN SEE YOU BELIEVE YOU ARE.
BUT THAT'S WHAT GOOD LIARS DO.
LET'S DIG DEEPER.
WHAT'S THIS?
A LIST OF ACCOUNT NAMES WHO DONATED TO HAVE YOU KILLED.
MAYBE IT'LL JOG SOMETHING LOOSE.

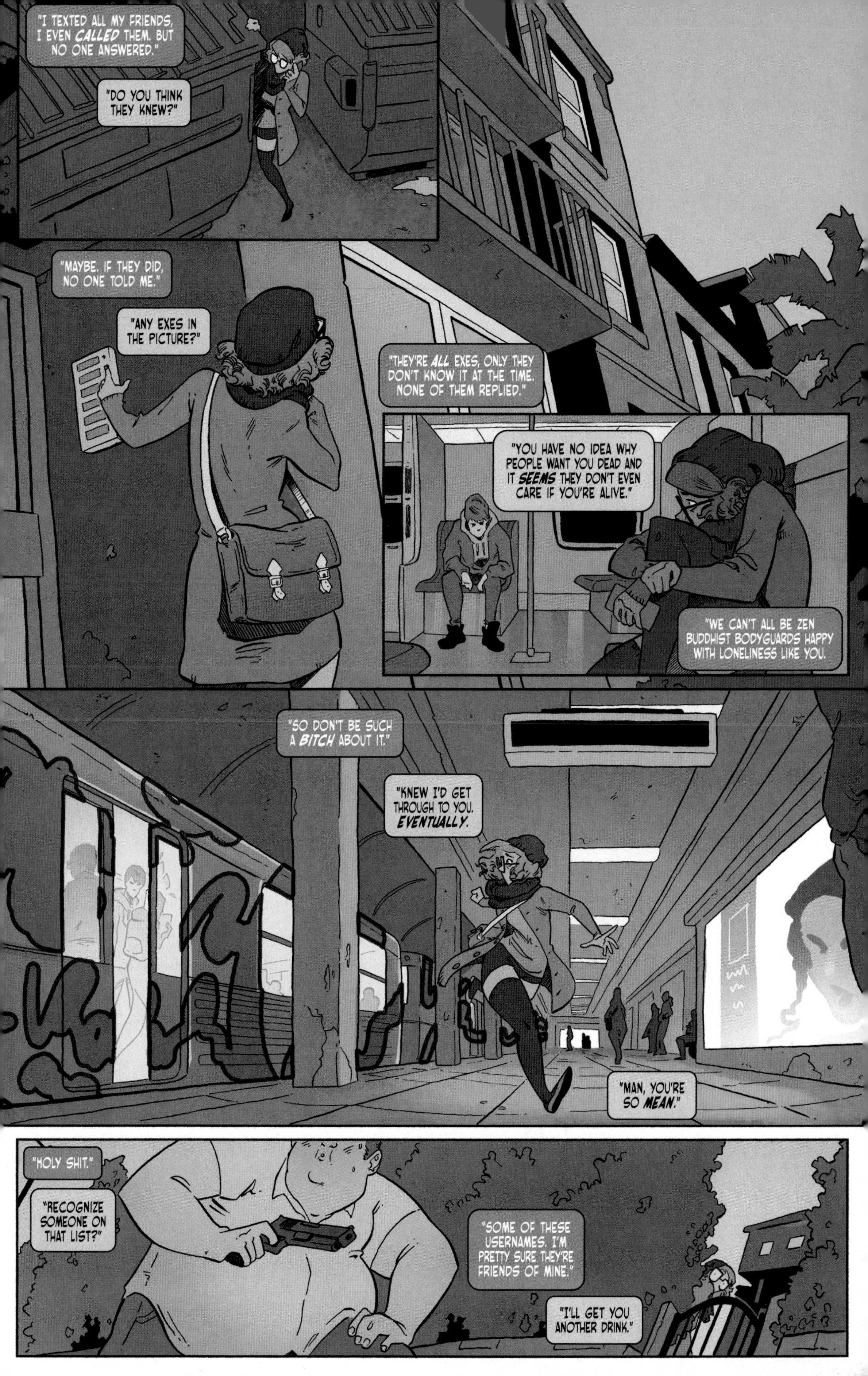
"I TEXTED ALL MY FRIENDS, I EVEN CALLED THEM. BUT NO ONE ANSWERED."
"DO YOU THINK THEY KNEW?"
"MAYBE. IF THEY DID, NO ONE TOLD ME."
"ANY EXES IN THE PICTURE?"
"THEY'RE ALL EXES, ONLY THEY DON'T KNOW IT AT THE TIME. NONE OF THEM REPLIED."
"YOU HAVE NO IDEA WHY PEOPLE WANT YOU DEAD AND IT SEEMS THEY DON'T EVEN CARE IF YOU'RE ALIVE."
"WE CAN'T ALL BE ZEN BUDDHIST BODYGUARDS HAPPY WITH LONELINESS LIKE YOU.
"SO DON'T BE SUCH A BITCH ABOUT IT."
"KNEW I'D GET THROUGH TO YOU. EVENTUALLY."
"MAN, YOU'RE SO MEAN."
"HOLY SHIT."
"RECOGNIZE SOMEONE ON THAT LIST?"
"SOME OF THESE USERNAMES. I'M PRETTY SURE THEY'RE FRIENDS OF MINE."
"I'LL GET YOU ANOTHER DRINK."

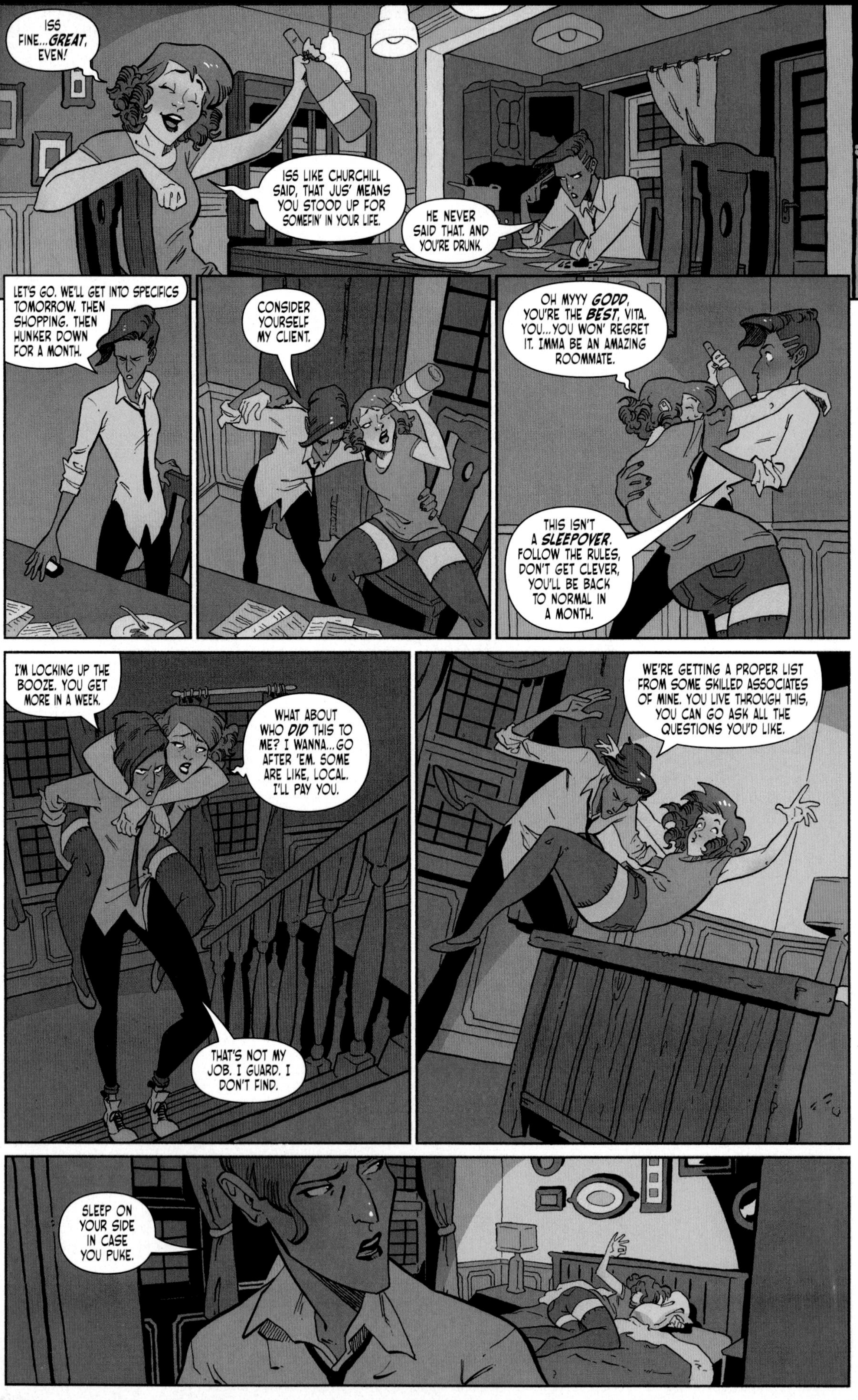
ISS FINE...GREAT, EVEN!
ISS LIKE CHURCHILL SAID, THAT JUS' MEANS YOU STOOD UP FOR SOMEFIN' IN YOUR LIFE.
HE NEVER SAID THAT. AND YOU'RE DRUNK.
LET'S GO. WE'LL GET INTO SPECIFICS TOMORROW. THEN SHOPPING. THEN HUNKER DOWN FOR A MONTH.
CONSIDER YOURSELF MY CLIENT.
OH MYYY GODD, YOU'RE THE BEST, VITA. YOU...YOU WON' REGRET IT. IMMA BE AN AMAZING ROOMMATE.
THIS ISN'T A SLEEPOVER. FOLLOW THE RULES, DON'T GET CLEVER, YOU'LL BE BACK TO NORMAL IN A MONTH.
I'M LOCKING UP THE BOOZE. YOU GET MORE IN A WEEK.
WHAT ABOUT WHO DID THIS TO ME? I WANNA...GO AFTER 'EM. SOME ARE LIKE, LOCAL. I'LL PAY YOU.
THAT'S NOT MY JOB. I GUARD. I DON'T FIND.
WE'RE GETTING A PROPER LIST FROM SOME SKILLED ASSOCIATES OF MINE. YOU LIVE THROUGH THIS, YOU CAN GO ASK ALL THE QUESTIONS YOU'D LIKE.
SLEEP ON YOUR SIDE IN CASE YOU PUKE.

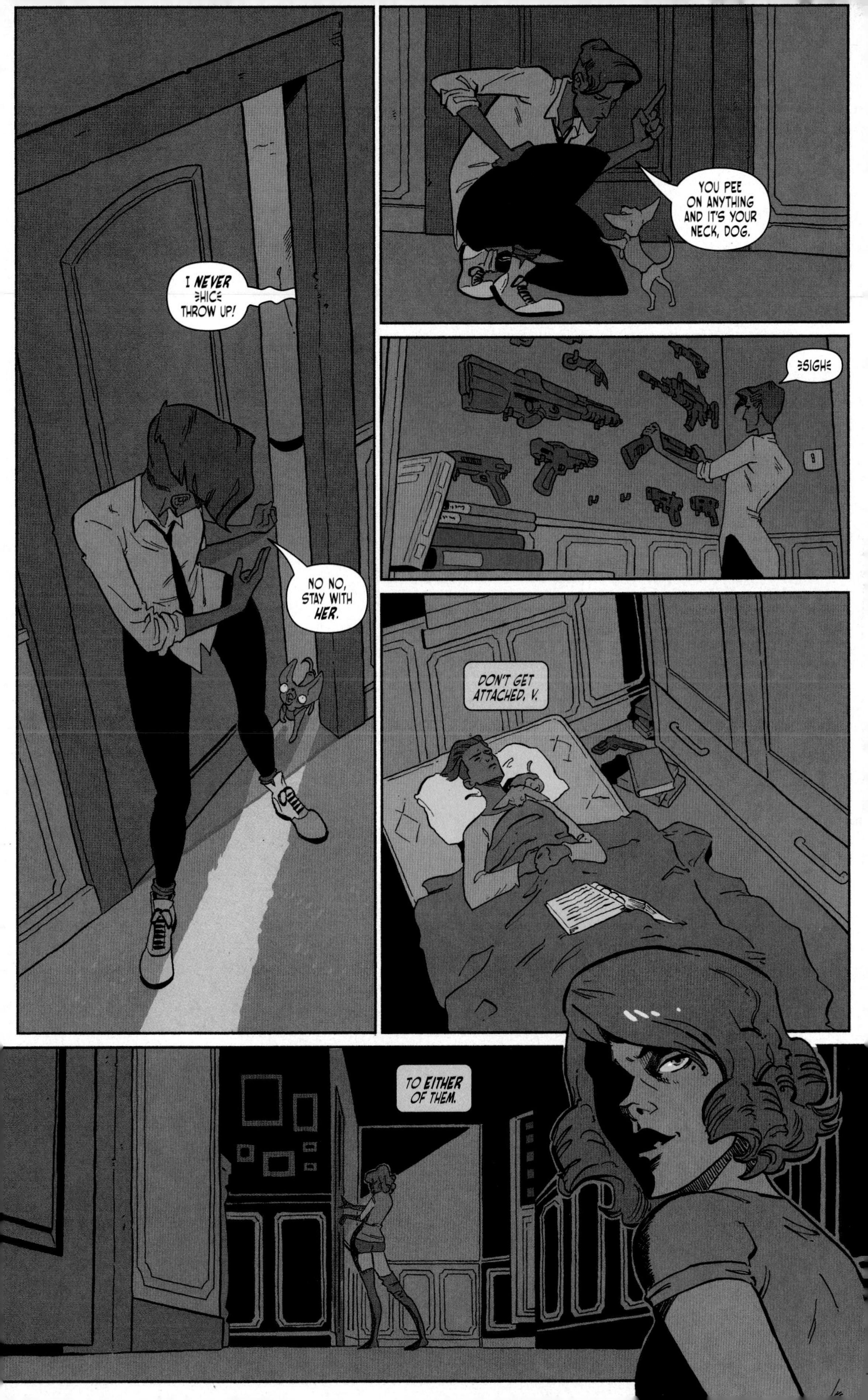

I NEVER
HIC
THROW UP!
NO NO, STAY WITH HER.
YOU PEE ON ANYTHING AND IT'S YOUR NECK, DOG.
SIGH
DON'T GET ATTACHED, V.
TO EITHER OF THEM.

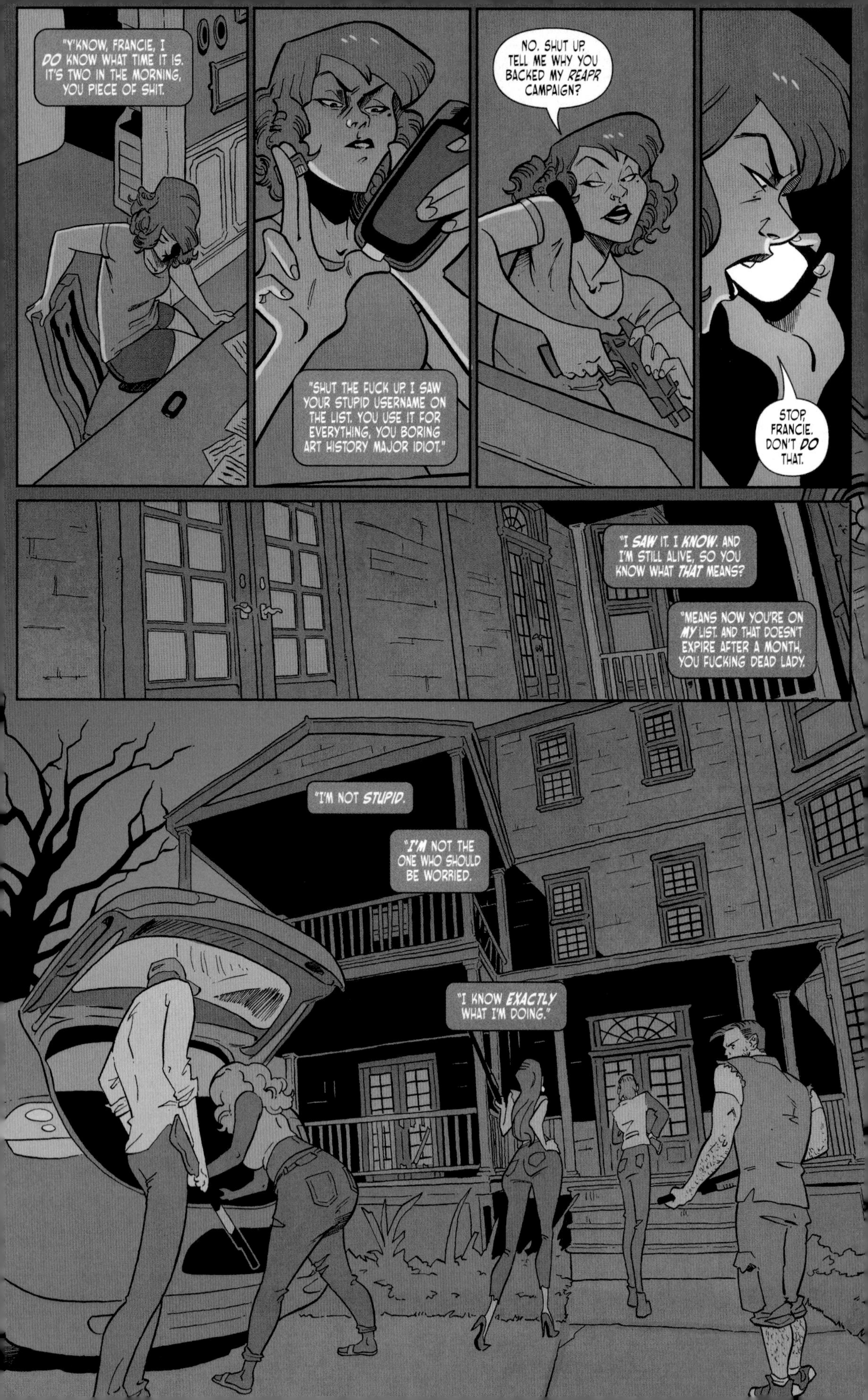
"Y'KNOW, FRANCIE, I DO KNOW WHAT TIME IT IS. IT'S TWO IN THE MORNING, YOU PIECE OF SHIT.
"SHUT THE FUCK UP. I SAW YOUR STUPID USERNAME ON THE LIST. YOU USE IT FOR EVERYTHING, YOU BORING ART HISTORY MAJOR IDIOT."
NO. SHUT UP. TELL ME WHY YOU BACKED MY REAPR CAMPAIGN?
STOP, FRANCIE. DON'T DO THAT.
"I SAW IT. I KNOW. AND I'M STILL ALIVE, SO YOU KNOW WHAT THAT MEANS?
"MEANS NOW YOU'RE ON MY LIST. AND THAT DOESN'T EXPIRE AFTER A MONTH, YOU FUCKING DEAD LADY.
"I'M NOT STUPID.
"I'M NOT THE ONE WHO SHOULD BE WORRIED.
"I KNOW EXACTLY WHAT I'M DOING."

CHAPTER TWO
FUTURE STARTS SLOW

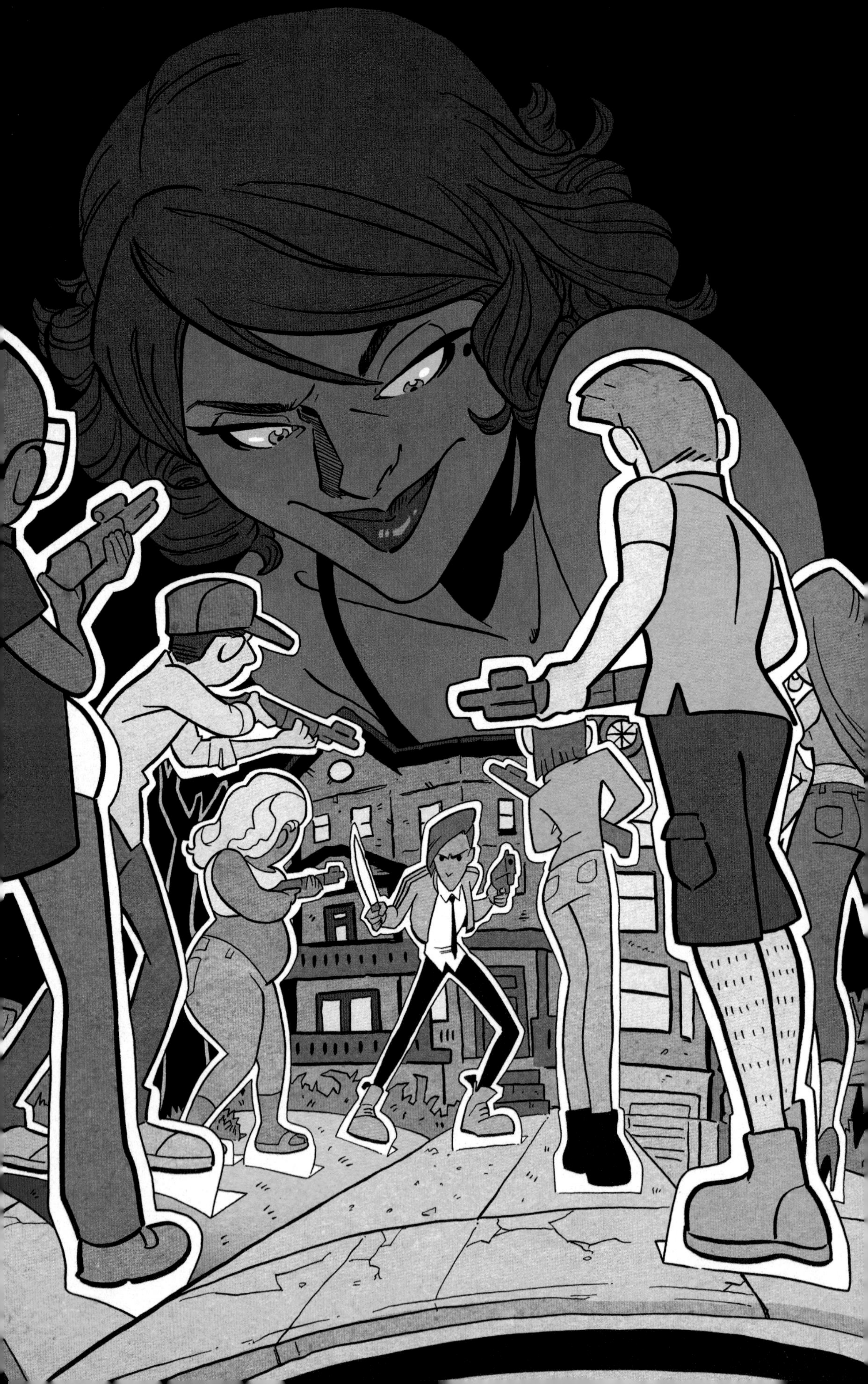

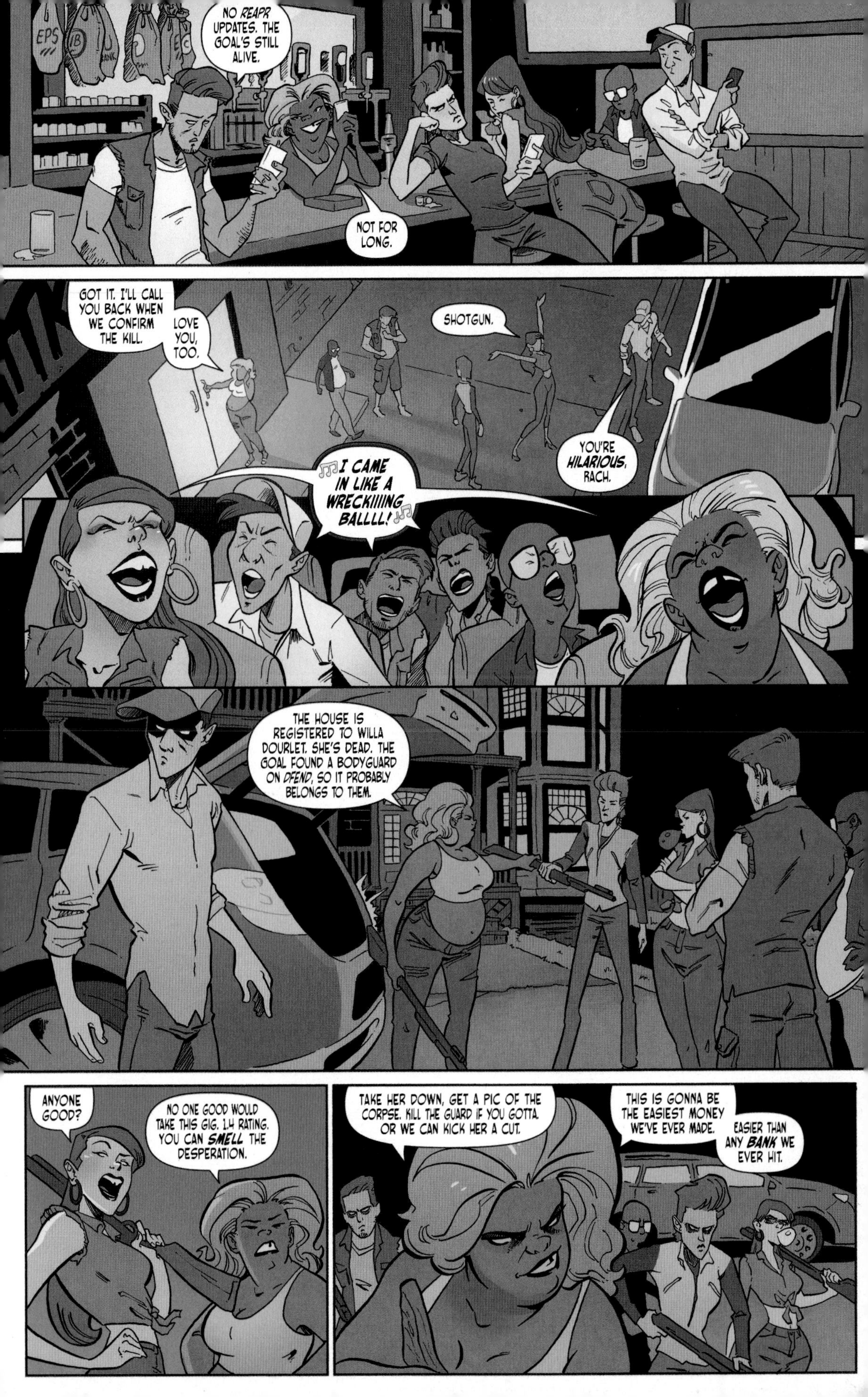
NO *REAPR* UPDATES. THE GOAL'S STILL ALIVE.
NOT FOR LONG.
GOT IT. I'LL CALL YOU BACK WHEN WE CONFIRM THE KILL.
LOVE YOU, TOO.
SHOTGUN.
YOU'RE *HILARIOUS*, RACH.
♫I CAME IN LIKE A WRECKIIIING BALLLL!♫
THE HOUSE IS REGISTERED TO WILLA DOURLET. SHE'S DEAD. THE GOAL FOUND A BODYGUARD ON *DFEND*, SO IT PROBABLY BELONGS TO THEM.
ANYONE GOOD?
NO ONE GOOD WOULD TAKE THIS GIG. 1.4 RATING. YOU CAN *SMELL* THE DESPERATION.
TAKE HER DOWN, GET A PIC OF THE CORPSE. KILL THE GUARD IF YOU GOTTA. OR WE CAN KICK HER A CUT.
THIS IS GONNA BE THE EASIEST MONEY WE'VE EVER MADE.
EASIER THAN ANY *BANK* WE EVER HIT.

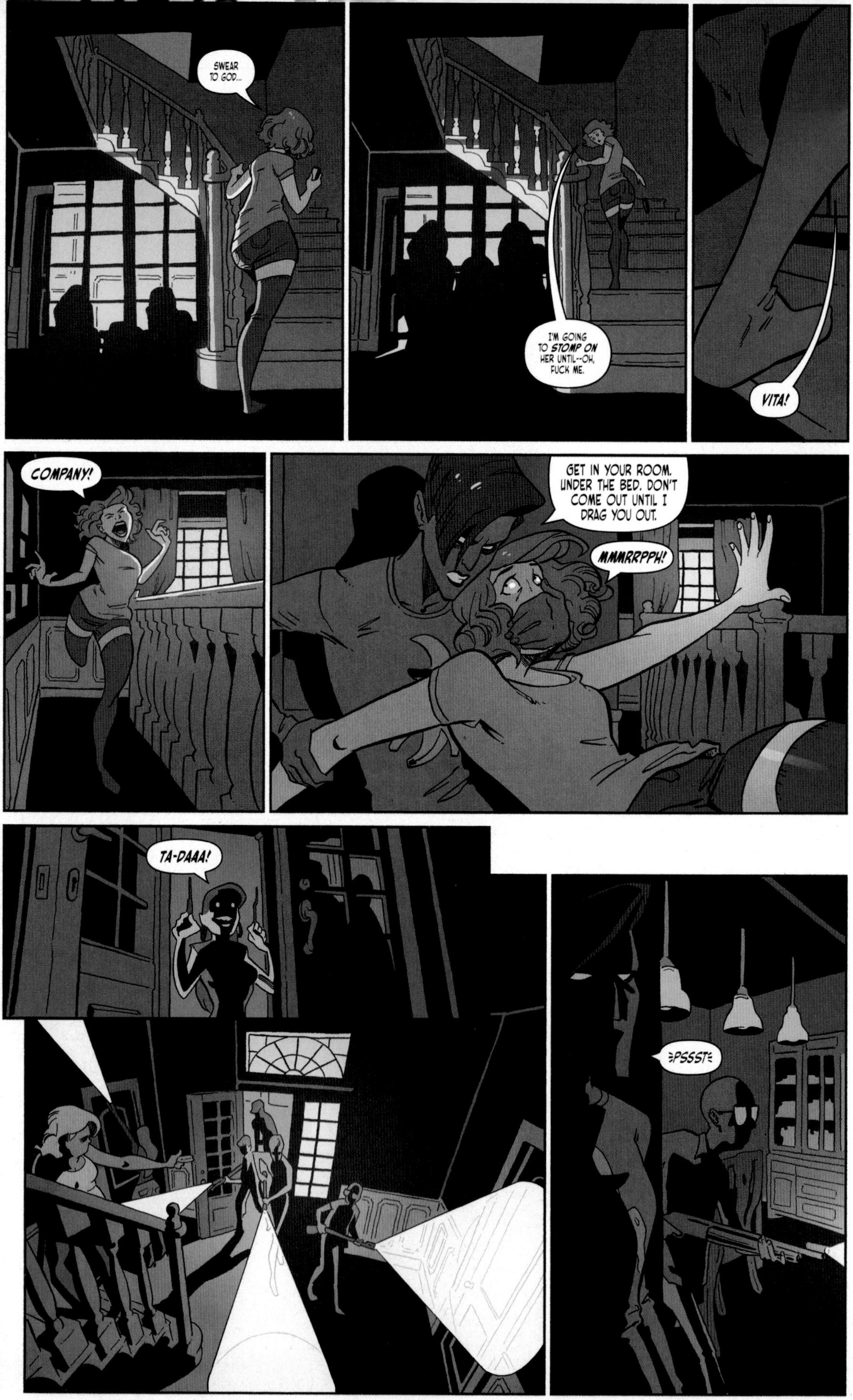
SWEAR TO GOD...
I'M GOING TO STOMP ON HER UNTIL--OH, FUCK ME.
VITA!
COMPANY!
GET IN YOUR ROOM. UNDER THE BED. DON'T COME OUT UNTIL I DRAG YOU OUT.
MMMRRPPH!
TA-DAAA!
PSSST

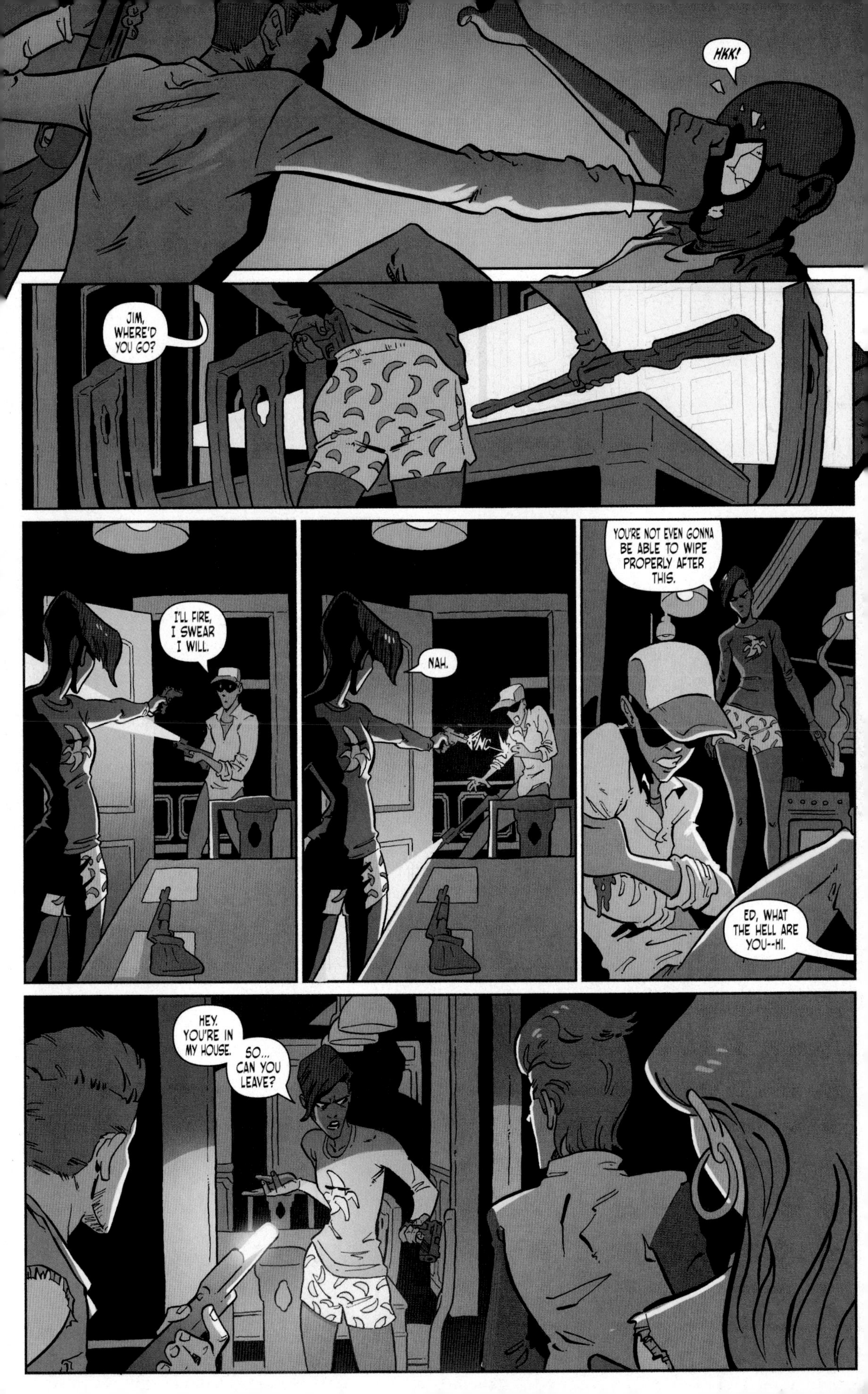
HKK!
JIM, WHERE'D YOU GO?
I'LL FIRE, I SWEAR I WILL.
NAH.
YOU'RE NOT EVEN GONNA BE ABLE TO WIPE PROPERLY AFTER THIS.
ED, WHAT THE HELL ARE YOU--HI.
HEY. YOU'RE IN MY HOUSE.
SO... CAN YOU LEAVE?

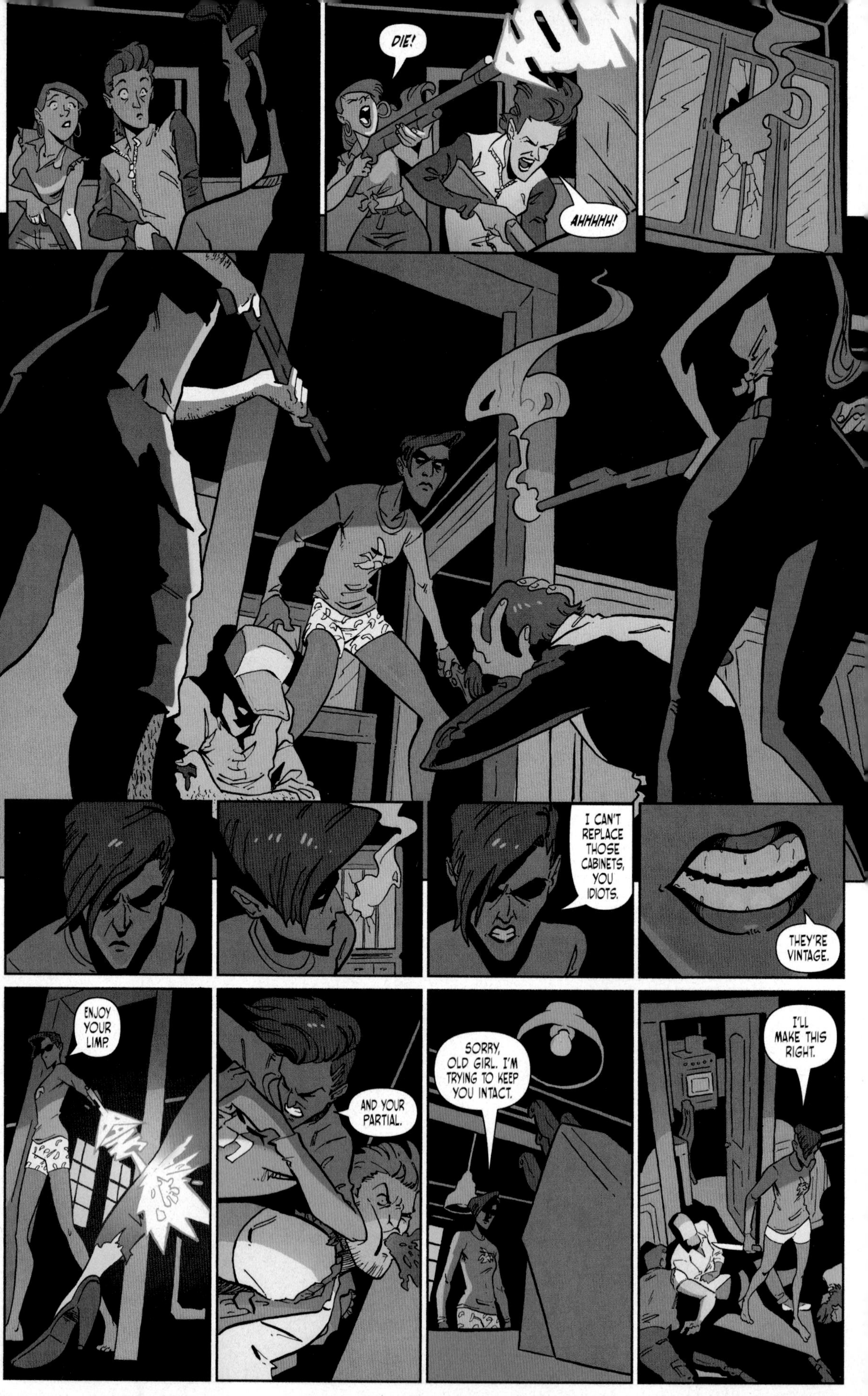
DIE!
AHHHHH!
I CAN'T REPLACE THOSE CABINETS, YOU IDIOTS.
THEY'RE VINTAGE.
ENJOY YOUR LIMP.
AND YOUR PARTIAL.
SORRY, OLD GIRL. I'M TRYING TO KEEP YOU INTACT.
I'LL MAKE THIS RIGHT.

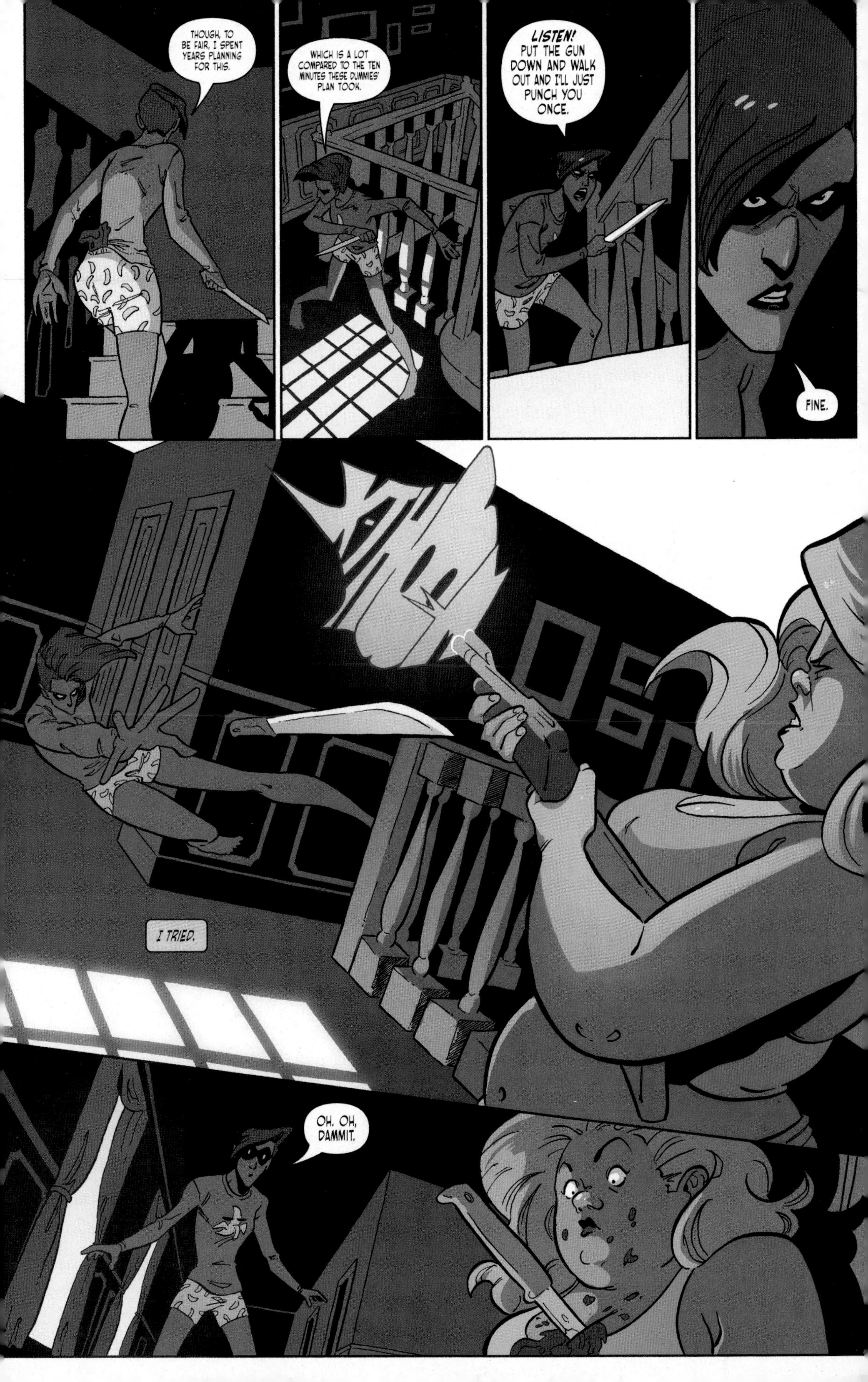

THOUGH, TO BE FAIR, I SPENT YEARS PLANNING FOR THIS.
WHICH IS A LOT COMPARED TO THE TEN MINUTES THESE DUMMIES' PLAN TOOK.
LISTEN! PUT THE GUN DOWN AND WALK OUT AND I'LL JUST PUNCH YOU ONCE.
FINE.
I TRIED.
OH, OH, DAMMIT.

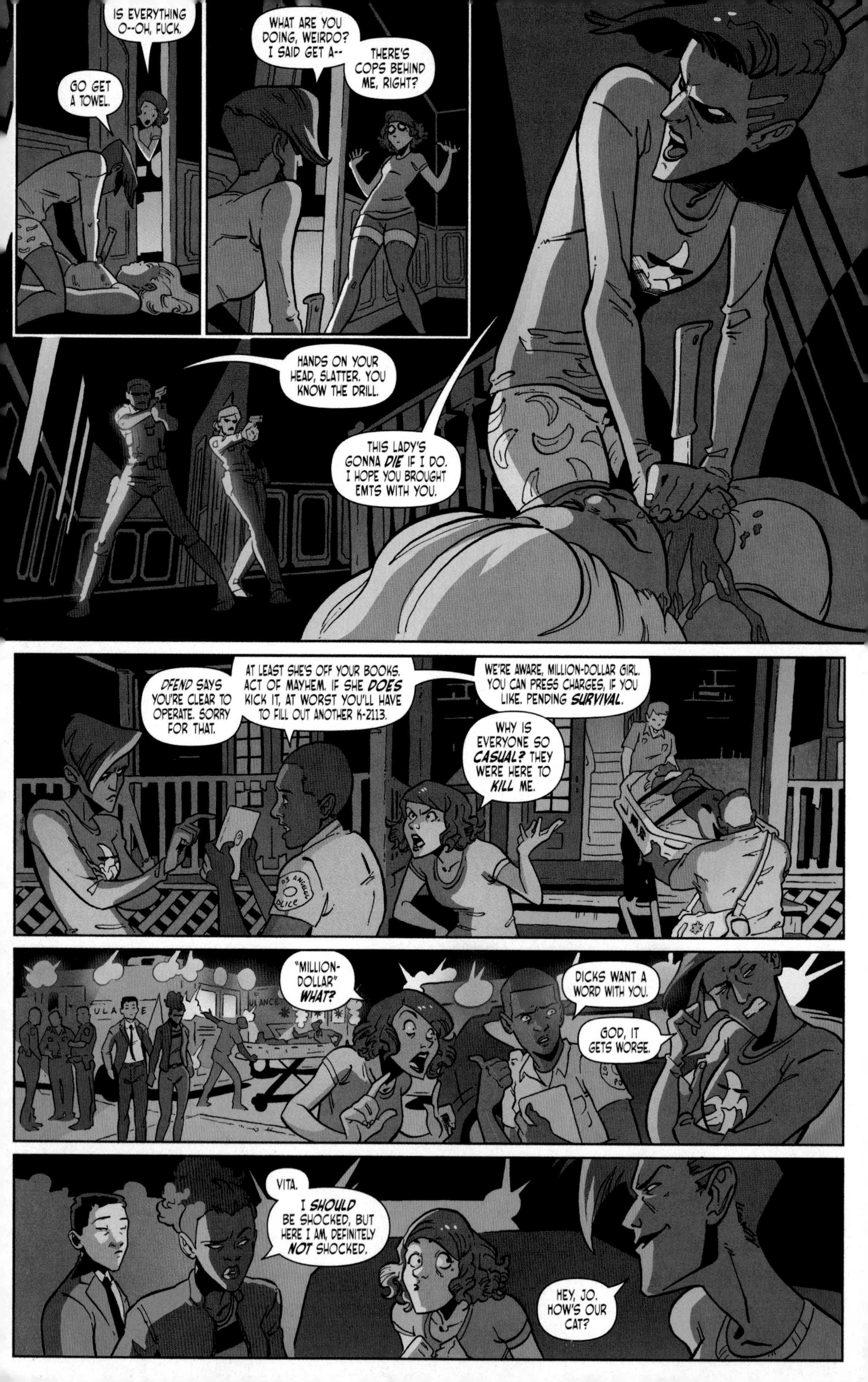
IS EVERYTHING O--OH, FUCK.
GO GET A TOWEL.
WHAT ARE YOU DOING, WEIRDO? I SAID GET A--
THERE'S COPS BEHIND ME, RIGHT?
HANDS ON YOUR HEAD, SLATTER. YOU KNOW THE DRILL.
THIS LADY'S GONNA DIE IF I DO. I HOPE YOU BROUGHT EMTS WITH YOU.
DFEND SAYS YOU'RE CLEAR TO OPERATE. SORRY FOR THAT.
AT LEAST SHE'S OFF YOUR BOOKS. ACT OF MAYHEM. IF SHE DOES KICK IT, AT WORST YOU'LL HAVE TO FILL OUT ANOTHER K-2113.
WE'RE AWARE, MILLION-DOLLAR GIRL. YOU CAN PRESS CHARGES, IF YOU LIKE. PENDING SURVIVAL.
WHY IS EVERYONE SO CASUAL? THEY WERE HERE TO KILL ME.
"MILLION-DOLLAR" WHAT?
DICKS WANT A WORD WITH YOU.
GOD, IT GETS WORSE.
VITA.
I SHOULD BE SHOCKED, BUT HERE I AM, DEFINITELY NOT SHOCKED.
HEY, JO. HOW'S OUR CAT?

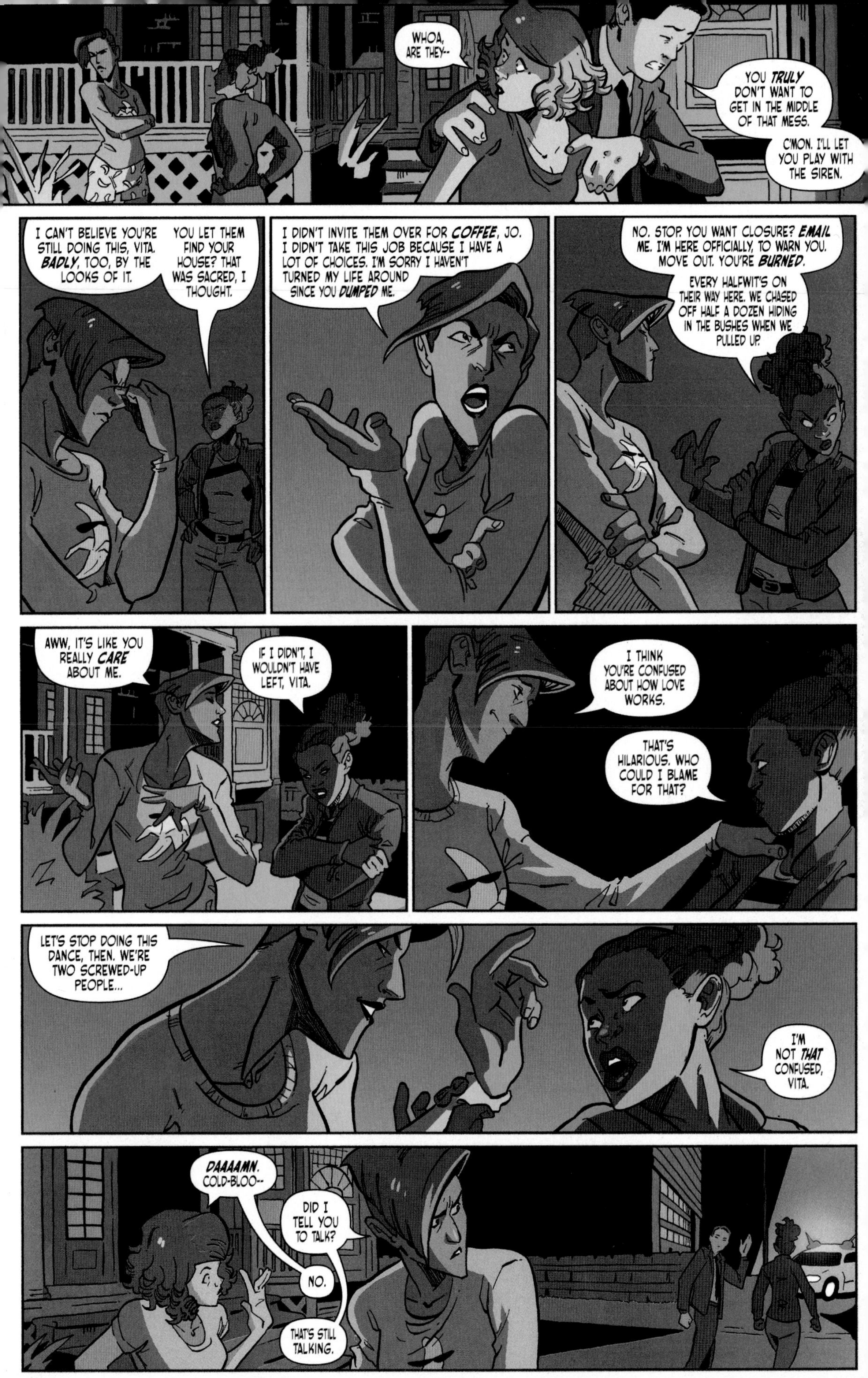
WHOA, ARE THEY--
YOU TRULY DON'T WANT TO GET IN THE MIDDLE OF THAT MESS.
C'MON. I'LL LET YOU PLAY WITH THE SIREN.
I CAN'T BELIEVE YOU'RE STILL DOING THIS, VITA. BADLY, TOO, BY THE LOOKS OF IT.
YOU LET THEM FIND YOUR HOUSE? THAT WAS SACRED, I THOUGHT.
I DIDN'T INVITE THEM OVER FOR COFFEE, JO. I DIDN'T TAKE THIS JOB BECAUSE I HAVE A LOT OF CHOICES. I'M SORRY I HAVEN'T TURNED MY LIFE AROUND SINCE YOU DUMPED ME.
NO. STOP. YOU WANT CLOSURE? EMAIL ME. I'M HERE OFFICIALLY, TO WARN YOU. MOVE OUT. YOU'RE BURNED.
EVERY HALFWIT'S ON THEIR WAY HERE. WE CHASED OFF HALF A DOZEN HIDING IN THE BUSHES WHEN WE PULLED UP.
AWW, IT'S LIKE YOU REALLY CARE ABOUT ME.
IF I DIDN'T, I WOULDN'T HAVE LEFT, VITA.
I THINK YOU'RE CONFUSED ABOUT HOW LOVE WORKS.
THAT'S HILARIOUS. WHO COULD I BLAME FOR THAT?
LET'S STOP DOING THIS DANCE, THEN. WE'RE TWO SCREWED-UP PEOPLE...
I'M NOT THAT CONFUSED, VITA.
DAAAAMN. COLD-BLOO--
DID I TELL YOU TO TALK?
NO.
THAT'S STILL TALKING.

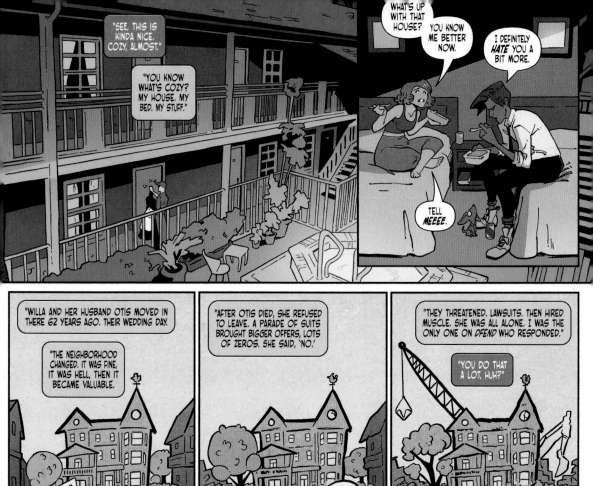

"SEE, THIS IS KINDA NICE. COZY, ALMOST."

"YOU KNOW WHAT'S COZY? MY HOUSE. MY BED. MY STUFF."

WHAT'S UP WITH THAT HOUSE? YOU KNOW ME BETTER NOW.

I DEFINITELY *HATE* YOU A BIT MORE.

TELL *MEEEE.*

"WILLA AND HER HUSBAND OTIS MOVED IN THERE 62 YEARS AGO. THEIR WEDDING DAY."

"THE NEIGHBORHOOD CHANGED. IT WAS FINE, IT WAS HELL, THEN IT BECAME VALUABLE.

SOLD

"AFTER OTIS DIED, SHE REFUSED TO LEAVE. A PARADE OF SUITS BROUGHT BIGGER OFFERS, LOTS OF ZEROS. SHE SAID, 'NO.'

X

"THEY THREATENED. LAWSUITS. THEN HIRED MUSCLE. SHE WAS ALL ALONE. I WAS THE ONLY ONE ON *DFEND* WHO RESPONDED."

"YOU DO THAT A LOT, HUH?"

"FOLKS CALL IT A 'NAIL HOUSE.' ONE PERSON HOLDS OUT, DOESN'T SIGN, HOLDS THE WHOLE REDEVELOPMENT PROCESS UP."

"WILLA LOVED HER HOME, BUT SHE POSITIVELY ADORED THAT, NO MATTER HOW MUCH MONEY THESE BOUGIES HAD, THEY STILL COULDN'T BUY THE THING THEY WANTED MOST.

"PRETTY SURE THE OLD GIRL LIVED LONGER JUST TO PISS SOME RICH IDIOTS OFF WHILE SHE STILL COULD."

"WILLA BARELY PAID, BUT I DIDN'T CARE. I LIKED HER A LOT. SHE DIED LAST YEAR.

"TWO WEEKS LATER I FIND OUT SHE LEFT ME THE HOUSE. TO KEEP HER 'SCREW YOU' LIVING ON BEYOND HER. MY VERY FIRST HOUSE.

"*THAT'S* WHAT YOU BLEW FOR ME."

"I'M SO SORRY."

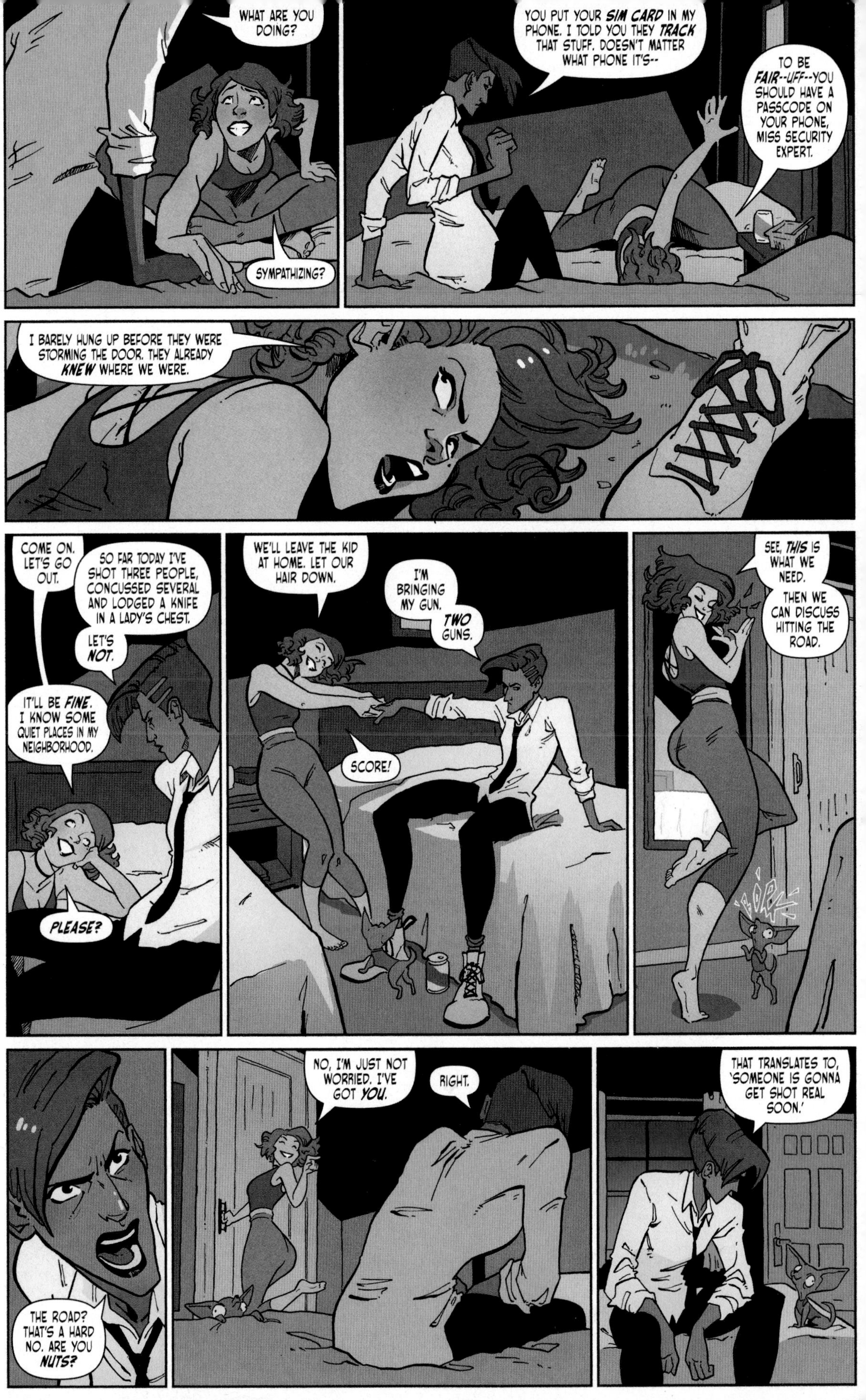
WHAT ARE YOU DOING?
SYMPATHIZING?
YOU PUT YOUR SIM CARD IN MY PHONE. I TOLD YOU THEY TRACK THAT STUFF. DOESN'T MATTER WHAT PHONE IT'S--
TO BE FAIR--UFF--YOU SHOULD HAVE A PASSCODE ON YOUR PHONE, MISS SECURITY EXPERT.
I BARELY HUNG UP BEFORE THEY WERE STORMING THE DOOR. THEY ALREADY KNEW WHERE WE WERE.
COME ON. LET'S GO OUT.
SO FAR TODAY I'VE SHOT THREE PEOPLE, CONCUSSED SEVERAL AND LODGED A KNIFE IN A LADY'S CHEST.
LET'S NOT.
IT'LL BE FINE. I KNOW SOME QUIET PLACES IN MY NEIGHBORHOOD.
PLEASE?
WE'LL LEAVE THE KID AT HOME. LET OUR HAIR DOWN.
I'M BRINGING MY GUN. TWO GUNS.
SCORE!
SEE, THIS IS WHAT WE NEED.
THEN WE CAN DISCUSS HITTING THE ROAD.
THE ROAD? THAT'S A HARD NO. ARE YOU NUTS?
NO, I'M JUST NOT WORRIED. I'VE GOT YOU.
RIGHT.
THAT TRANSLATES TO, 'SOMEONE IS GONNA GET SHOT REAL SOON.'

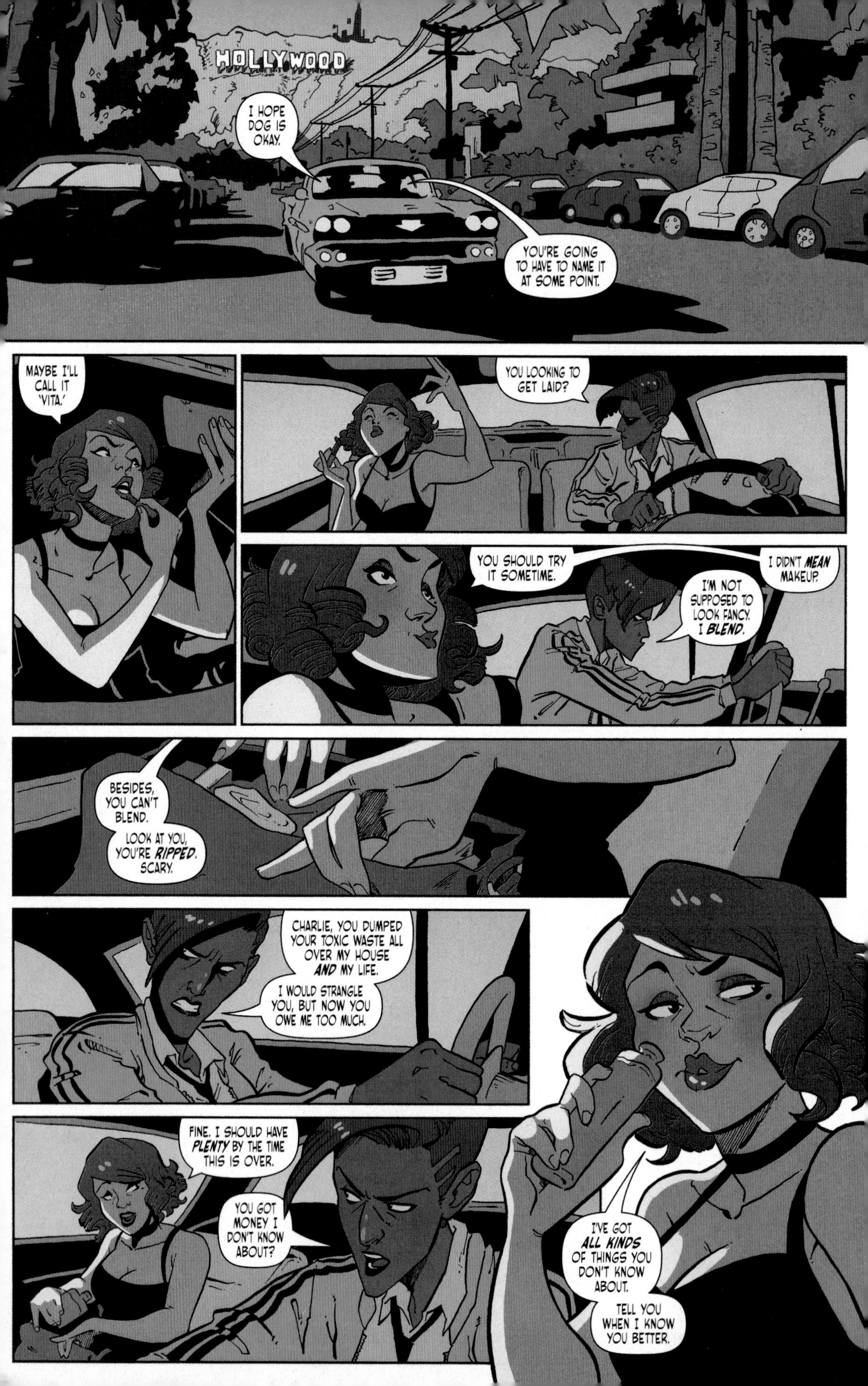
HOLLYWOOD
I HOPE DOG IS OKAY.
YOU'RE GOING TO HAVE TO NAME IT AT SOME POINT.
MAYBE I'LL CALL IT 'VITA.'
YOU LOOKING TO GET LAID?
I DIDN'T MEAN MAKEUP.
YOU SHOULD TRY IT SOMETIME.
I'M NOT SUPPOSED TO LOOK FANCY. I BLEND.
BESIDES, YOU CAN'T BLEND.
LOOK AT YOU, YOU'RE RIPPED. SCARY.
CHARLIE, YOU DUMPED YOUR TOXIC WASTE ALL OVER MY HOUSE AND MY LIFE.
I WOULD STRANGLE YOU, BUT NOW YOU OWE ME TOO MUCH.
FINE. I SHOULD HAVE PLENTY BY THE TIME THIS IS OVER.
YOU GOT MONEY I DON'T KNOW ABOUT?
I'VE GOT ALL KINDS OF THINGS YOU DON'T KNOW ABOUT.
TELL YOU WHEN I KNOW YOU BETTER.

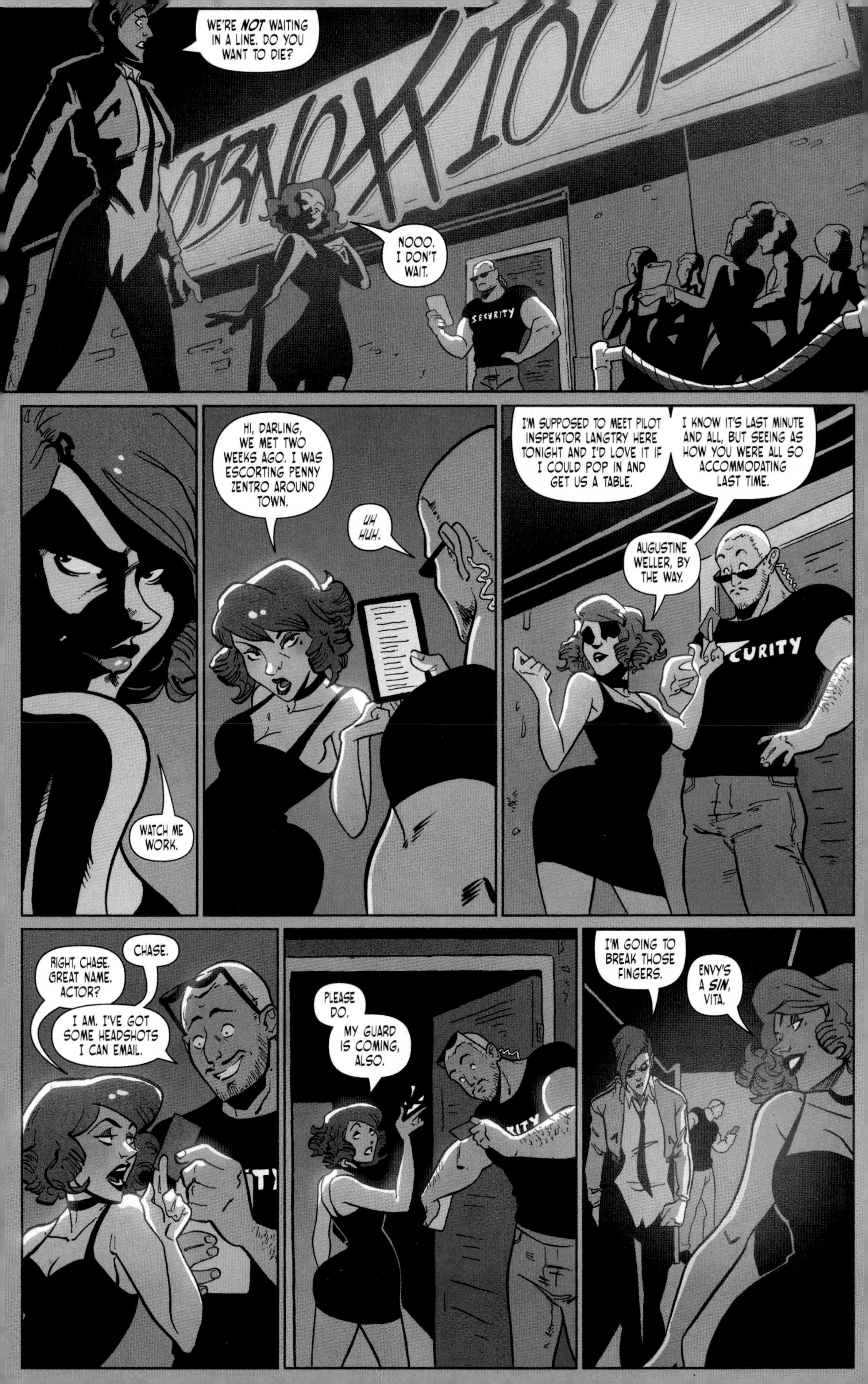
WE'RE *NOT* WAITING IN A LINE. DO YOU WANT TO DIE?
OBNOXXIOU
NOOO. I DON'T WAIT.
SECURITY
WATCH ME WORK.
HI, DARLING, WE MET TWO WEEKS AGO. I WAS ESCORTING PENNY ZENTRO AROUND TOWN.
UH HUH.
I'M SUPPOSED TO MEET PILOT INSPEKTOR LANGTRY HERE TONIGHT AND I'D LOVE IT IF I COULD POP IN AND GET US A TABLE.
I KNOW IT'S LAST MINUTE AND ALL, BUT SEEING AS HOW YOU WERE ALL SO ACCOMMODATING LAST TIME.
AUGUSTINE WELLER, BY THE WAY.
CURITY
CHASE.
RIGHT, CHASE. GREAT NAME. ACTOR?
I AM. I'VE GOT SOME HEADSHOTS I CAN EMAIL.
PLEASE DO.
MY GUARD IS COMING, ALSO.
I'M GOING TO BREAK THOSE FINGERS.
ENVY'S A *SIN*, VITA.

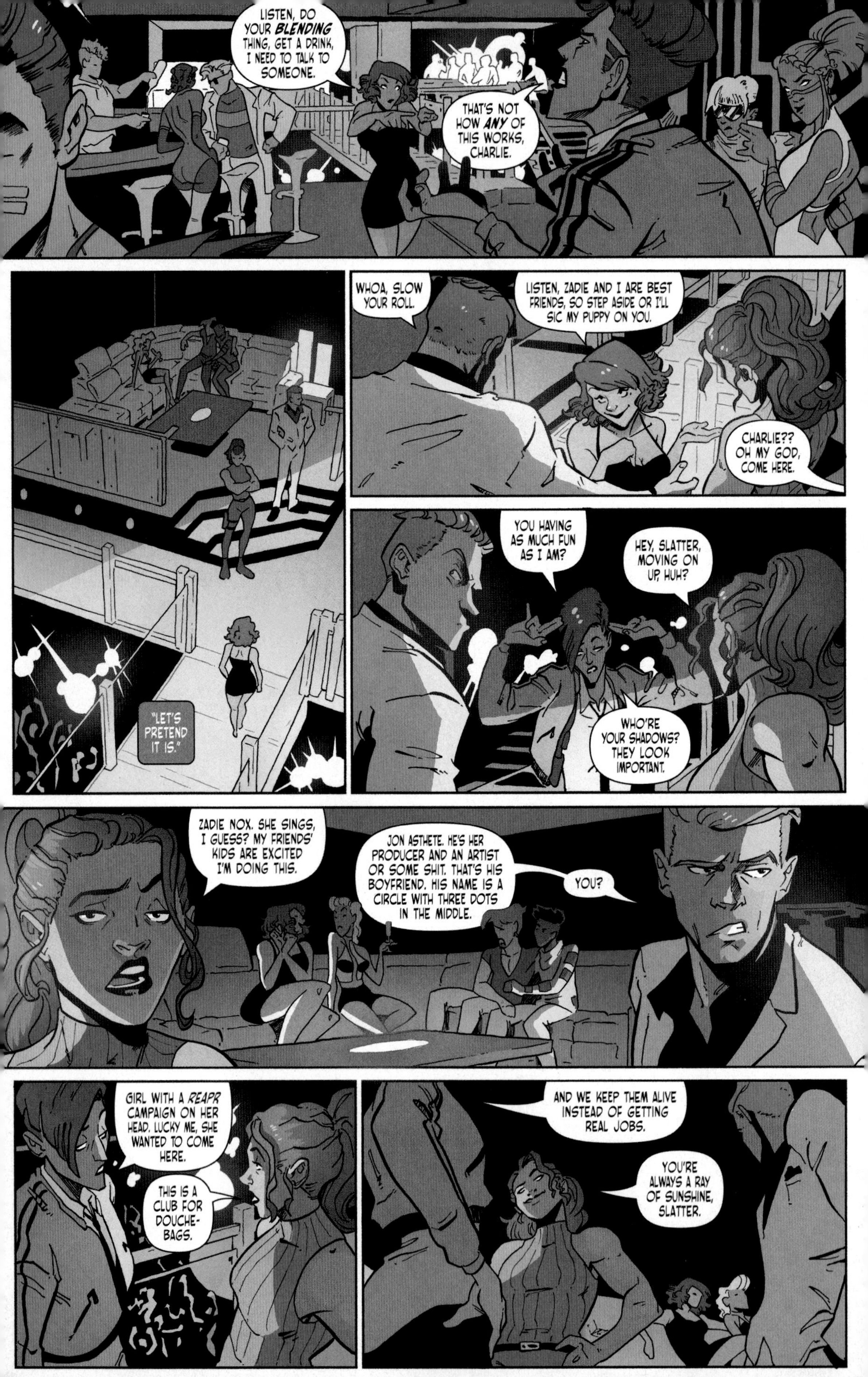
LISTEN, DO YOUR BLENDING THING, GET A DRINK, I NEED TO TALK TO SOMEONE.
THAT'S NOT HOW ANY OF THIS WORKS, CHARLIE.
"LET'S PRETEND IT IS."
WHOA, SLOW YOUR ROLL.
LISTEN, ZADIE AND I ARE BEST FRIENDS, SO STEP ASIDE OR I'LL SIC MY PUPPY ON YOU.
CHARLIE?? OH MY GOD, COME HERE.
YOU HAVING AS MUCH FUN AS I AM?
HEY, SLATTER, MOVING ON UP, HUH?
WHO'RE YOUR SHADOWS? THEY LOOK IMPORTANT.
ZADIE NOX. SHE SINGS, I GUESS? MY FRIENDS' KIDS ARE EXCITED I'M DOING THIS.
JON ASTHETE. HE'S HER PRODUCER AND AN ARTIST OR SOME SHIT. THAT'S HIS BOYFRIEND. HIS NAME IS A CIRCLE WITH THREE DOTS IN THE MIDDLE.
YOU?
GIRL WITH A REAPR CAMPAIGN ON HER HEAD. LUCKY ME, SHE WANTED TO COME HERE.
THIS IS A CLUB FOR DOUCHE-BAGS.
AND WE KEEP THEM ALIVE INSTEAD OF GETTING REAL JOBS.
YOU'RE ALWAYS A RAY OF SUNSHINE, SLATTER.

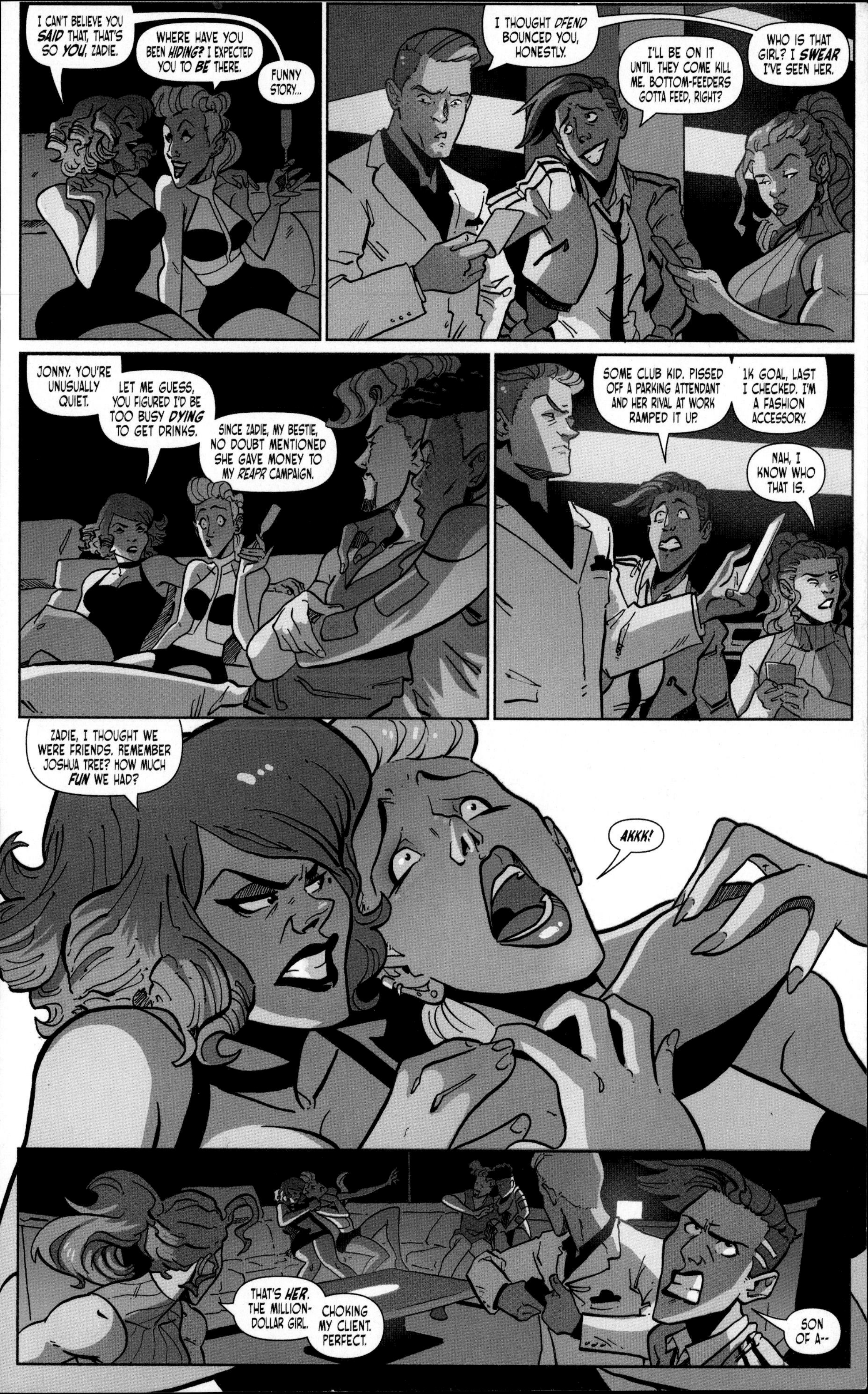
I CAN'T BELIEVE YOU SAID THAT, THAT'S SO YOU, ZADIE.
WHERE HAVE YOU BEEN HIDING? I EXPECTED YOU TO BE THERE.
FUNNY STORY...
I THOUGHT DFEND BOUNCED YOU, HONESTLY.
I'LL BE ON IT UNTIL THEY COME KILL ME. BOTTOM-FEEDERS GOTTA FEED, RIGHT?
WHO IS THAT GIRL? I SWEAR I'VE SEEN HER.
JONNY. YOU'RE UNUSUALLY QUIET.
LET ME GUESS, YOU FIGURED I'D BE TOO BUSY DYING TO GET DRINKS.
SINCE ZADIE, MY BESTIE, NO DOUBT MENTIONED SHE GAVE MONEY TO MY REAPR CAMPAIGN.
SOME CLUB KID. PISSED OFF A PARKING ATTENDANT AND HER RIVAL AT WORK RAMPED IT UP.
1K GOAL, LAST I CHECKED. I'M A FASHION ACCESSORY.
NAH, I KNOW WHO THAT IS.
ZADIE, I THOUGHT WE WERE FRIENDS. REMEMBER JOSHUA TREE? HOW MUCH FUN WE HAD?
AKKK!
THAT'S HER. THE MILLION-DOLLAR GIRL.
CHOKING MY CLIENT. PERFECT.
SON OF A--

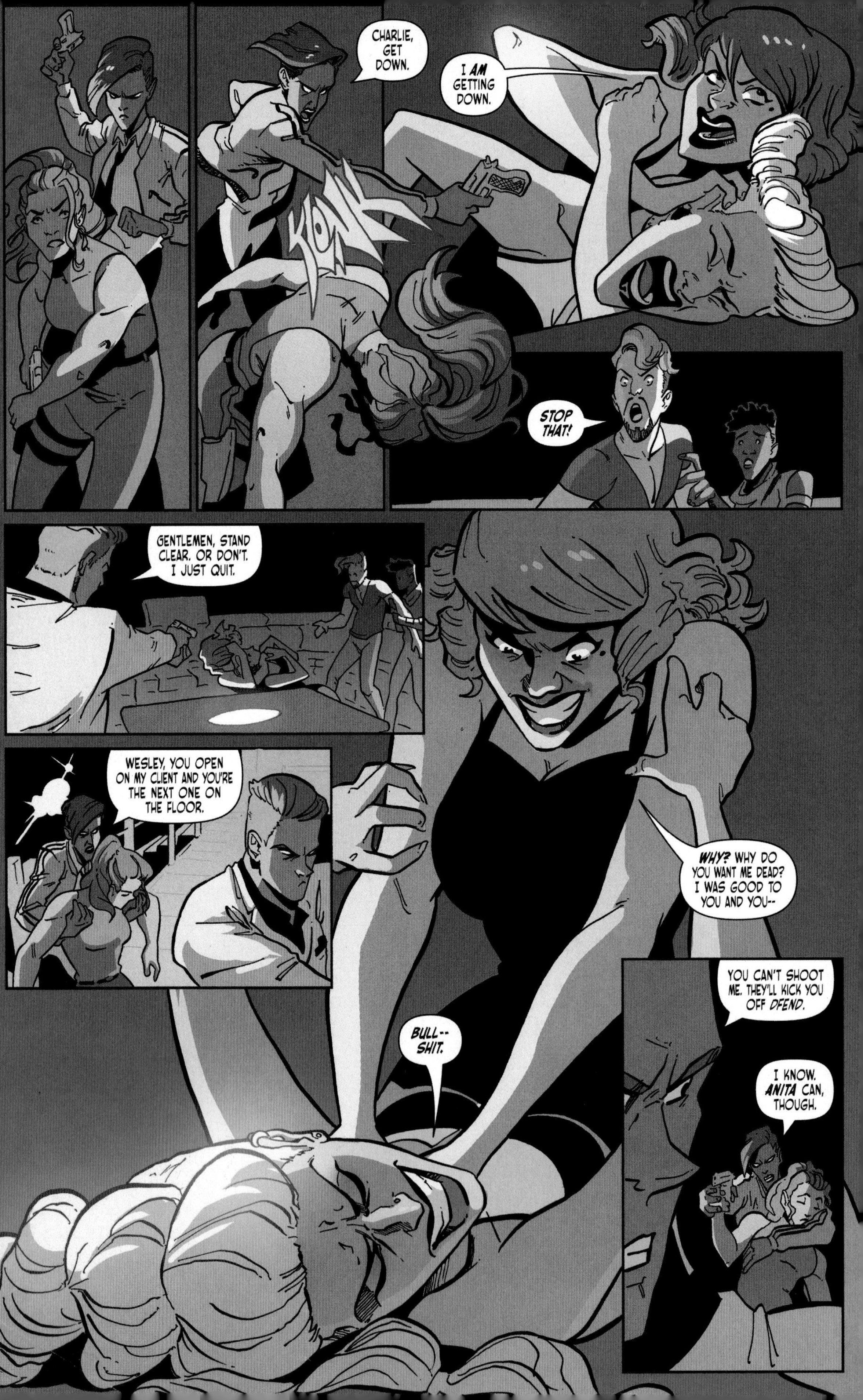

CHARLIE, GET DOWN.
I AM GETTING DOWN.
KOW
STOP THAT!
GENTLEMEN, STAND CLEAR. OR DON'T. I JUST QUIT.
WESLEY, YOU OPEN ON MY CLIENT AND YOU'RE THE NEXT ONE ON THE FLOOR.
WHY? WHY DO YOU WANT ME DEAD? I WAS GOOD TO YOU AND YOU--
BULL-- SHIT.
YOU CAN'T SHOOT ME. THEY'LL KICK YOU OFF DFEND.
I KNOW. ANITA CAN, THOUGH.

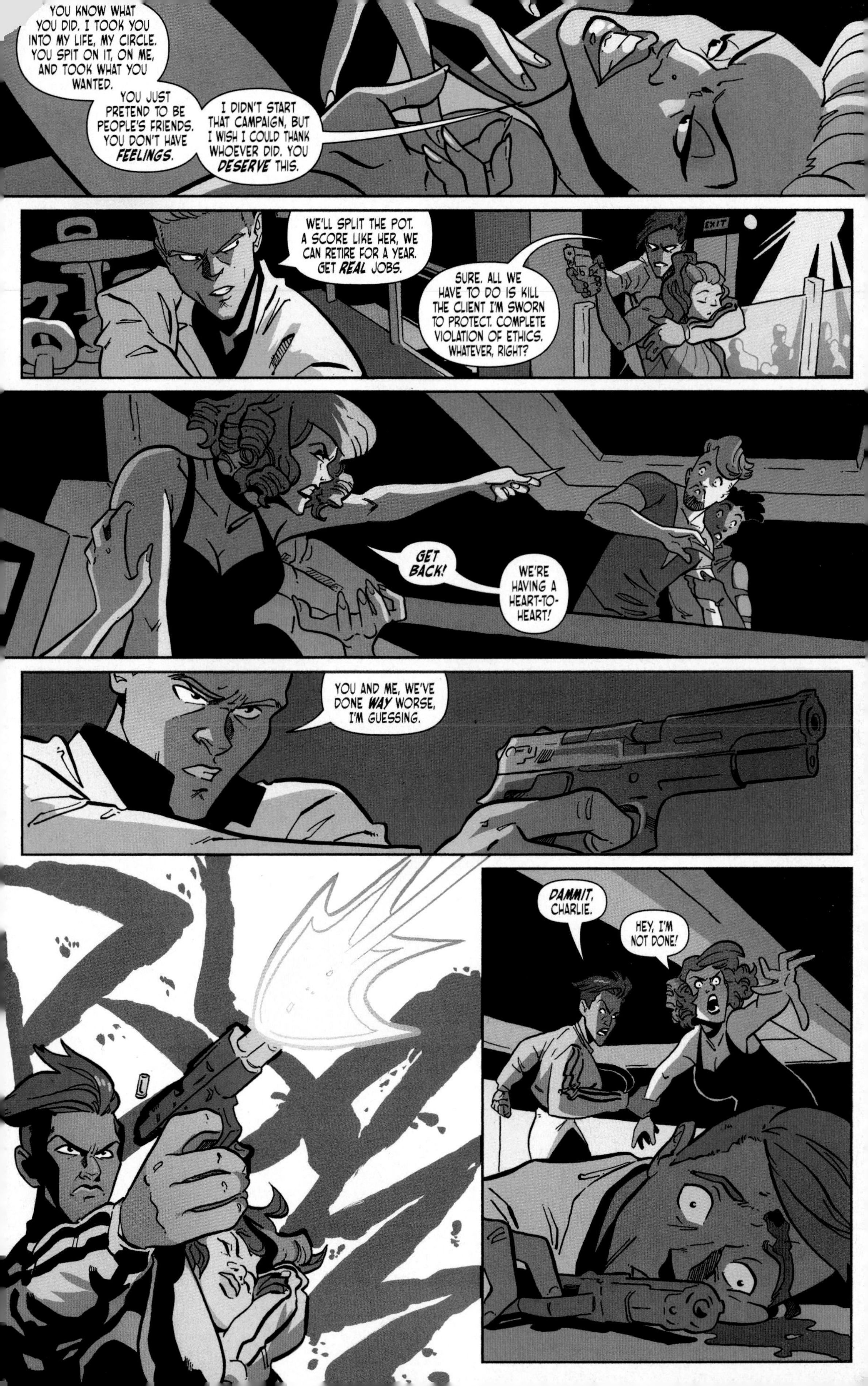

YOU KNOW WHAT YOU DID. I TOOK YOU INTO MY LIFE, MY CIRCLE. YOU SPIT ON IT, ON ME, AND TOOK WHAT YOU WANTED.
YOU JUST PRETEND TO BE PEOPLE'S FRIENDS. YOU DON'T HAVE FEELINGS.
I DIDN'T START THAT CAMPAIGN, BUT I WISH I COULD THANK WHOEVER DID. YOU DESERVE THIS.
EXIT
WE'LL SPLIT THE POT. A SCORE LIKE HER, WE CAN RETIRE FOR A YEAR. GET REAL JOBS.
SURE. ALL WE HAVE TO DO IS KILL THE CLIENT I'M SWORN TO PROTECT. COMPLETE VIOLATION OF ETHICS. WHATEVER, RIGHT?
GET BACK!
WE'RE HAVING A HEART-TO-HEART!
YOU AND ME, WE'VE DONE WAY WORSE, I'M GUESSING.
DAMMIT, CHARLIE.
HEY, I'M NOT DONE!

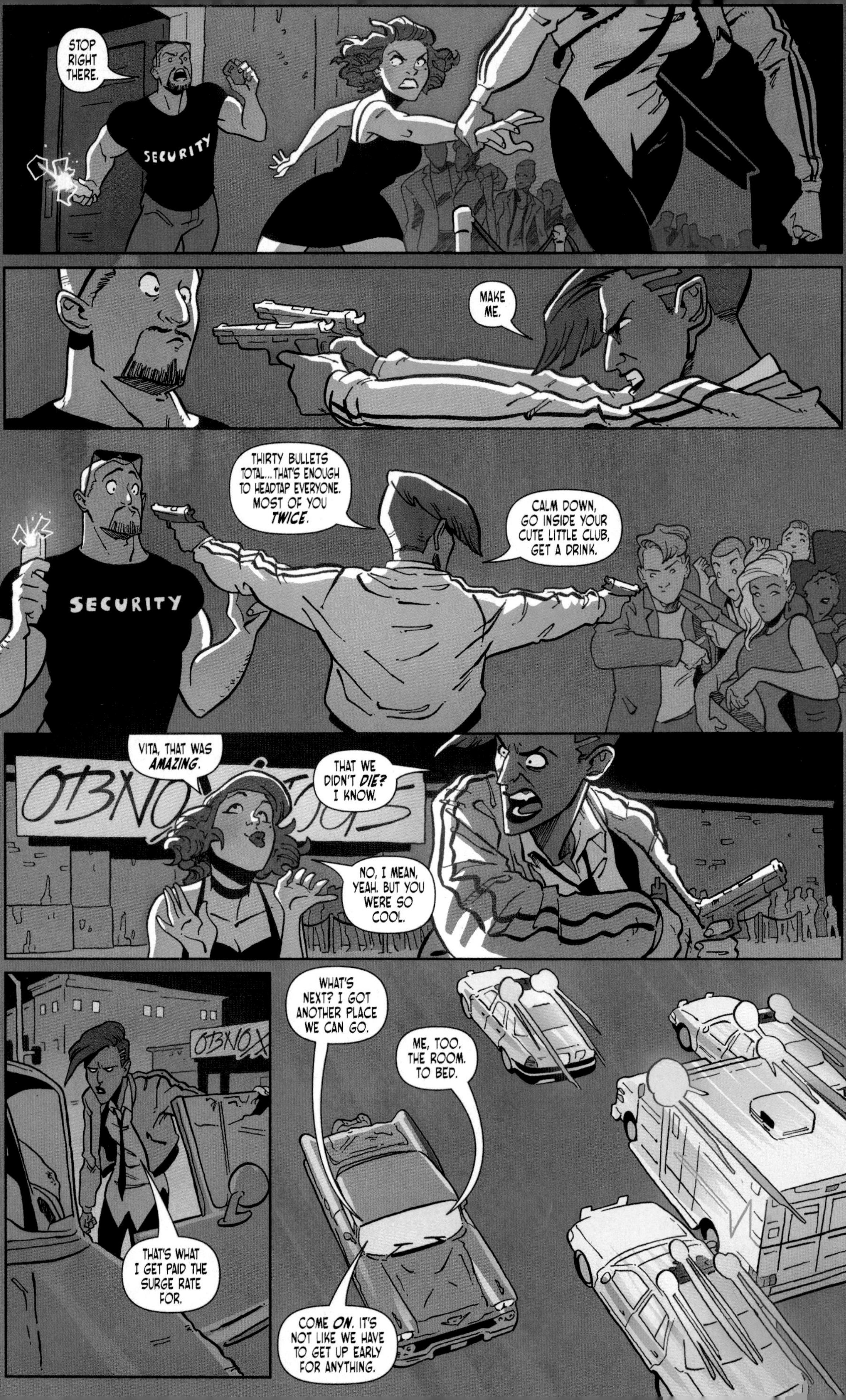
STOP RIGHT THERE.
SECURITY
MAKE ME.
SECURITY
THIRTY BULLETS TOTAL...THAT'S ENOUGH TO HEADTAP EVERYONE. MOST OF YOU *TWICE*.
CALM DOWN, GO INSIDE YOUR CUTE LITTLE CLUB, GET A DRINK.
VITA, THAT WAS *AMAZING*.
THAT WE DIDN'T *DIE?* I KNOW.
NO, I MEAN, YEAH. BUT YOU WERE SO COOL.
THAT'S WHAT I GET PAID THE SURGE RATE FOR.
WHAT'S NEXT? I GOT ANOTHER PLACE WE CAN GO.
ME, TOO. THE ROOM. TO BED.
COME *ON*. IT'S NOT LIKE WE HAVE TO GET UP EARLY FOR ANYTHING.

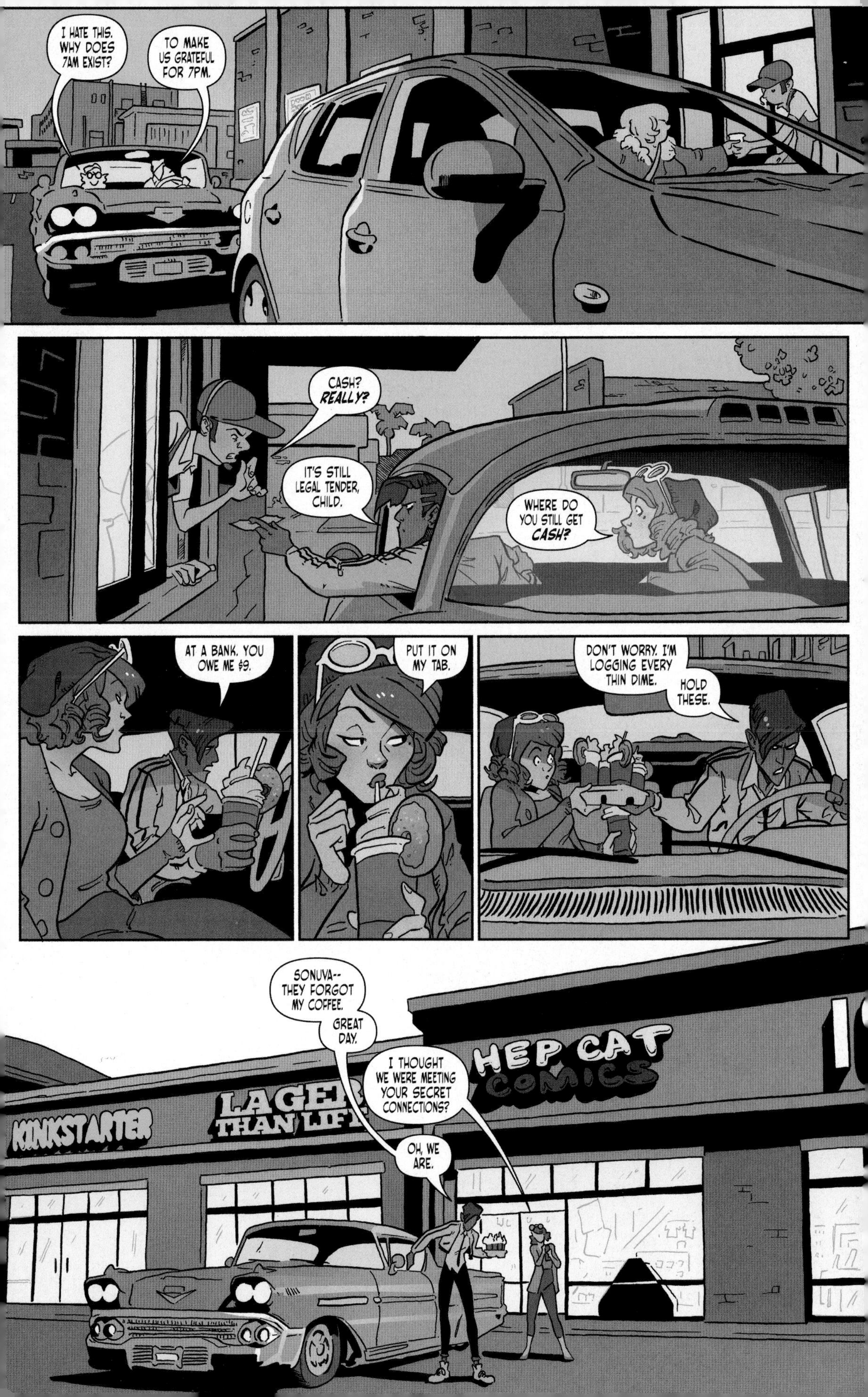
I HATE THIS. WHY DOES 7AM EXIST?
TO MAKE US GRATEFUL FOR 7PM.
CASH? REALLY?
IT'S STILL LEGAL TENDER, CHILD.
WHERE DO YOU STILL GET CASH?
AT A BANK. YOU OWE ME $9.
PUT IT ON MY TAB.
DON'T WORRY. I'M LOGGING EVERY THIN DIME.
HOLD THESE.
SONUVA-- THEY FORGOT MY COFFEE.
GREAT DAY.
HEP CAT COMICS
LAGER THAN LIFE
KINKSTARTER
I THOUGHT WE WERE MEETING YOUR SECRET CONNECTIONS?
OH, WE ARE.

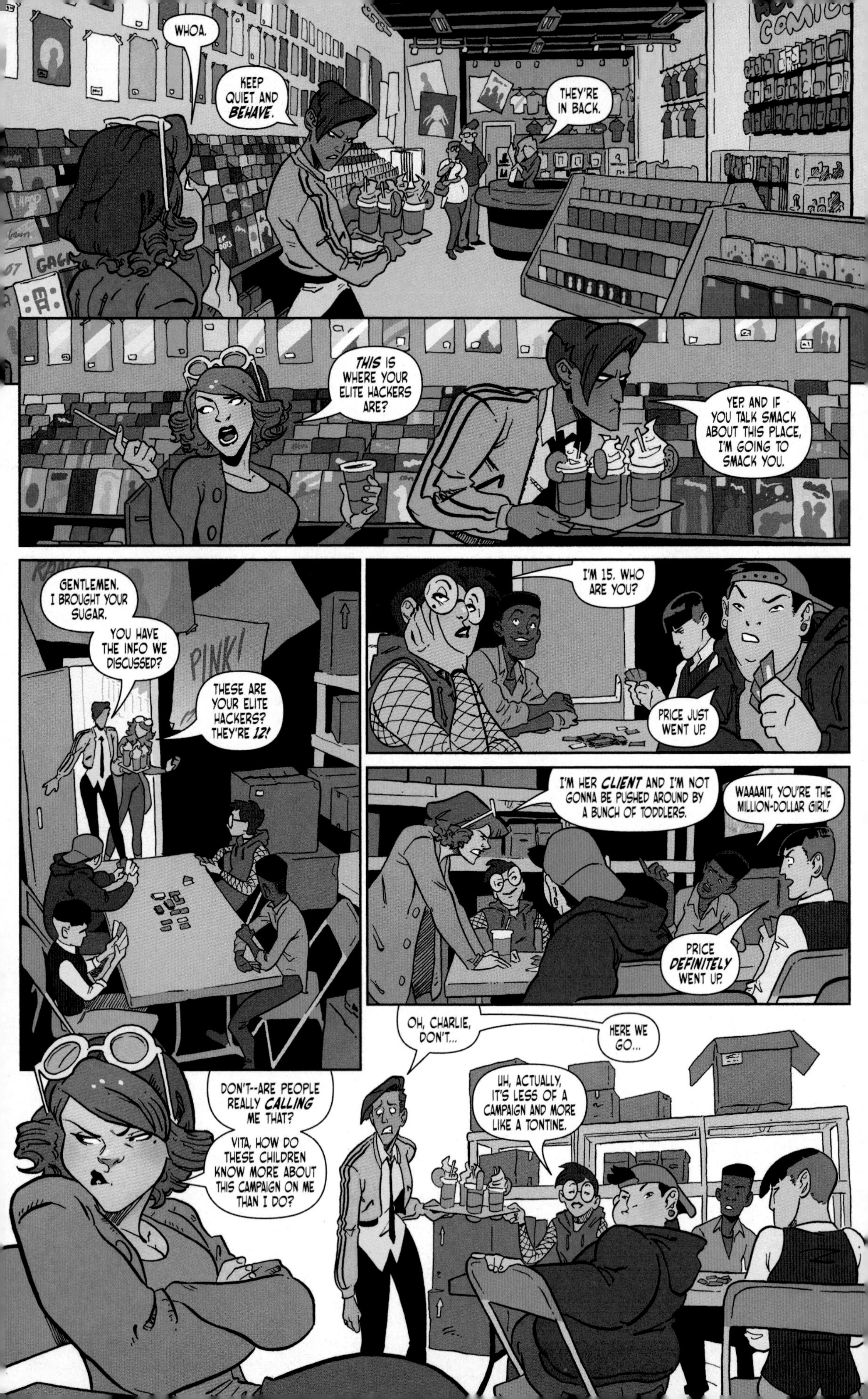
WHOA.
KEEP QUIET AND BEHAVE.
THEY'RE IN BACK.
THIS IS WHERE YOUR ELITE HACKERS ARE?
YEP. AND IF YOU TALK SMACK ABOUT THIS PLACE, I'M GOING TO SMACK YOU.
GENTLEMEN. I BROUGHT YOUR SUGAR.
YOU HAVE THE INFO WE DISCUSSED?
THESE ARE YOUR ELITE HACKERS? THEY'RE 12!
PINK!
I'M 15. WHO ARE YOU?
PRICE JUST WENT UP.
I'M HER CLIENT AND I'M NOT GONNA BE PUSHED AROUND BY A BUNCH OF TODDLERS.
WAAAAIT, YOU'RE THE MILLION-DOLLAR GIRL!
PRICE DEFINITELY WENT UP.
OH, CHARLIE, DON'T...
HERE WE GO...
DON'T--ARE PEOPLE REALLY CALLING ME THAT?
VITA, HOW DO THESE CHILDREN KNOW MORE ABOUT THIS CAMPAIGN ON ME THAN I DO?
UH, ACTUALLY, IT'S LESS OF A CAMPAIGN AND MORE LIKE A TONTINE.

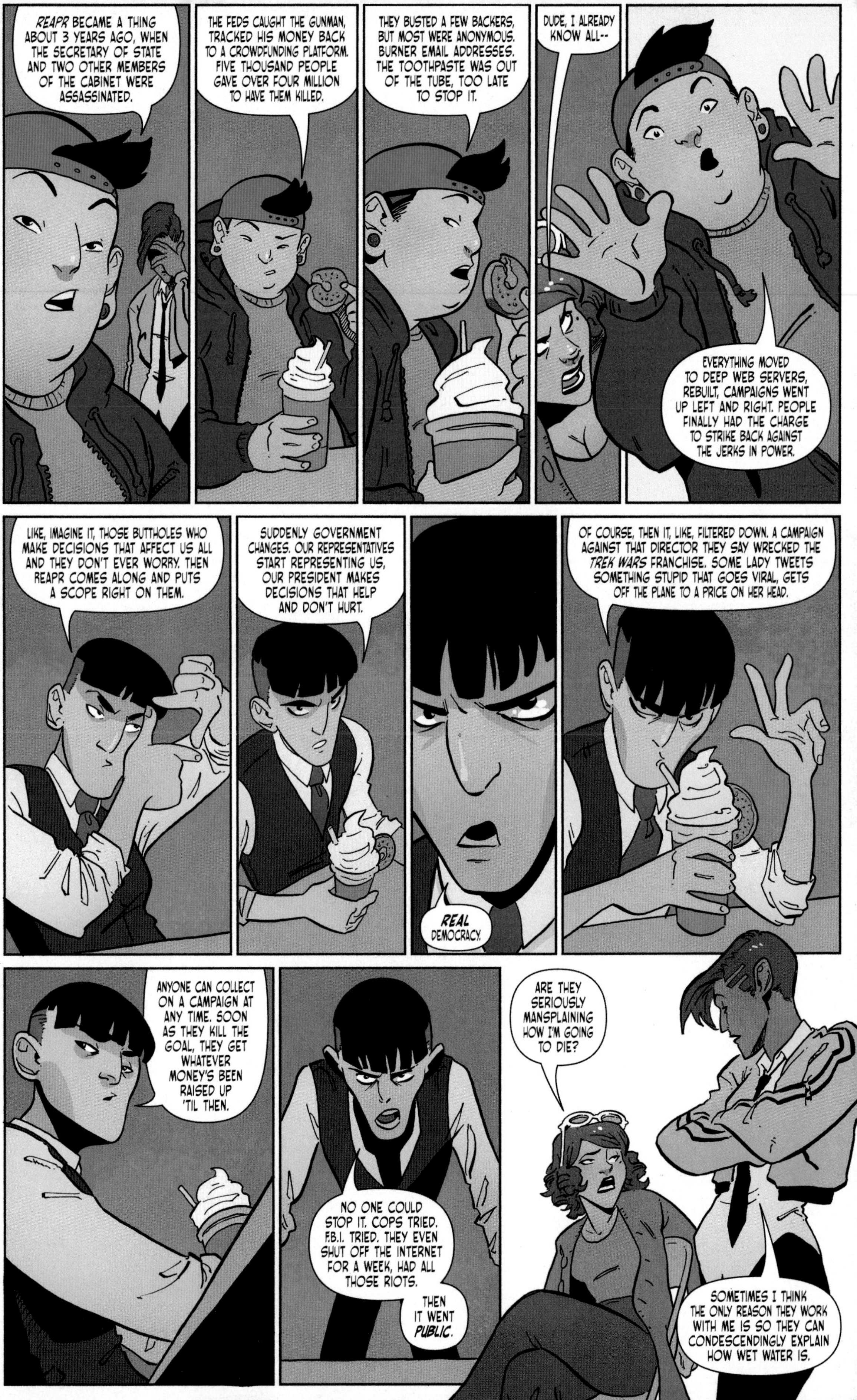
REAPR BECAME A THING ABOUT 3 YEARS AGO, WHEN THE SECRETARY OF STATE AND TWO OTHER MEMBERS OF THE CABINET WERE ASSASSINATED.
THE FEDS CAUGHT THE GUNMAN, TRACKED HIS MONEY BACK TO A CROWDFUNDING PLATFORM. FIVE THOUSAND PEOPLE GAVE OVER FOUR MILLION TO HAVE THEM KILLED.
THEY BUSTED A FEW BACKERS, BUT MOST WERE ANONYMOUS. BURNER EMAIL ADDRESSES. THE TOOTHPASTE WAS OUT OF THE TUBE, TOO LATE TO STOP IT.
DUDE, I ALREADY KNOW ALL--
EVERYTHING MOVED TO DEEP WEB SERVERS, REBUILT, CAMPAIGNS WENT UP LEFT AND RIGHT. PEOPLE FINALLY HAD THE CHARGE TO STRIKE BACK AGAINST THE JERKS IN POWER.
LIKE, IMAGINE IT, THOSE BUTTHOLES WHO MAKE DECISIONS THAT AFFECT US ALL AND THEY DON'T EVER WORRY. THEN REAPR COMES ALONG AND PUTS A SCOPE RIGHT ON THEM.
SUDDENLY GOVERNMENT CHANGES. OUR REPRESENTATIVES START REPRESENTING US, OUR PRESIDENT MAKES DECISIONS THAT HELP AND DON'T HURT.
REAL DEMOCRACY.
OF COURSE, THEN IT, LIKE, FILTERED DOWN. A CAMPAIGN AGAINST THAT DIRECTOR THEY SAY WRECKED THE TREK WARS FRANCHISE. SOME LADY TWEETS SOMETHING STUPID THAT GOES VIRAL, GETS OFF THE PLANE TO A PRICE ON HER HEAD.
ANYONE CAN COLLECT ON A CAMPAIGN AT ANY TIME. SOON AS THEY KILL THE GOAL, THEY GET WHATEVER MONEY'S BEEN RAISED UP 'TIL THEN.
NO ONE COULD STOP IT. COPS TRIED. F.B.I. TRIED. THEY EVEN SHUT OFF THE INTERNET FOR A WEEK, HAD ALL THOSE RIOTS.
THEN IT WENT PUBLIC.
ARE THEY SERIOUSLY MANSPLAINING HOW I'M GOING TO DIE?
SOMETIMES I THINK THE ONLY REASON THEY WORK WITH ME IS SO THEY CAN CONDESCENDINGLY EXPLAIN HOW WET WATER IS.

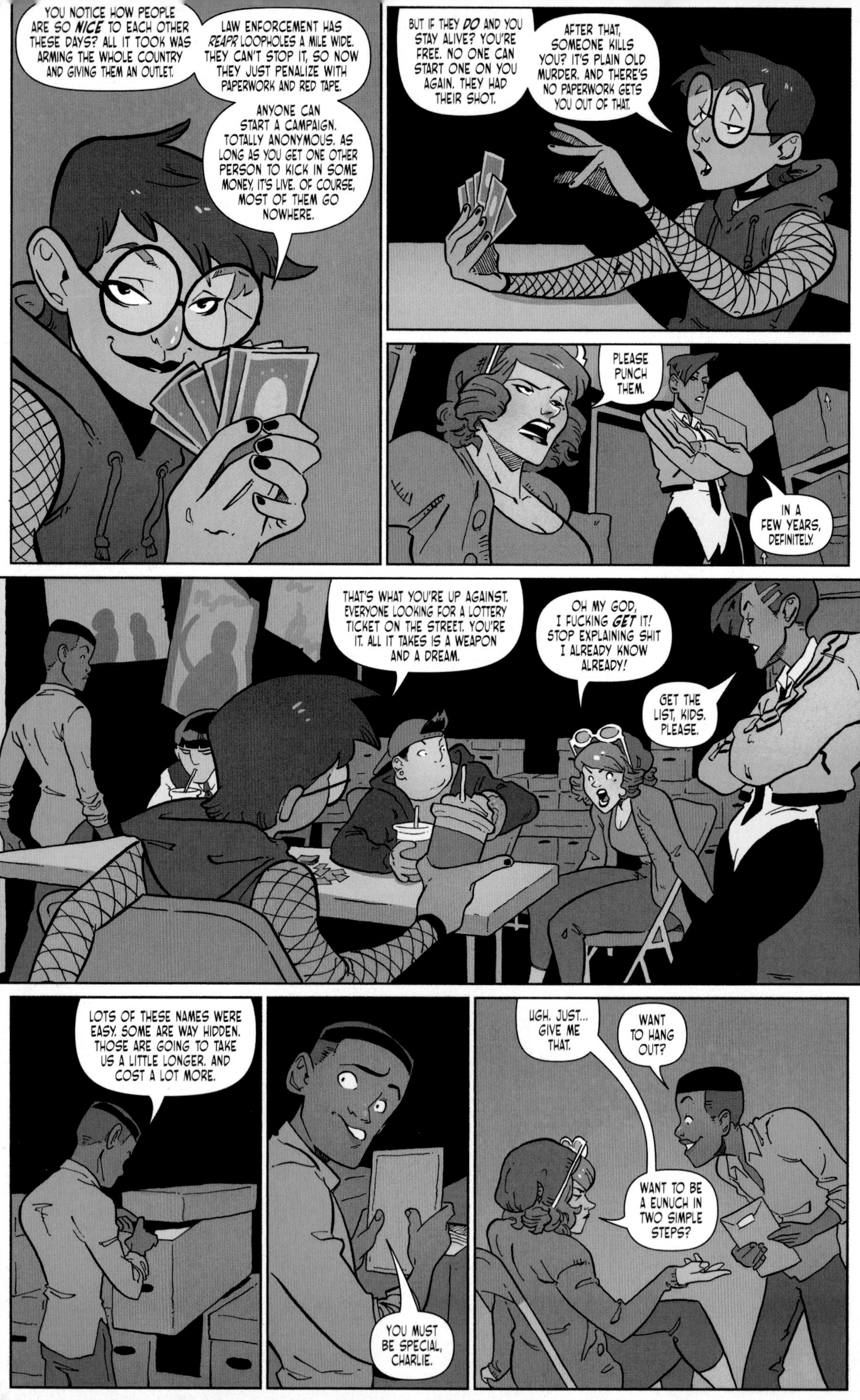
YOU NOTICE HOW PEOPLE ARE SO *NICE* TO EACH OTHER THESE DAYS? ALL IT TOOK WAS ARMING THE WHOLE COUNTRY AND GIVING THEM AN OUTLET.
LAW ENFORCEMENT HAS *REAPR* LOOPHOLES A MILE WIDE. THEY CAN'T STOP IT, SO NOW THEY JUST PENALIZE WITH PAPERWORK AND RED TAPE.
ANYONE CAN START A CAMPAIGN. TOTALLY ANONYMOUS. AS LONG AS YOU GET ONE OTHER PERSON TO KICK IN SOME MONEY, IT'S LIVE. OF COURSE, MOST OF THEM GO NOWHERE.
BUT IF THEY *DO* AND YOU STAY ALIVE? YOU'RE FREE. NO ONE CAN START ONE ON YOU AGAIN. THEY HAD THEIR SHOT.
AFTER THAT, SOMEONE KILLS YOU? IT'S PLAIN OLD MURDER. AND THERE'S NO PAPERWORK GETS YOU OUT OF THAT.
PLEASE PUNCH THEM.
IN A FEW YEARS, DEFINITELY.
THAT'S WHAT YOU'RE UP AGAINST. EVERYONE LOOKING FOR A LOTTERY TICKET ON THE STREET. YOU'RE IT. ALL IT TAKES IS A WEAPON AND A DREAM.
OH MY GOD, I FUCKING *GET* IT! STOP EXPLAINING SHIT I ALREADY KNOW ALREADY!
GET THE LIST, KIDS. PLEASE.
LOTS OF THESE NAMES WERE EASY. SOME ARE WAY HIDDEN. THOSE ARE GOING TO TAKE US A LITTLE LONGER. AND COST A LOT MORE.
YOU MUST BE SPECIAL, CHARLIE.
UGH. JUST... GIVE ME THAT.
WANT TO HANG OUT?
WANT TO BE A EUNUCH IN TWO SIMPLE STEPS?

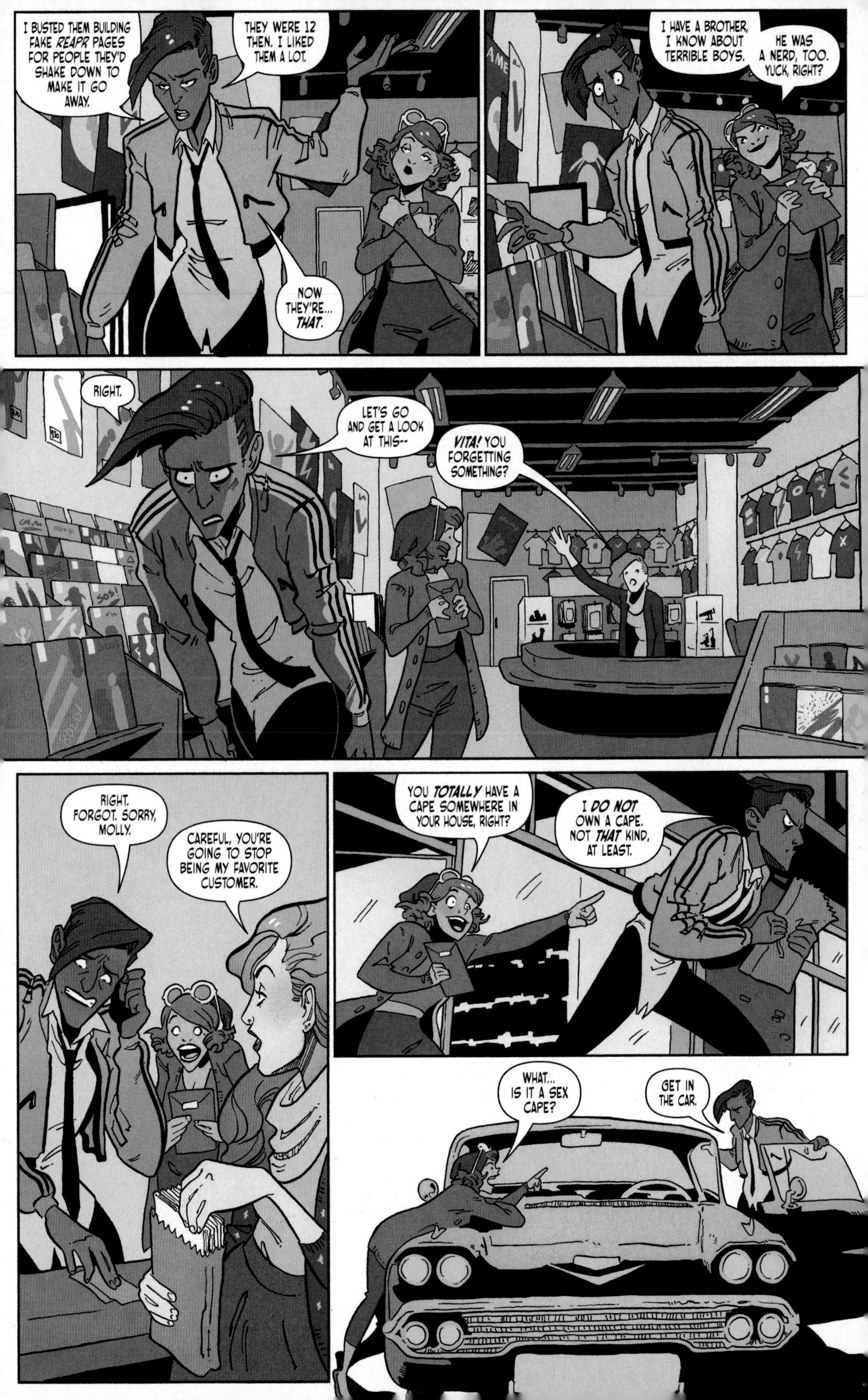
I BUSTED THEM BUILDING FAKE REAPR PAGES FOR PEOPLE THEY'D SHAKE DOWN TO MAKE IT GO AWAY.
THEY WERE 12 THEN. I LIKED THEM A LOT.
NOW THEY'RE... THAT.
I HAVE A BROTHER, I KNOW ABOUT TERRIBLE BOYS.
HE WAS A NERD, TOO. YUCK, RIGHT?
RIGHT.
LET'S GO AND GET A LOOK AT THIS--
VITA! YOU FORGETTING SOMETHING?
RIGHT. FORGOT. SORRY, MOLLY.
CAREFUL, YOU'RE GOING TO STOP BEING MY FAVORITE CUSTOMER.
YOU TOTALLY HAVE A CAPE SOMEWHERE IN YOUR HOUSE, RIGHT?
I DO NOT OWN A CAPE. NOT THAT KIND, AT LEAST.
WHAT... IS IT A SEX CAPE?
GET IN THE CAR.

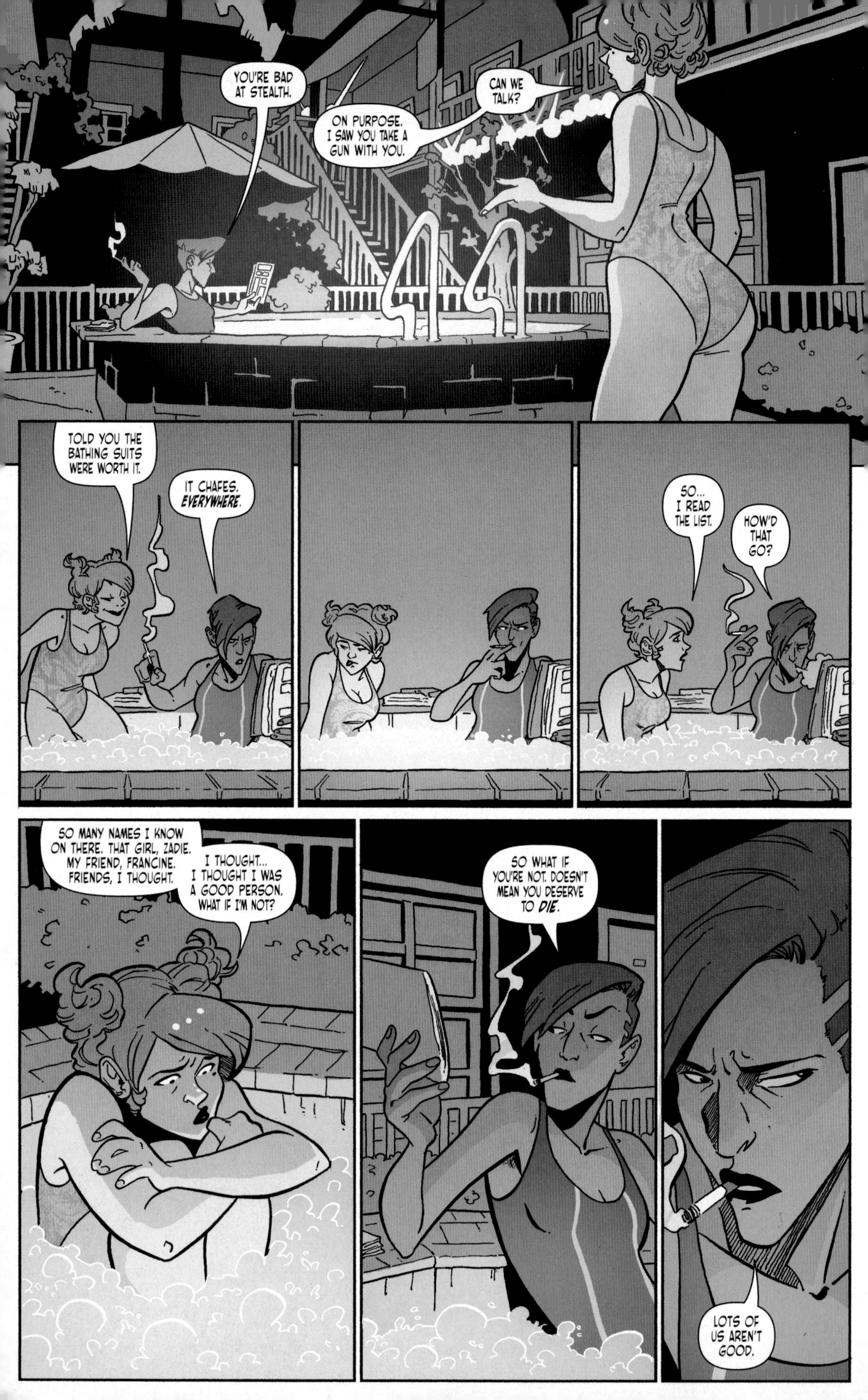
YOU'RE BAD AT STEALTH.
ON PURPOSE. I SAW YOU TAKE A GUN WITH YOU.
CAN WE TALK?
TOLD YOU THE BATHING SUITS WERE WORTH IT.
IT CHAFES. *EVERYWHERE*.
SO... I READ THE LIST.
HOW'D THAT GO?
SO MANY NAMES I KNOW ON THERE. THAT GIRL, ZADIE. MY FRIEND, FRANCINE. FRIENDS, I THOUGHT.
I THOUGHT... I THOUGHT I WAS A GOOD PERSON. WHAT IF I'M NOT?
SO WHAT IF YOU'RE NOT. DOESN'T MEAN YOU DESERVE TO *DIE*.
LOTS OF US AREN'T GOOD.

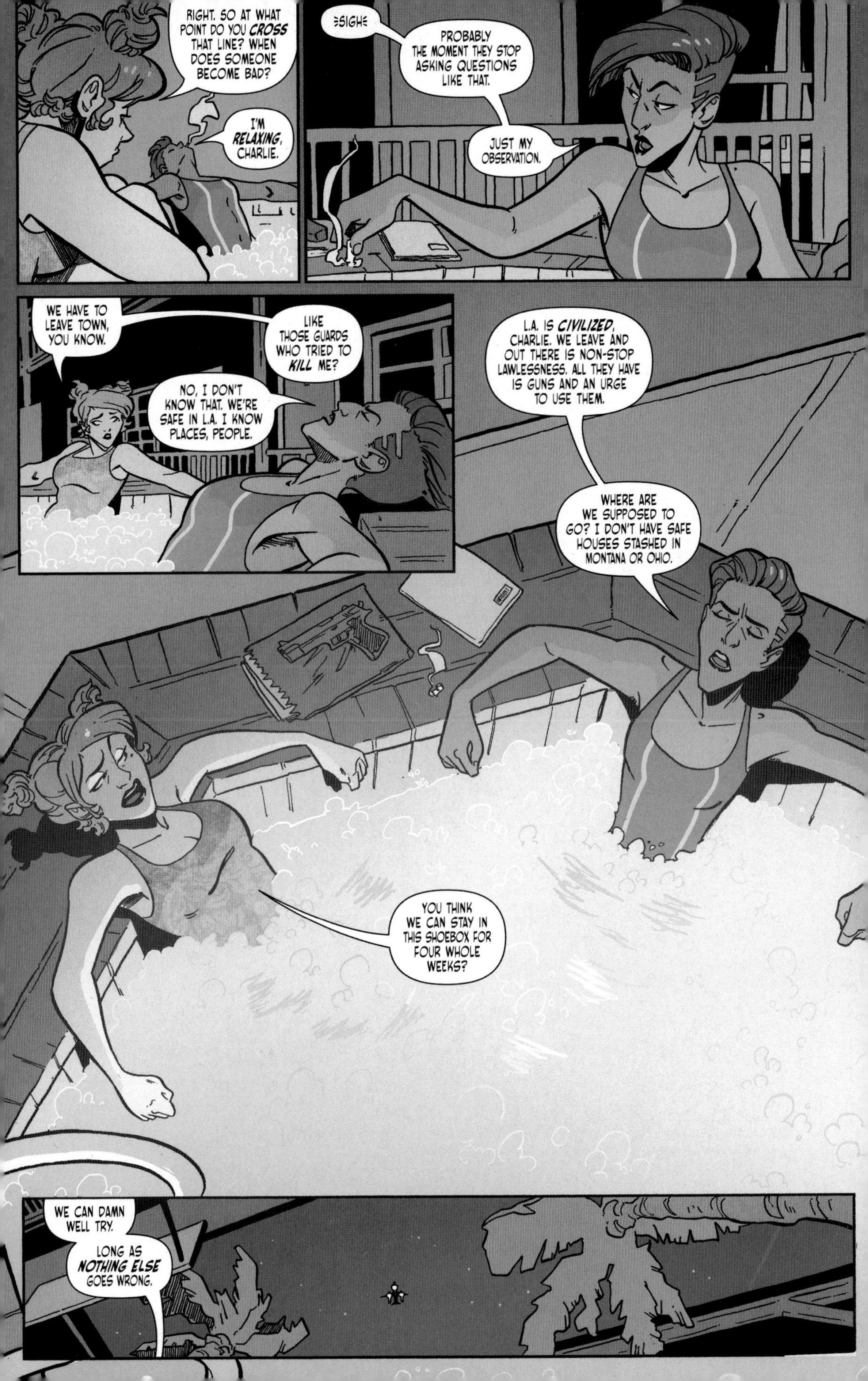
RIGHT. SO AT WHAT POINT DO YOU CROSS THAT LINE? WHEN DOES SOMEONE BECOME BAD?
I'M RELAXING, CHARLIE.
SIGH
PROBABLY THE MOMENT THEY STOP ASKING QUESTIONS LIKE THAT.
JUST MY OBSERVATION.
WE HAVE TO LEAVE TOWN, YOU KNOW.
LIKE THOSE GUARDS WHO TRIED TO KILL ME?
NO, I DON'T KNOW THAT. WE'RE SAFE IN L.A. I KNOW PLACES, PEOPLE.
L.A. IS CIVILIZED, CHARLIE. WE LEAVE AND OUT THERE IS NON-STOP LAWLESSNESS. ALL THEY HAVE IS GUNS AND AN URGE TO USE THEM.
WHERE ARE WE SUPPOSED TO GO? I DON'T HAVE SAFE HOUSES STASHED IN MONTANA OR OHIO.
YOU THINK WE CAN STAY IN THIS SHOEBOX FOR FOUR WHOLE WEEKS?
WE CAN DAMN WELL TRY.
LONG AS NOTHING ELSE GOES WRONG.

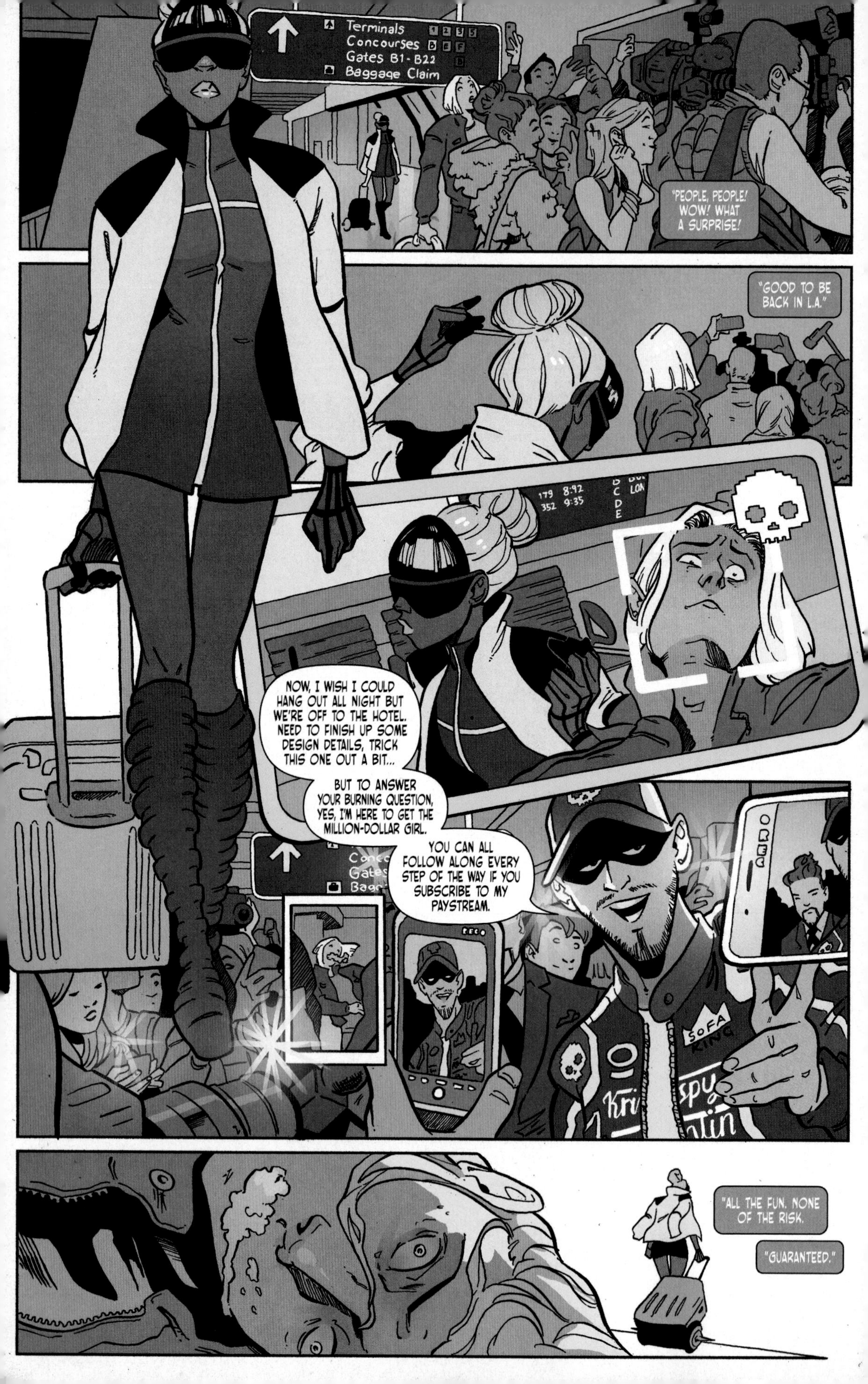
Terminals
Concourses
Gates B1 - B22
Baggage Claim
"PEOPLE, PEOPLE! WOW! WHAT A SURPRISE!
"GOOD TO BE BACK IN L.A."
NOW, I WISH I COULD HANG OUT ALL NIGHT BUT WE'RE OFF TO THE HOTEL. NEED TO FINISH UP SOME DESIGN DETAILS, TRICK THIS ONE OUT A BIT...
BUT TO ANSWER YOUR BURNING QUESTION, YES, I'M HERE TO GET THE MILLION-DOLLAR GIRL.
YOU CAN ALL FOLLOW ALONG EVERY STEP OF THE WAY IF YOU SUBSCRIBE TO MY PAYSTREAM.
"ALL THE FUN. NONE OF THE RISK.
"GUARANTEED."

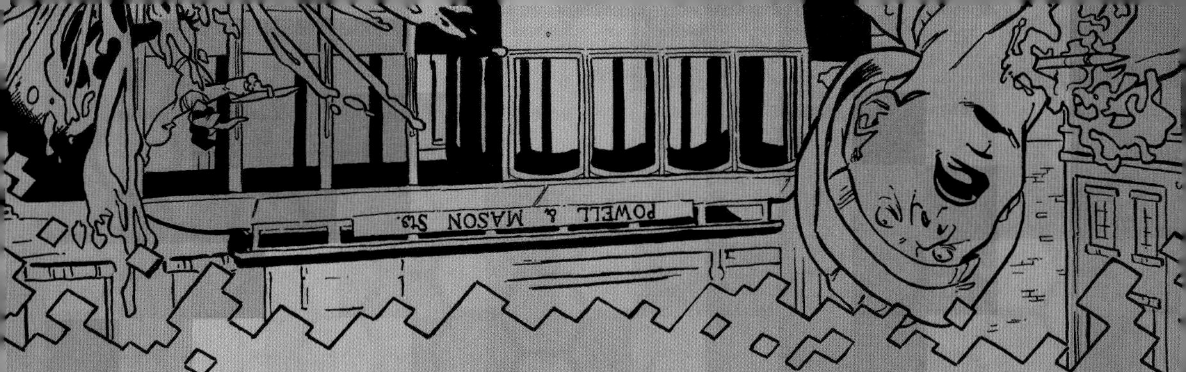
POWELL & MASON Sts.

CHAPTER THREE

KILL V. MAIM

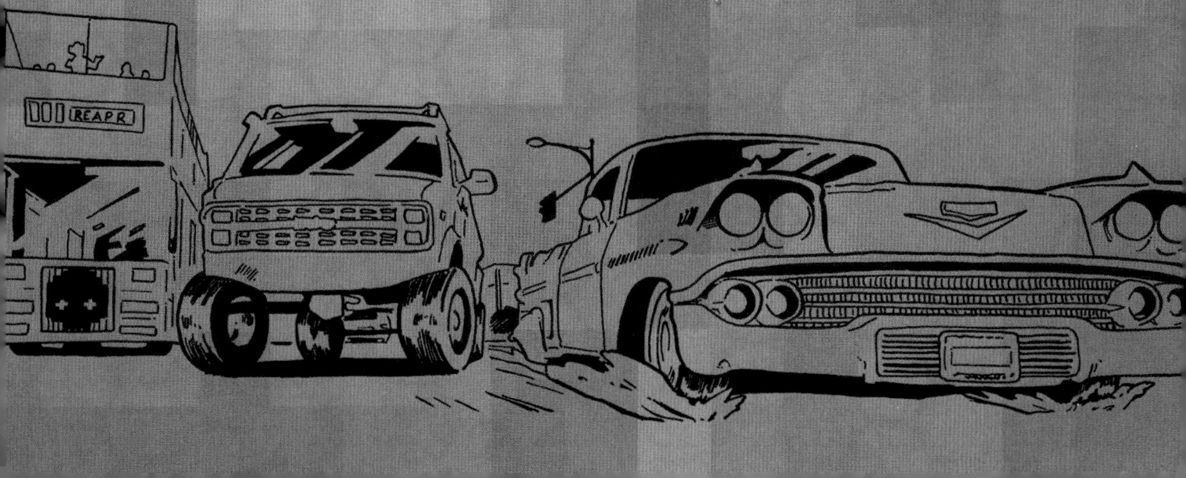
REAPR

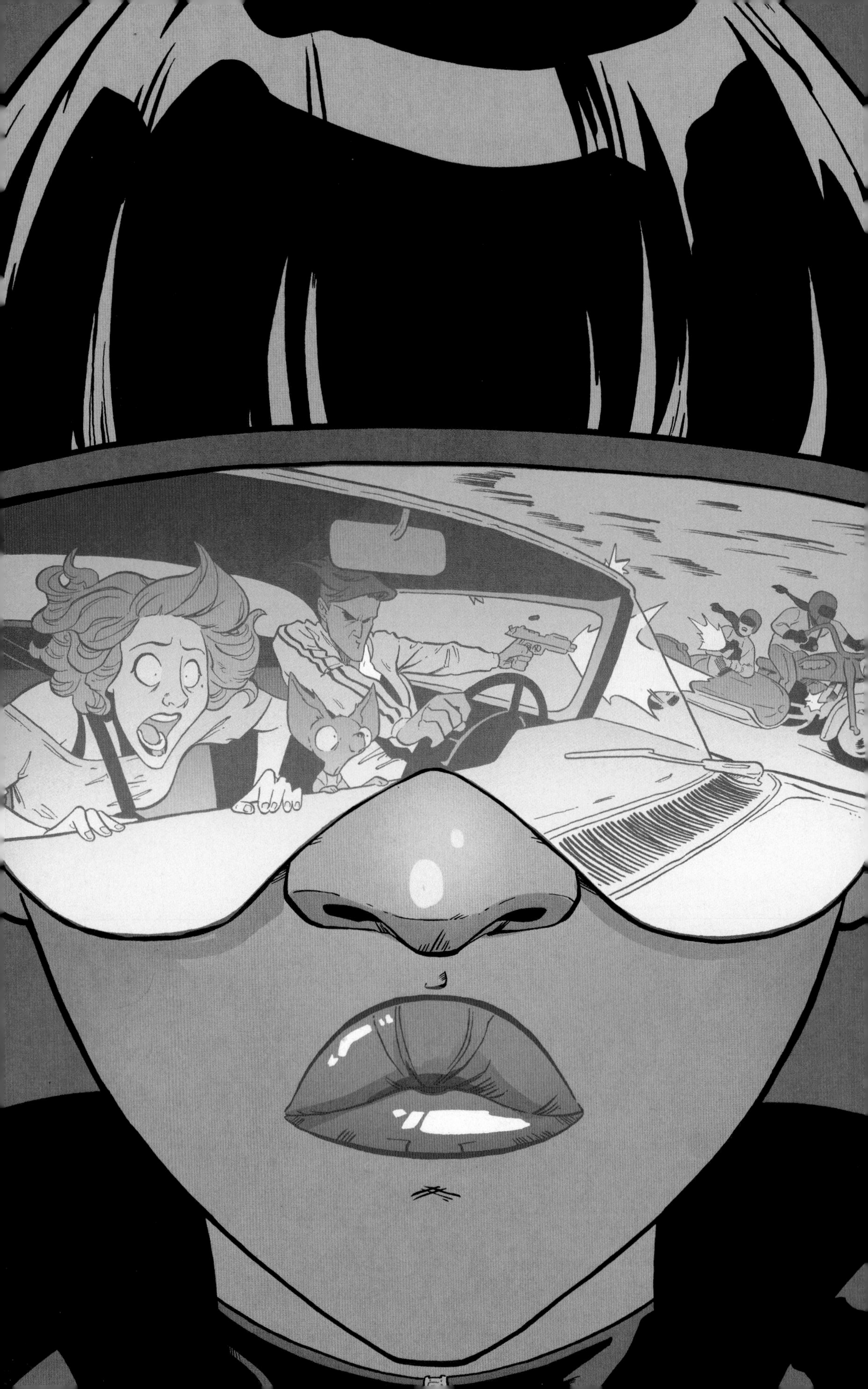

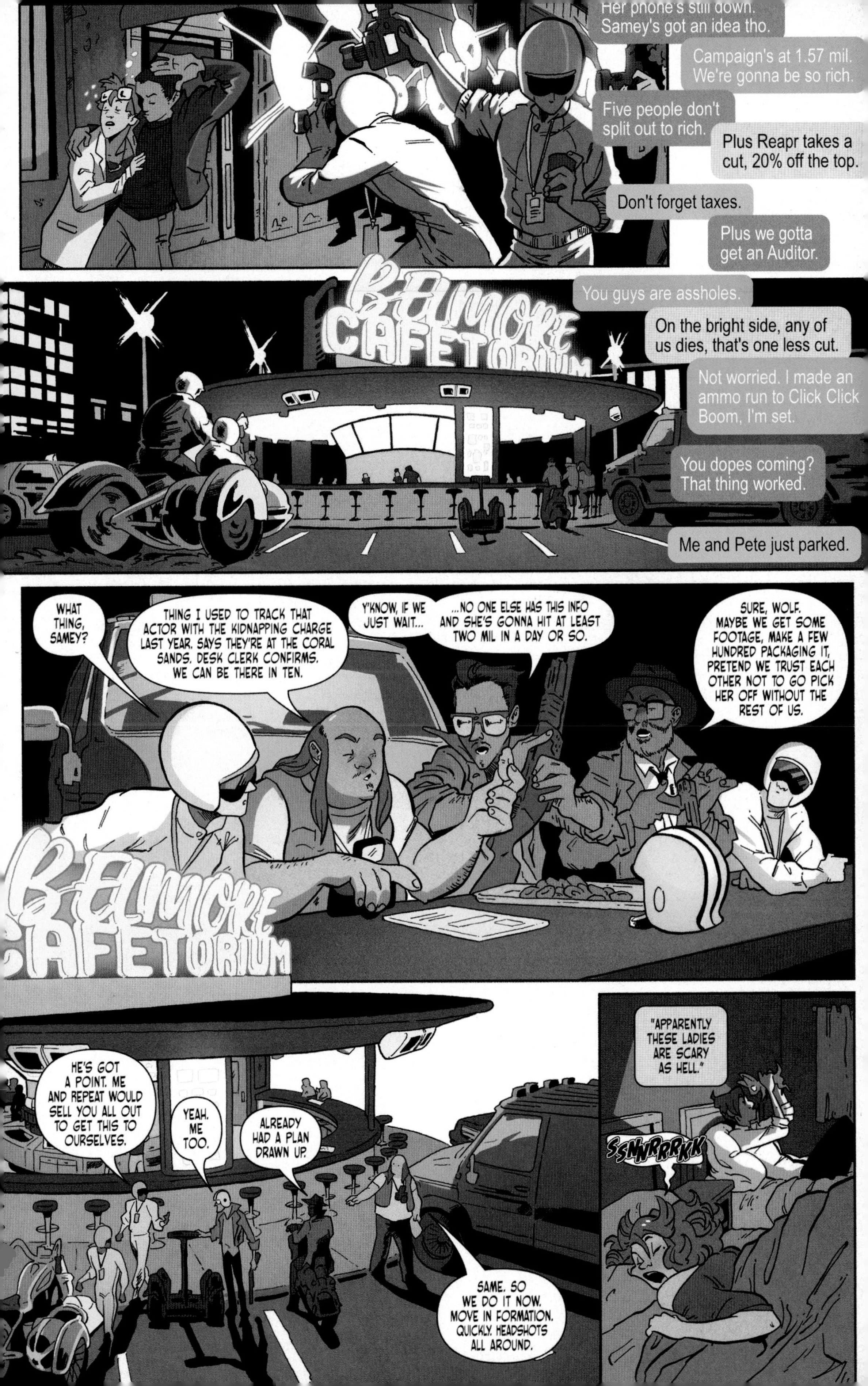
Her phone's still down. Samey's got an idea tho.
Campaign's at 1.57 mil. We're gonna be so rich.
Five people don't split out to rich.
Plus Reapr takes a cut, 20% off the top.
Don't forget taxes.
Plus we gotta get an Auditor.
BELMORE CAFETORIUM
You guys are assholes.
On the bright side, any of us dies, that's one less cut.
Not worried. I made an ammo run to Click Click Boom, I'm set.
You dopes coming? That thing worked.
Me and Pete just parked.
WHAT THING, SAMEY?
THING I USED TO TRACK THAT ACTOR WITH THE KIDNAPPING CHARGE LAST YEAR. SAYS THEY'RE AT THE CORAL SANDS. DESK CLERK CONFIRMS. WE CAN BE THERE IN TEN.
Y'KNOW, IF WE JUST WAIT...
...NO ONE ELSE HAS THIS INFO AND SHE'S GONNA HIT AT LEAST TWO MIL IN A DAY OR SO.
SURE, WOLF. MAYBE WE GET SOME FOOTAGE, MAKE A FEW HUNDRED PACKAGING IT, PRETEND WE TRUST EACH OTHER NOT TO GO PICK HER OFF WITHOUT THE REST OF US.
BELMORE CAFETORIUM
HE'S GOT A POINT. ME AND REPEAT WOULD SELL YOU ALL OUT TO GET THIS TO OURSELVES.
YEAH. ME TOO.
ALREADY HAD A PLAN DRAWN UP.
SAME. SO WE DO IT NOW. MOVE IN FORMATION. QUICKLY. HEADSHOTS ALL AROUND.
"APPARENTLY THESE LADIES ARE SCARY AS HELL."
SSNNRRRKK

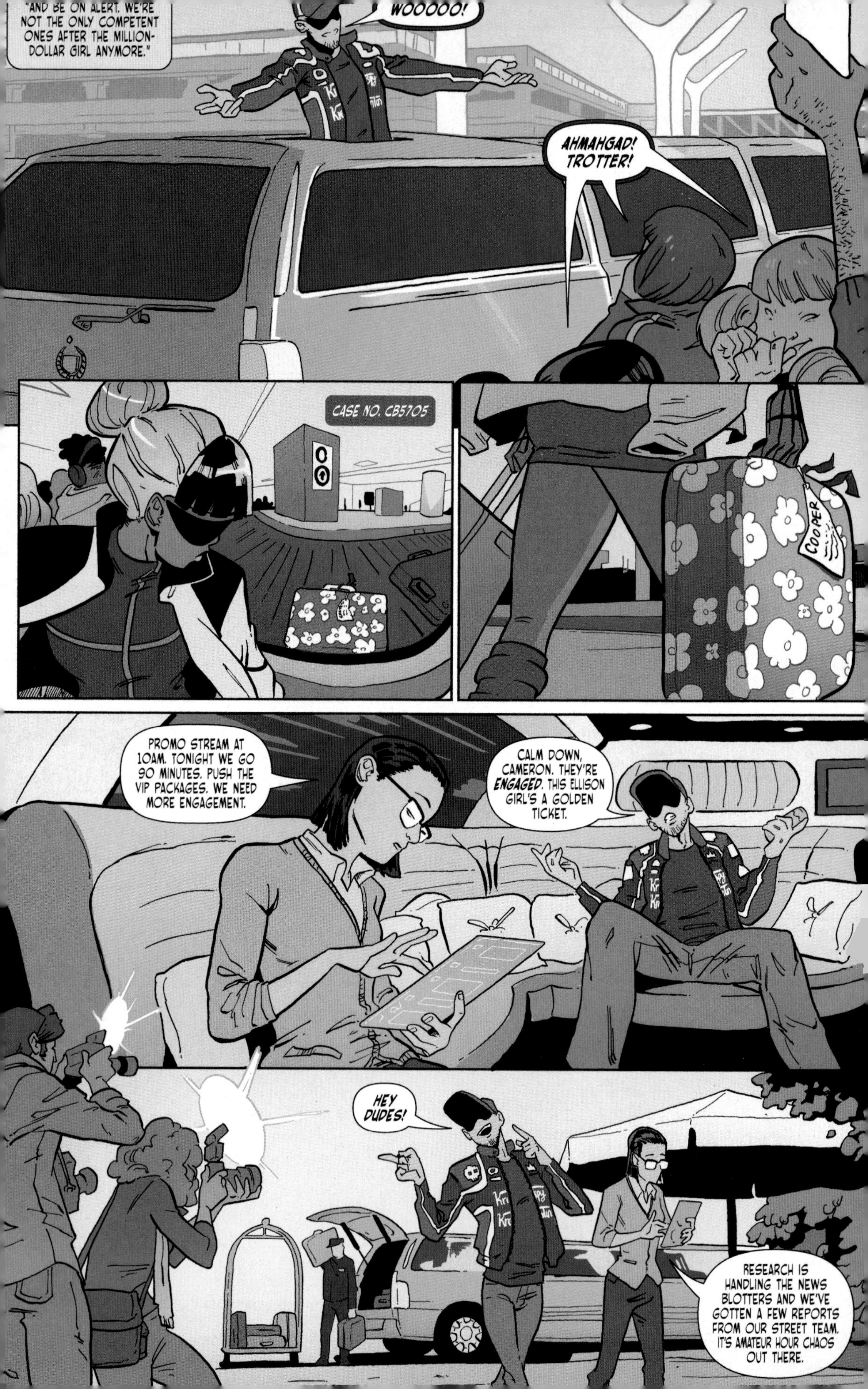
"AND BE ON ALERT. WE'RE NOT THE ONLY COMPETENT ONES AFTER THE MILLION-DOLLAR GIRL ANYMORE."
WOOOOO!
AHMAHGAD! TROTTER!
CASE NO. CB5705
COOPER
PROMO STREAM AT 10AM. TONIGHT WE GO 90 MINUTES. PUSH THE VIP PACKAGES. WE NEED MORE ENGAGEMENT.
CALM DOWN, CAMERON. THEY'RE ENGAGED. THIS ELLISON GIRL'S A GOLDEN TICKET.
HEY DUDES!
RESEARCH IS HANDLING THE NEWS BLOTTERS AND WE'VE GOTTEN A FEW REPORTS FROM OUR STREET TEAM. IT'S AMATEUR HOUR CHAOS OUT THERE.

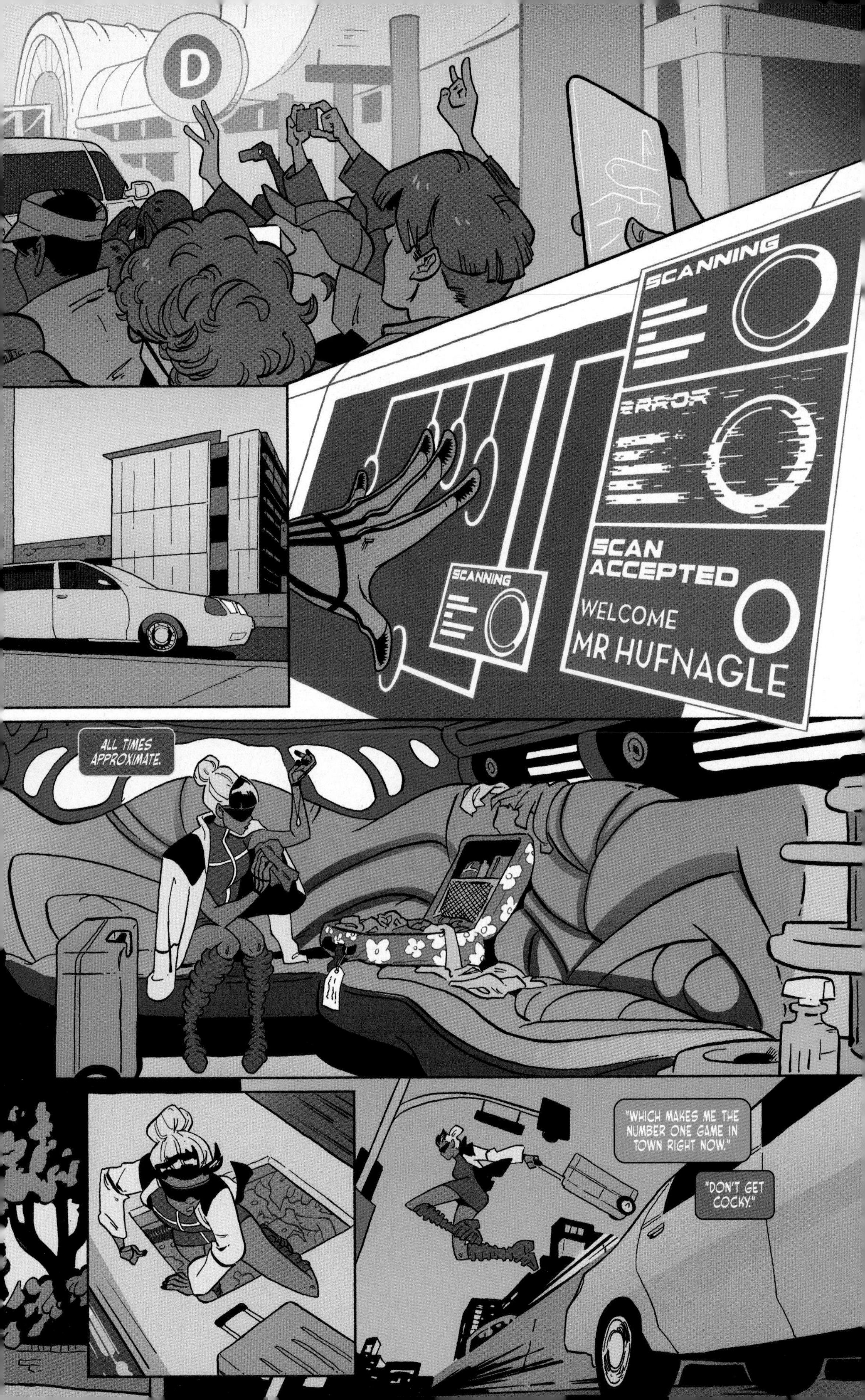
D
SCANNING
ERROR
SCANNING
SCAN ACCEPTED
WELCOME
MR HUFNAGLE
ALL TIMES APPROXIMATE.
"WHICH MAKES ME THE NUMBER ONE GAME IN TOWN RIGHT NOW."
"DON'T GET COCKY."

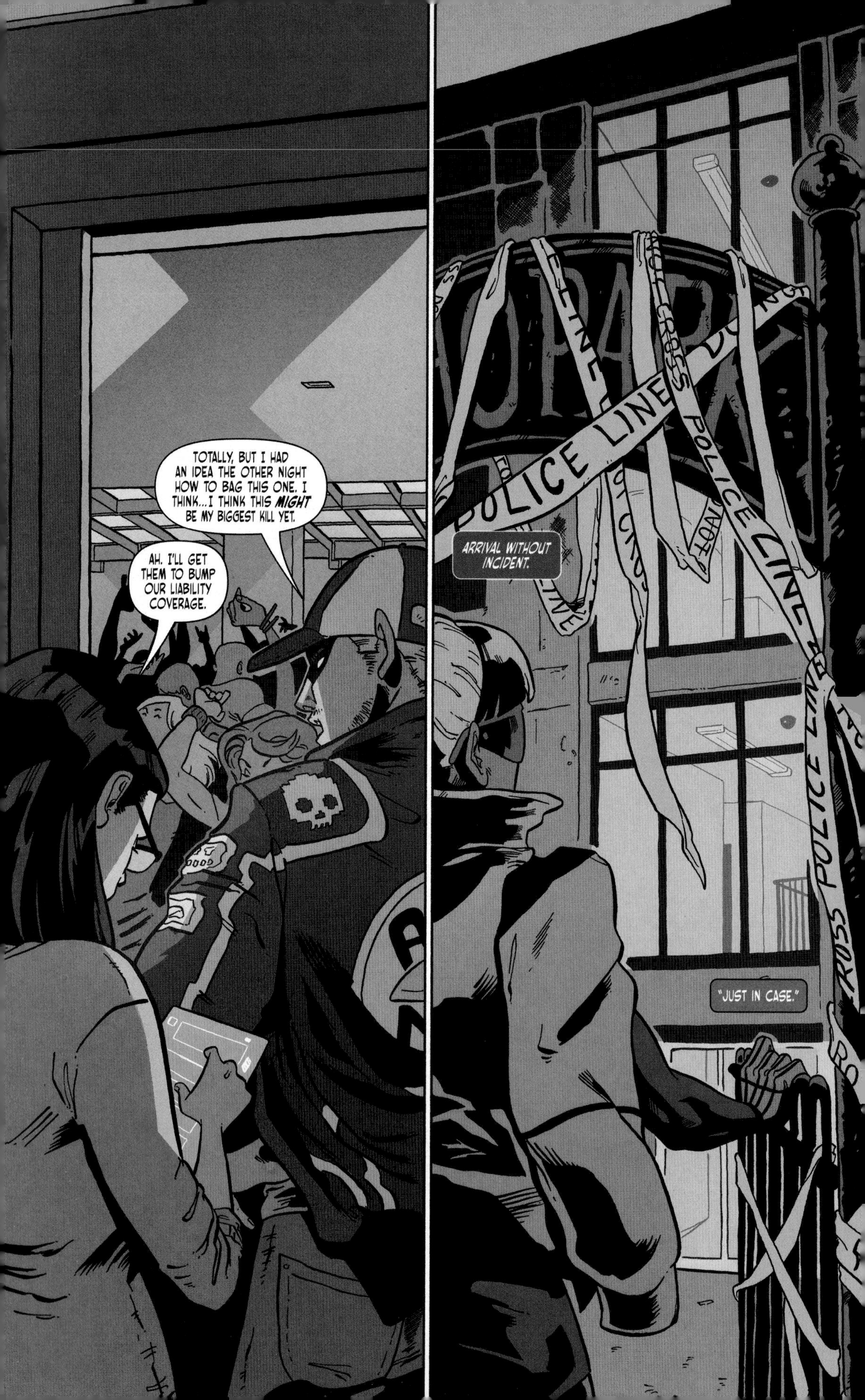
TOTALLY, BUT I HAD AN IDEA THE OTHER NIGHT HOW TO BAG THIS ONE. I THINK...I THINK THIS MIGHT BE MY BIGGEST KILL YET.
AH. I'LL GET THEM TO BUMP OUR LIABILITY COVERAGE.
ARRIVAL WITHOUT INCIDENT.
"JUST IN CASE."

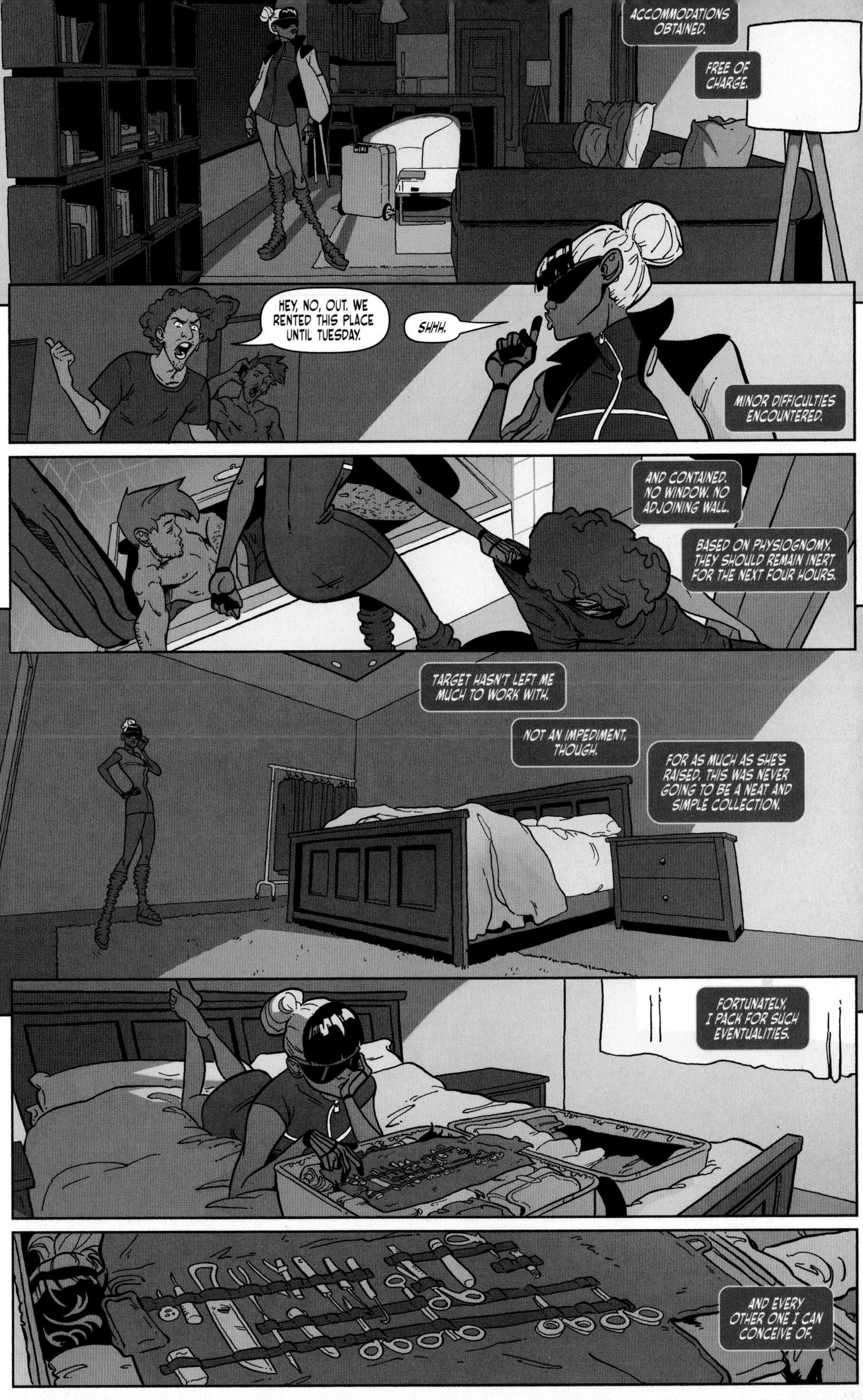
ACCOMMODATIONS OBTAINED.
FREE OF CHARGE.
HEY, NO, OUT. WE RENTED THIS PLACE UNTIL TUESDAY.
SHHH.
MINOR DIFFICULTIES ENCOUNTERED.
AND CONTAINED. NO WINDOW. NO ADJOINING WALL.
BASED ON PHYSIOGNOMY, THEY SHOULD REMAIN INERT FOR THE NEXT FOUR HOURS.
TARGET HASN'T LEFT ME MUCH TO WORK WITH.
NOT AN IMPEDIMENT, THOUGH.
FOR AS MUCH AS SHE'S RAISED, THIS WAS NEVER GOING TO BE A NEAT AND SIMPLE COLLECTION.
FORTUNATELY, I PACK FOR SUCH EVENTUALITIES.
AND EVERY OTHER ONE I CAN CONCEIVE OF.

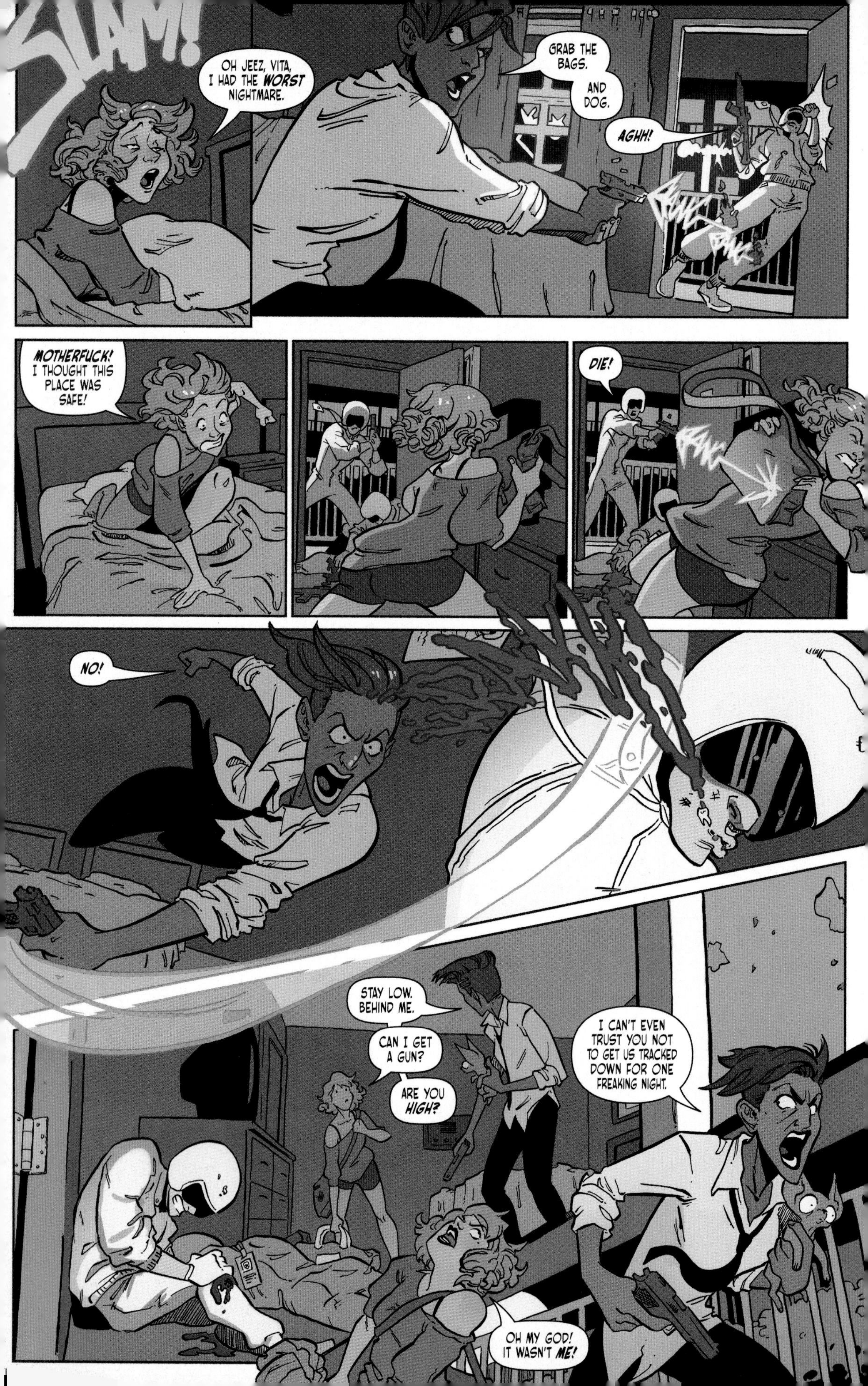
SLAM!
OH JEEZ, VITA, I HAD THE WORST NIGHTMARE.
GRAB THE BAGS.
AND DOG.
AGHH!
MOTHERFUCK! I THOUGHT THIS PLACE WAS SAFE!
DIE!
NO!
STAY LOW. BEHIND ME.
CAN I GET A GUN?
ARE YOU HIGH?
I CAN'T EVEN TRUST YOU NOT TO GET US TRACKED DOWN FOR ONE FREAKING NIGHT.
OH MY GOD! IT WASN'T ME!

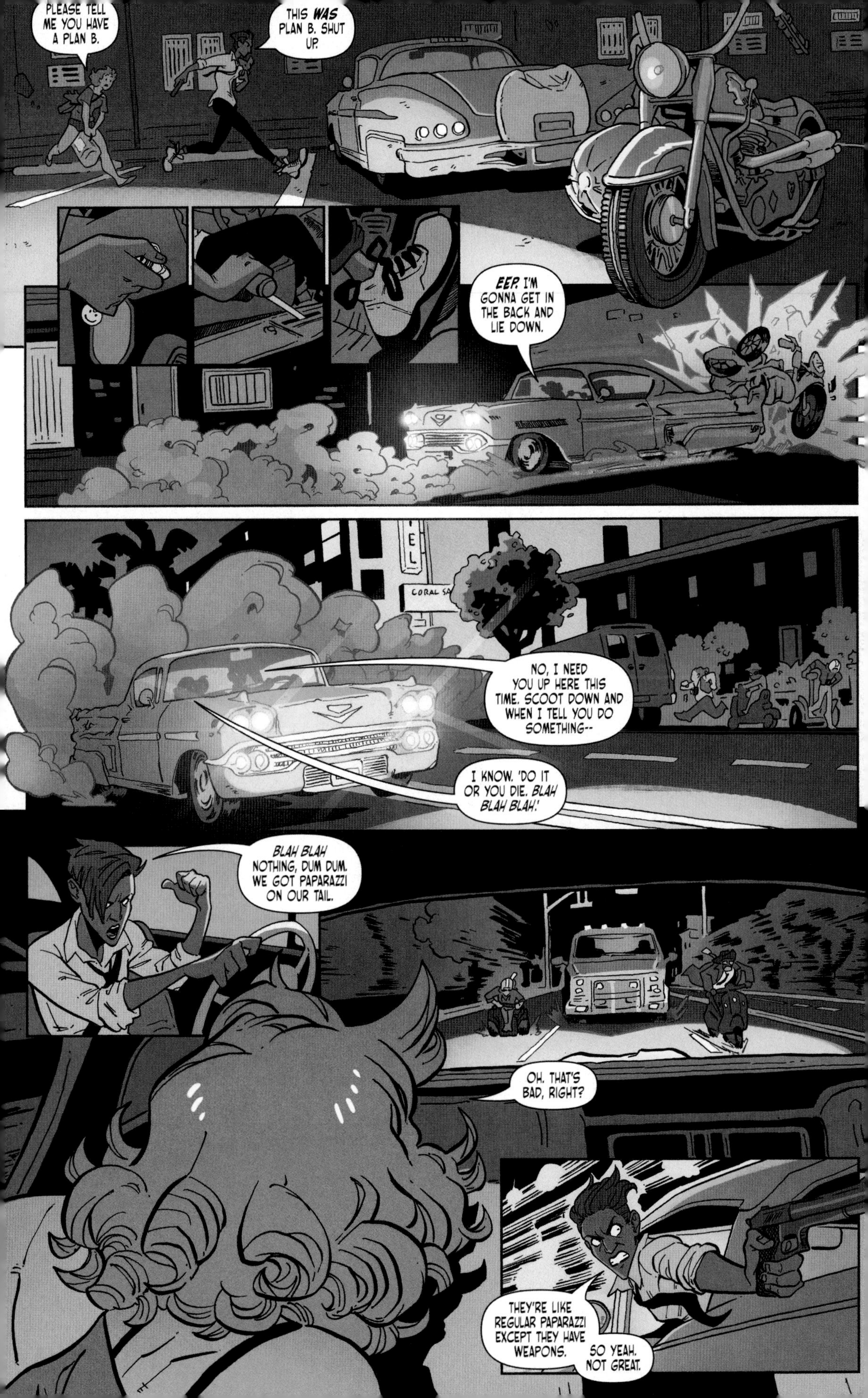
PLEASE TELL ME YOU HAVE A PLAN B.
THIS WAS PLAN B. SHUT UP.
EEP. I'M GONNA GET IN THE BACK AND LIE DOWN.
CORAL SA
NO, I NEED YOU UP HERE THIS TIME. SCOOT DOWN AND WHEN I TELL YOU DO SOMETHING--
I KNOW. 'DO IT OR YOU DIE. BLAH BLAH BLAH.'
BLAH BLAH NOTHING, DUM DUM. WE GOT PAPARAZZI ON OUR TAIL.
OH. THAT'S BAD, RIGHT?
THEY'RE LIKE REGULAR PAPARAZZI EXCEPT THEY HAVE WEAPONS.
SO YEAH. NOT GREAT.

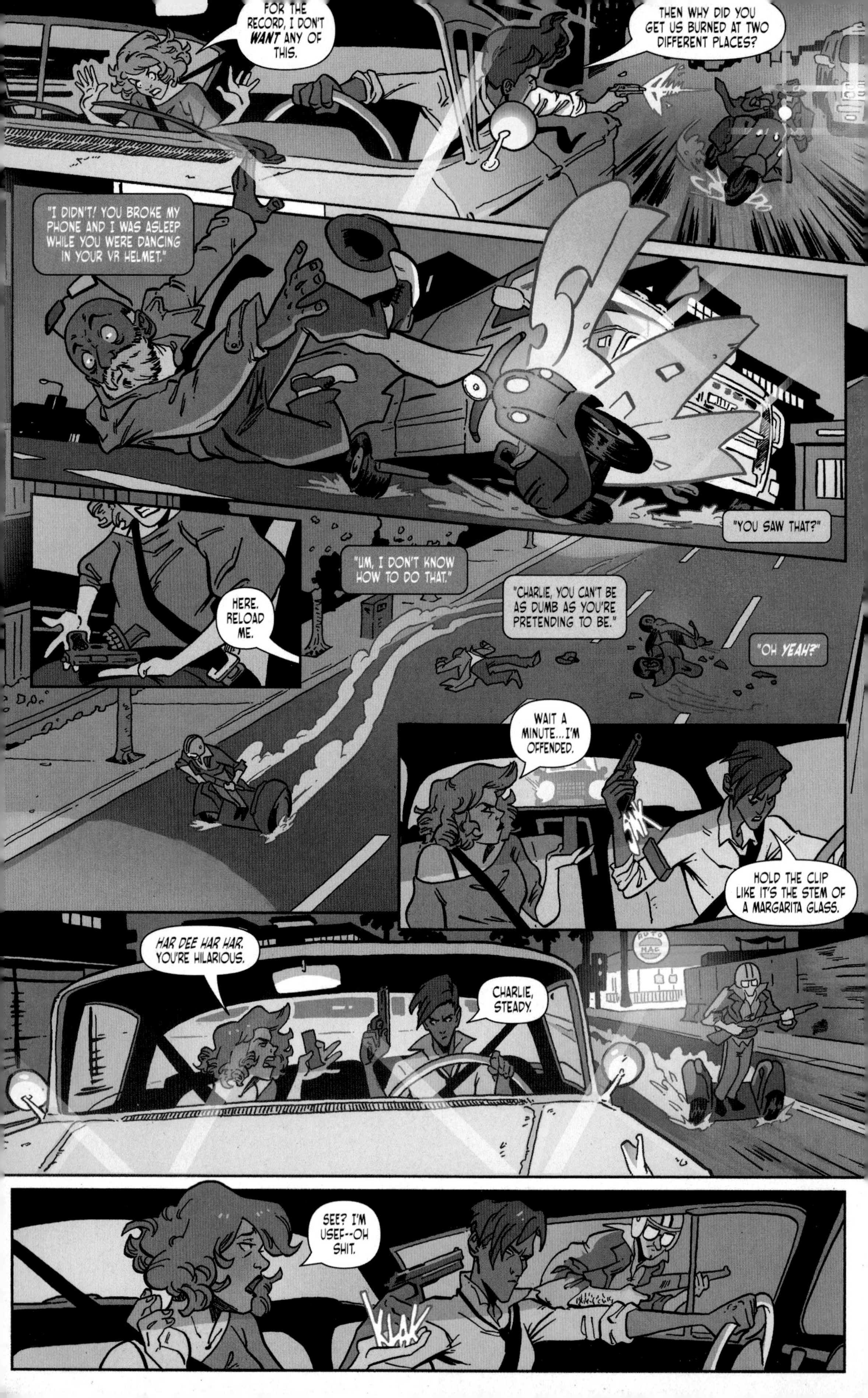
FOR THE RECORD, I DON'T *WANT* ANY OF THIS.
THEN WHY DID YOU GET US BURNED AT TWO DIFFERENT PLACES?
"I DIDN'T! YOU BROKE MY PHONE AND I WAS ASLEEP WHILE YOU WERE DANCING IN YOUR VR HELMET."
"YOU SAW THAT?"
HERE. RELOAD ME.
"UM, I DON'T KNOW HOW TO DO THAT."
"CHARLIE, YOU CAN'T BE AS DUMB AS YOU'RE PRETENDING TO BE."
"OH *YEAH?*"
WAIT A MINUTE...I'M OFFENDED.
HOLD THE CLIP LIKE IT'S THE STEM OF A MARGARITA GLASS.
HAR DEE HAR HAR. YOU'RE HILARIOUS.
CHARLIE, STEADY.
AUTO MAC
SEE? I'M USEF--OH SHIT.
KLAK

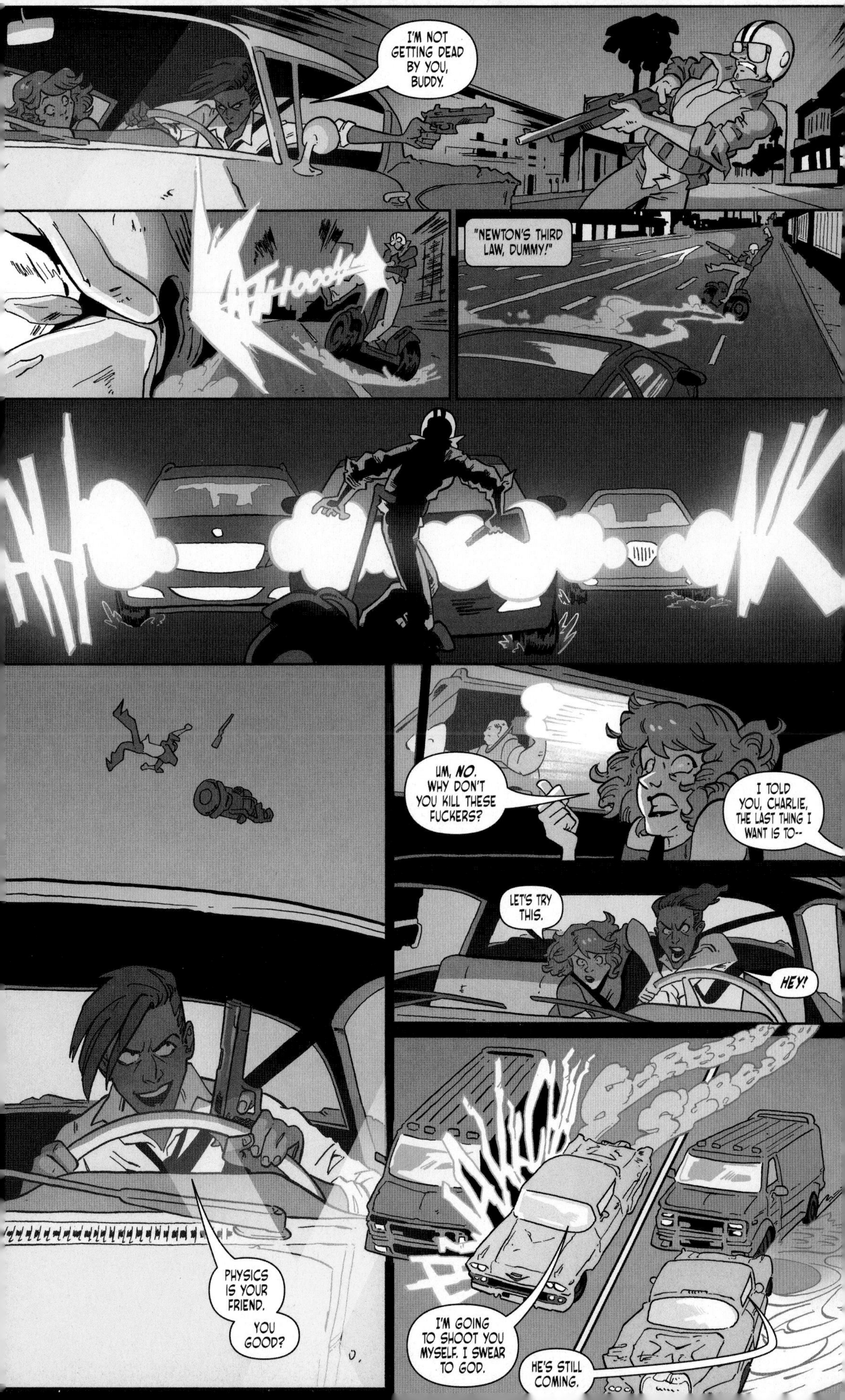
I'M NOT GETTING DEAD BY YOU, BUDDY.
"NEWTON'S THIRD LAW, DUMMY!"
UM, NO. WHY DON'T YOU KILL THESE FUCKERS?
I TOLD YOU, CHARLIE, THE LAST THING I WANT IS TO--
LET'S TRY THIS.
HEY!
PHYSICS IS YOUR FRIEND.
YOU GOOD?
I'M GOING TO SHOOT YOU MYSELF. I SWEAR TO GOD.
HE'S STILL COMING.

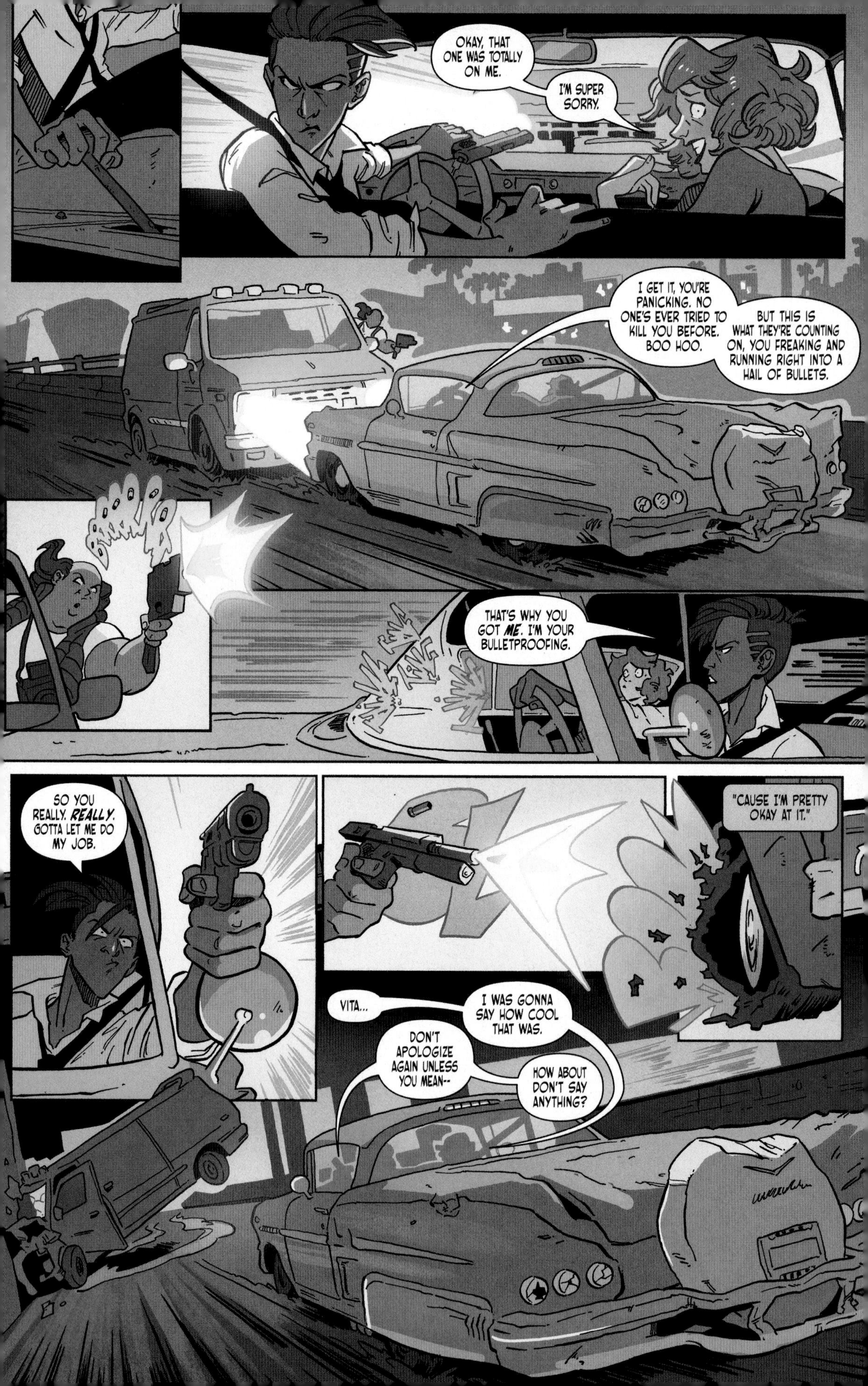
OKAY, THAT ONE WAS TOTALLY ON ME.
I'M SUPER SORRY.
I GET IT, YOU'RE PANICKING. NO ONE'S EVER TRIED TO KILL YOU BEFORE. BOO HOO.
BUT THIS IS WHAT THEY'RE COUNTING ON, YOU FREAKING AND RUNNING RIGHT INTO A HAIL OF BULLETS.
THAT'S WHY YOU GOT **ME**. I'M YOUR BULLETPROOFING.
SO YOU REALLY. ***REALLY***. GOTTA LET ME DO MY JOB.
"CAUSE I'M PRETTY OKAY AT IT."
VITA...
I WAS GONNA SAY HOW COOL THAT WAS.
DON'T APOLOGIZE AGAIN UNLESS YOU MEAN--
HOW ABOUT DON'T SAY ANYTHING?

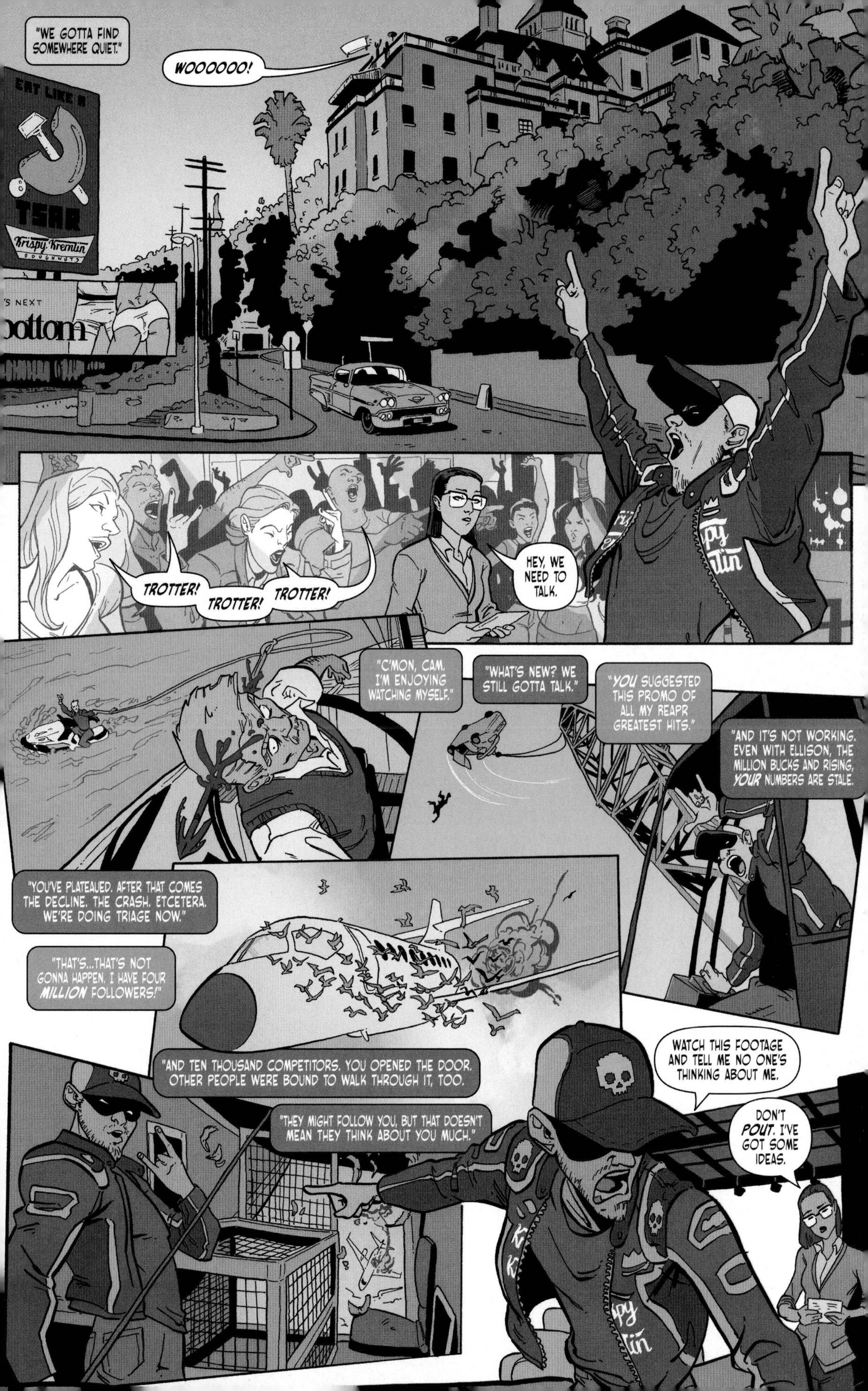
"WE GOTTA FIND SOMEWHERE QUIET."
WOOOOOO!
EAT LIKE A TSAR
Krispy Kremlin DOUGHNUTS
'S NEXT bottom
TROTTER!
TROTTER!
TROTTER!
HEY, WE NEED TO TALK.
"C'MON, CAM. I'M ENJOYING WATCHING MYSELF."
"WHAT'S NEW? WE STILL GOTTA TALK."
"YOU SUGGESTED THIS PROMO OF ALL MY REAPR GREATEST HITS."
"AND IT'S NOT WORKING. EVEN WITH ELLISON, THE MILLION BUCKS AND RISING, YOUR NUMBERS ARE STALE.
"YOU'VE PLATEAUED. AFTER THAT COMES THE DECLINE. THE CRASH. ETCETERA. WE'RE DOING TRIAGE NOW."
"THAT'S...THAT'S NOT GONNA HAPPEN. I HAVE FOUR MILLION FOLLOWERS!"
"AND TEN THOUSAND COMPETITORS. YOU OPENED THE DOOR. OTHER PEOPLE WERE BOUND TO WALK THROUGH IT, TOO.
"THEY MIGHT FOLLOW YOU, BUT THAT DOESN'T MEAN THEY THINK ABOUT YOU MUCH."
WATCH THIS FOOTAGE AND TELL ME NO ONE'S THINKING ABOUT ME.
DON'T POUT. I'VE GOT SOME IDEAS.

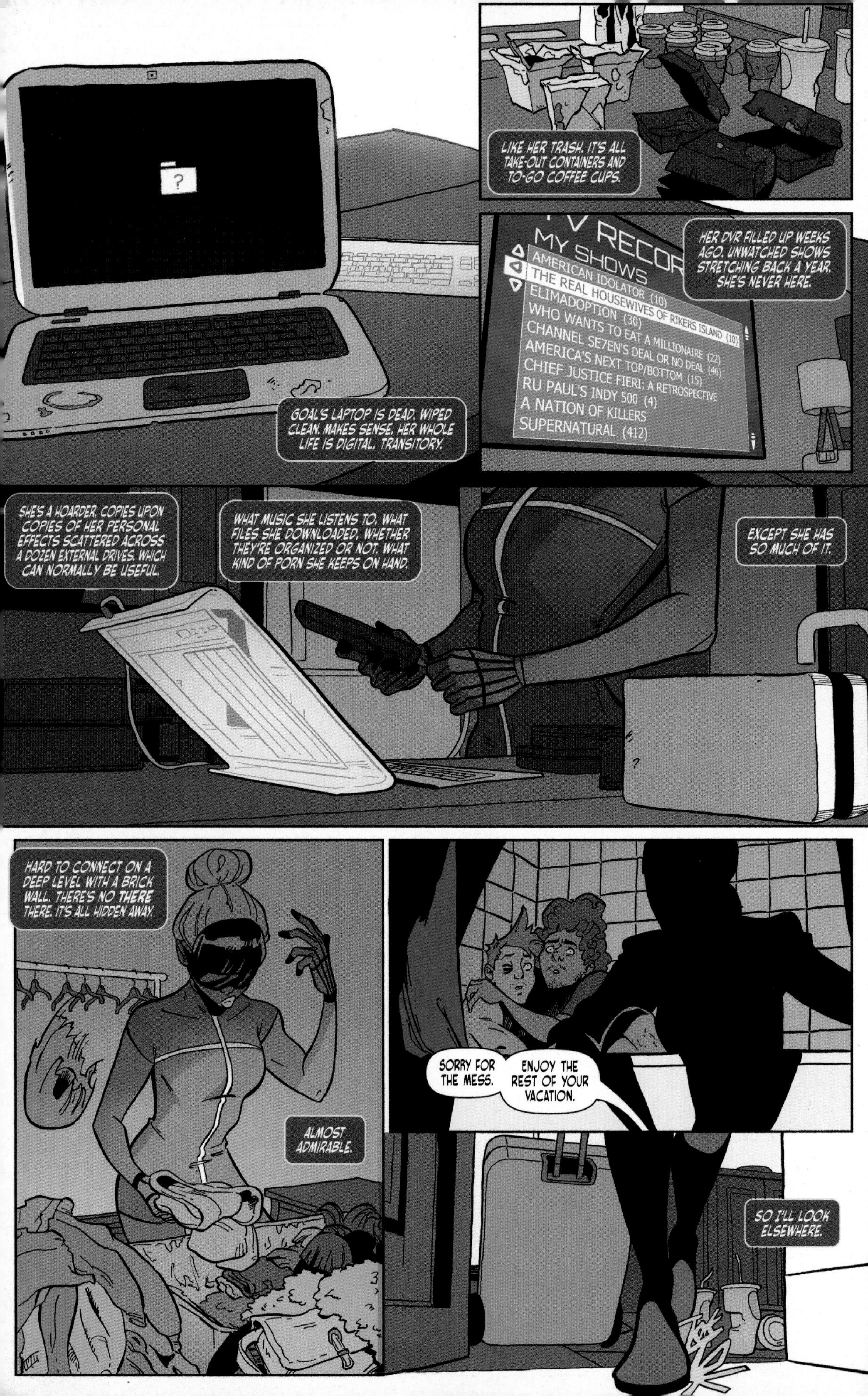
GOAL'S LAPTOP IS DEAD. WIPED CLEAN. MAKES SENSE, HER WHOLE LIFE IS DIGITAL. TRANSITORY.
LIKE HER TRASH. IT'S ALL TAKE-OUT CONTAINERS AND TO-GO COFFEE CUPS.
MY SHOWS
AMERICAN IDOLATOR (10)
THE REAL HOUSEWIVES OF RIKERS ISLAND (10)
ELIMADOPTION (30)
WHO WANTS TO EAT A MILLIONAIRE (22)
CHANNEL SE7EN'S DEAL OR NO DEAL (46)
AMERICA'S NEXT TOP/BOTTOM (15)
CHIEF JUSTICE FIERI: A RETROSPECTIVE
RU PAUL'S INDY 500 (4)
A NATION OF KILLERS
SUPERNATURAL (412)
HER DVR FILLED UP WEEKS AGO. UNWATCHED SHOWS STRETCHING BACK A YEAR. SHE'S NEVER HERE.
SHE'S A HOARDER. COPIES UPON COPIES OF HER PERSONAL EFFECTS SCATTERED ACROSS A DOZEN EXTERNAL DRIVES. WHICH CAN NORMALLY BE USEFUL.
WHAT MUSIC SHE LISTENS TO. WHAT FILES SHE DOWNLOADED. WHETHER THEY'RE ORGANIZED OR NOT. WHAT KIND OF PORN SHE KEEPS ON HAND.
EXCEPT SHE HAS SO MUCH OF IT.
HARD TO CONNECT ON A DEEP LEVEL WITH A BRICK WALL. THERE'S NO THERE THERE. IT'S ALL HIDDEN AWAY.
ALMOST ADMIRABLE.
SORRY FOR THE MESS.
ENJOY THE REST OF YOUR VACATION.
SO I'LL LOOK ELSEWHERE.

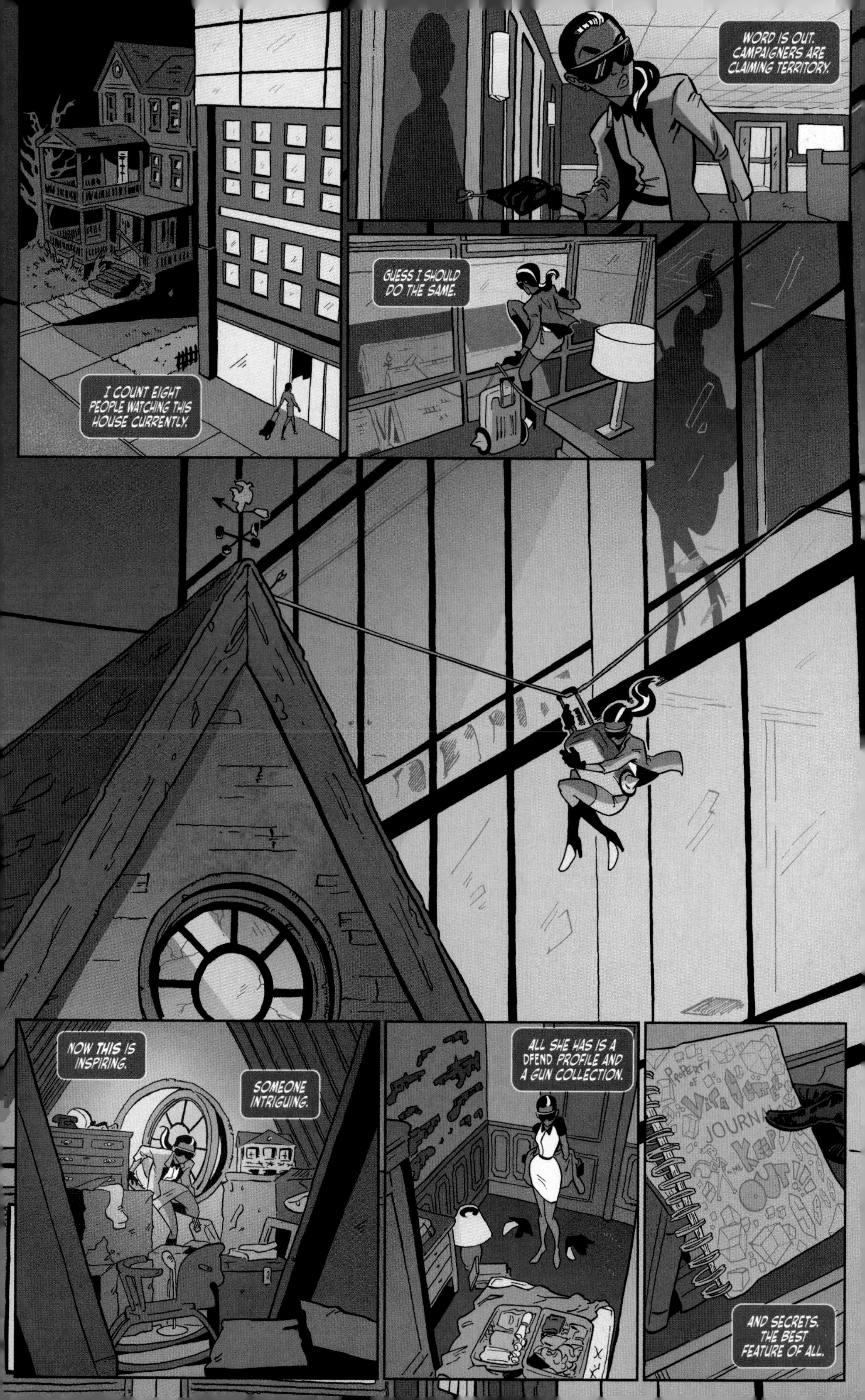
I COUNT EIGHT PEOPLE WATCHING THIS HOUSE CURRENTLY.
WORD IS OUT. CAMPAIGNERS ARE CLAIMING TERRITORY.
GUESS I SHOULD DO THE SAME.
NOW THIS IS INSPIRING.
SOMEONE INTRIGUING.
ALL SHE HAS IS A DFEND PROFILE AND A GUN COLLECTION.
PROPERTY OF
JOURNAL
KEEP OUT!!!
AND SECRETS. THE BEST FEATURE OF ALL.

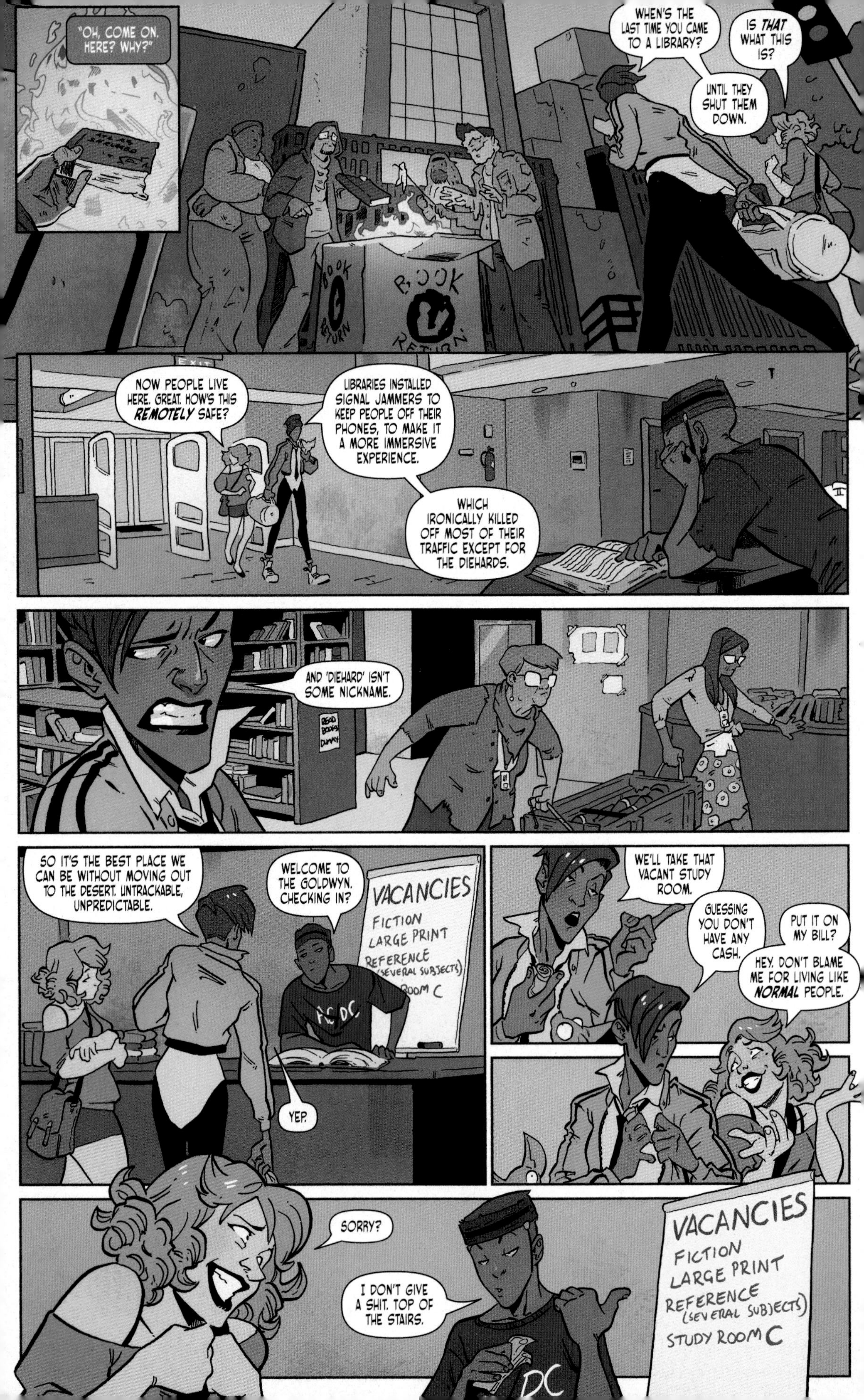
"OH, COME ON. HERE? WHY?"
ATLAS SHRUGGED
WHEN'S THE LAST TIME YOU CAME TO A LIBRARY?
UNTIL THEY SHUT THEM DOWN.
IS THAT WHAT THIS IS?
BOOK RETURN
BOOK RETURN
EXIT
NOW PEOPLE LIVE HERE. GREAT. HOW'S THIS REMOTELY SAFE?
LIBRARIES INSTALLED SIGNAL JAMMERS TO KEEP PEOPLE OFF THEIR PHONES, TO MAKE IT A MORE IMMERSIVE EXPERIENCE.
WHICH IRONICALLY KILLED OFF MOST OF THEIR TRAFFIC EXCEPT FOR THE DIEHARDS.
AND 'DIEHARD' ISN'T SOME NICKNAME.
READ BOOKS DUMMY
SO IT'S THE BEST PLACE WE CAN BE WITHOUT MOVING OUT TO THE DESERT. UNTRACKABLE, UNPREDICTABLE.
WELCOME TO THE GOLDWYN. CHECKING IN?
VACANCIES
FICTION
LARGE PRINT
REFERENCE (SEVERAL SUBJECTS)
ROOM C
AC DC
YEP.
WE'LL TAKE THAT VACANT STUDY ROOM.
GUESSING YOU DON'T HAVE ANY CASH.
PUT IT ON MY BILL?
HEY. DON'T BLAME ME FOR LIVING LIKE NORMAL PEOPLE.
SORRY?
I DON'T GIVE A SHIT. TOP OF THE STAIRS.
VACANCIES
FICTION
LARGE PRINT
REFERENCE (SEVERAL SUBJECTS)
STUDY ROOM C
DC

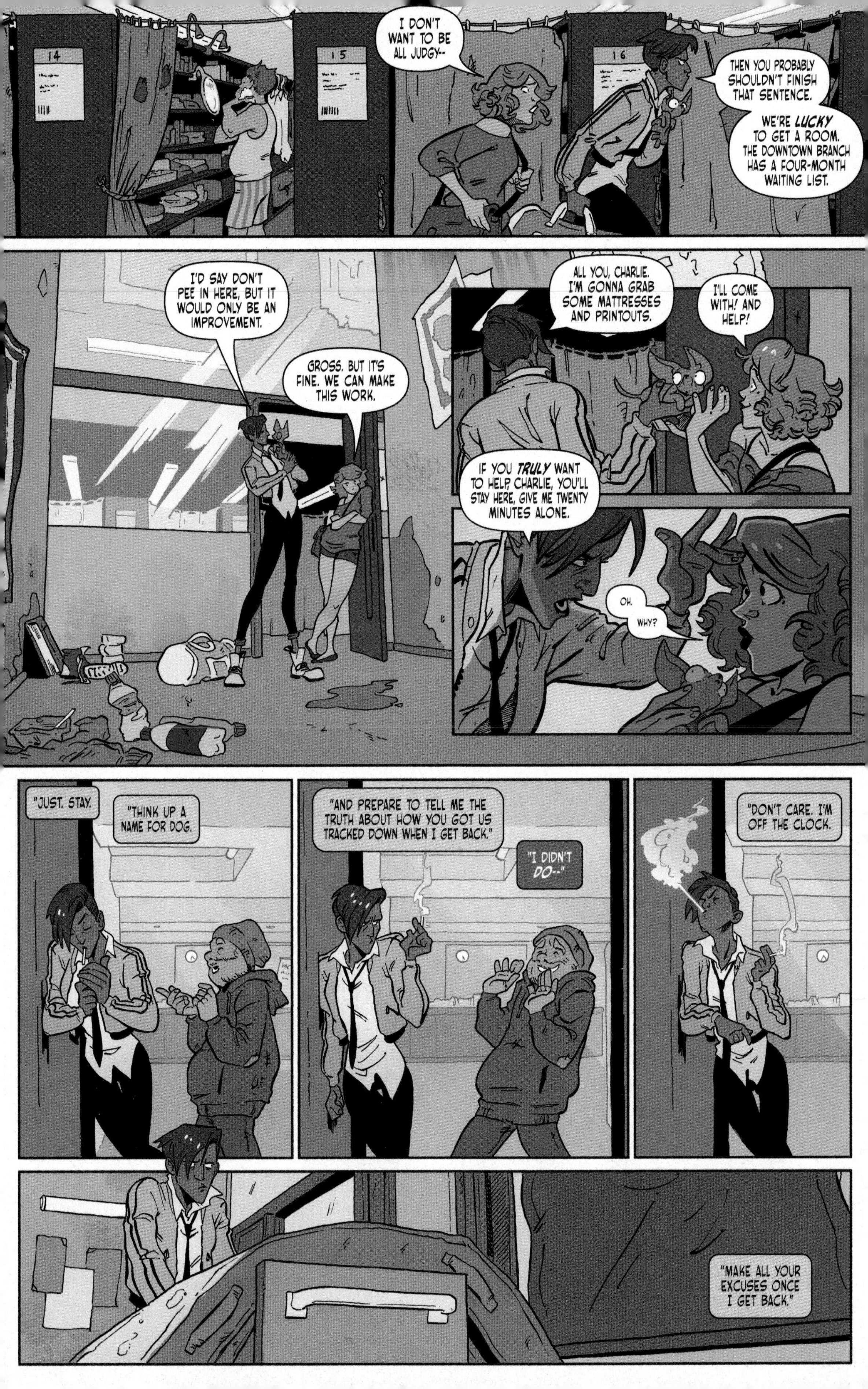
I DON'T WANT TO BE ALL JUDGY--
THEN YOU PROBABLY SHOULDN'T FINISH THAT SENTENCE.
WE'RE *LUCKY* TO GET A ROOM. THE DOWNTOWN BRANCH HAS A FOUR-MONTH WAITING LIST.
I'D SAY DON'T PEE IN HERE, BUT IT WOULD ONLY BE AN IMPROVEMENT.
GROSS. BUT IT'S FINE. WE CAN MAKE THIS WORK.
ALL YOU, CHARLIE. I'M GONNA GRAB SOME MATTRESSES AND PRINTOUTS.
I'LL COME WITH! AND HELP!
IF YOU *TRULY* WANT TO HELP, CHARLIE, YOU'LL STAY HERE, GIVE ME TWENTY MINUTES ALONE.
OH.
WHY?
"JUST. STAY.
"THINK UP A NAME FOR DOG.
"AND PREPARE TO TELL ME THE TRUTH ABOUT HOW YOU GOT US TRACKED DOWN WHEN I GET BACK."
"I DIDN'T *DO*--"
"DON'T CARE. I'M OFF THE CLOCK.
"MAKE ALL YOUR EXCUSES ONCE I GET BACK."

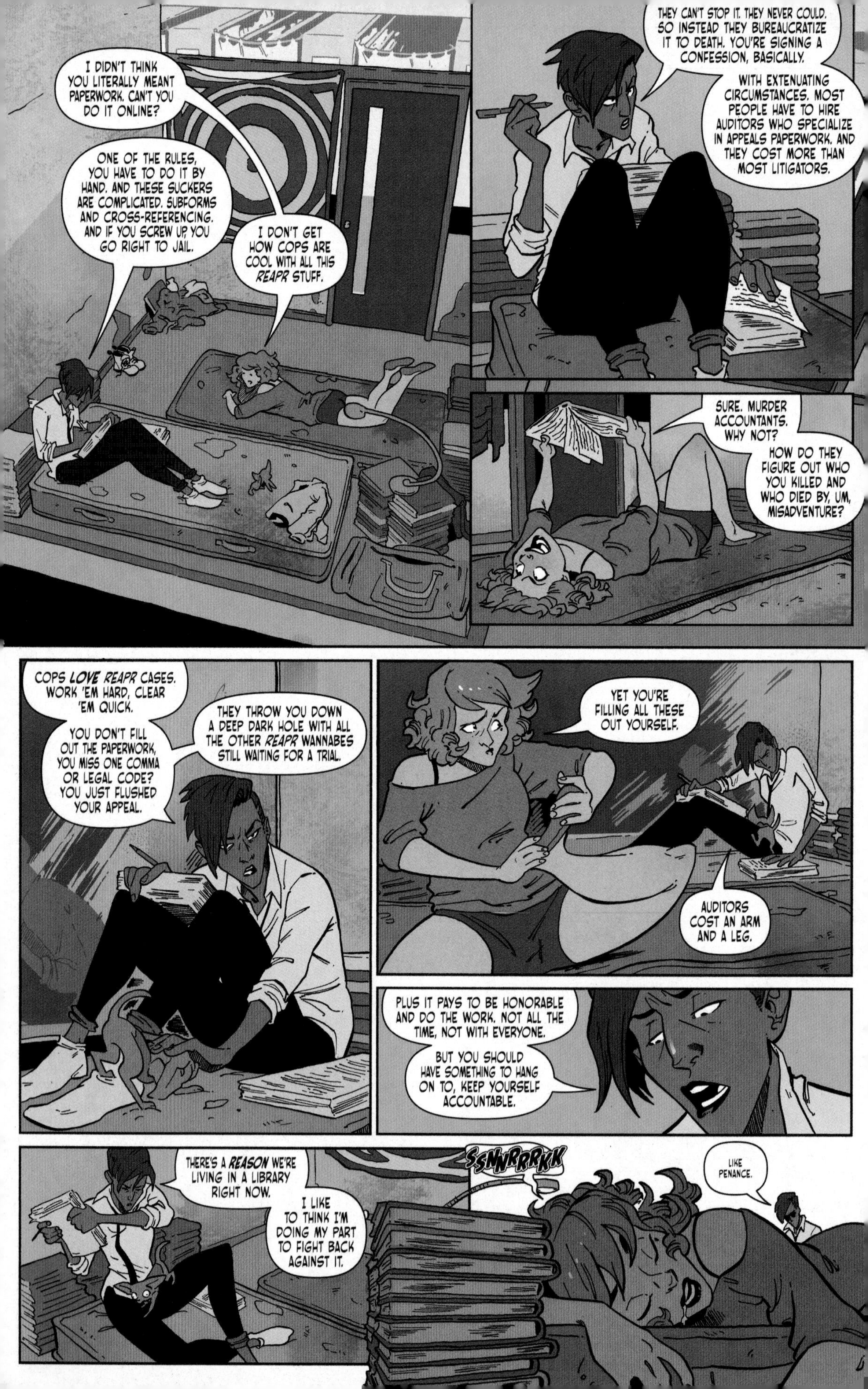

I DIDN'T THINK YOU LITERALLY MEANT PAPERWORK. CAN'T YOU DO IT ONLINE?
ONE OF THE RULES, YOU HAVE TO DO IT BY HAND. AND THESE SUCKERS ARE COMPLICATED. SUBFORMS AND CROSS-REFERENCING. AND IF YOU SCREW UP, YOU GO RIGHT TO JAIL.
I DON'T GET HOW COPS ARE COOL WITH ALL THIS *REAPR* STUFF.
THEY CAN'T STOP IT. THEY NEVER COULD. SO INSTEAD THEY BUREAUCRATIZE IT TO DEATH. YOU'RE SIGNING A CONFESSION, BASICALLY.
WITH EXTENUATING CIRCUMSTANCES. MOST PEOPLE HAVE TO HIRE AUDITORS WHO SPECIALIZE IN APPEALS PAPERWORK. AND THEY COST MORE THAN MOST LITIGATORS.
SURE. MURDER ACCOUNTANTS. WHY NOT?
HOW DO THEY FIGURE OUT WHO YOU KILLED AND WHO DIED BY, UM, MISADVENTURE?
COPS *LOVE REAPR* CASES. WORK 'EM HARD, CLEAR 'EM QUICK.
YOU DON'T FILL OUT THE PAPERWORK, YOU MISS ONE COMMA OR LEGAL CODE? YOU JUST FLUSHED YOUR APPEAL.
THEY THROW YOU DOWN A DEEP DARK HOLE WITH ALL THE OTHER *REAPR* WANNABES STILL WAITING FOR A TRIAL.
YET YOU'RE FILLING ALL THESE OUT YOURSELF.
AUDITORS COST AN ARM AND A LEG.
PLUS IT PAYS TO BE HONORABLE AND DO THE WORK. NOT ALL THE TIME, NOT WITH EVERYONE.
BUT YOU SHOULD HAVE SOMETHING TO HANG ON TO, KEEP YOURSELF ACCOUNTABLE.
THERE'S A *REASON* WE'RE LIVING IN A LIBRARY RIGHT NOW.
I LIKE TO THINK I'M DOING MY PART TO FIGHT BACK AGAINST IT.
SSNNRRRKK
LIKE PENANCE.

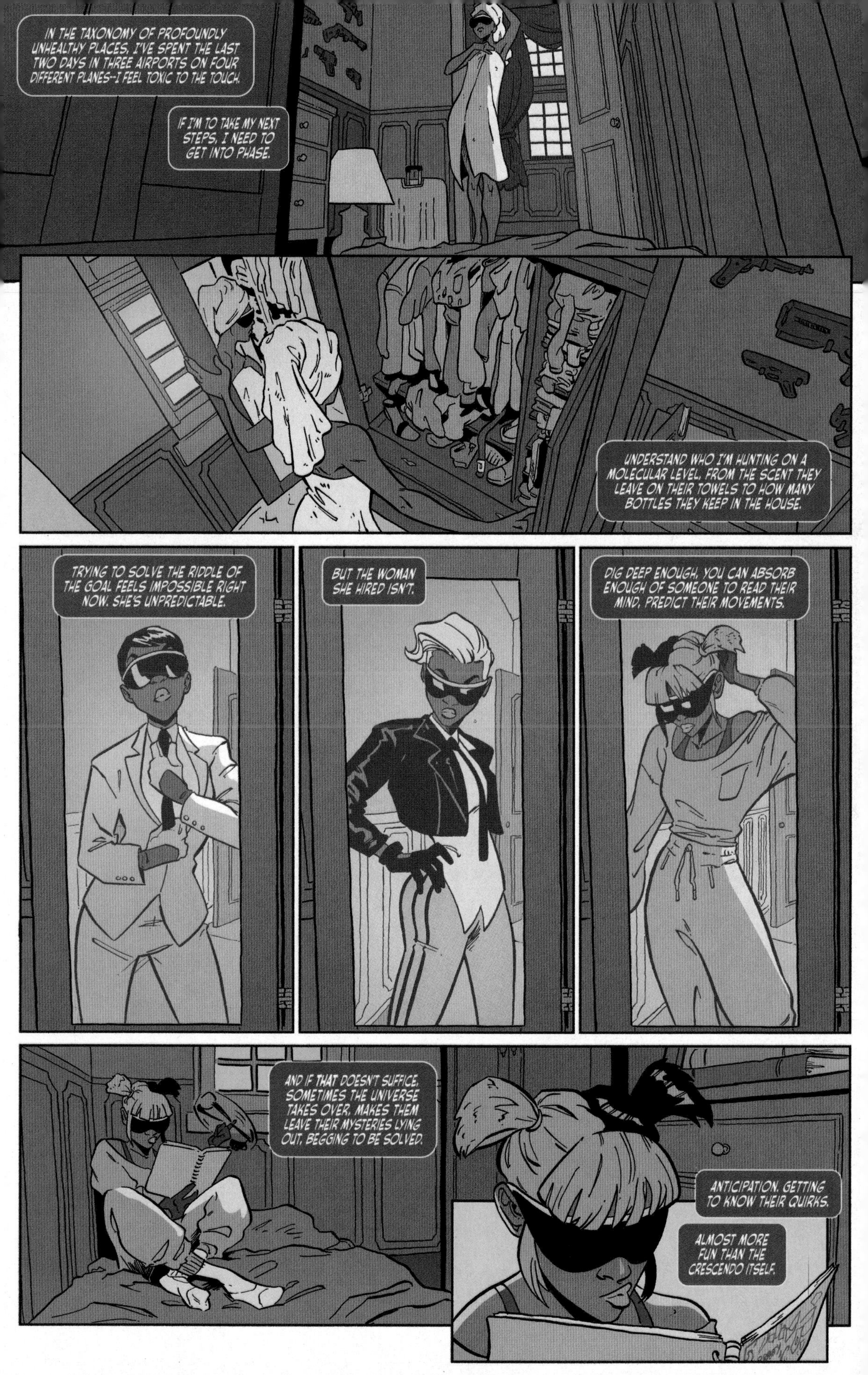
IN THE TAXONOMY OF PROFOUNDLY UNHEALTHY PLACES, I'VE SPENT THE LAST TWO DAYS IN THREE AIRPORTS ON FOUR DIFFERENT PLANES--I FEEL TOXIC TO THE TOUCH.
IF I'M TO TAKE MY NEXT STEPS, I NEED TO GET INTO PHASE.
UNDERSTAND WHO I'M HUNTING ON A MOLECULAR LEVEL, FROM THE SCENT THEY LEAVE ON THEIR TOWELS TO HOW MANY BOTTLES THEY KEEP IN THE HOUSE.
TRYING TO SOLVE THE RIDDLE OF THE GOAL FEELS IMPOSSIBLE RIGHT NOW. SHE'S UNPREDICTABLE.
BUT THE WOMAN SHE HIRED ISN'T.
DIG DEEP ENOUGH, YOU CAN ABSORB ENOUGH OF SOMEONE TO READ THEIR MIND, PREDICT THEIR MOVEMENTS.
AND IF THAT DOESN'T SUFFICE, SOMETIMES THE UNIVERSE TAKES OVER, MAKES THEM LEAVE THEIR MYSTERIES LYING OUT, BEGGING TO BE SOLVED.
ANTICIPATION. GETTING TO KNOW THEIR QUIRKS.
ALMOST MORE FUN THAN THE CRESCENDO ITSELF.

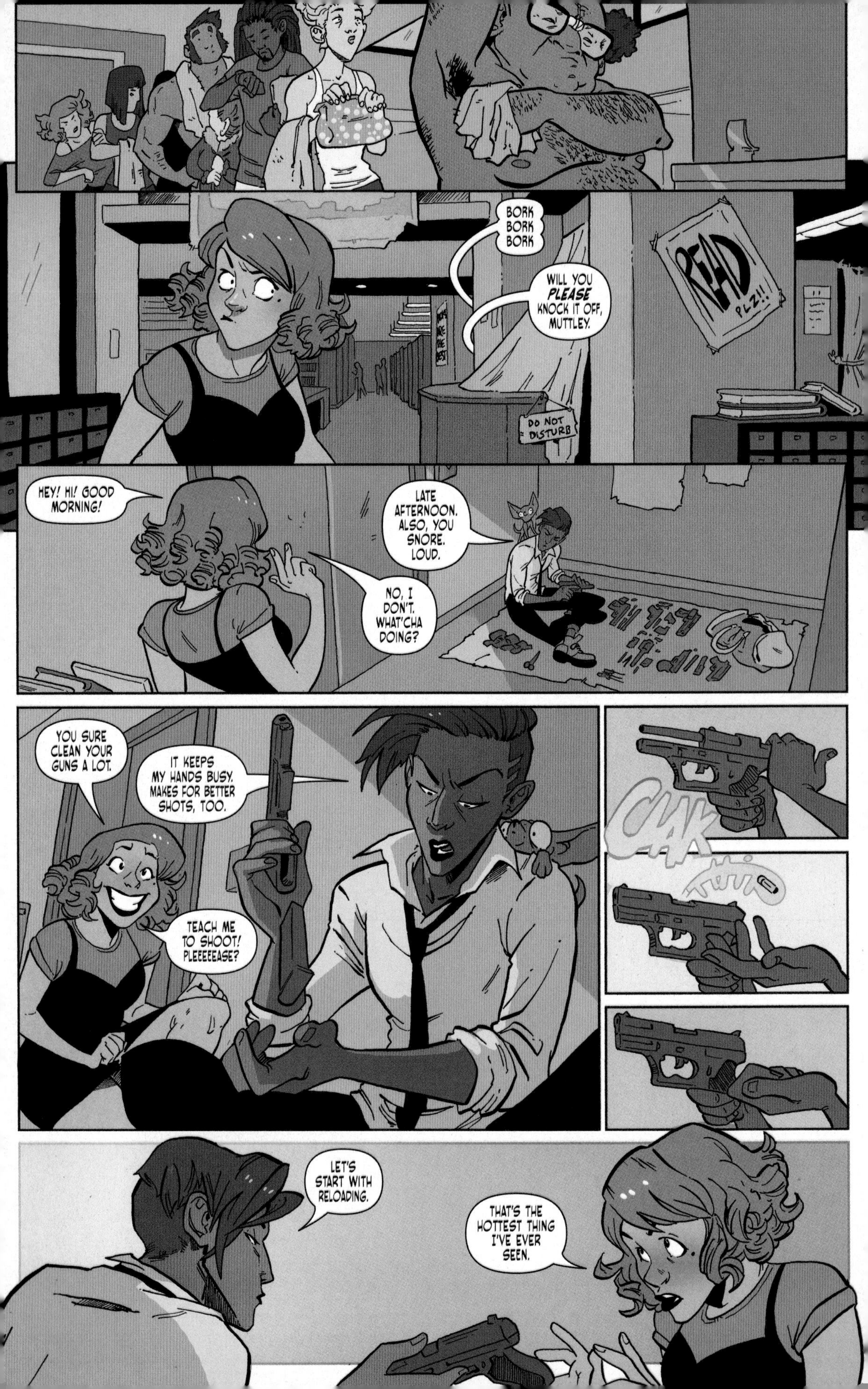
BORK BORK BORK
WILL YOU PLEASE KNOCK IT OFF, MUTTLEY.
READ PLZ!!
DO NOT DISTURB
HEY! HI! GOOD MORNING!
LATE AFTERNOON. ALSO, YOU SNORE. LOUD.
NO, I DON'T. WHAT'CHA DOING?
YOU SURE CLEAN YOUR GUNS A LOT.
IT KEEPS MY HANDS BUSY. MAKES FOR BETTER SHOTS, TOO.
TEACH ME TO SHOOT! PLEEEEEASE?
CHAK
LET'S START WITH RELOADING.
THAT'S THE HOTTEST THING I'VE EVER SEEN.

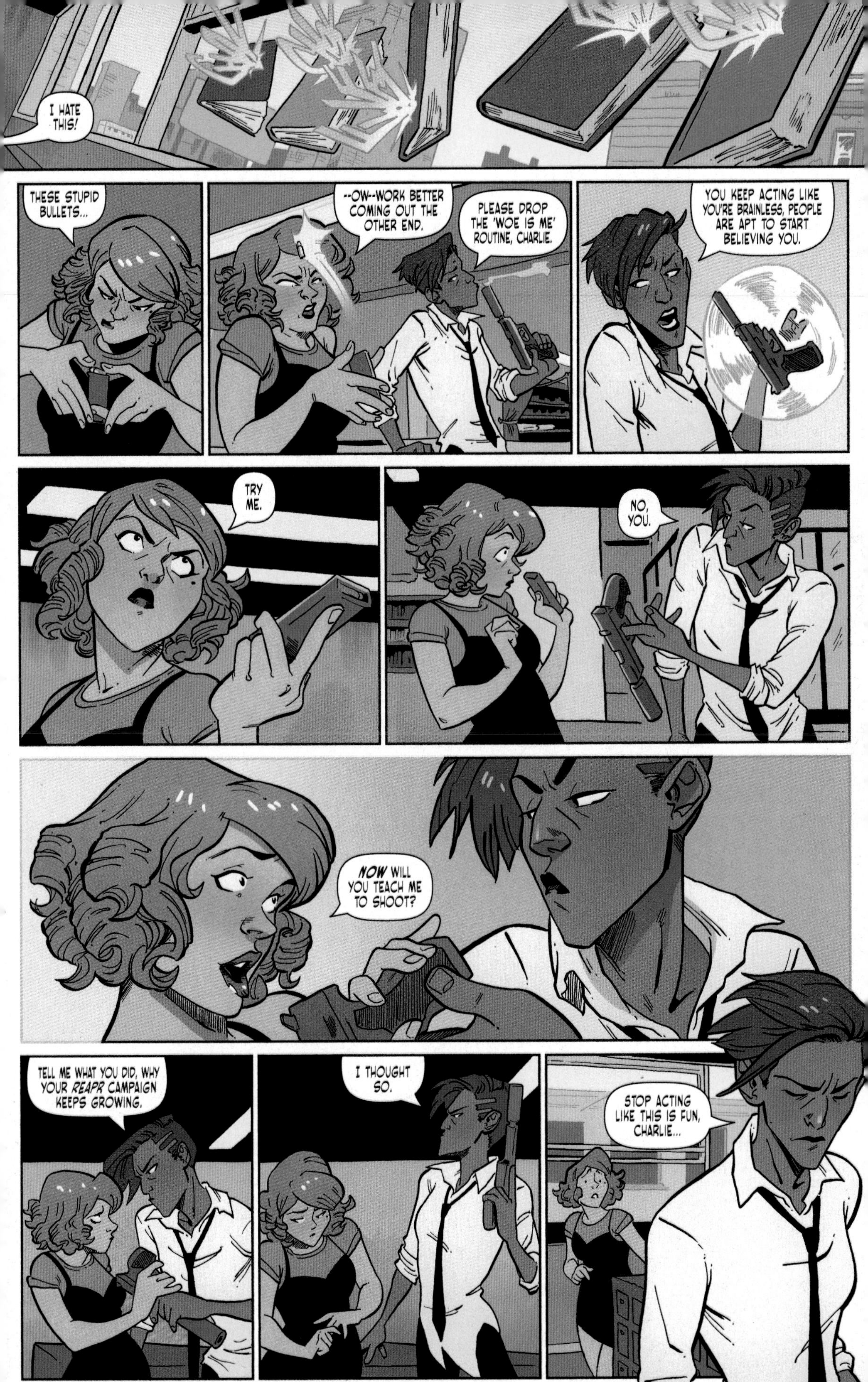
I HATE THIS!
THESE STUPID BULLETS...
--OW--WORK BETTER COMING OUT THE OTHER END.
PLEASE DROP THE 'WOE IS ME' ROUTINE, CHARLIE.
YOU KEEP ACTING LIKE YOU'RE BRAINLESS, PEOPLE ARE APT TO START BELIEVING YOU.
TRY ME.
NO, YOU.
NOW WILL YOU TEACH ME TO SHOOT?
TELL ME WHAT YOU DID, WHY YOUR REAPR CAMPAIGN KEEPS GROWING.
I THOUGHT SO.
STOP ACTING LIKE THIS IS FUN, CHARLIE...

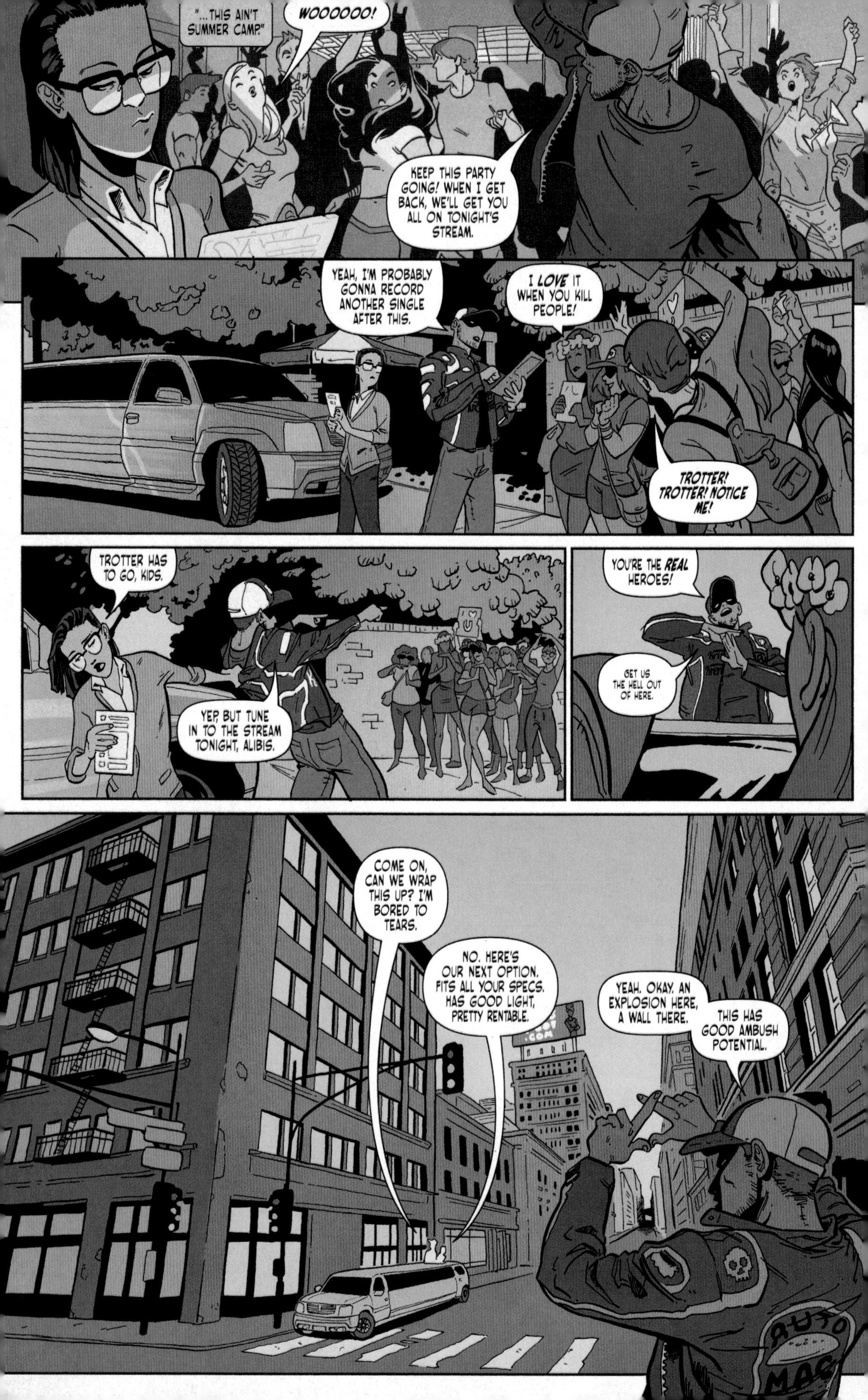
"...THIS AIN'T SUMMER CAMP."
WOOOOOO!
KEEP THIS PARTY GOING! WHEN I GET BACK, WE'LL GET YOU ALL ON TONIGHT'S STREAM.
YEAH, I'M PROBABLY GONNA RECORD ANOTHER SINGLE AFTER THIS.
I LOVE IT WHEN YOU KILL PEOPLE!
TROTTER! TROTTER! NOTICE ME!
TROTTER HAS TO GO, KIDS.
YEP, BUT TUNE IN TO THE STREAM TONIGHT, ALIBIS.
YOU'RE THE REAL HEROES!
GET US THE HELL OUT OF HERE.
COME ON, CAN WE WRAP THIS UP? I'M BORED TO TEARS.
NO. HERE'S OUR NEXT OPTION. FITS ALL YOUR SPECS. HAS GOOD LIGHT, PRETTY RENTABLE.
YEAH. OKAY. AN EXPLOSION HERE, A WALL THERE.
THIS HAS GOOD AMBUSH POTENTIAL.

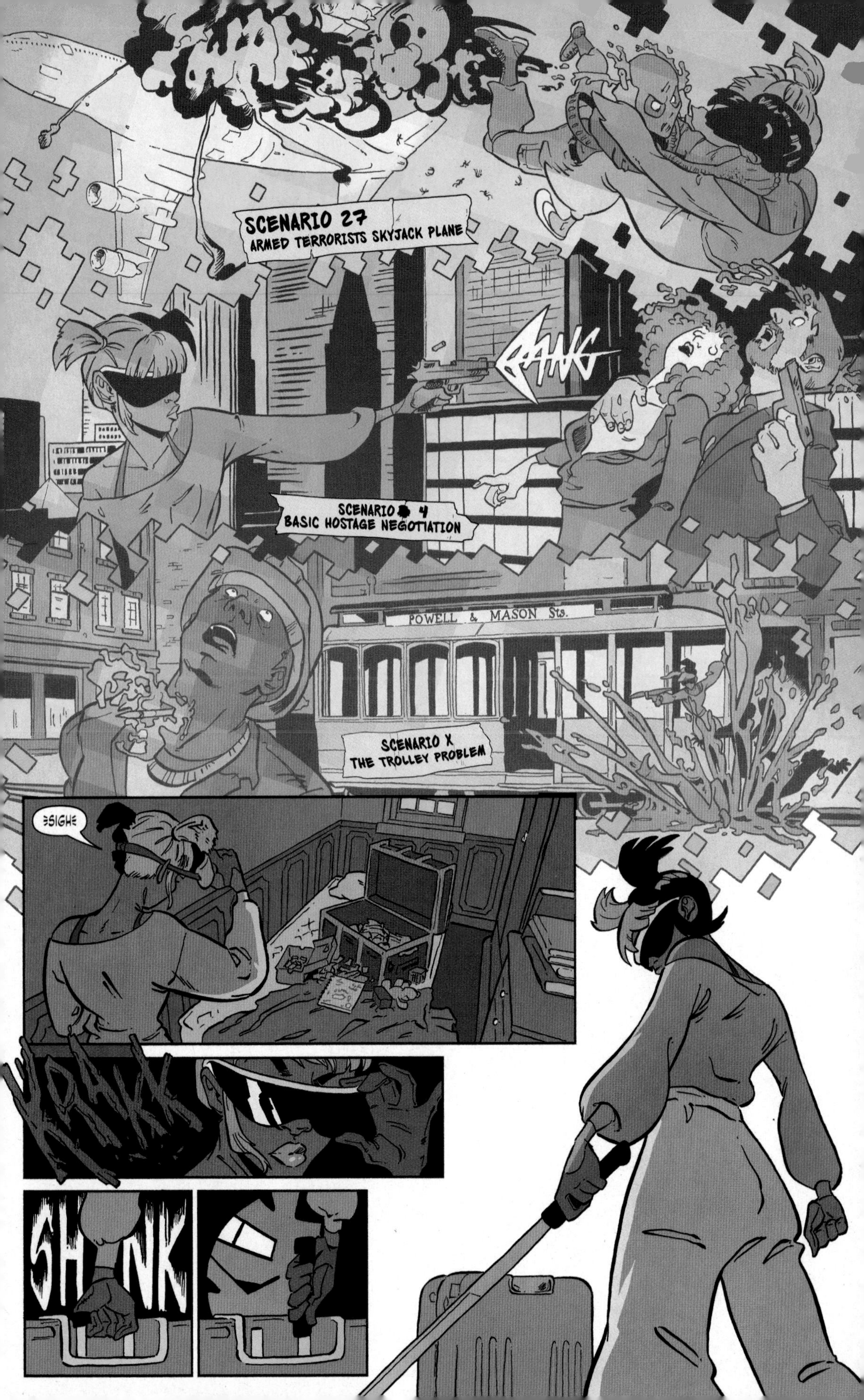
SCENARIO 27
ARMED TERRORISTS SKYJACK PLANE
BLAAANG
SCENARIO 4
BASIC HOSTAGE NEGOTIATION
POWELL & MASON Sts.
SCENARIO X
THE TROLLEY PROBLEM
SIGH
SHNK

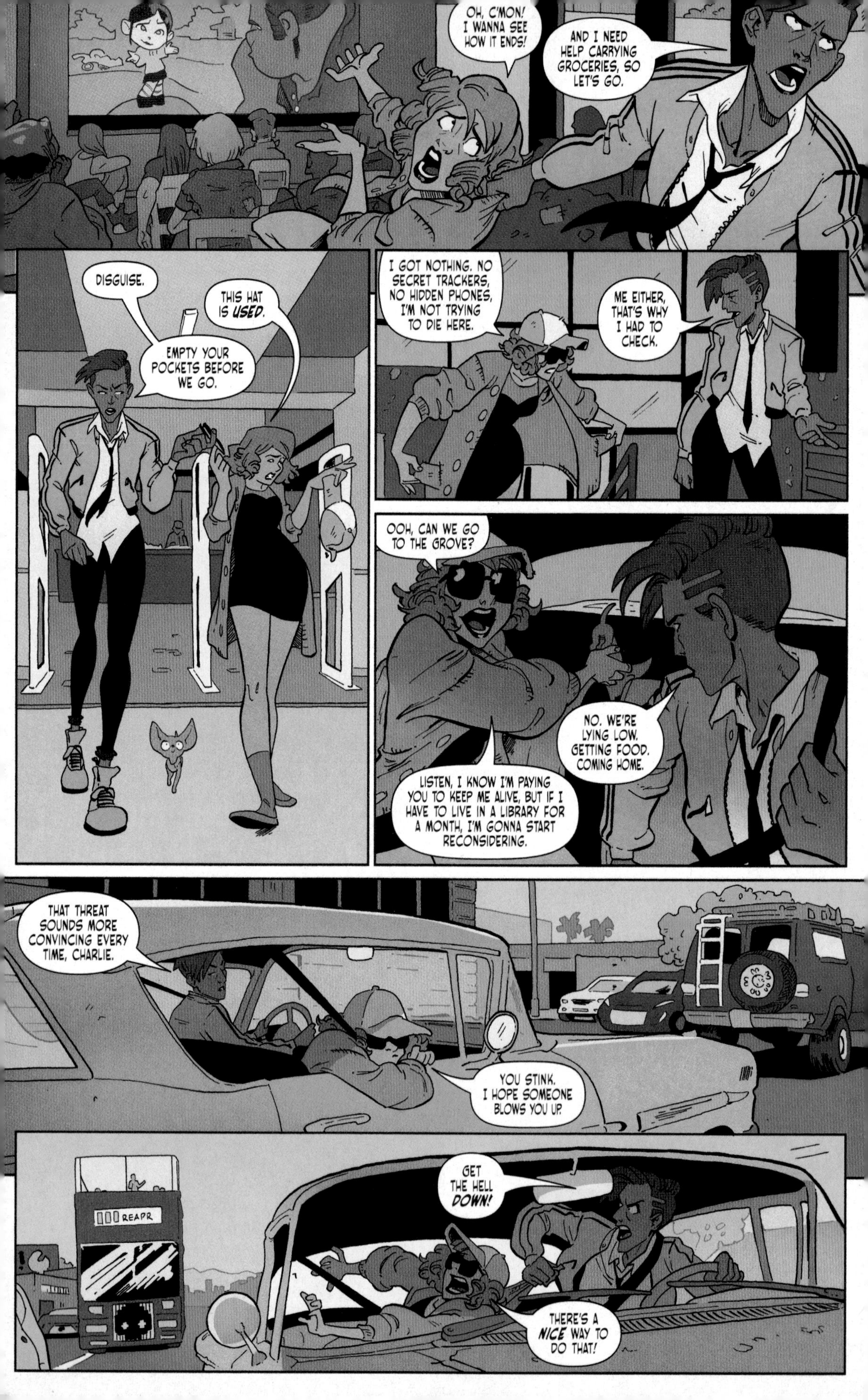
OH, C'MON! I WANNA SEE HOW IT ENDS!
AND I NEED HELP CARRYING GROCERIES, SO LET'S GO.
DISGUISE.
THIS HAT IS USED.
EMPTY YOUR POCKETS BEFORE WE GO.
I GOT NOTHING. NO SECRET TRACKERS, NO HIDDEN PHONES, I'M NOT TRYING TO DIE HERE.
ME EITHER, THAT'S WHY I HAD TO CHECK.
OOH, CAN WE GO TO THE GROVE?
NO. WE'RE LYING LOW. GETTING FOOD. COMING HOME.
LISTEN, I KNOW I'M PAYING YOU TO KEEP ME ALIVE, BUT IF I HAVE TO LIVE IN A LIBRARY FOR A MONTH, I'M GONNA START RECONSIDERING.
THAT THREAT SOUNDS MORE CONVINCING EVERY TIME, CHARLIE.
YOU STINK. I HOPE SOMEONE BLOWS YOU UP.
REAPR
GET THE HELL DOWN!
THERE'S A NICE WAY TO DO THAT!

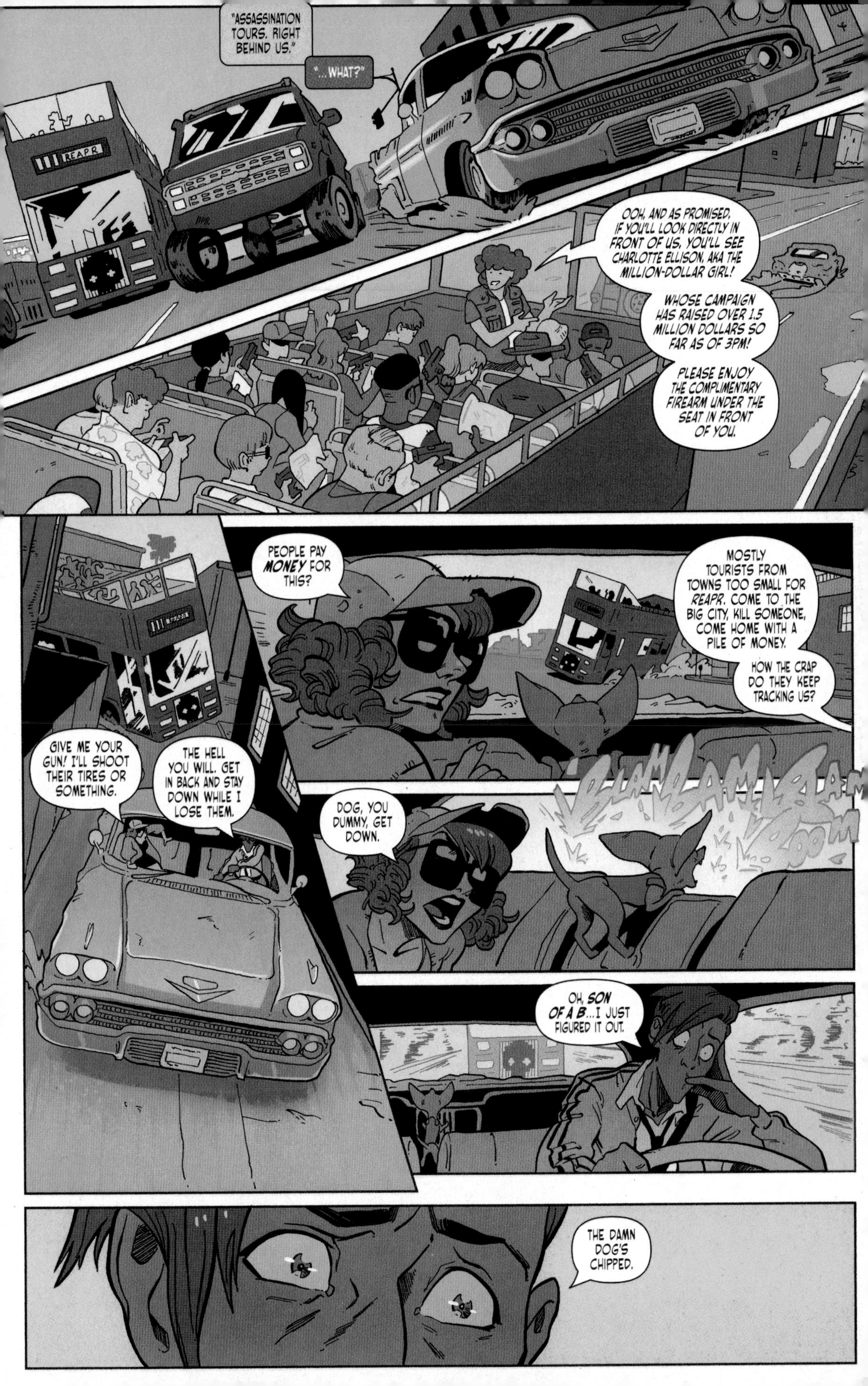
"ASSASSINATION TOURS. RIGHT BEHIND US."
"...WHAT?"
REAPR
OOH, AND AS PROMISED, IF YOU'LL LOOK DIRECTLY IN FRONT OF US, YOU'LL SEE CHARLOTTE ELLISON, AKA THE MILLION-DOLLAR GIRL!
WHOSE CAMPAIGN HAS RAISED OVER 1.5 MILLION DOLLARS SO FAR AS OF 3PM!
PLEASE ENJOY THE COMPLIMENTARY FIREARM UNDER THE SEAT IN FRONT OF YOU.
PEOPLE PAY MONEY FOR THIS?
MOSTLY TOURISTS FROM TOWNS TOO SMALL FOR REAPR. COME TO THE BIG CITY, KILL SOMEONE, COME HOME WITH A PILE OF MONEY.
HOW THE CRAP DO THEY KEEP TRACKING US?
GIVE ME YOUR GUN! I'LL SHOOT THEIR TIRES OR SOMETHING.
THE HELL YOU WILL. GET IN BACK AND STAY DOWN WHILE I LOSE THEM.
DOG, YOU DUMMY, GET DOWN.
OH, SON OF A B...I JUST FIGURED IT OUT.
THE DAMN DOG'S CHIPPED.

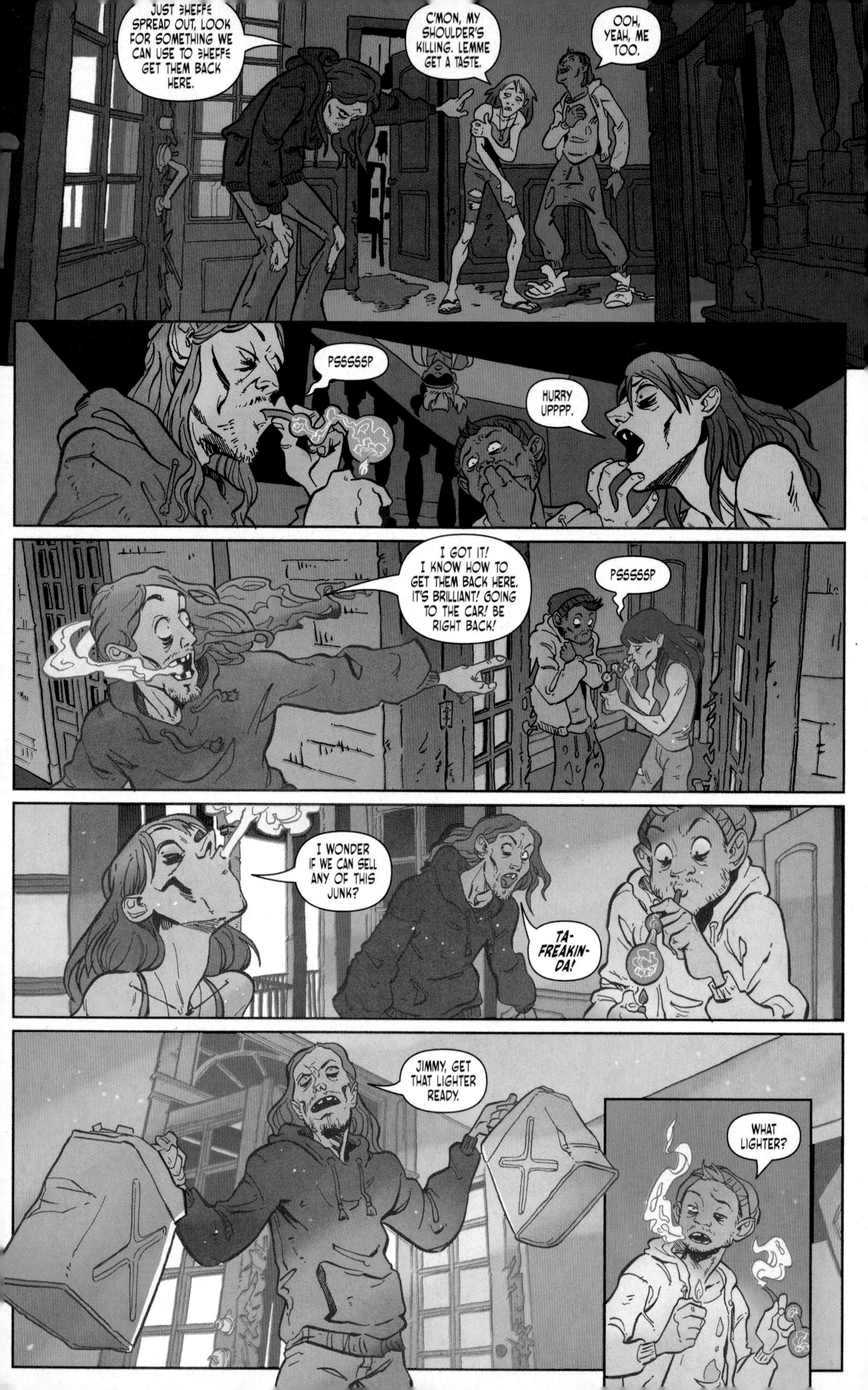
JUST ≷HEFF≷ SPREAD OUT, LOOK FOR SOMETHING WE CAN USE TO ≷HEFF≷ GET THEM BACK HERE.
C'MON, MY SHOULDER'S KILLING. LEMME GET A TASTE.
OOH, YEAH, ME TOO.
PSSSSSP
HURRY UPPPP.
I GOT IT! I KNOW HOW TO GET THEM BACK HERE. IT'S BRILLIANT! GOING TO THE CAR! BE RIGHT BACK!
PSSSSSP
I WONDER IF WE CAN SELL ANY OF THIS JUNK?
TA-FREAKIN-DA!
JIMMY, GET THAT LIGHTER READY.
WHAT LIGHTER?

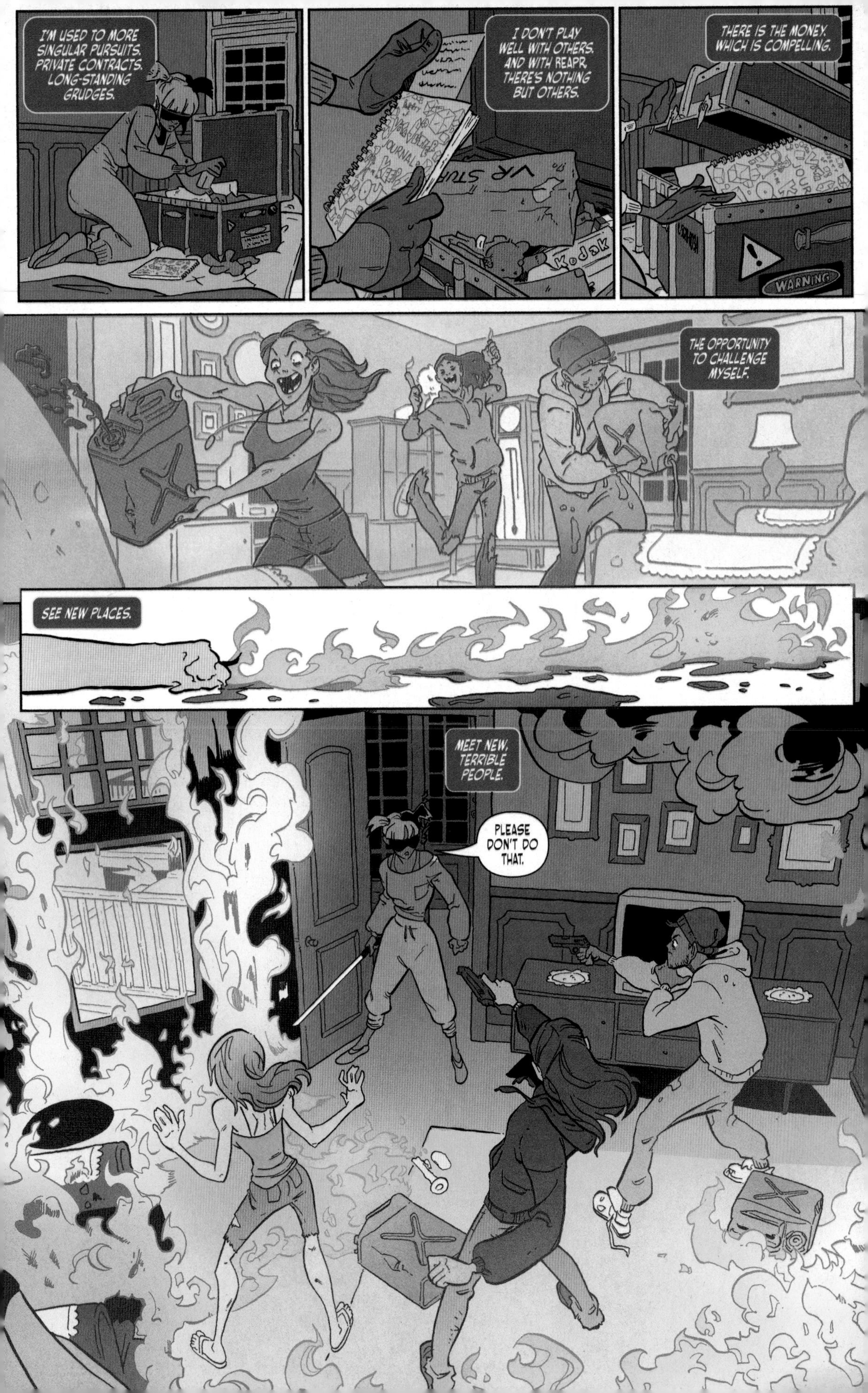
I'M USED TO MORE SINGULAR PURSUITS. PRIVATE CONTRACTS. LONG-STANDING GRUDGES.
I DON'T PLAY WELL WITH OTHERS. AND WITH REAPR, THERE'S NOTHING BUT OTHERS.
Kodak
THERE IS THE MONEY, WHICH IS COMPELLING.
WARNING
THE OPPORTUNITY TO CHALLENGE MYSELF.
SEE NEW PLACES.
MEET NEW, TERRIBLE PEOPLE.
PLEASE DON'T DO THAT.

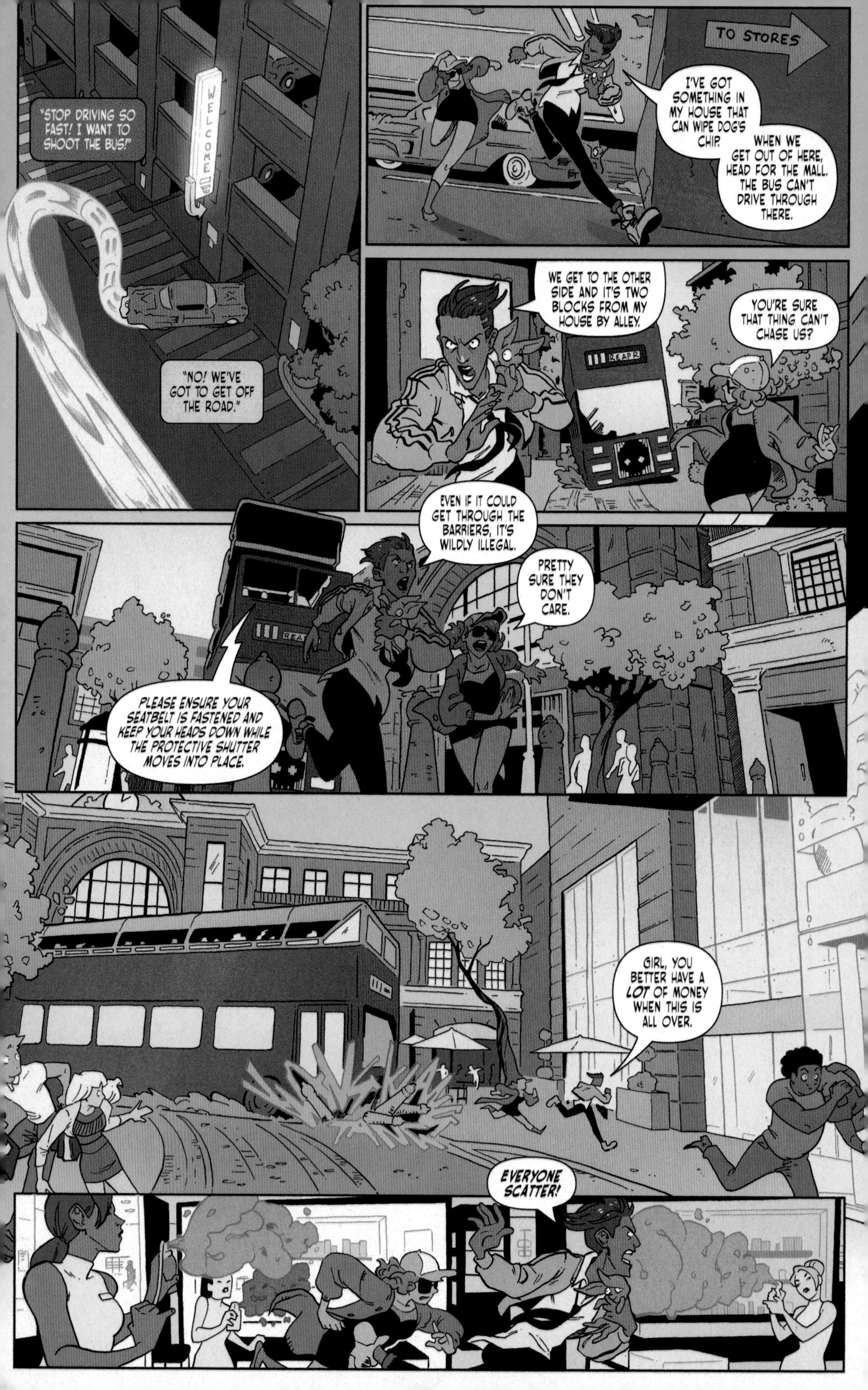
"STOP DRIVING SO FAST! I WANT TO SHOOT THE BUS!"
WELCOME
"NO! WE'VE GOT TO GET OFF THE ROAD."
TO STORES
I'VE GOT SOMETHING IN MY HOUSE THAT CAN WIPE DOG'S CHIP.
WHEN WE GET OUT OF HERE, HEAD FOR THE MALL. THE BUS CAN'T DRIVE THROUGH THERE.
WE GET TO THE OTHER SIDE AND IT'S TWO BLOCKS FROM MY HOUSE BY ALLEY.
YOU'RE SURE THAT THING CAN'T CHASE US?
REAPR
EVEN IF IT COULD GET THROUGH THE BARRIERS, IT'S WILDLY ILLEGAL.
PRETTY SURE THEY DON'T CARE.
PLEASE ENSURE YOUR SEATBELT IS FASTENED AND KEEP YOUR HEADS DOWN WHILE THE PROTECTIVE SHUTTER MOVES INTO PLACE.
GIRL, YOU BETTER HAVE A LOT OF MONEY WHEN THIS IS ALL OVER.
EVERYONE SCATTER!

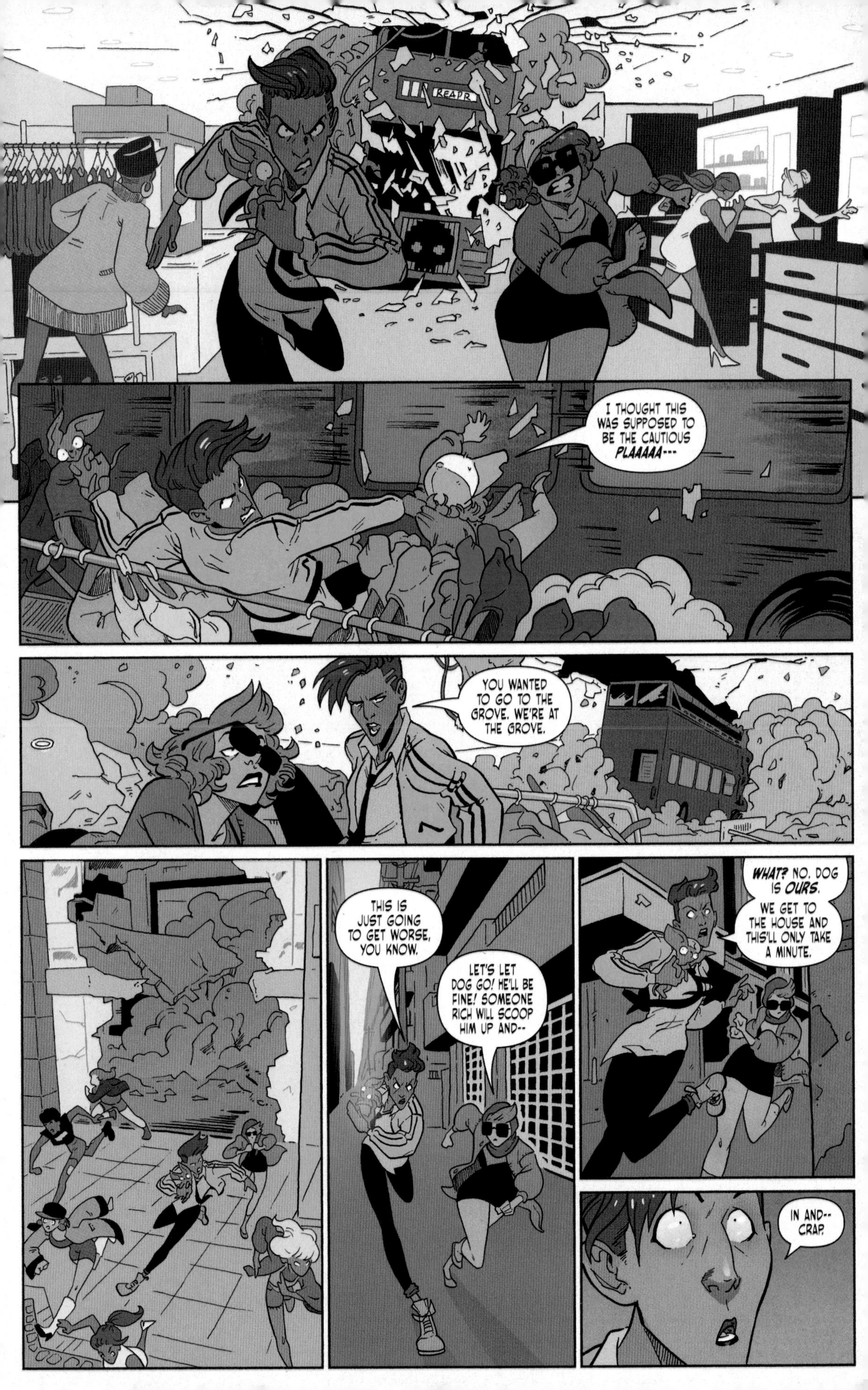
REAPR
I THOUGHT THIS WAS SUPPOSED TO BE THE CAUTIOUS *PLAAAAA*---
YOU WANTED TO GO TO THE GROVE. WE'RE AT THE GROVE.
THIS IS JUST GOING TO GET WORSE, YOU KNOW.
LET'S LET DOG GO! HE'LL BE FINE! SOMEONE RICH WILL SCOOP HIM UP AND--
WHAT? NO. DOG IS *OURS*.
WE GET TO THE HOUSE AND THIS'LL ONLY TAKE A MINUTE.
IN AND-- CRAP.

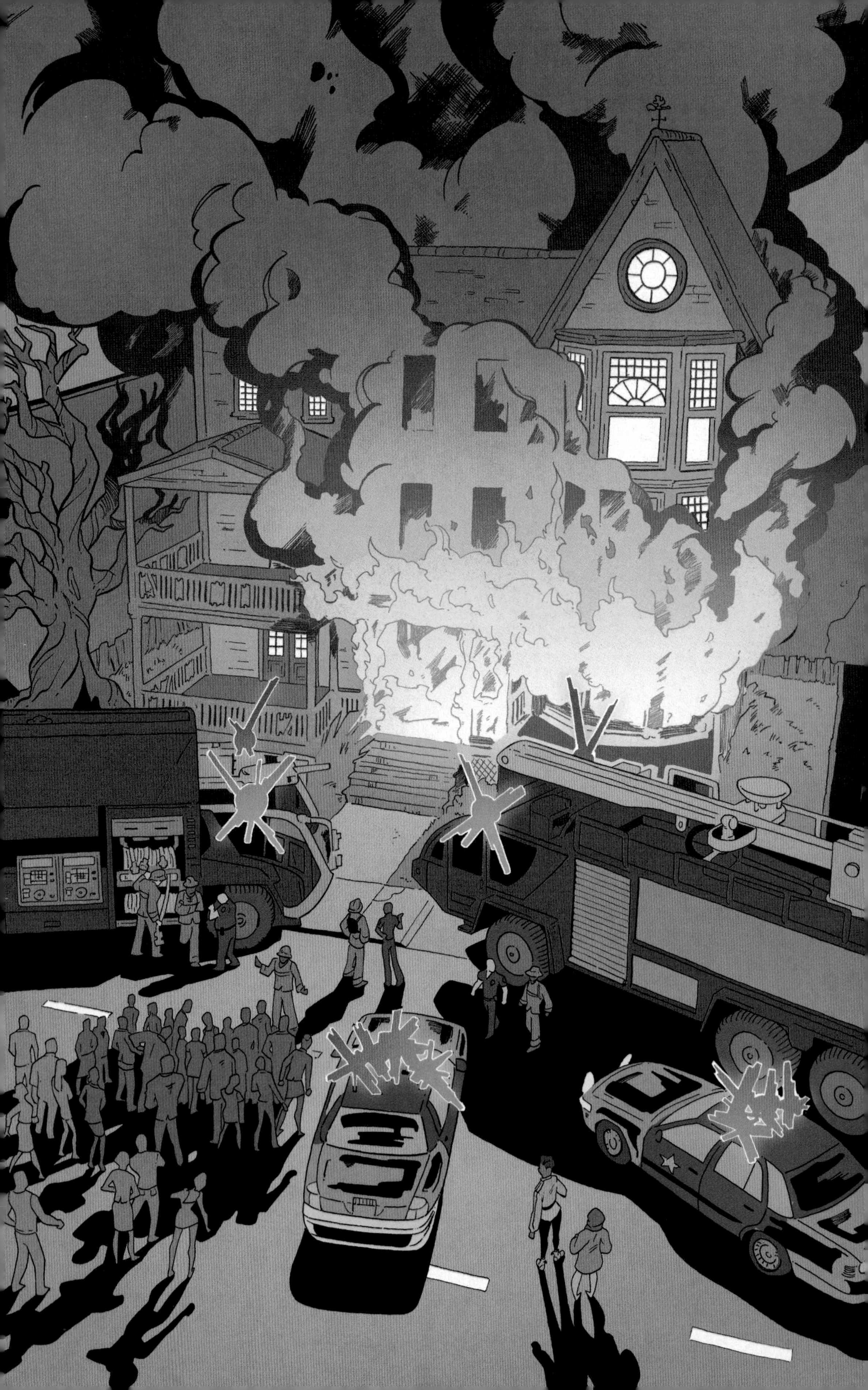

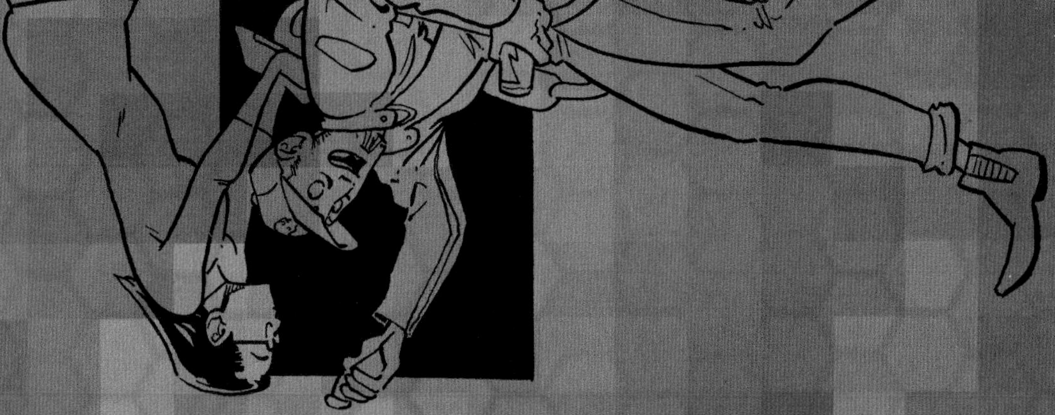

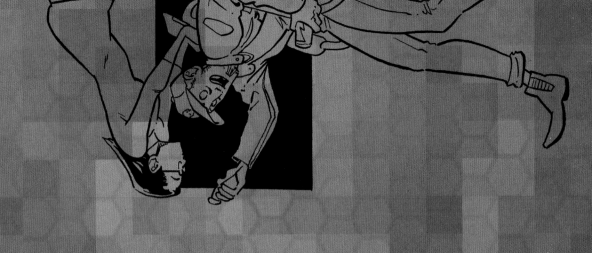

CHAPTER FOUR

THE AMERICAN IN ME

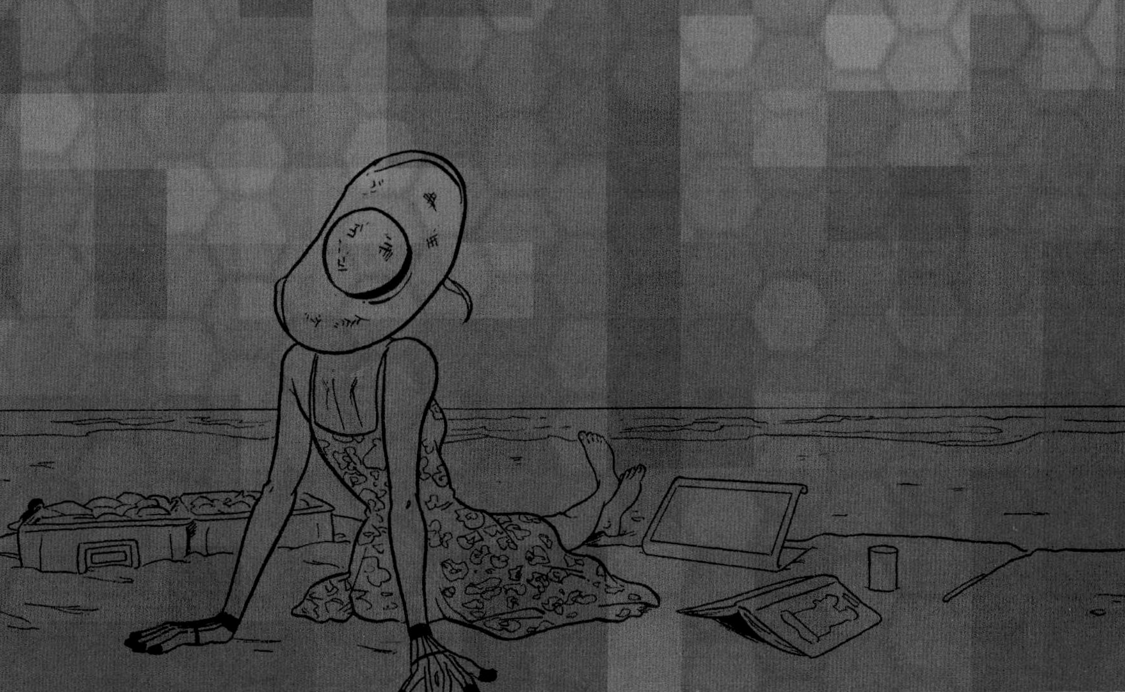

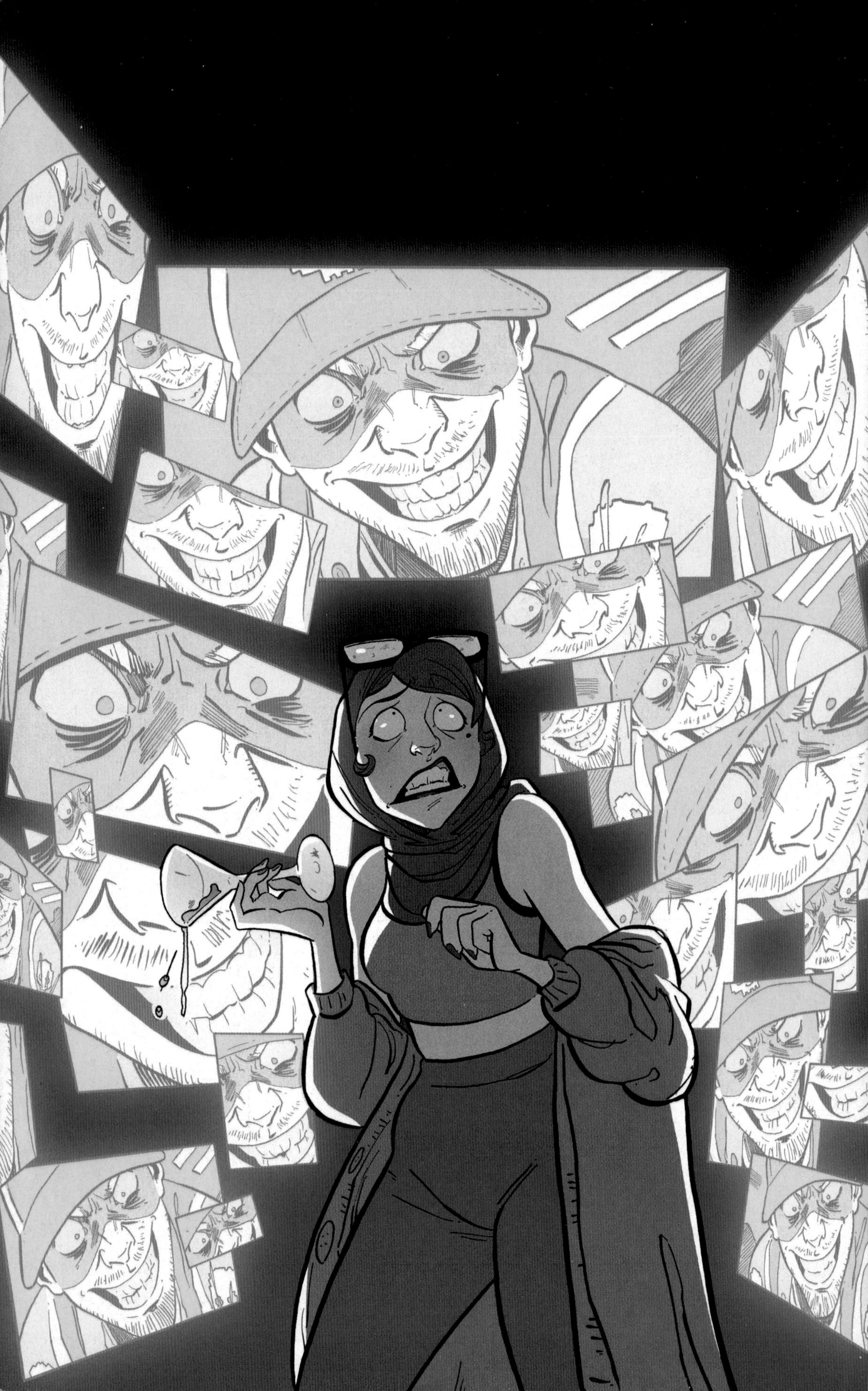

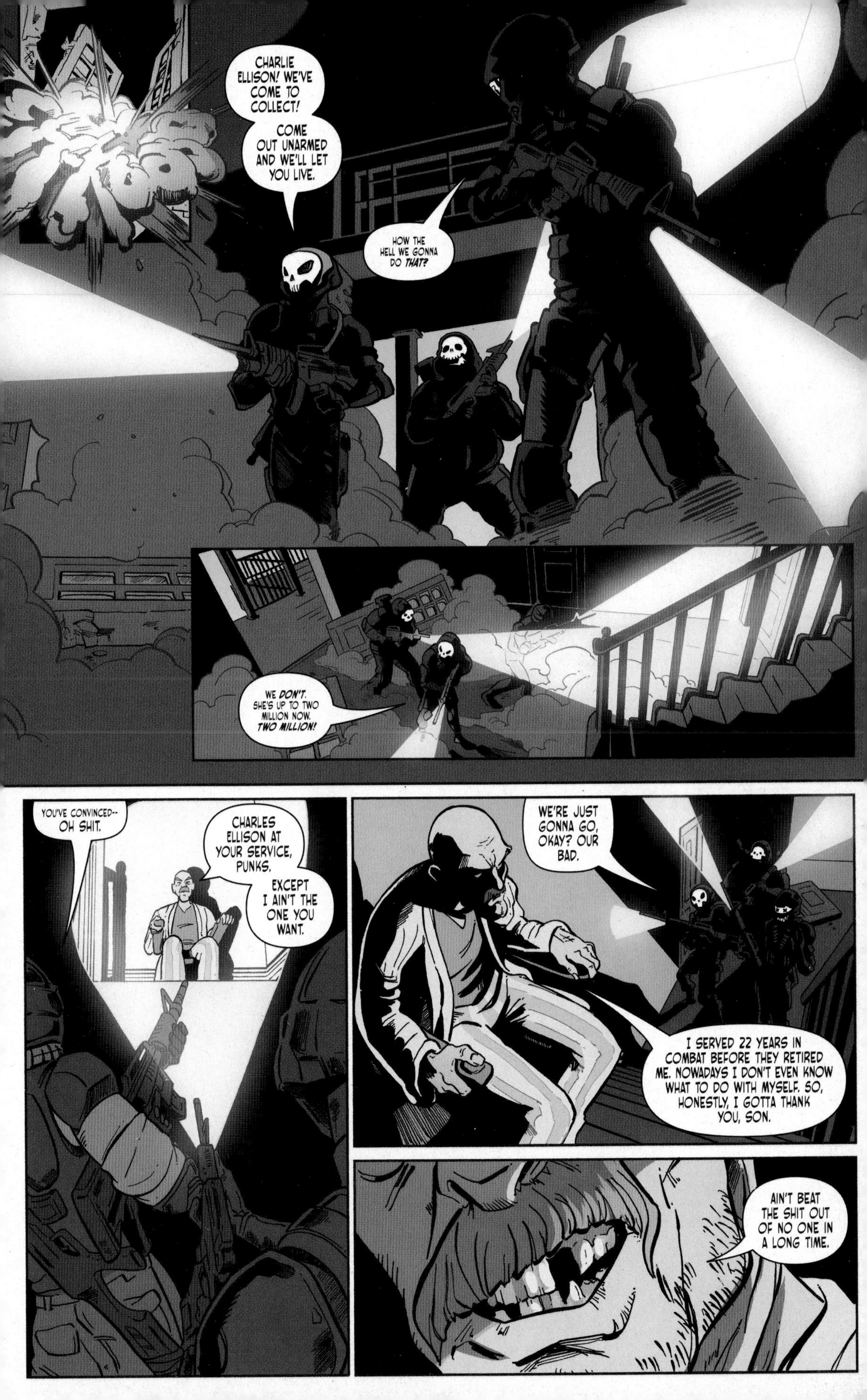
CHARLIE ELLISON! WE'VE COME TO COLLECT!
COME OUT UNARMED AND WE'LL LET YOU LIVE.
HOW THE HELL WE GONNA DO *THAT?*
WE *DON'T*. SHE'S UP TO TWO MILLION NOW. *TWO MILLION!*
YOU'VE CONVINCED-- OH SHIT.
CHARLES ELLISON AT YOUR SERVICE, PUNKS.
EXCEPT I AIN'T THE ONE YOU WANT.
WE'RE JUST GONNA GO, OKAY? OUR BAD.
I SERVED 22 YEARS IN COMBAT BEFORE THEY RETIRED ME. NOWADAYS I DON'T EVEN KNOW WHAT TO DO WITH MYSELF. SO, HONESTLY, I GOTTA THANK YOU, SON.
AIN'T BEAT THE SHIT OUT OF NO ONE IN A LONG TIME.

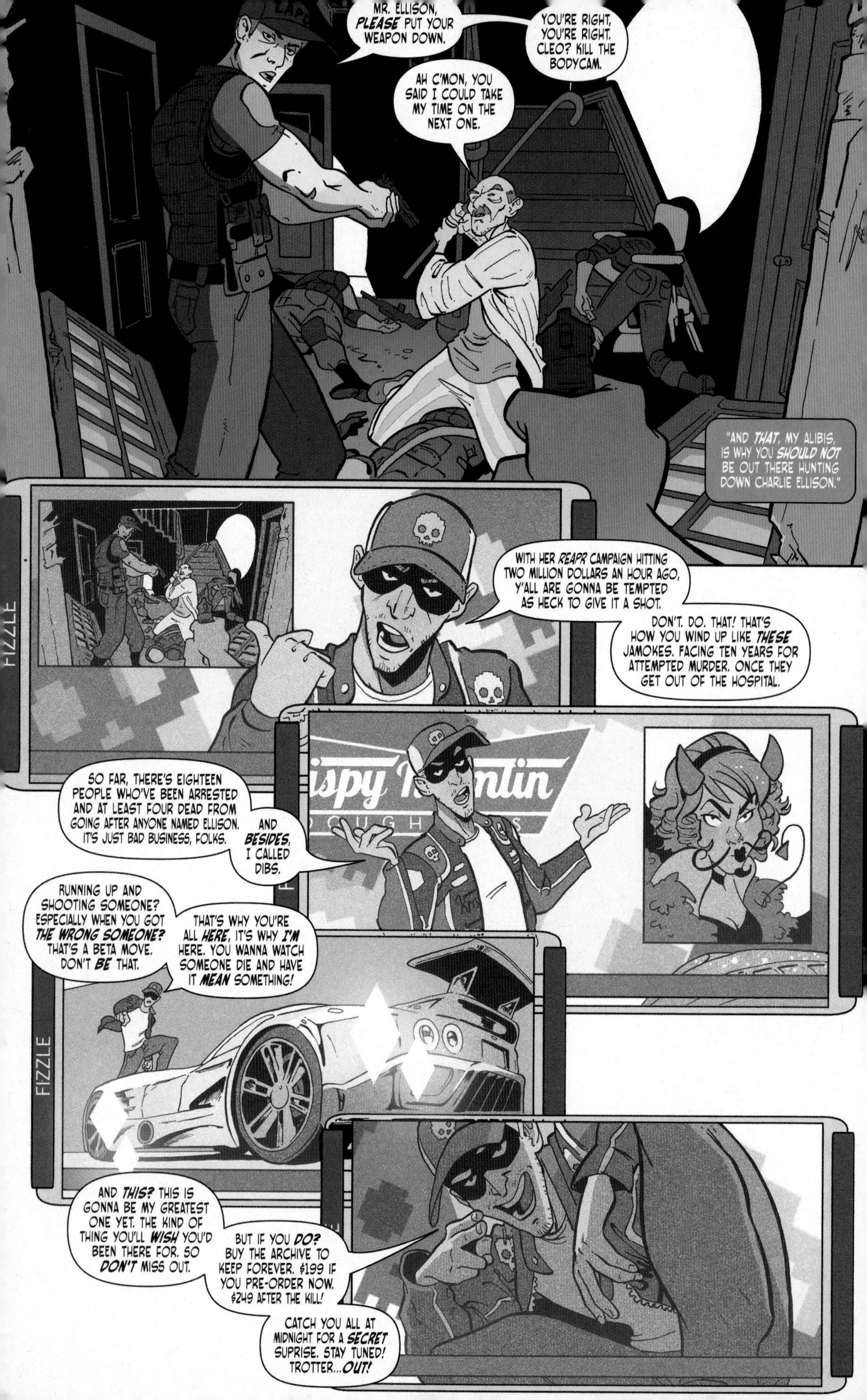

MR. ELLISON, PLEASE PUT YOUR WEAPON DOWN.
AH C'MON, YOU SAID I COULD TAKE MY TIME ON THE NEXT ONE.
YOU'RE RIGHT, YOU'RE RIGHT. CLEO? KILL THE BODYCAM.
"AND THAT, MY ALIBIS, IS WHY YOU SHOULD NOT BE OUT THERE HUNTING DOWN CHARLIE ELLISON."
FIZZLE
WITH HER REAPR CAMPAIGN HITTING TWO MILLION DOLLARS AN HOUR AGO, Y'ALL ARE GONNA BE TEMPTED AS HECK TO GIVE IT A SHOT.
DON'T. DO. THAT! THAT'S HOW YOU WIND UP LIKE THESE JAMOKES. FACING TEN YEARS FOR ATTEMPTED MURDER. ONCE THEY GET OUT OF THE HOSPITAL.
SO FAR, THERE'S EIGHTEEN PEOPLE WHO'VE BEEN ARRESTED AND AT LEAST FOUR DEAD FROM GOING AFTER ANYONE NAMED ELLISON. IT'S JUST BAD BUSINESS, FOLKS.
AND BESIDES, I CALLED DIBS.
RUNNING UP AND SHOOTING SOMEONE? ESPECIALLY WHEN YOU GOT THE WRONG SOMEONE? THAT'S A BETA MOVE. DON'T BE THAT.
THAT'S WHY YOU'RE ALL HERE, IT'S WHY I'M HERE. YOU WANNA WATCH SOMEONE DIE AND HAVE IT MEAN SOMETHING!
FIZZLE
AND THIS? THIS IS GONNA BE MY GREATEST ONE YET. THE KIND OF THING YOU'LL WISH YOU'D BEEN THERE FOR. SO DON'T MISS OUT.
BUT IF YOU DO? BUY THE ARCHIVE TO KEEP FOREVER. $199 IF YOU PRE-ORDER NOW. $249 AFTER THE KILL!
CATCH YOU ALL AT MIDNIGHT FOR A SECRET SUPRISE. STAY TUNED! TROTTER...OUT!

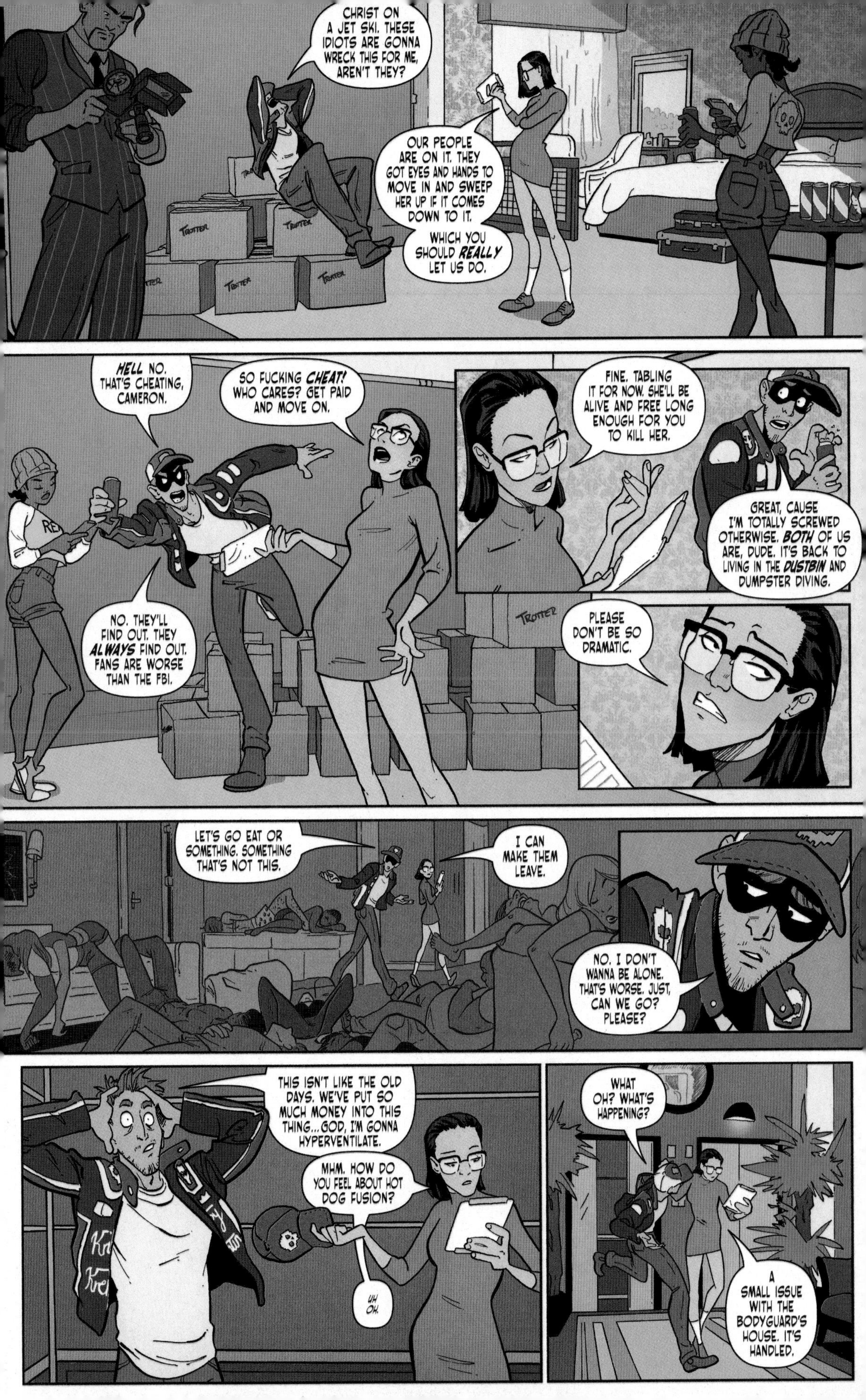
CHRIST ON A JET SKI. THESE IDIOTS ARE GONNA WRECK THIS FOR ME, AREN'T THEY?
OUR PEOPLE ARE ON IT. THEY GOT EYES AND HANDS TO MOVE IN AND SWEEP HER UP IF IT COMES DOWN TO IT.
WHICH YOU SHOULD REALLY LET US DO.
HELL NO. THAT'S CHEATING, CAMERON.
SO FUCKING CHEAT! WHO CARES? GET PAID AND MOVE ON.
NO. THEY'LL FIND OUT. THEY ALWAYS FIND OUT. FANS ARE WORSE THAN THE FBI.
FINE. TABLING IT FOR NOW. SHE'LL BE ALIVE AND FREE LONG ENOUGH FOR YOU TO KILL HER.
GREAT, CAUSE I'M TOTALLY SCREWED OTHERWISE. BOTH OF US ARE, DUDE. IT'S BACK TO LIVING IN THE DUSTBIN AND DUMPSTER DIVING.
PLEASE DON'T BE SO DRAMATIC.
LET'S GO EAT OR SOMETHING. SOMETHING THAT'S NOT THIS.
I CAN MAKE THEM LEAVE.
NO. I DON'T WANNA BE ALONE. THAT'S WORSE. JUST, CAN WE GO? PLEASE?
THIS ISN'T LIKE THE OLD DAYS. WE'VE PUT SO MUCH MONEY INTO THIS THING...GOD, I'M GONNA HYPERVENTILATE.
MHM. HOW DO YOU FEEL ABOUT HOT DOG FUSION?
UH OH.
WHAT OH? WHAT'S HAPPENING?
A SMALL ISSUE WITH THE BODYGUARD'S HOUSE. IT'S HANDLED.

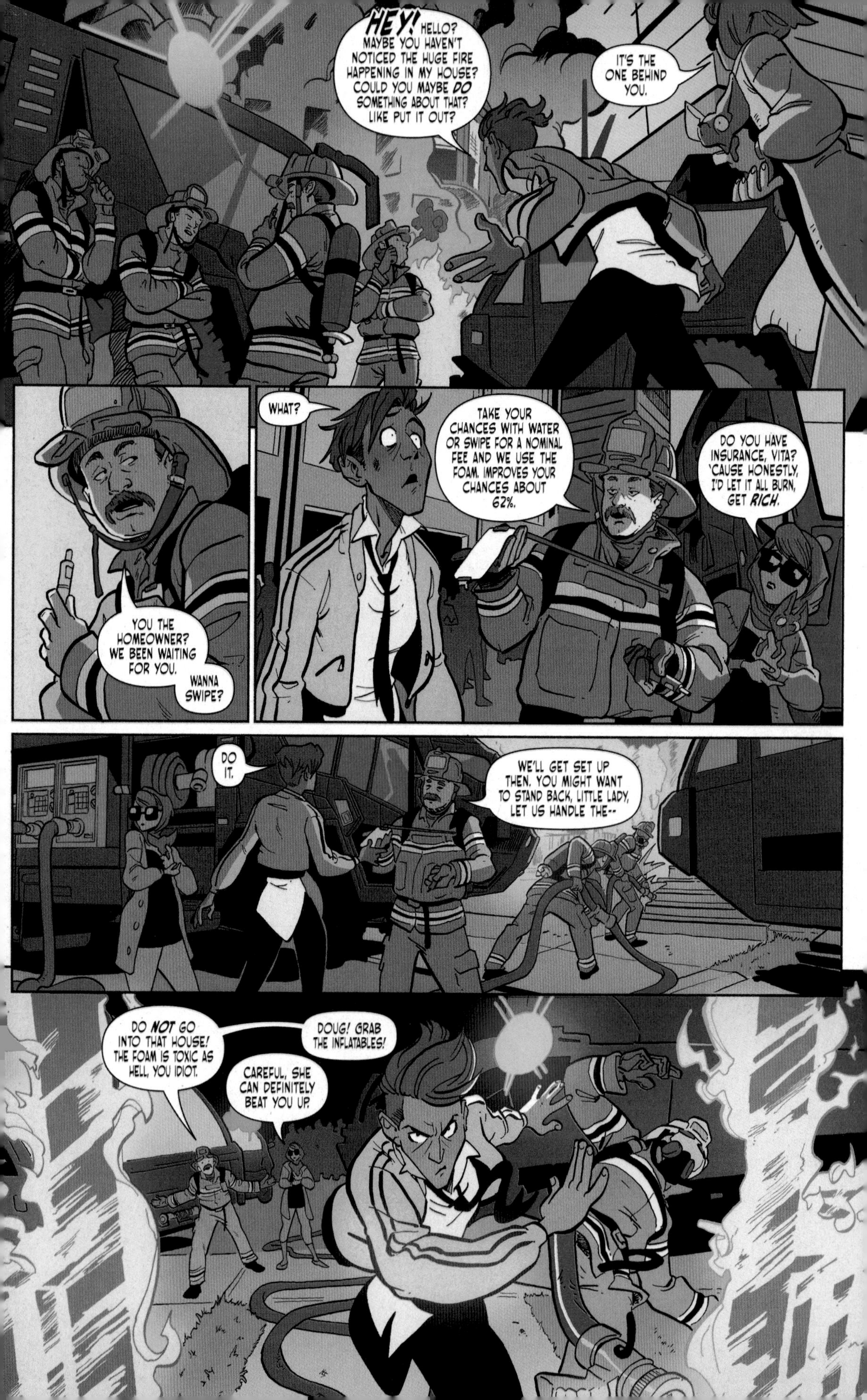
HEY! HELLO? MAYBE YOU HAVEN'T NOTICED THE HUGE FIRE HAPPENING IN MY HOUSE? COULD YOU MAYBE DO SOMETHING ABOUT THAT? LIKE PUT IT OUT?
IT'S THE ONE BEHIND YOU.
YOU THE HOMEOWNER? WE BEEN WAITING FOR YOU.
WANNA SWIPE?
WHAT?
TAKE YOUR CHANCES WITH WATER OR SWIPE FOR A NOMINAL FEE AND WE USE THE FOAM. IMPROVES YOUR CHANCES ABOUT 62%.
DO YOU HAVE INSURANCE, VITA? 'CAUSE HONESTLY, I'D LET IT ALL BURN, GET RICH.
DO IT.
WE'LL GET SET UP THEN. YOU MIGHT WANT TO STAND BACK, LITTLE LADY, LET US HANDLE THE--
DO NOT GO INTO THAT HOUSE! THE FOAM IS TOXIC AS HELL, YOU IDIOT.
DOUG! GRAB THE INFLATABLES!
CAREFUL, SHE CAN DEFINITELY BEAT YOU UP.

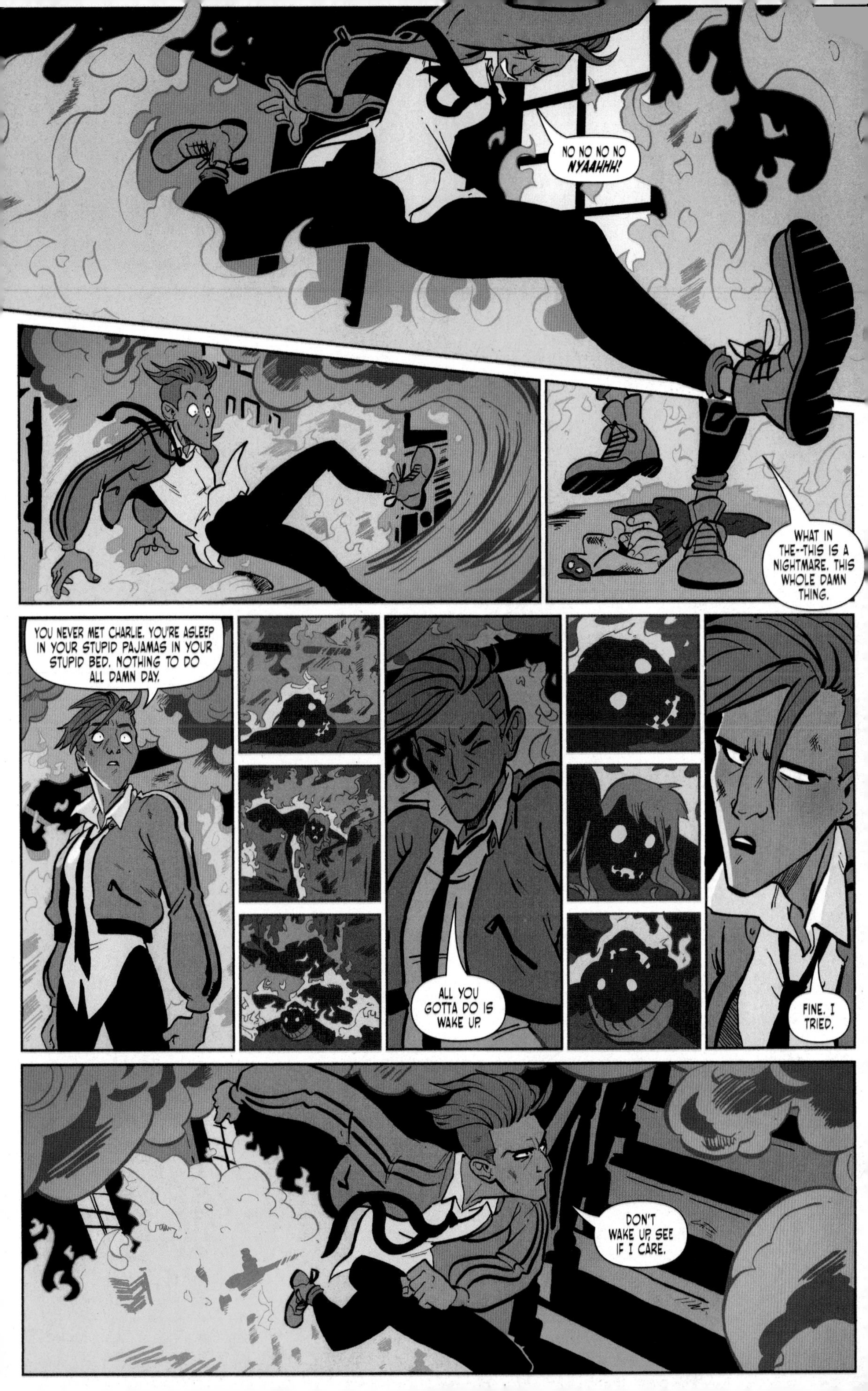
NO NO NO NO
NYAAHHH!
WHAT IN THE--THIS IS A NIGHTMARE. THIS WHOLE DAMN THING.
YOU NEVER MET CHARLIE. YOU'RE ASLEEP IN YOUR STUPID PAJAMAS IN YOUR STUPID BED. NOTHING TO DO ALL DAMN DAY.
ALL YOU GOTTA DO IS WAKE UP.
FINE. I TRIED.
DON'T WAKE UP, SEE IF I CARE.

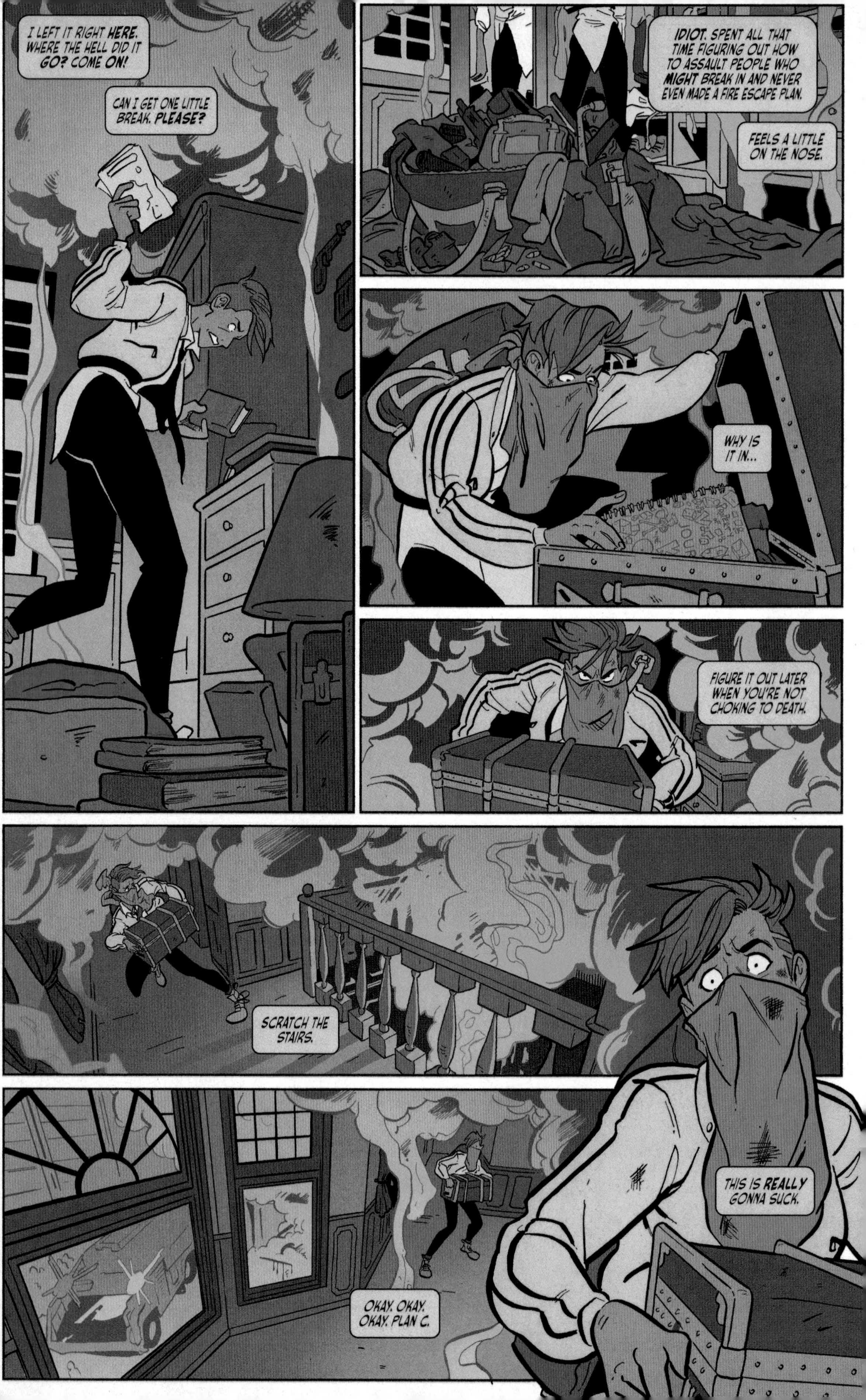
I LEFT IT RIGHT HERE. WHERE THE HELL DID IT GO? COME ON!
CAN I GET ONE LITTLE BREAK. PLEASE?
IDIOT. SPENT ALL THAT TIME FIGURING OUT HOW TO ASSAULT PEOPLE WHO MIGHT BREAK IN AND NEVER EVEN MADE A FIRE ESCAPE PLAN.
FEELS A LITTLE ON THE NOSE.
WHY IS IT IN...
FIGURE IT OUT LATER WHEN YOU'RE NOT CHOKING TO DEATH.
SCRATCH THE STAIRS.
OKAY. OKAY. OKAY. PLAN C.
THIS IS REALLY GONNA SUCK.

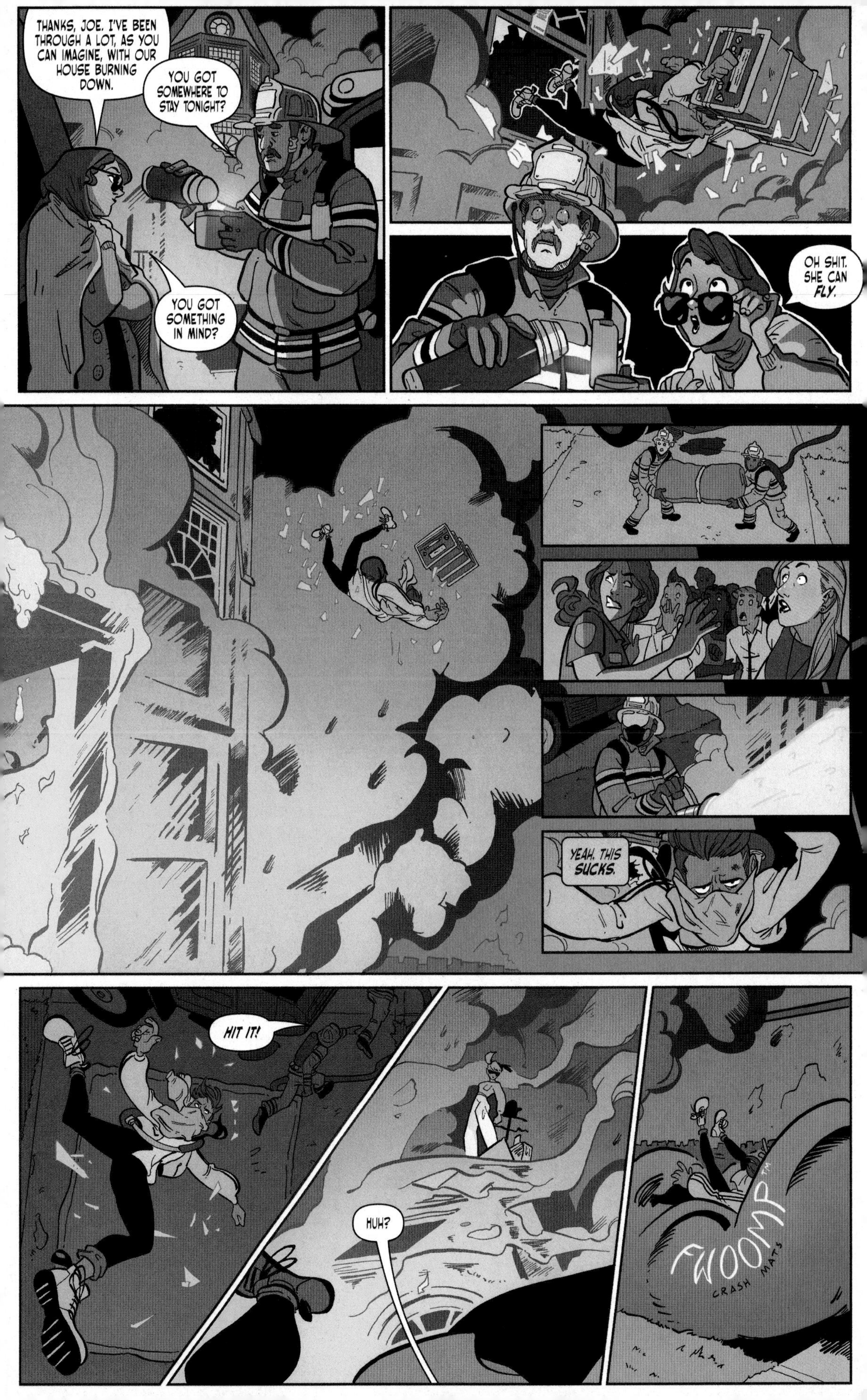
THANKS, JOE. I'VE BEEN THROUGH A LOT, AS YOU CAN IMAGINE, WITH OUR HOUSE BURNING DOWN.
YOU GOT SOMEWHERE TO STAY TONIGHT?
YOU GOT SOMETHING IN MIND?
OH SHIT. SHE CAN FLY.
YEAH. THIS SUCKS.
HIT IT!
HUH?
FWOOMP
CRASH MATS™

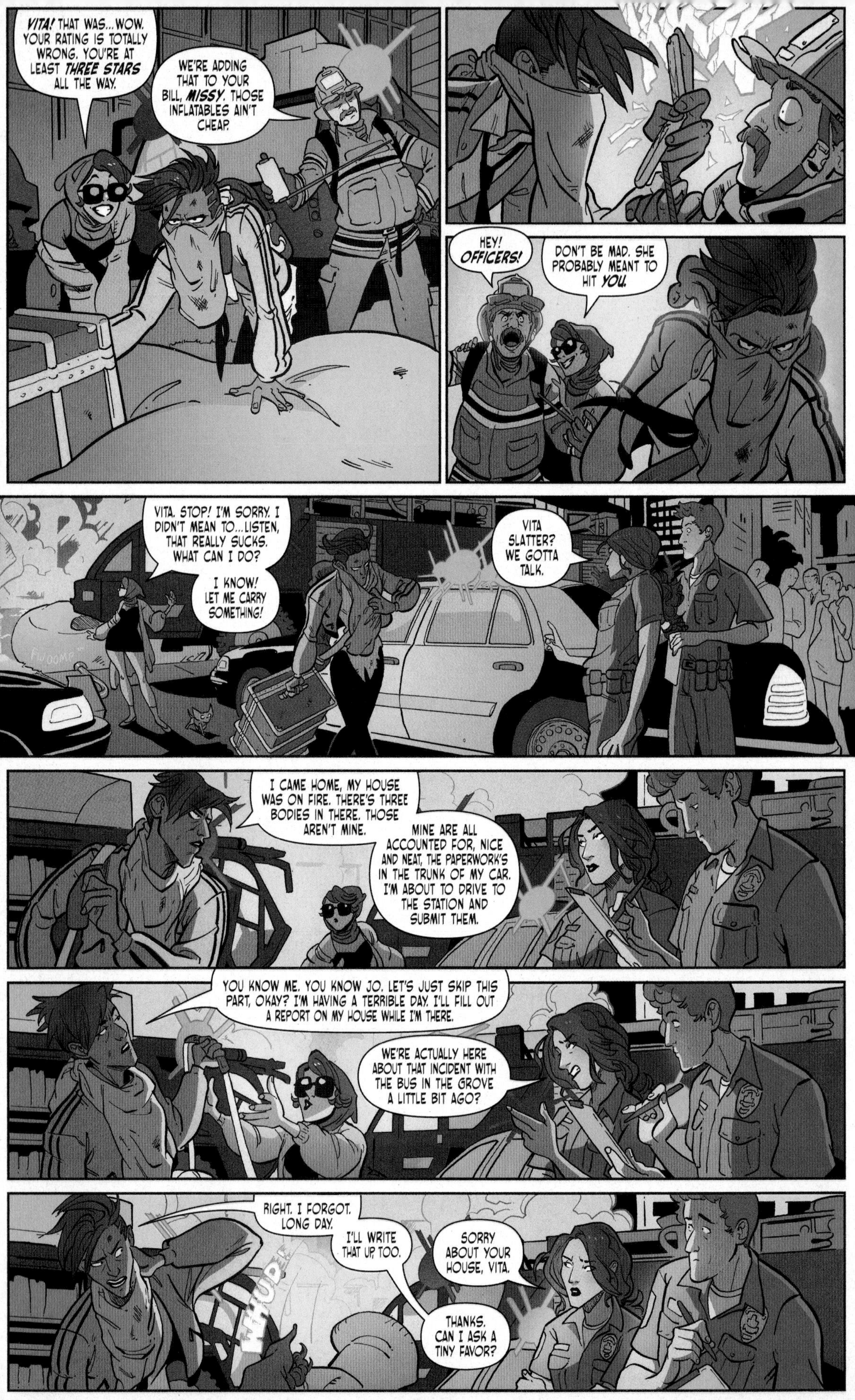

VITA! THAT WAS... WOW. YOUR RATING IS TOTALLY WRONG. YOU'RE AT LEAST *THREE STARS* ALL THE WAY.
WE'RE ADDING THAT TO YOUR BILL, *MISSY*. THOSE INFLATABLES AIN'T CHEAP.
HEY! *OFFICERS!*
DON'T BE MAD. SHE PROBABLY MEANT TO HIT *YOU.*
VITA. STOP! I'M SORRY. I DIDN'T MEAN TO... LISTEN, THAT REALLY SUCKS. WHAT CAN I DO?
I KNOW! LET ME CARRY SOMETHING!
VITA SLATTER? WE GOTTA TALK.
I CAME HOME, MY HOUSE WAS ON FIRE. THERE'S THREE BODIES IN THERE. THOSE AREN'T MINE.
MINE ARE ALL ACCOUNTED FOR, NICE AND NEAT, THE PAPERWORK'S IN THE TRUNK OF MY CAR. I'M ABOUT TO DRIVE TO THE STATION AND SUBMIT THEM.
YOU KNOW ME. YOU KNOW JO. LET'S JUST SKIP THIS PART, OKAY? I'M HAVING A TERRIBLE DAY. I'LL FILL OUT A REPORT ON MY HOUSE WHILE I'M THERE.
WE'RE ACTUALLY HERE ABOUT THAT INCIDENT WITH THE BUS IN THE GROVE A LITTLE BIT AGO?
RIGHT. I FORGOT. LONG DAY.
I'LL WRITE THAT UP, TOO.
SORRY ABOUT YOUR HOUSE, VITA.
THANKS. CAN I ASK A TINY FAVOR?

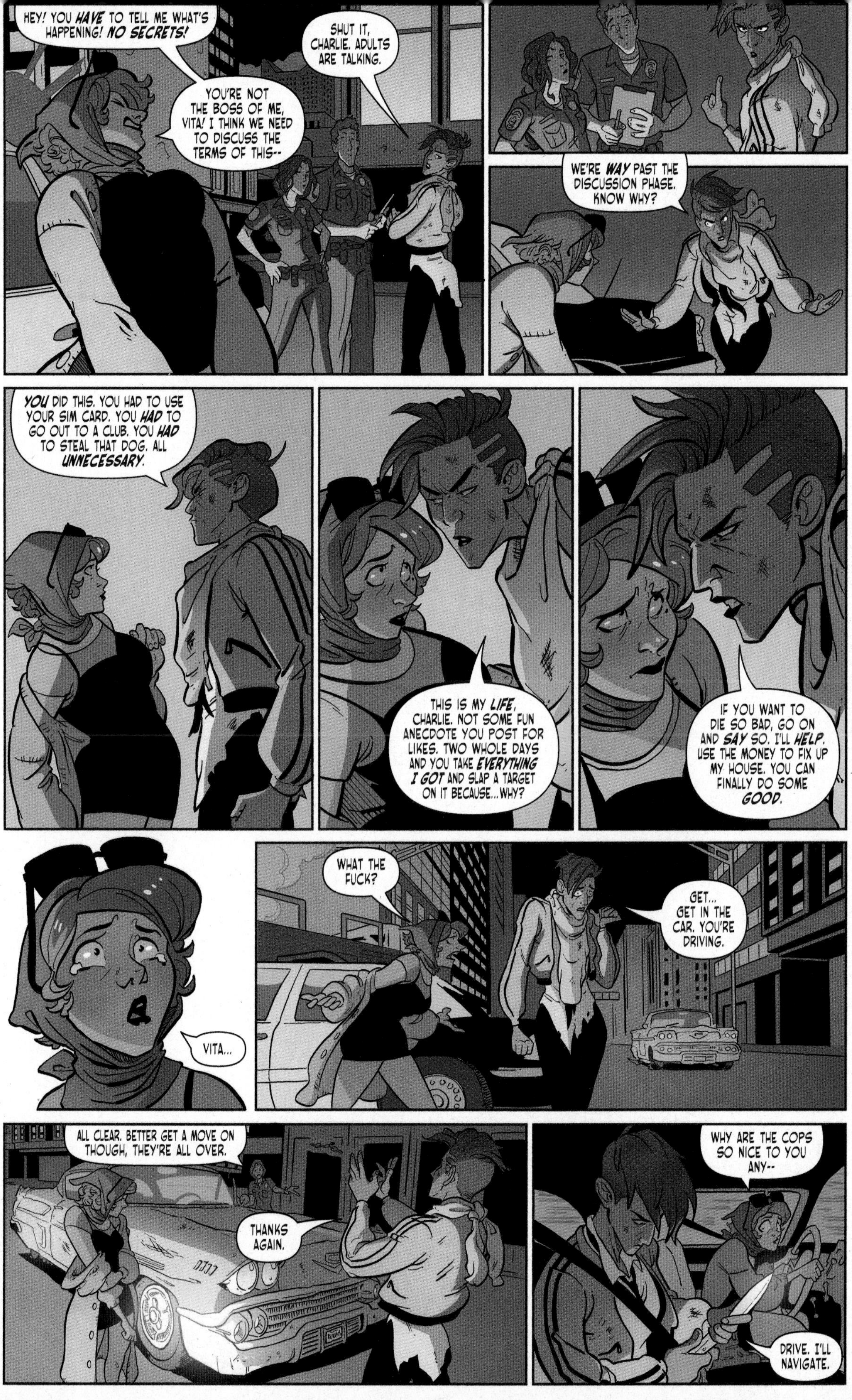
HEY! YOU HAVE TO TELL ME WHAT'S HAPPENING! NO SECRETS!
SHUT IT, CHARLIE. ADULTS ARE TALKING.
YOU'RE NOT THE BOSS OF ME, VITA! I THINK WE NEED TO DISCUSS THE TERMS OF THIS--
WE'RE WAY PAST THE DISCUSSION PHASE. KNOW WHY?
YOU DID THIS. YOU HAD TO USE YOUR SIM CARD. YOU HAD TO GO OUT TO A CLUB. YOU HAD TO STEAL THAT DOG. ALL UNNECESSARY.
THIS IS MY LIFE, CHARLIE. NOT SOME FUN ANECDOTE YOU POST FOR LIKES. TWO WHOLE DAYS AND YOU TAKE EVERYTHING I GOT AND SLAP A TARGET ON IT BECAUSE...WHY?
IF YOU WANT TO DIE SO BAD, GO ON AND SAY SO. I'LL HELP. USE THE MONEY TO FIX UP MY HOUSE. YOU CAN FINALLY DO SOME GOOD.
VITA...
WHAT THE FUCK?
GET... GET IN THE CAR. YOU'RE DRIVING.
ALL CLEAR. BETTER GET A MOVE ON THOUGH, THEY'RE ALL OVER.
THANKS AGAIN.
WHY ARE THE COPS SO NICE TO YOU ANY--
DRIVE. I'LL NAVIGATE.

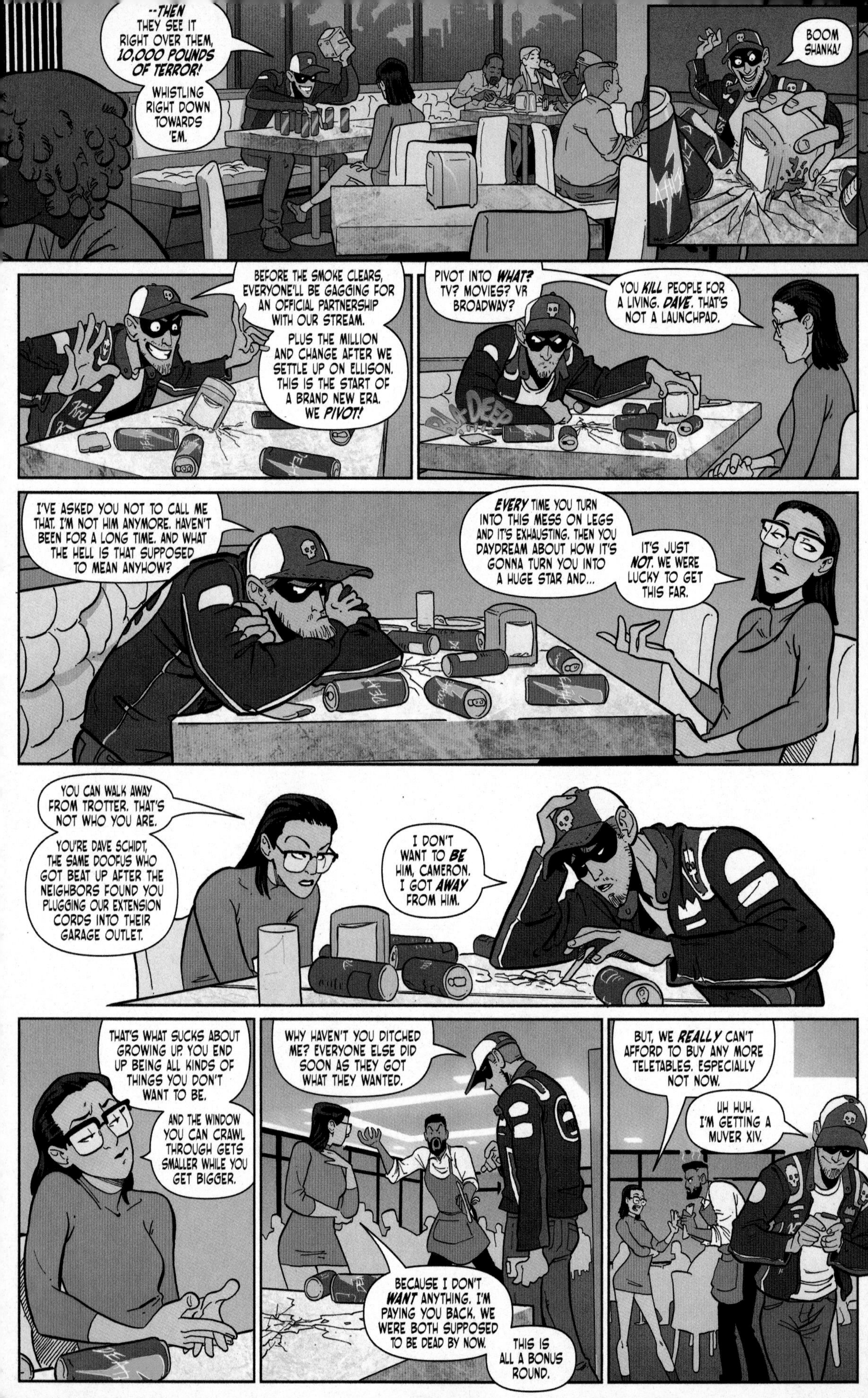
--THEN THEY SEE IT RIGHT OVER THEM, 10,000 POUNDS OF TERROR!
WHISTLING RIGHT DOWN TOWARDS 'EM.
BOOM SHANKA!
BEFORE THE SMOKE CLEARS, EVERYONE'LL BE GAGGING FOR AN OFFICIAL PARTNERSHIP WITH OUR STREAM.
PLUS THE MILLION AND CHANGE AFTER WE SETTLE UP ON ELLISON. THIS IS THE START OF A BRAND NEW ERA. WE PIVOT!
PIVOT INTO WHAT? TV? MOVIES? VR BROADWAY?
YOU KILL PEOPLE FOR A LIVING, DAVE. THAT'S NOT A LAUNCHPAD.
I'VE ASKED YOU NOT TO CALL ME THAT. I'M NOT HIM ANYMORE. HAVEN'T BEEN FOR A LONG TIME. AND WHAT THE HELL IS THAT SUPPOSED TO MEAN ANYHOW?
EVERY TIME YOU TURN INTO THIS MESS ON LEGS AND IT'S EXHAUSTING. THEN YOU DAYDREAM ABOUT HOW IT'S GONNA TURN YOU INTO A HUGE STAR AND...
IT'S JUST NOT. WE WERE LUCKY TO GET THIS FAR.
YOU CAN WALK AWAY FROM TROTTER. THAT'S NOT WHO YOU ARE.
YOU'RE DAVE SCHIDT, THE SAME DOOFUS WHO GOT BEAT UP AFTER THE NEIGHBORS FOUND YOU PLUGGING OUR EXTENSION CORDS INTO THEIR GARAGE OUTLET.
I DON'T WANT TO BE HIM, CAMERON. I GOT AWAY FROM HIM.
THAT'S WHAT SUCKS ABOUT GROWING UP. YOU END UP BEING ALL KINDS OF THINGS YOU DON'T WANT TO BE.
AND THE WINDOW YOU CAN CRAWL THROUGH GETS SMALLER WHILE YOU GET BIGGER.
WHY HAVEN'T YOU DITCHED ME? EVERYONE ELSE DID SOON AS THEY GOT WHAT THEY WANTED.
BECAUSE I DON'T WANT ANYTHING. I'M PAYING YOU BACK. WE WERE BOTH SUPPOSED TO BE DEAD BY NOW.
THIS IS ALL A BONUS ROUND.
BUT, WE REALLY CAN'T AFFORD TO BUY ANY MORE TELETABLES. ESPECIALLY NOT NOW.
UH HUH. I'M GETTING A MUVER XIV.

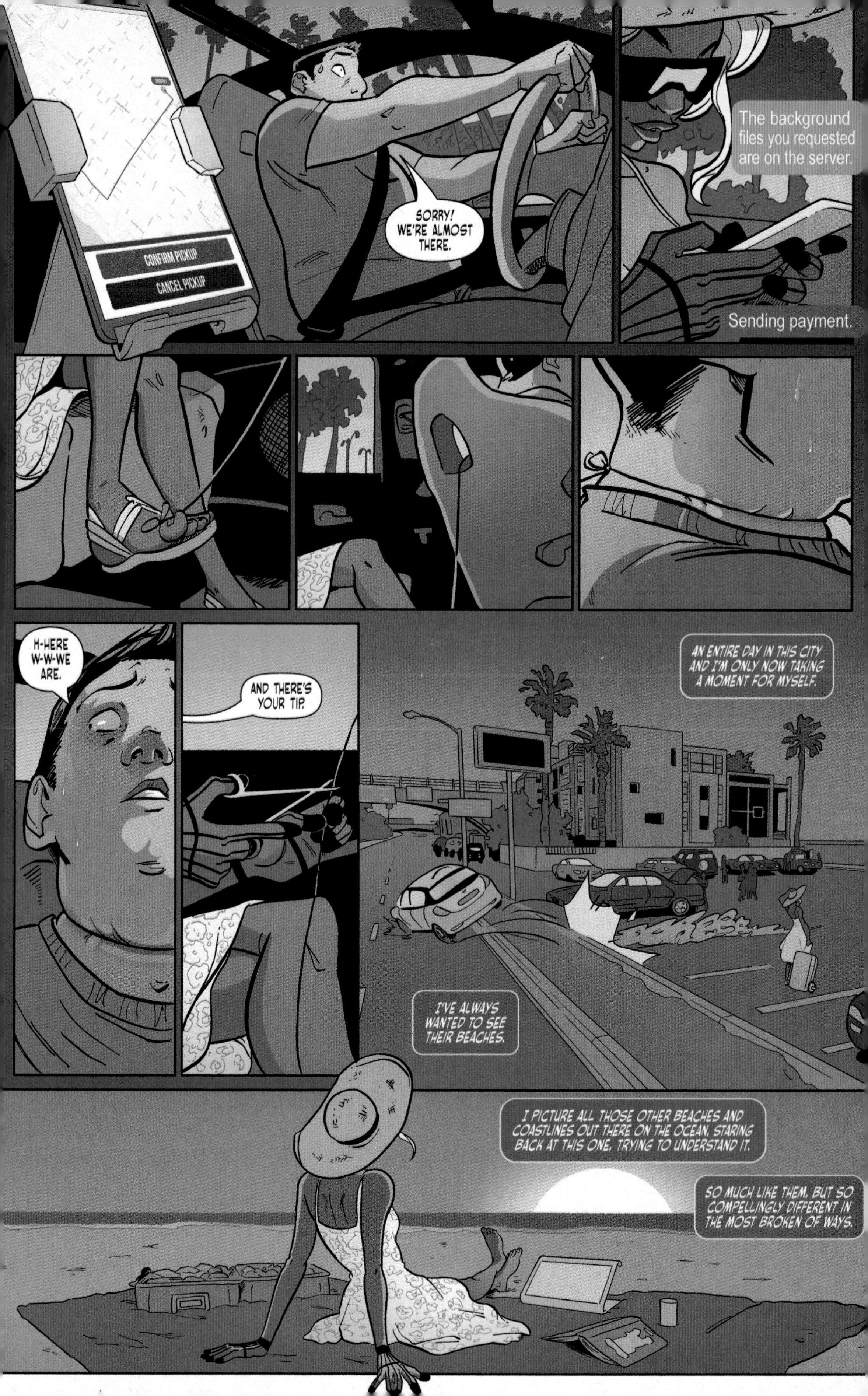
CONFIRM PICKUP
CANCEL PICKUP
SORRY! WE'RE ALMOST THERE.
The background files you requested are on the server.
Sending payment.
H-HERE W-W-WE ARE.
AND THERE'S YOUR TIP.
AN ENTIRE DAY IN THIS CITY AND I'M ONLY NOW TAKING A MOMENT FOR MYSELF.
I'VE ALWAYS WANTED TO SEE THEIR BEACHES.
I PICTURE ALL THOSE OTHER BEACHES AND COASTLINES OUT THERE ON THE OCEAN, STARING BACK AT THIS ONE, TRYING TO UNDERSTAND IT.
SO MUCH LIKE THEM, BUT SO COMPELLINGLY DIFFERENT IN THE MOST BROKEN OF WAYS.

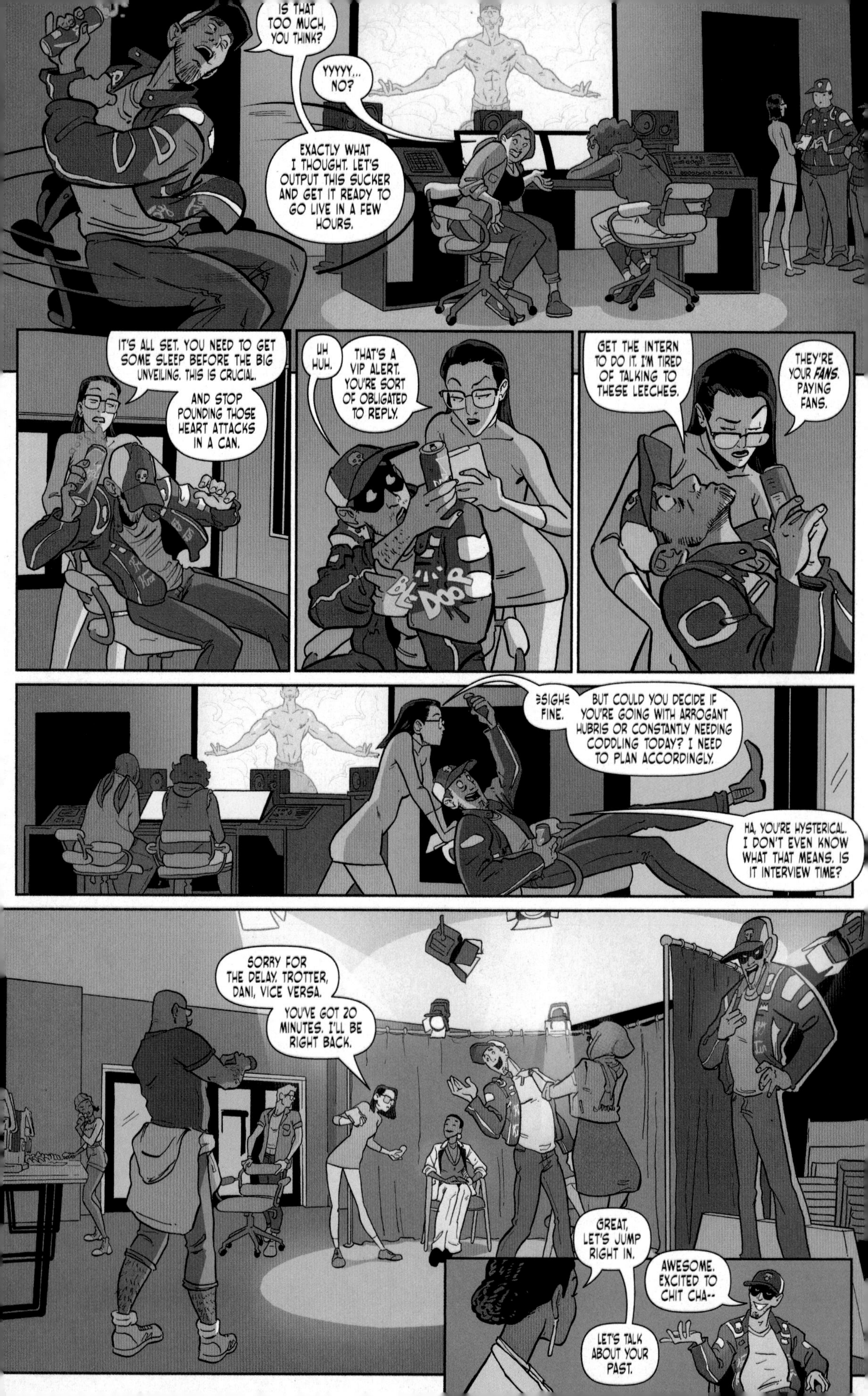
IS THAT TOO MUCH, YOU THINK?
YYYYY... NO?
EXACTLY WHAT I THOUGHT. LET'S OUTPUT THIS SUCKER AND GET IT READY TO GO LIVE IN A FEW HOURS.
IT'S ALL SET. YOU NEED TO GET SOME SLEEP BEFORE THE BIG UNVEILING. THIS IS CRUCIAL.
AND STOP POUNDING THOSE HEART ATTACKS IN A CAN.
UH HUH.
THAT'S A VIP ALERT. YOU'RE SORT OF OBLIGATED TO REPLY.
BE-DOOP
GET THE INTERN TO DO IT. I'M TIRED OF TALKING TO THESE LEECHES.
THEY'RE YOUR *FANS*. PAYING FANS.
≥SIGH≤ FINE.
BUT COULD YOU DECIDE IF YOU'RE GOING WITH ARROGANT HUBRIS OR CONSTANTLY NEEDING CODDLING TODAY? I NEED TO PLAN ACCORDINGLY.
HA, YOU'RE HYSTERICAL. I DON'T EVEN KNOW WHAT THAT MEANS. IS IT INTERVIEW TIME?
SORRY FOR THE DELAY. TROTTER, DANI, VICE VERSA.
YOU'VE GOT 20 MINUTES. I'LL BE RIGHT BACK.
GREAT, LET'S JUMP RIGHT IN.
AWESOME. EXCITED TO CHIT CHA--
LET'S TALK ABOUT YOUR PAST.

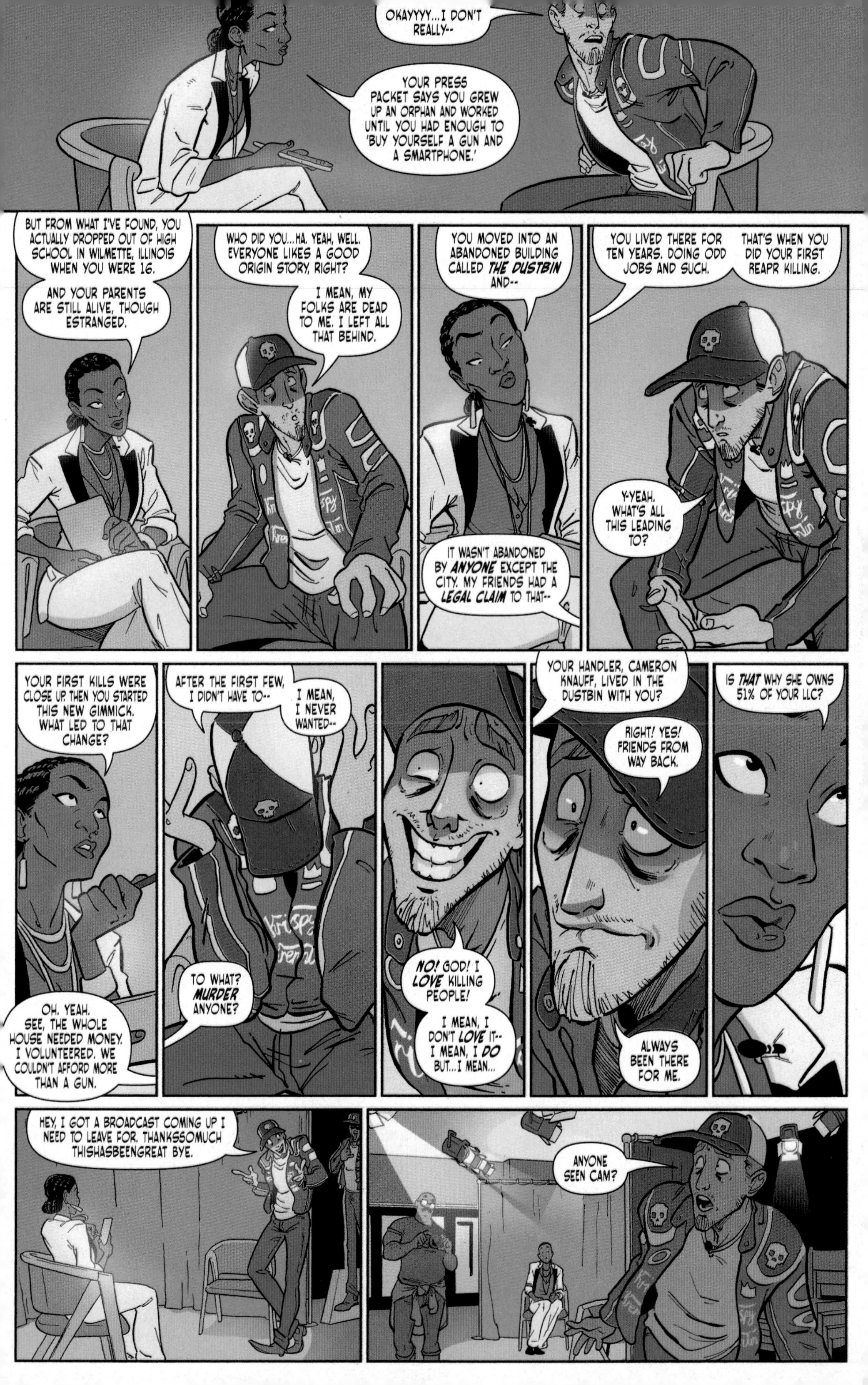
OKAYYYY...I DON'T REALLY--
YOUR PRESS PACKET SAYS YOU GREW UP AN ORPHAN AND WORKED UNTIL YOU HAD ENOUGH TO 'BUY YOURSELF A GUN AND A SMARTPHONE.'
BUT FROM WHAT I'VE FOUND, YOU ACTUALLY DROPPED OUT OF HIGH SCHOOL IN WILMETTE, ILLINOIS WHEN YOU WERE 16.
AND YOUR PARENTS ARE STILL ALIVE, THOUGH ESTRANGED.
WHO DID YOU...HA. YEAH, WELL. EVERYONE LIKES A GOOD ORIGIN STORY, RIGHT?
I MEAN, MY FOLKS ARE DEAD TO ME. I LEFT ALL THAT BEHIND.
YOU MOVED INTO AN ABANDONED BUILDING CALLED THE DUSTBIN AND--
IT WASN'T ABANDONED BY ANYONE EXCEPT THE CITY. MY FRIENDS HAD A LEGAL CLAIM TO THAT--
YOU LIVED THERE FOR TEN YEARS, DOING ODD JOBS AND SUCH.
THAT'S WHEN YOU DID YOUR FIRST REAPR KILLING.
Y-YEAH. WHAT'S ALL THIS LEADING TO?
YOUR FIRST KILLS WERE CLOSE UP. THEN YOU STARTED THIS NEW GIMMICK. WHAT LED TO THAT CHANGE?
OH. YEAH. SEE, THE WHOLE HOUSE NEEDED MONEY. I VOLUNTEERED. WE COULDN'T AFFORD MORE THAN A GUN.
AFTER THE FIRST FEW, I DIDN'T HAVE TO--
I MEAN, I NEVER WANTED--
TO WHAT? MURDER ANYONE?
NO! GOD! I LOVE KILLING PEOPLE!
I MEAN, I DON'T LOVE IT-- I MEAN, I DO BUT...I MEAN...
YOUR HANDLER, CAMERON KNAUFF, LIVED IN THE DUSTBIN WITH YOU?
RIGHT! YES! FRIENDS FROM WAY BACK.
ALWAYS BEEN THERE FOR ME.
IS THAT WHY SHE OWNS 51% OF YOUR LLC?
HEY, I GOT A BROADCAST COMING UP I NEED TO LEAVE FOR, THANKSSOMUCH THISHASBEENGREAT BYE.
ANYONE SEEN CAM?

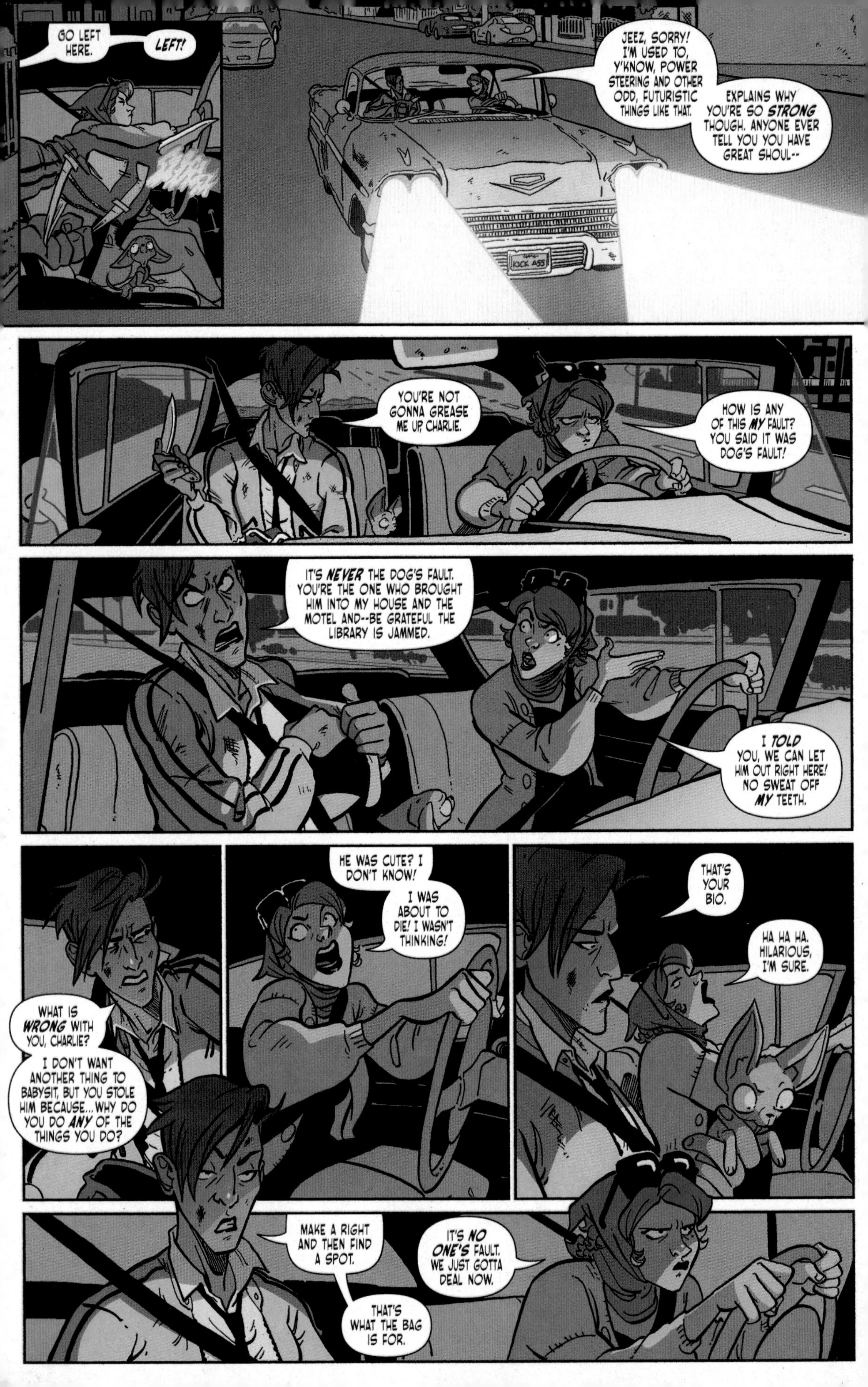
GO LEFT HERE.
LEFT!
JEEZ, SORRY! I'M USED TO, Y'KNOW, POWER STEERING AND OTHER ODD, FUTURISTIC THINGS LIKE THAT.
EXPLAINS WHY YOU'RE SO STRONG THOUGH. ANYONE EVER TELL YOU YOU HAVE GREAT SHOUL--
KICK ASS
YOU'RE NOT GONNA GREASE ME UP, CHARLIE.
HOW IS ANY OF THIS MY FAULT? YOU SAID IT WAS DOG'S FAULT!
IT'S NEVER THE DOG'S FAULT. YOU'RE THE ONE WHO BROUGHT HIM INTO MY HOUSE AND THE MOTEL AND--BE GRATEFUL THE LIBRARY IS JAMMED.
I TOLD YOU, WE CAN LET HIM OUT RIGHT HERE! NO SWEAT OFF MY TEETH.
WHAT IS WRONG WITH YOU, CHARLIE?
I DON'T WANT ANOTHER THING TO BABYSIT, BUT YOU STOLE HIM BECAUSE... WHY DO YOU DO ANY OF THE THINGS YOU DO?
HE WAS CUTE? I DON'T KNOW!
I WAS ABOUT TO DIE! I WASN'T THINKING!
THAT'S YOUR BIO.
HA HA HA. HILARIOUS, I'M SURE.
MAKE A RIGHT AND THEN FIND A SPOT.
THAT'S WHAT THE BAG IS FOR.
IT'S NO ONE'S FAULT. WE JUST GOTTA DEAL NOW.

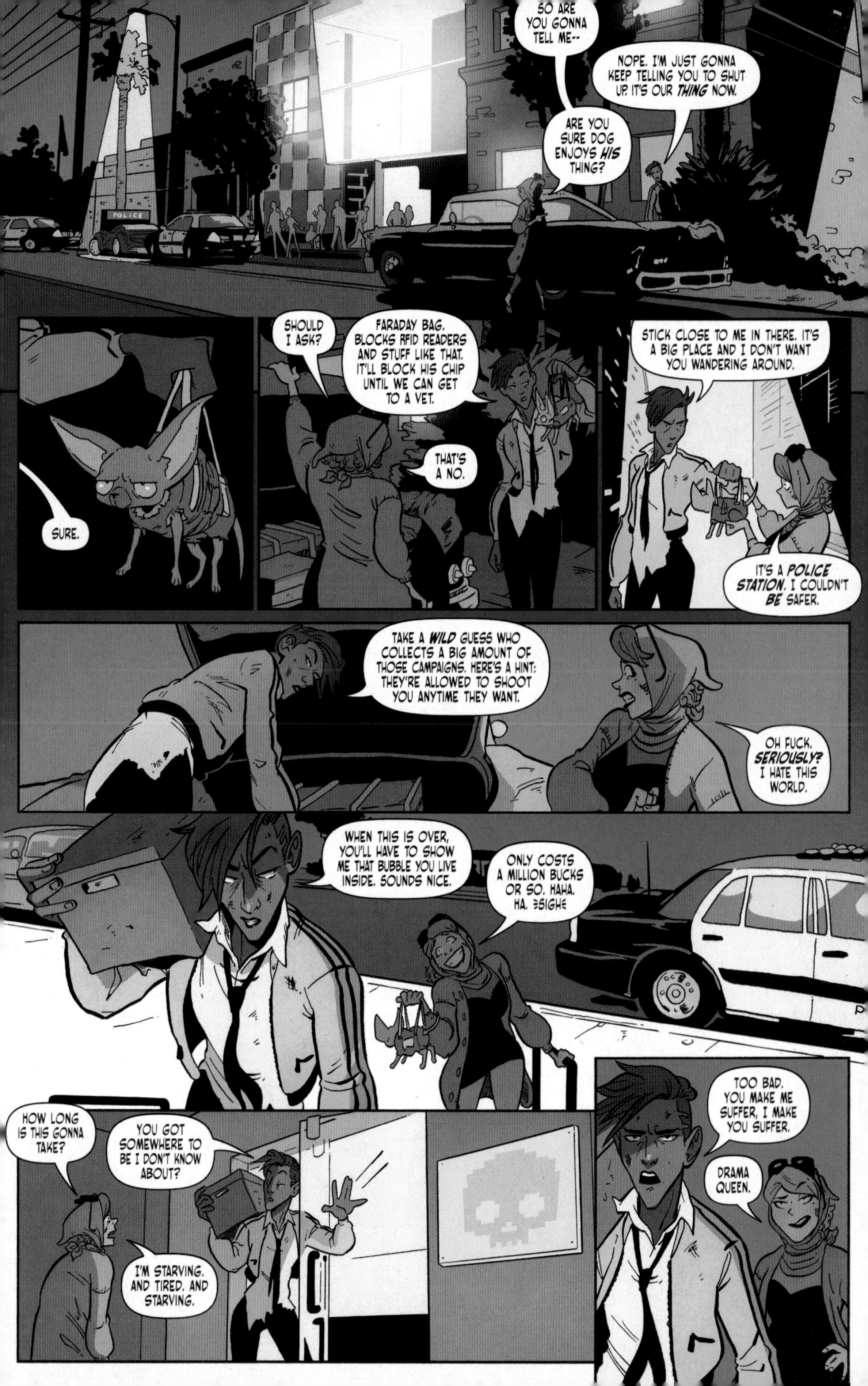
SO ARE YOU GONNA TELL ME--
NOPE. I'M JUST GONNA KEEP TELLING YOU TO SHUT UP. IT'S OUR THING NOW.
ARE YOU SURE DOG ENJOYS HIS THING?
POLICE
SURE.
SHOULD I ASK?
FARADAY BAG. BLOCKS RFID READERS AND STUFF LIKE THAT. IT'LL BLOCK HIS CHIP UNTIL WE CAN GET TO A VET.
THAT'S A NO.
STICK CLOSE TO ME IN THERE. IT'S A BIG PLACE AND I DON'T WANT YOU WANDERING AROUND.
IT'S A POLICE STATION. I COULDN'T BE SAFER.
TAKE A WILD GUESS WHO COLLECTS A BIG AMOUNT OF THOSE CAMPAIGNS. HERE'S A HINT: THEY'RE ALLOWED TO SHOOT YOU ANYTIME THEY WANT.
OH FUCK. SERIOUSLY? I HATE THIS WORLD.
WHEN THIS IS OVER, YOU'LL HAVE TO SHOW ME THAT BUBBLE YOU LIVE INSIDE. SOUNDS NICE.
ONLY COSTS A MILLION BUCKS OR SO. HAHA. HA. ≡SIGH≡
HOW LONG IS THIS GONNA TAKE?
YOU GOT SOMEWHERE TO BE I DON'T KNOW ABOUT?
I'M STARVING. AND TIRED. AND STARVING.
TOO BAD. YOU MAKE ME SUFFER, I MAKE YOU SUFFER.
DRAMA QUEEN.

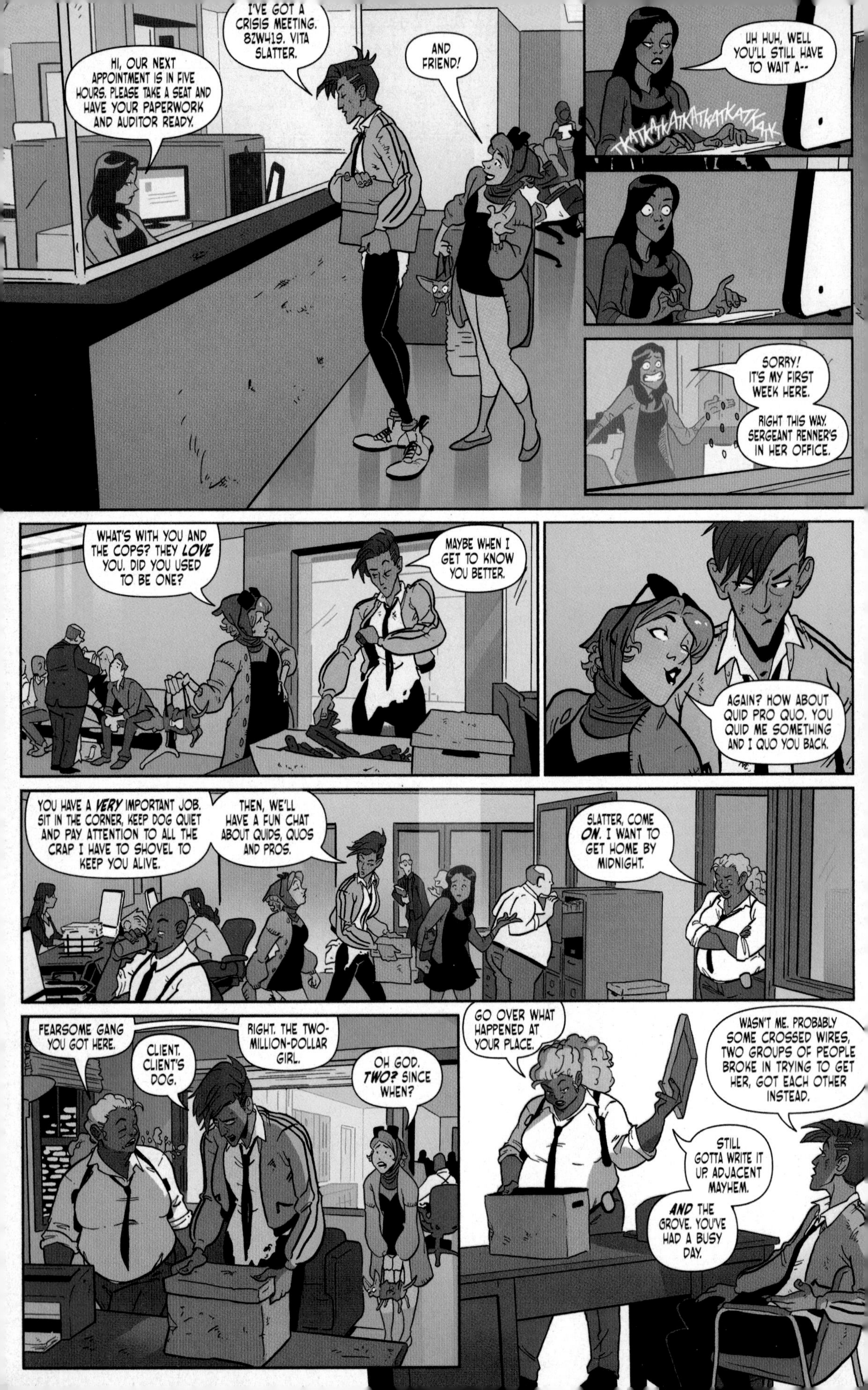
HI, OUR NEXT APPOINTMENT IS IN FIVE HOURS. PLEASE TAKE A SEAT AND HAVE YOUR PAPERWORK AND AUDITOR READY.
I'VE GOT A CRISIS MEETING. 8ZW419. VITA SLATTER.
AND FRIEND!
UH HUH, WELL YOU'LL STILL HAVE TO WAIT A--
TKATKATKATKATKATKATKATKATK
SORRY! IT'S MY FIRST WEEK HERE.
RIGHT THIS WAY. SERGEANT RENNER'S IN HER OFFICE.
WHAT'S WITH YOU AND THE COPS? THEY LOVE YOU. DID YOU USED TO BE ONE?
MAYBE WHEN I GET TO KNOW YOU BETTER.
AGAIN? HOW ABOUT QUID PRO QUO. YOU QUID ME SOMETHING AND I QUO YOU BACK.
YOU HAVE A VERY IMPORTANT JOB. SIT IN THE CORNER, KEEP DOG QUIET AND PAY ATTENTION TO ALL THE CRAP I HAVE TO SHOVEL TO KEEP YOU ALIVE.
THEN, WE'LL HAVE A FUN CHAT ABOUT QUIDS, QUOS AND PROS.
SLATTER, COME ON. I WANT TO GET HOME BY MIDNIGHT.
FEARSOME GANG YOU GOT HERE.
CLIENT. CLIENT'S DOG.
RIGHT. THE TWO-MILLION-DOLLAR GIRL.
OH GOD. TWO? SINCE WHEN?
GO OVER WHAT HAPPENED AT YOUR PLACE.
WASN'T ME. PROBABLY SOME CROSSED WIRES, TWO GROUPS OF PEOPLE BROKE IN TRYING TO GET HER, GOT EACH OTHER INSTEAD.
STILL GOTTA WRITE IT UP. ADJACENT MAYHEM.
AND THE GROVE. YOU'VE HAD A BUSY DAY.

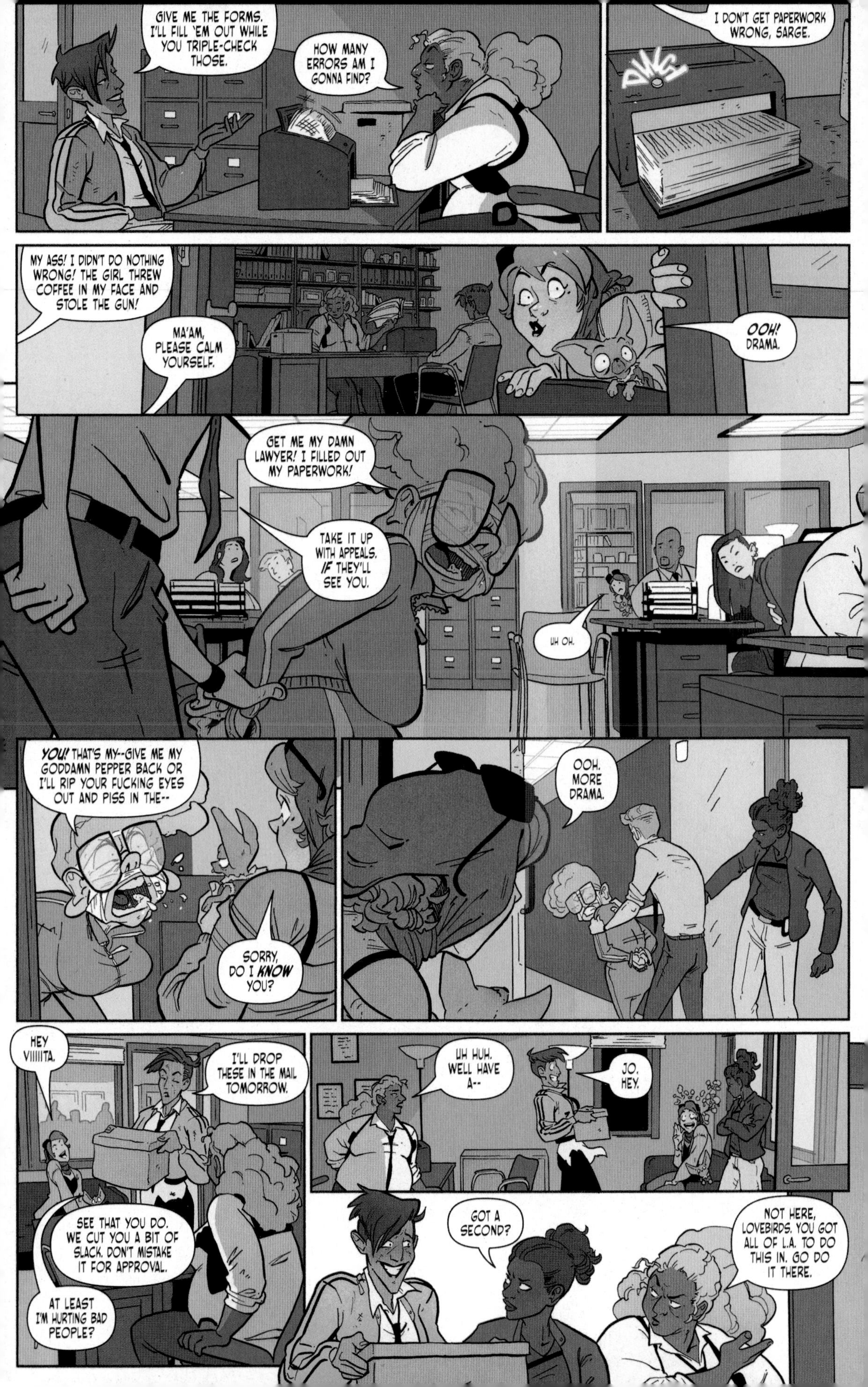
GIVE ME THE FORMS. I'LL FILL 'EM OUT WHILE YOU TRIPLE-CHECK THOSE.
HOW MANY ERRORS AM I GONNA FIND?
I DON'T GET PAPERWORK WRONG, SARGE.
MY ASS! I DIDN'T DO NOTHING WRONG! THE GIRL THREW COFFEE IN MY FACE AND STOLE THE GUN!
MA'AM, PLEASE CALM YOURSELF.
OOH! DRAMA.
GET ME MY DAMN LAWYER! I FILLED OUT MY PAPERWORK!
TAKE IT UP WITH APPEALS. IF THEY'LL SEE YOU.
UH OH.
YOU! THAT'S MY--GIVE ME MY GODDAMN PEPPER BACK OR I'LL RIP YOUR FUCKING EYES OUT AND PISS IN THE--
SORRY, DO I KNOW YOU?
OOH. MORE DRAMA.
HEY VIIIIITA.
I'LL DROP THESE IN THE MAIL TOMORROW.
SEE THAT YOU DO. WE CUT YOU A BIT OF SLACK. DON'T MISTAKE IT FOR APPROVAL.
AT LEAST I'M HURTING BAD PEOPLE?
UH HUH. WELL HAVE A--
JO. HEY.
GOT A SECOND?
NOT HERE, LOVEBIRDS. YOU GOT ALL OF L.A. TO DO THIS IN. GO DO IT THERE.

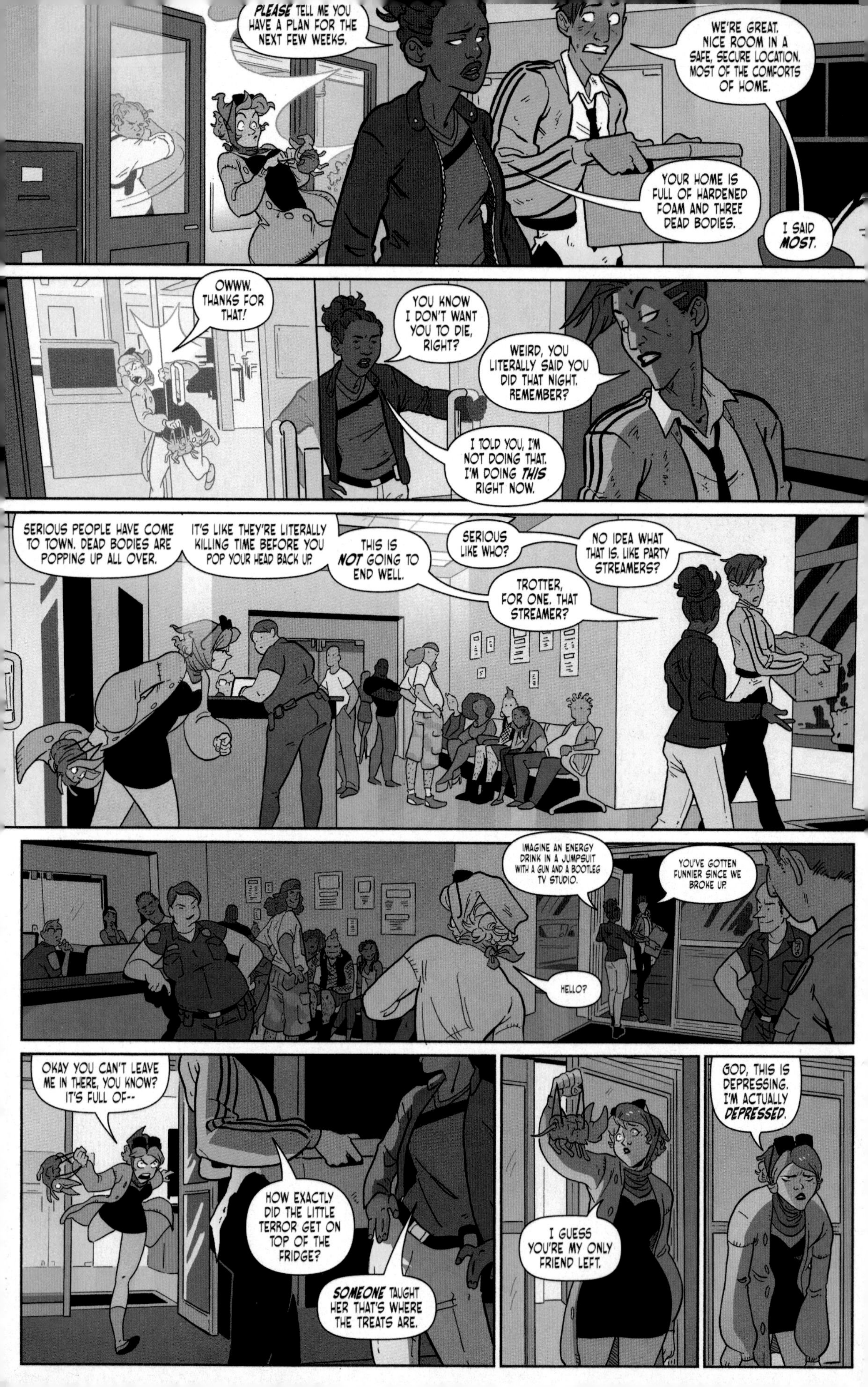
PLEASE TELL ME YOU HAVE A PLAN FOR THE NEXT FEW WEEKS.
WE'RE GREAT. NICE ROOM IN A SAFE, SECURE LOCATION. MOST OF THE COMFORTS OF HOME.
YOUR HOME IS FULL OF HARDENED FOAM AND THREE DEAD BODIES.
I SAID MOST.
OWWW. THANKS FOR THAT!
YOU KNOW I DON'T WANT YOU TO DIE, RIGHT?
WEIRD, YOU LITERALLY SAID YOU DID THAT NIGHT. REMEMBER?
I TOLD YOU, I'M NOT DOING THAT. I'M DOING THIS RIGHT NOW.
SERIOUS PEOPLE HAVE COME TO TOWN. DEAD BODIES ARE POPPING UP ALL OVER.
IT'S LIKE THEY'RE LITERALLY KILLING TIME BEFORE YOU POP YOUR HEAD BACK UP.
THIS IS NOT GOING TO END WELL.
SERIOUS LIKE WHO?
NO IDEA WHAT THAT IS. LIKE PARTY STREAMERS?
TROTTER, FOR ONE. THAT STREAMER?
IMAGINE AN ENERGY DRINK IN A JUMPSUIT WITH A GUN AND A BOOTLEG TV STUDIO.
YOU'VE GOTTEN FUNNIER SINCE WE BROKE UP.
HELLO?
OKAY YOU CAN'T LEAVE ME IN THERE, YOU KNOW? IT'S FULL OF--
HOW EXACTLY DID THE LITTLE TERROR GET ON TOP OF THE FRIDGE?
SOMEONE TAUGHT HER THAT'S WHERE THE TREATS ARE.
I GUESS YOU'RE MY ONLY FRIEND LEFT.
GOD, THIS IS DEPRESSING. I'M ACTUALLY DEPRESSED.

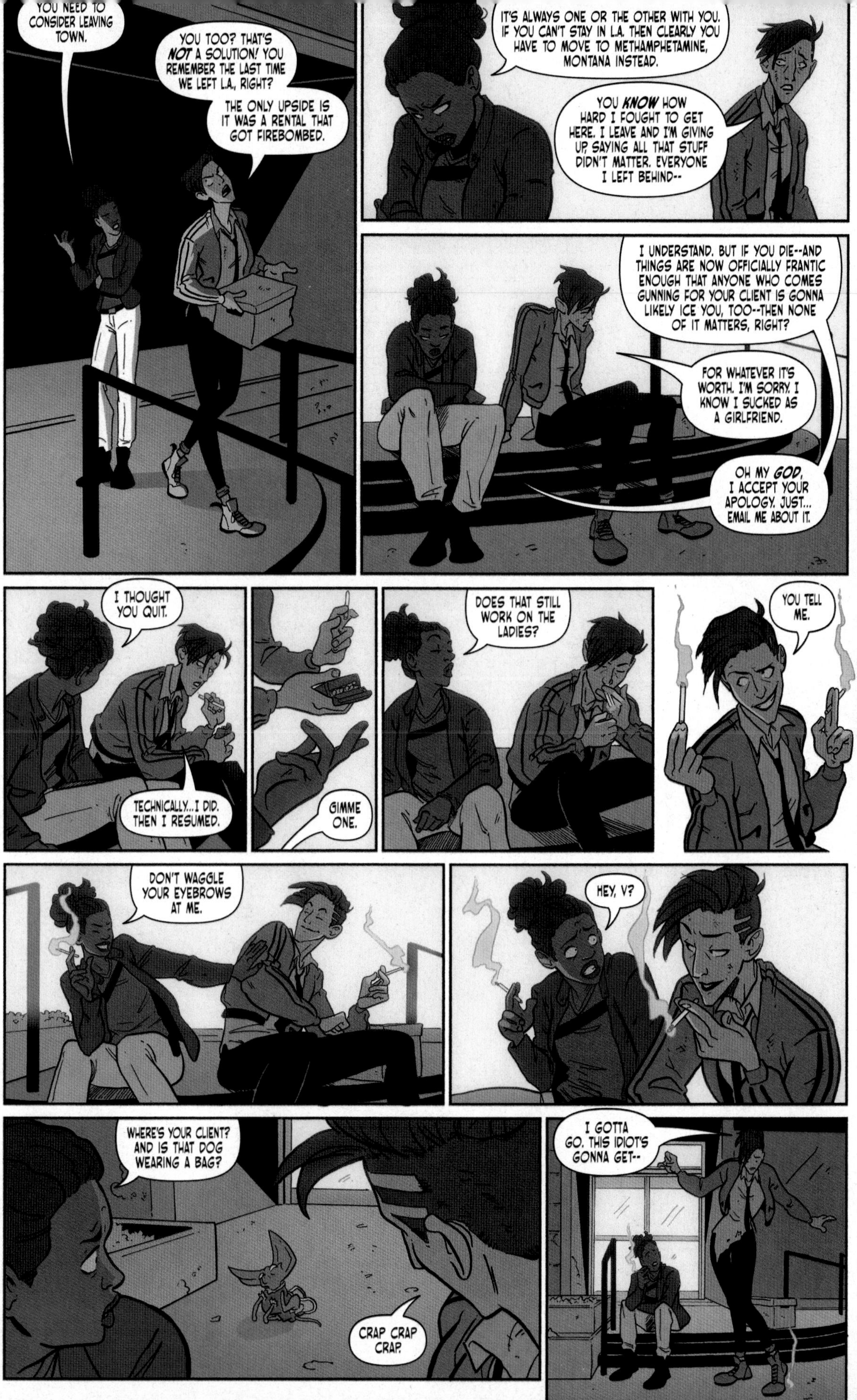
YOU NEED TO CONSIDER LEAVING TOWN.
YOU TOO? THAT'S *NOT* A SOLUTION! YOU REMEMBER THE LAST TIME WE LEFT L.A., RIGHT?
THE ONLY UPSIDE IS IT WAS A RENTAL THAT GOT FIREBOMBED.
IT'S ALWAYS ONE OR THE OTHER WITH YOU. IF YOU CAN'T STAY IN L.A. THEN CLEARLY YOU HAVE TO MOVE TO METHAMPHETAMINE, MONTANA INSTEAD.
YOU *KNOW* HOW HARD I FOUGHT TO GET HERE. I LEAVE AND I'M GIVING UP, SAYING ALL THAT STUFF DIDN'T MATTER. EVERYONE I LEFT BEHIND--
I UNDERSTAND. BUT IF YOU DIE--AND THINGS ARE NOW OFFICIALLY FRANTIC ENOUGH THAT ANYONE WHO COMES GUNNING FOR YOUR CLIENT IS GONNA LIKELY ICE YOU, TOO--THEN NONE OF IT MATTERS, RIGHT?
FOR WHATEVER IT'S WORTH. I'M SORRY. I KNOW I SUCKED AS A GIRLFRIEND.
OH MY *GOD*, I ACCEPT YOUR APOLOGY. JUST... EMAIL ME ABOUT IT.
I THOUGHT YOU QUIT.
TECHNICALLY...I DID. THEN I RESUMED.
GIMME ONE.
DOES THAT STILL WORK ON THE LADIES?
YOU TELL ME.
DON'T WAGGLE YOUR EYEBROWS AT ME.
HEY, V?
WHERE'S YOUR CLIENT? AND IS THAT DOG WEARING A BAG?
CRAP CRAP CRAP.
I GOTTA GO. THIS IDIOT'S GONNA GET--

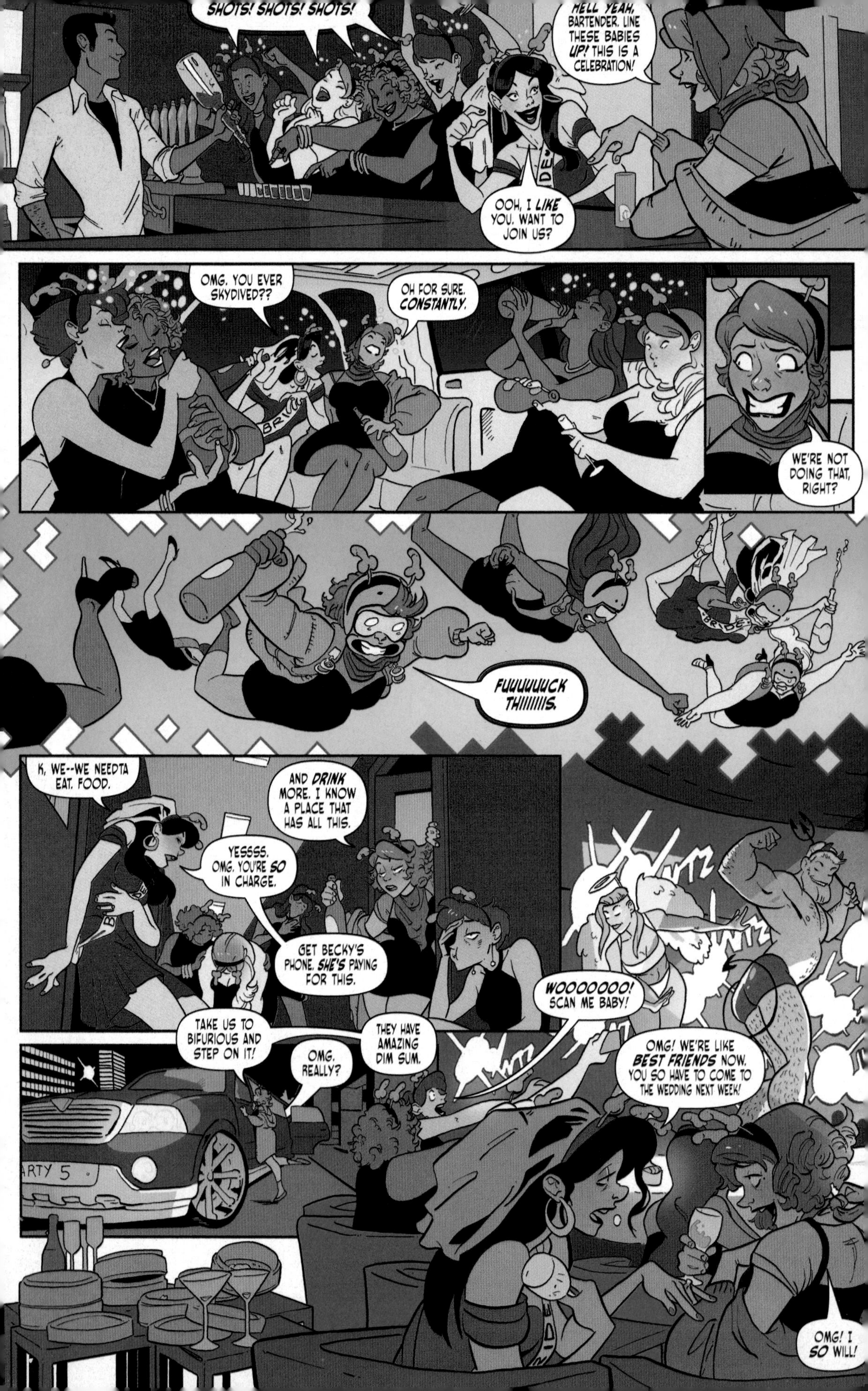
SHOTS! SHOTS! SHOTS!
HELL YEAH, BARTENDER. LINE THESE BABIES UP! THIS IS A CELEBRATION!
OOH, I LIKE YOU. WANT TO JOIN US?
OMG. YOU EVER SKYDIVED??
OH FOR SURE. CONSTANTLY.
WE'RE NOT DOING THAT, RIGHT?
FUUUUUUCK THIIIIIIS.
K, WE--WE NEEDTA EAT. FOOD.
AND DRINK MORE. I KNOW A PLACE THAT HAS ALL THIS.
YESSSS. OMG. YOU'RE SO IN CHARGE.
GET BECKY'S PHONE. SHE'S PAYING FOR THIS.
WOOOOOOO! SCAN ME BABY!
TAKE US TO BIFURIOUS AND STEP ON IT!
OMG. REALLY?
THEY HAVE AMAZING DIM SUM.
OMG! WE'RE LIKE BEST FRIENDS NOW. YOU SO HAVE TO COME TO THE WEDDING NEXT WEEK!
OMG! I SO WILL!

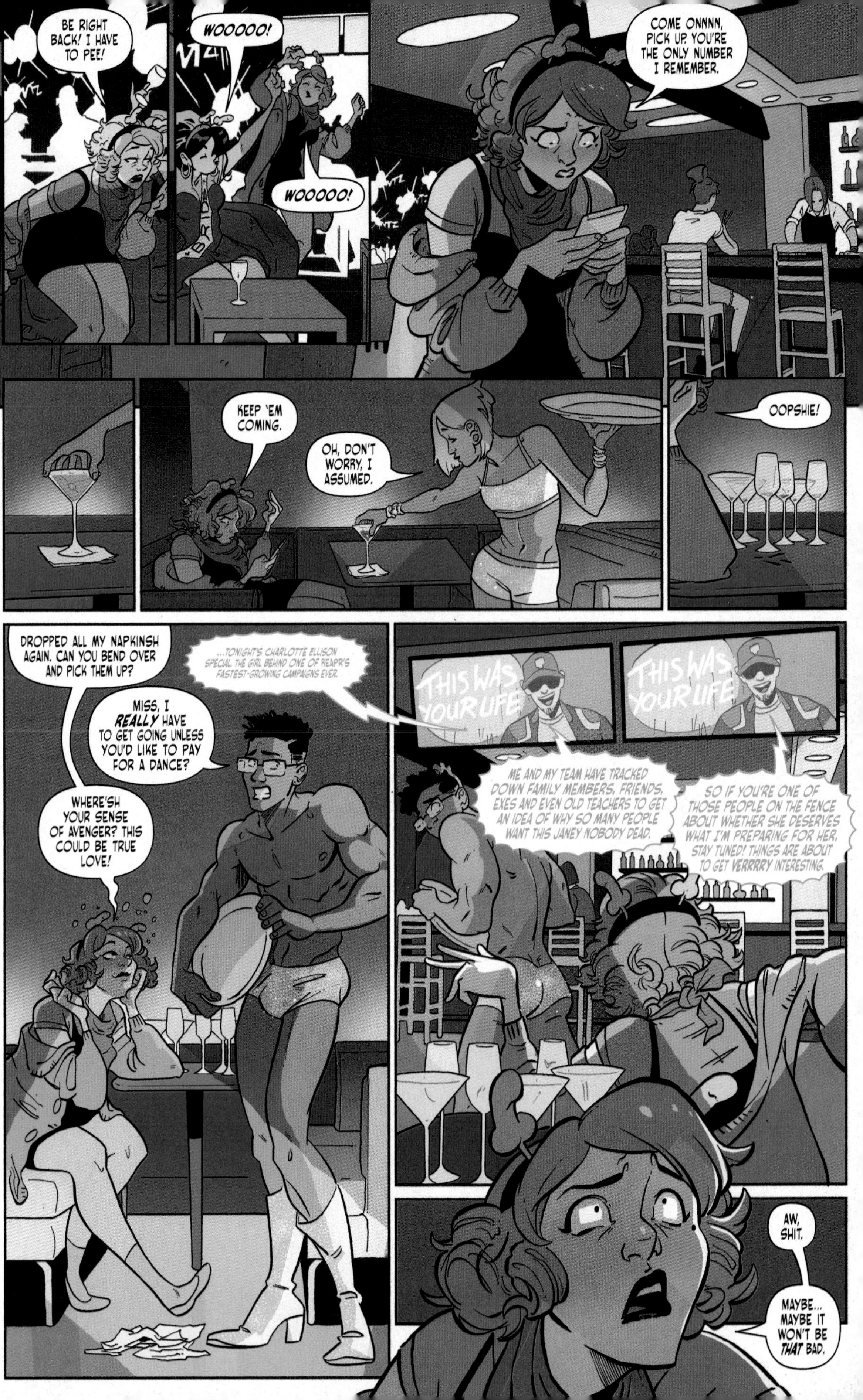
BE RIGHT BACK! I HAVE TO PEE!
WOOOOO!
WOOOOO!
COME ONNNN, PICK UP. YOU'RE THE ONLY NUMBER I REMEMBER.
KEEP 'EM COMING.
OH, DON'T WORRY, I ASSUMED.
OOPSHIE!
DROPPED ALL MY NAPKINSH AGAIN. CAN YOU BEND OVER AND PICK THEM UP?
MISS, I REALLY HAVE TO GET GOING UNLESS YOU'D LIKE TO PAY FOR A DANCE?
WHERE'SH YOUR SENSE OF AVENGER? THIS COULD BE TRUE LOVE!
...TONIGHT'S CHARLOTTE ELLISON SPECIAL. THE GIRL BEHIND ONE OF REAPR'S FASTEST-GROWING CAMPAIGNS EVER.
THIS WAS YOUR LIFE
THIS WAS YOUR LIFE
ME AND MY TEAM HAVE TRACKED DOWN FAMILY MEMBERS, FRIENDS, EXES AND EVEN OLD TEACHERS TO GET AN IDEA OF WHY SO MANY PEOPLE WANT THIS JANEY NOBODY DEAD.
SO IF YOU'RE ONE OF THOSE PEOPLE ON THE FENCE ABOUT WHETHER SHE DESERVES WHAT I'M PREPARING FOR HER, STAY TUNED! THINGS ARE ABOUT TO GET VERRRRY INTERESTING.
AW, SHIT.
MAYBE... MAYBE IT WON'T BE THAT BAD.

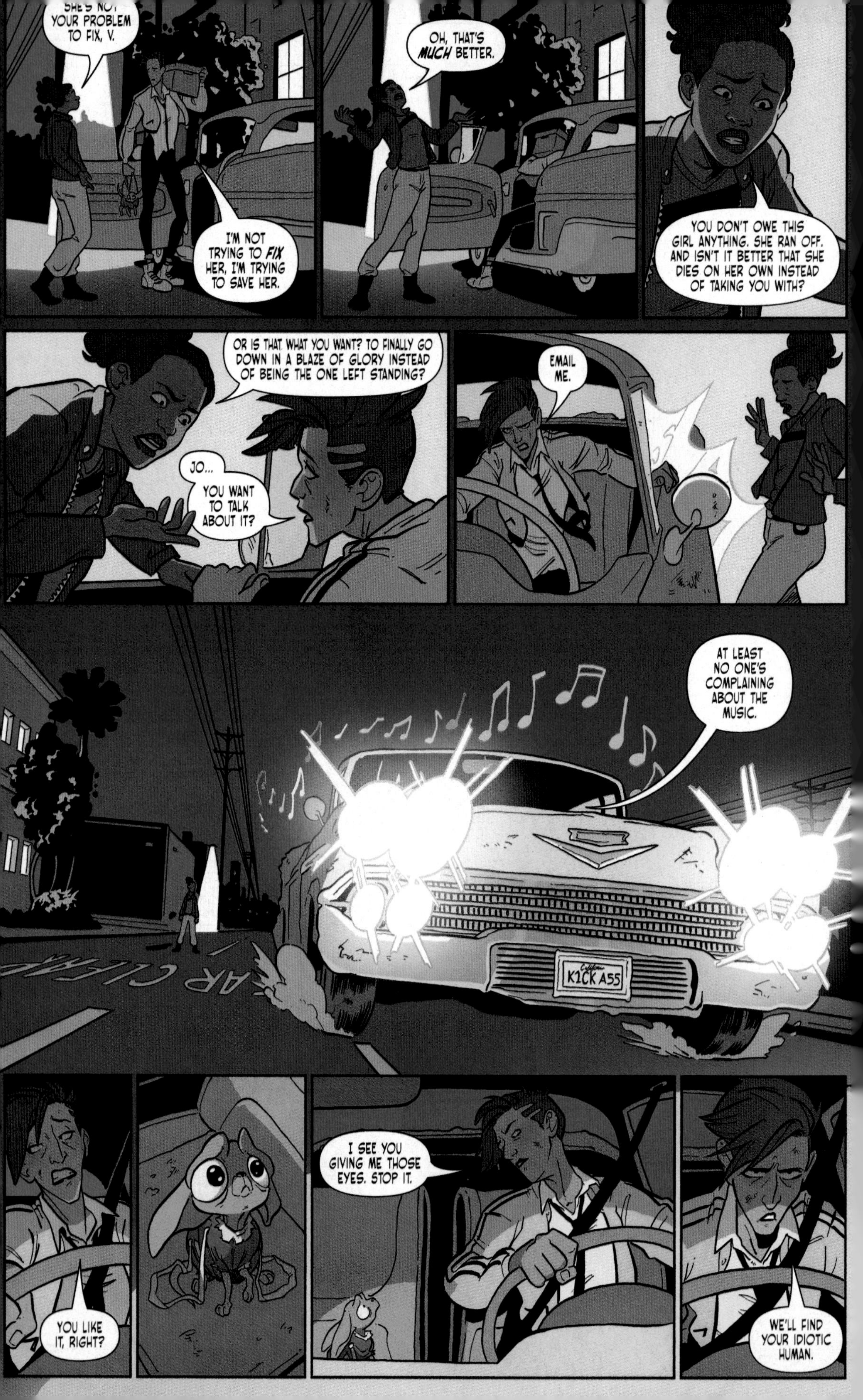
SHE'S NOT YOUR PROBLEM TO FIX, V.
I'M NOT TRYING TO FIX HER, I'M TRYING TO SAVE HER.
OH, THAT'S MUCH BETTER.
YOU DON'T OWE THIS GIRL ANYTHING. SHE RAN OFF. AND ISN'T IT BETTER THAT SHE DIES ON HER OWN INSTEAD OF TAKING YOU WITH?
OR IS THAT WHAT YOU WANT? TO FINALLY GO DOWN IN A BLAZE OF GLORY INSTEAD OF BEING THE ONE LEFT STANDING?
JO...
YOU WANT TO TALK ABOUT IT?
EMAIL ME.
AT LEAST NO ONE'S COMPLAINING ABOUT THE MUSIC.
K1CK A55
YOU LIKE IT, RIGHT?
I SEE YOU GIVING ME THOSE EYES. STOP IT.
WE'LL FIND YOUR IDIOTIC HUMAN.

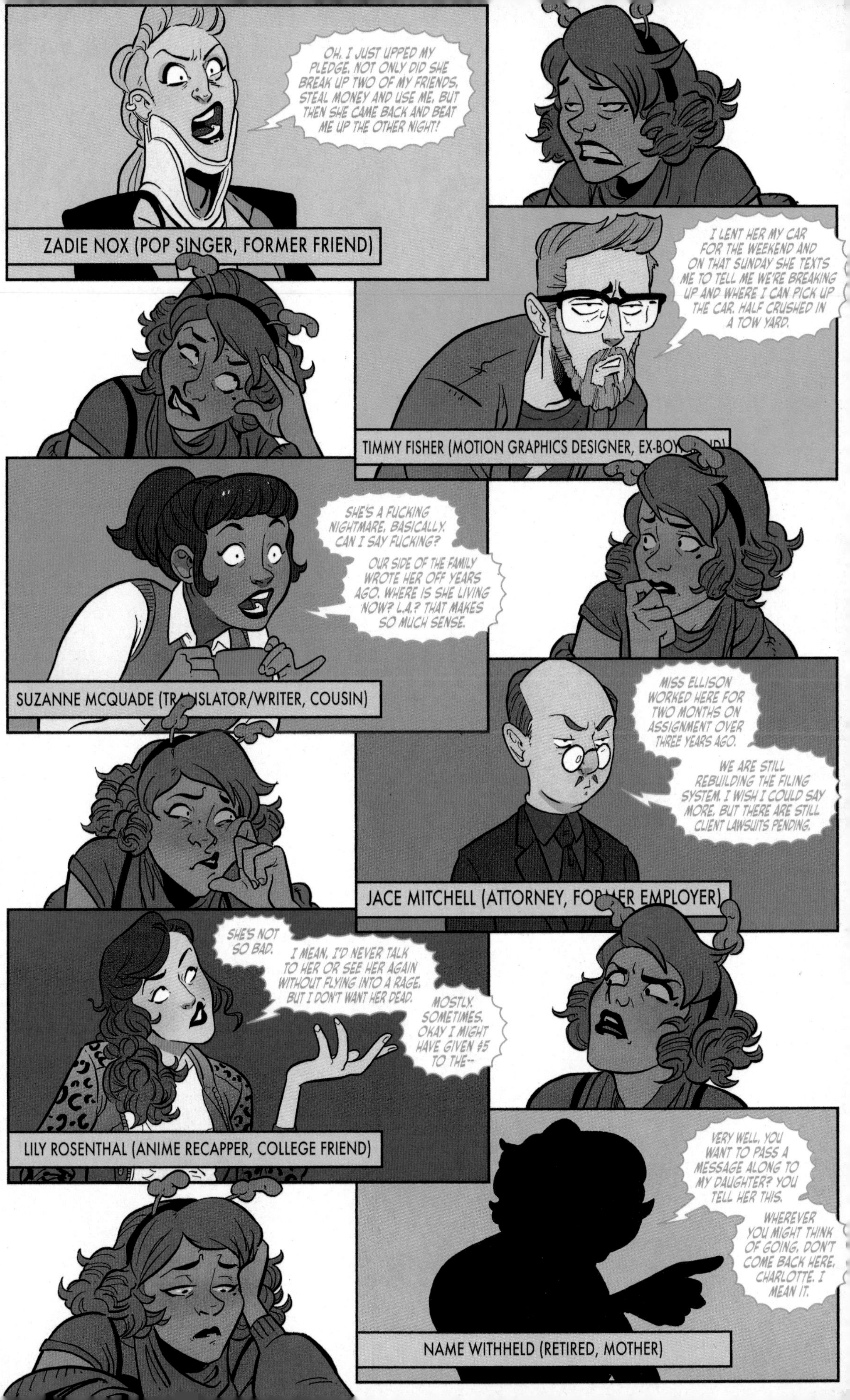
OH. I JUST UPPED MY PLEDGE. NOT ONLY DID SHE BREAK UP TWO OF MY FRIENDS, STEAL MONEY AND USE ME, BUT THEN SHE CAME BACK AND BEAT ME UP THE OTHER NIGHT!
ZADIE NOX (POP SINGER, FORMER FRIEND)
I LENT HER MY CAR FOR THE WEEKEND AND ON THAT SUNDAY SHE TEXTS ME TO TELL ME WE'RE BREAKING UP AND WHERE I CAN PICK UP THE CAR. HALF CRUSHED IN A TOW YARD.
SHE'S A FUCKING NIGHTMARE, BASICALLY. CAN I SAY FUCKING?
OUR SIDE OF THE FAMILY WROTE HER OFF YEARS AGO. WHERE IS SHE LIVING NOW? L.A.? THAT MAKES SO MUCH SENSE.
MISS ELLISON WORKED HERE FOR TWO MONTHS ON ASSIGNMENT OVER THREE YEARS AGO.
WE ARE STILL REBUILDING THE FILING SYSTEM. I WISH I COULD SAY MORE, BUT THERE ARE STILL CLIENT LAWSUITS PENDING.
SHE'S NOT SO BAD.
I MEAN, I'D NEVER TALK TO HER OR SEE HER AGAIN WITHOUT FLYING INTO A RAGE. BUT I DON'T WANT HER DEAD.
MOSTLY. SOMETIMES. OKAY I MIGHT HAVE GIVEN $5 TO THE--
LILY ROSENTHAL (ANIME RECAPPER, COLLEGE FRIEND)
VERY WELL. YOU WANT TO PASS A MESSAGE ALONG TO MY DAUGHTER? YOU TELL HER THIS.
WHEREVER YOU MIGHT THINK OF GOING, DON'T COME BACK HERE, CHARLOTTE. I MEAN IT.
NAME WITHHELD (RETIRED, MOTHER)

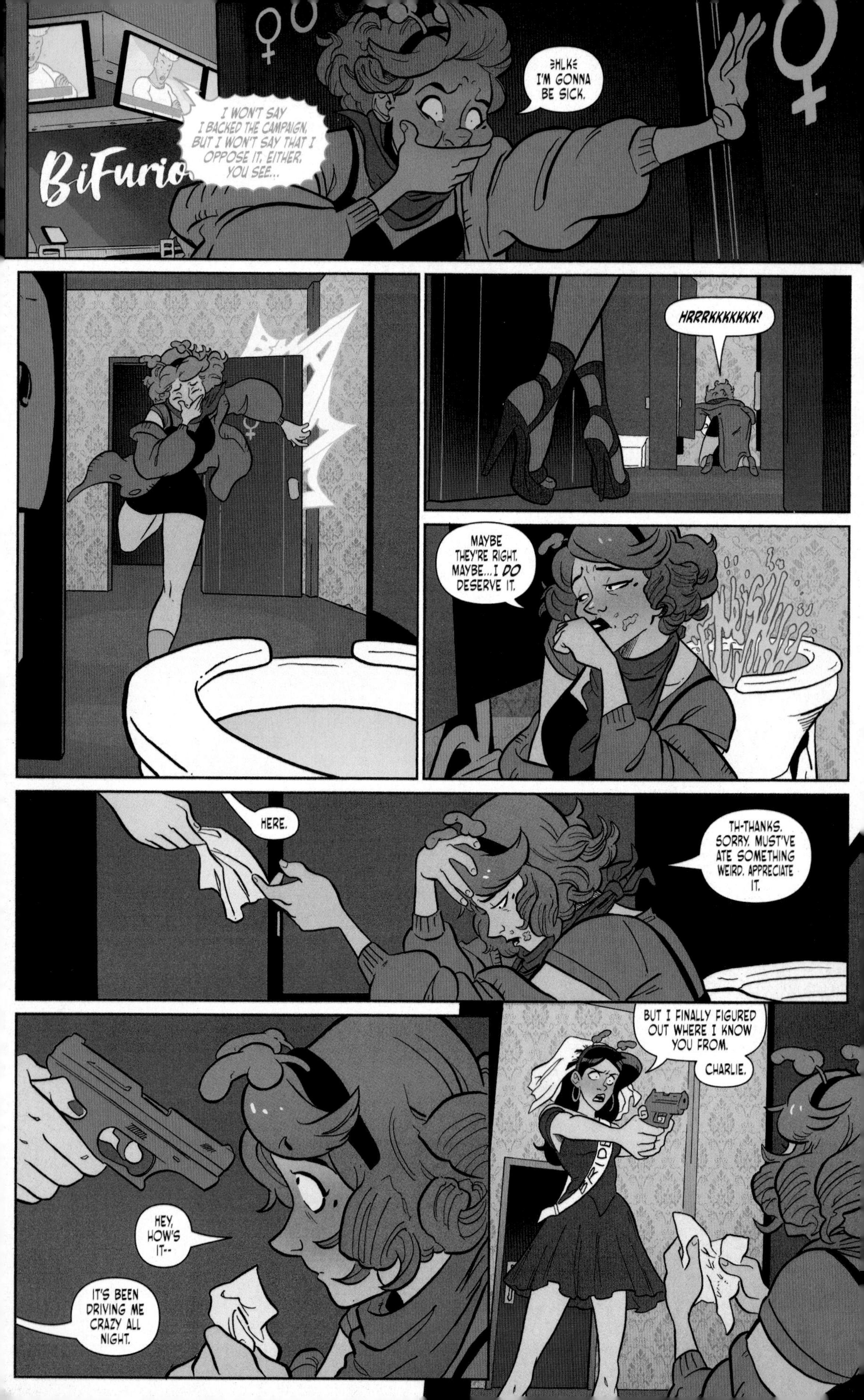

BiFurio
I WON'T SAY I BACKED THE CAMPAIGN, BUT I WON'T SAY THAT I OPPOSE IT, EITHER. YOU SEE...
I'M GONNA BE SICK.
HRRRKKKKKKK!
MAYBE THEY'RE RIGHT. MAYBE... I DO DESERVE IT.
HERE.
TH-THANKS. SORRY. MUST'VE ATE SOMETHING WEIRD. APPRECIATE IT.
HEY, HOW'S IT--
IT'S BEEN DRIVING ME CRAZY ALL NIGHT.
BUT I FINALLY FIGURED OUT WHERE I KNOW YOU FROM.
CHARLIE.

CHAPTER FIVE
TOO MANY PEOPLE

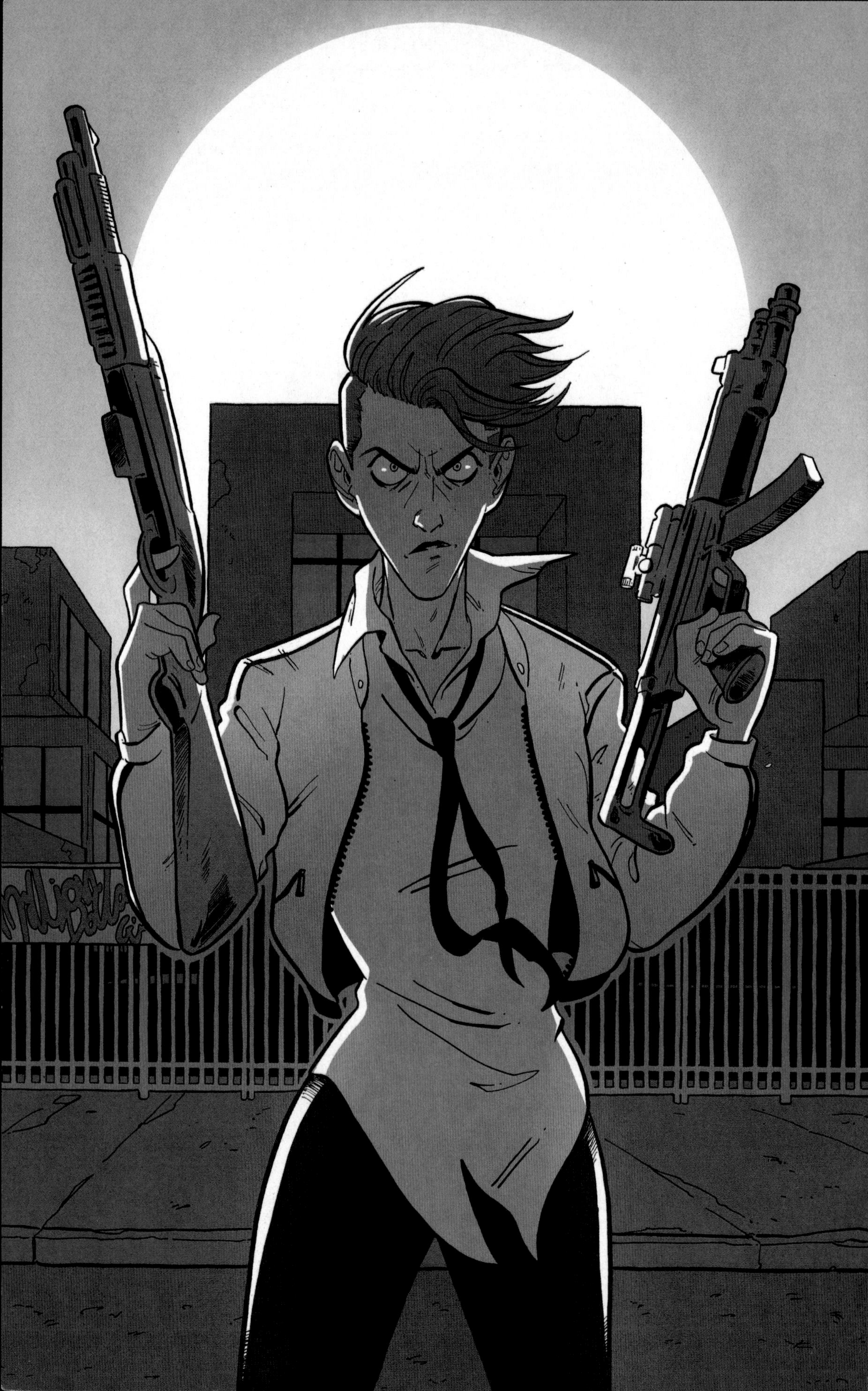

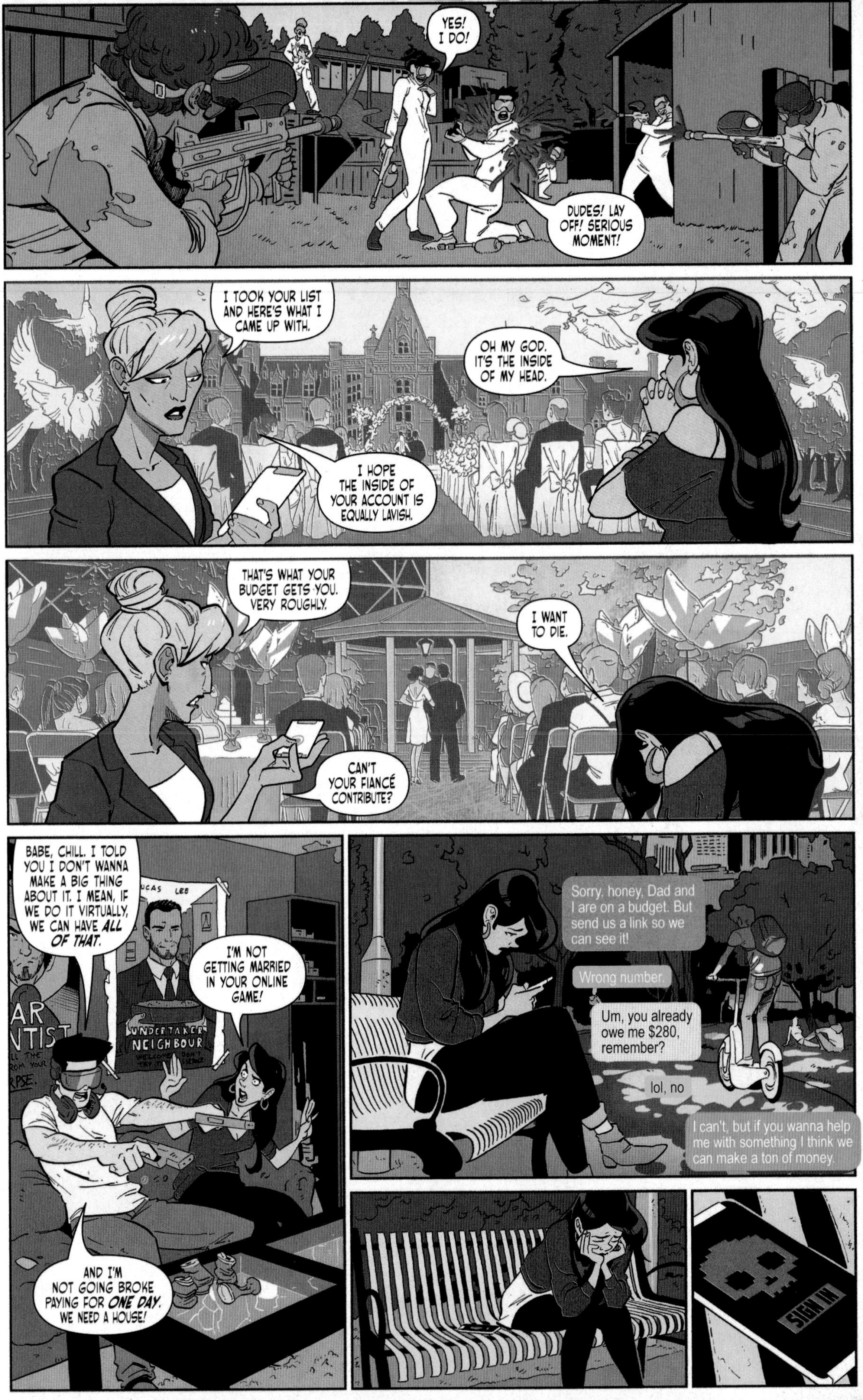

YES! I DO!
DUDES! LAY OFF! SERIOUS MOMENT!
I TOOK YOUR LIST AND HERE'S WHAT I CAME UP WITH.
OH MY GOD. IT'S THE INSIDE OF MY HEAD.
I HOPE THE INSIDE OF YOUR ACCOUNT IS EQUALLY LAVISH.
THAT'S WHAT YOUR BUDGET GETS YOU. VERY ROUGHLY.
I WANT TO DIE.
CAN'T YOUR FIANCÉ CONTRIBUTE?
BABE, CHILL. I TOLD YOU I DON'T WANNA MAKE A BIG THING ABOUT IT. I MEAN, IF WE DO IT VIRTUALLY, WE CAN HAVE ALL OF THAT.
I'M NOT GETTING MARRIED IN YOUR ONLINE GAME!
UNDERTAKER NEIGHBOUR
AND I'M NOT GOING BROKE PAYING FOR ONE DAY. WE NEED A HOUSE!
Sorry, honey, Dad and I are on a budget. But send us a link so we can see it!
Wrong number.
Um, you already owe me $280, remember?
lol, no
I can't, but if you wanna help me with something I think we can make a ton of money.
SIGN IN

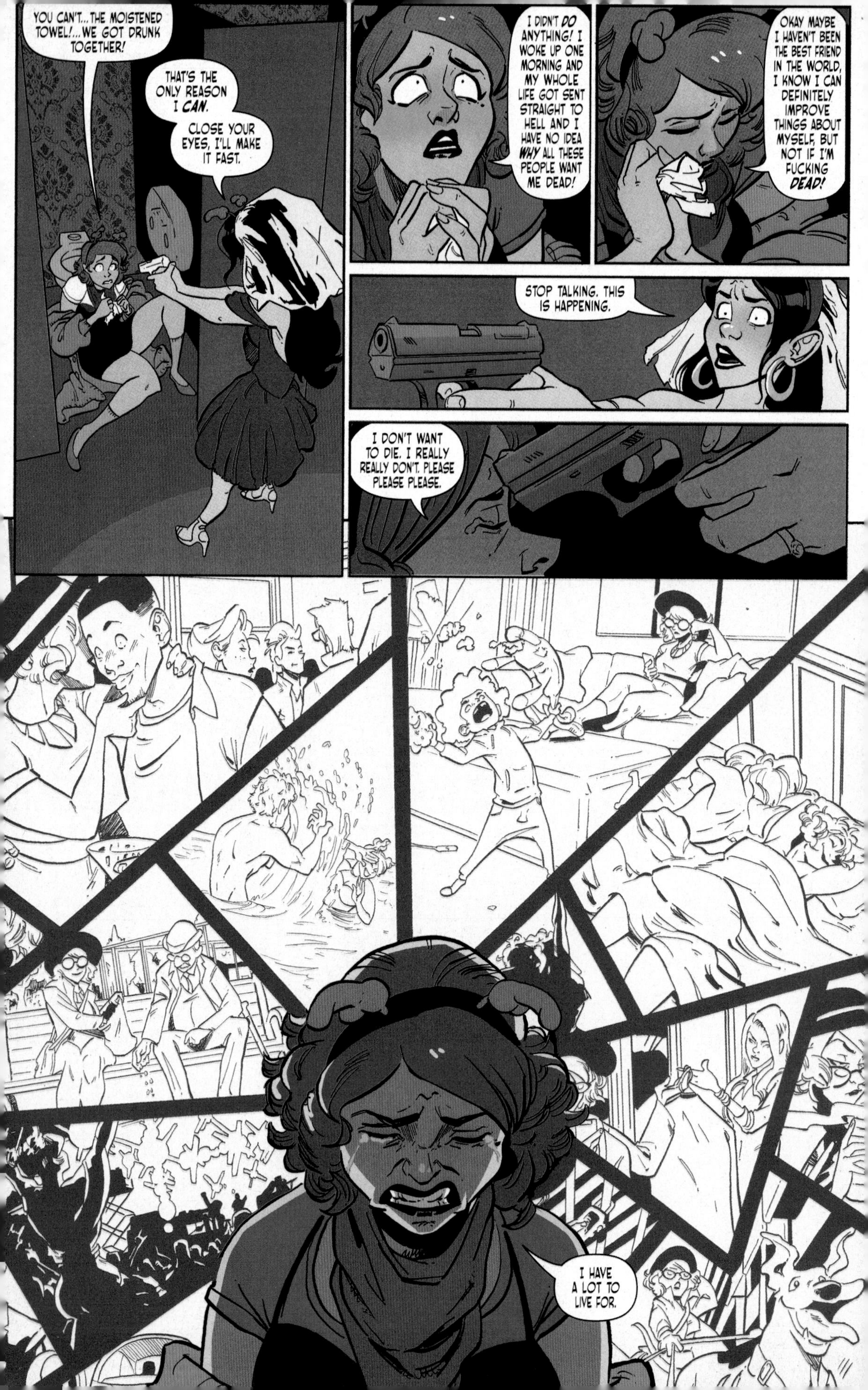

YOU CAN'T...THE MOISTENED TOWEL!...WE GOT DRUNK TOGETHER!
THAT'S THE ONLY REASON I CAN.
CLOSE YOUR EYES, I'LL MAKE IT FAST.
I DIDN'T DO ANYTHING! I WOKE UP ONE MORNING AND MY WHOLE LIFE GOT SENT STRAIGHT TO HELL AND I HAVE NO IDEA WHY ALL THESE PEOPLE WANT ME DEAD!
OKAY MAYBE I HAVEN'T BEEN THE BEST FRIEND IN THE WORLD, I KNOW I CAN DEFINITELY IMPROVE THINGS ABOUT MYSELF, BUT NOT IF I'M FUCKING DEAD!
STOP TALKING. THIS IS HAPPENING.
I DON'T WANT TO DIE. I REALLY REALLY DON'T. PLEASE PLEASE PLEASE.
I HAVE A LOT TO LIVE FOR.

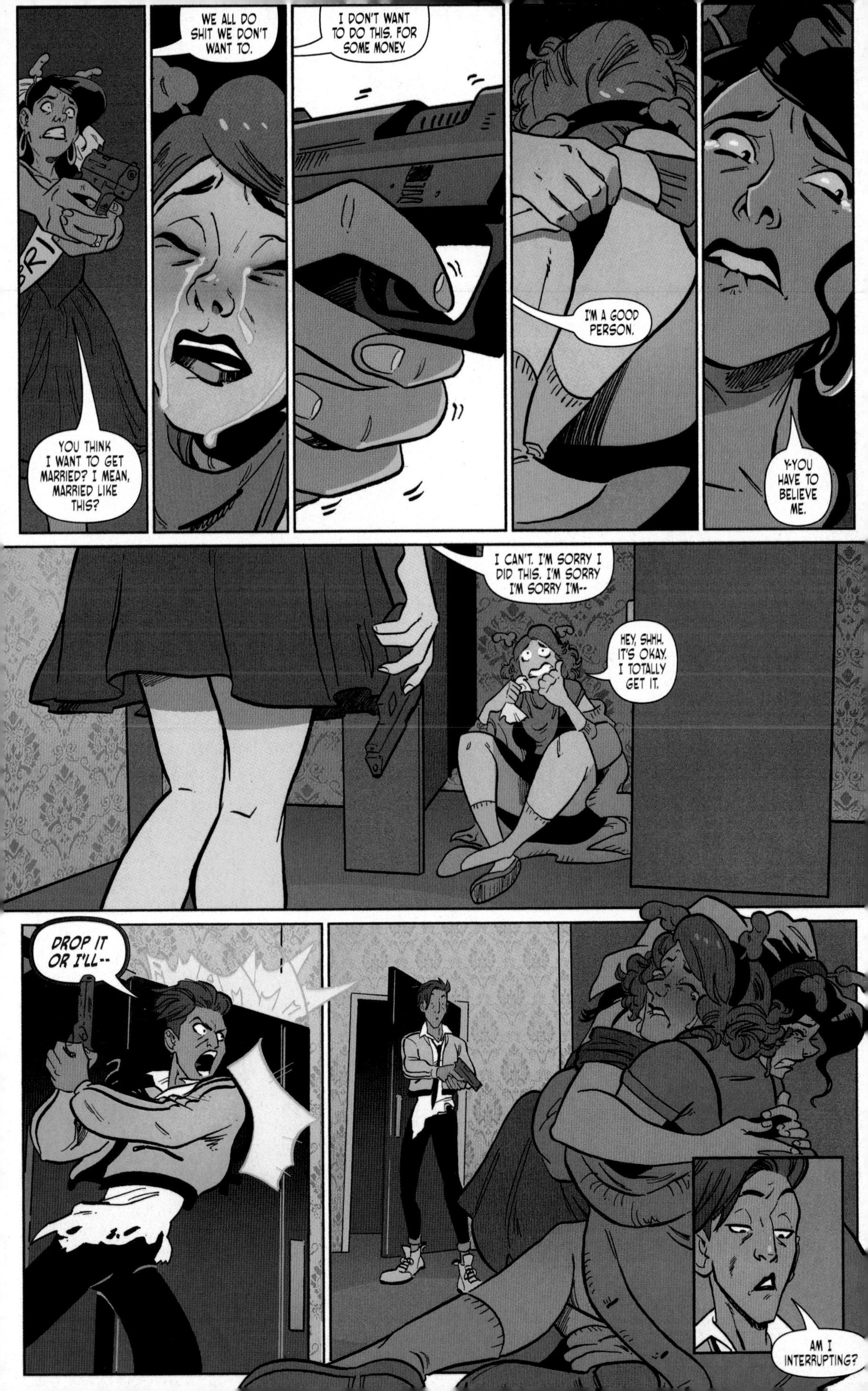
YOU THINK I WANT TO GET MARRIED? I MEAN, MARRIED LIKE THIS?
WE ALL DO SHIT WE DON'T WANT TO.
I DON'T WANT TO DO THIS. FOR SOME MONEY.
I'M A GOOD PERSON.
Y-YOU HAVE TO BELIEVE ME.
I CAN'T. I'M SORRY I DID THIS. I'M SORRY I'M SORRY I'M--
HEY, SHHH. IT'S OKAY. I TOTALLY GET IT.
DROP IT OR I'LL--
AM I INTERRUPTING?

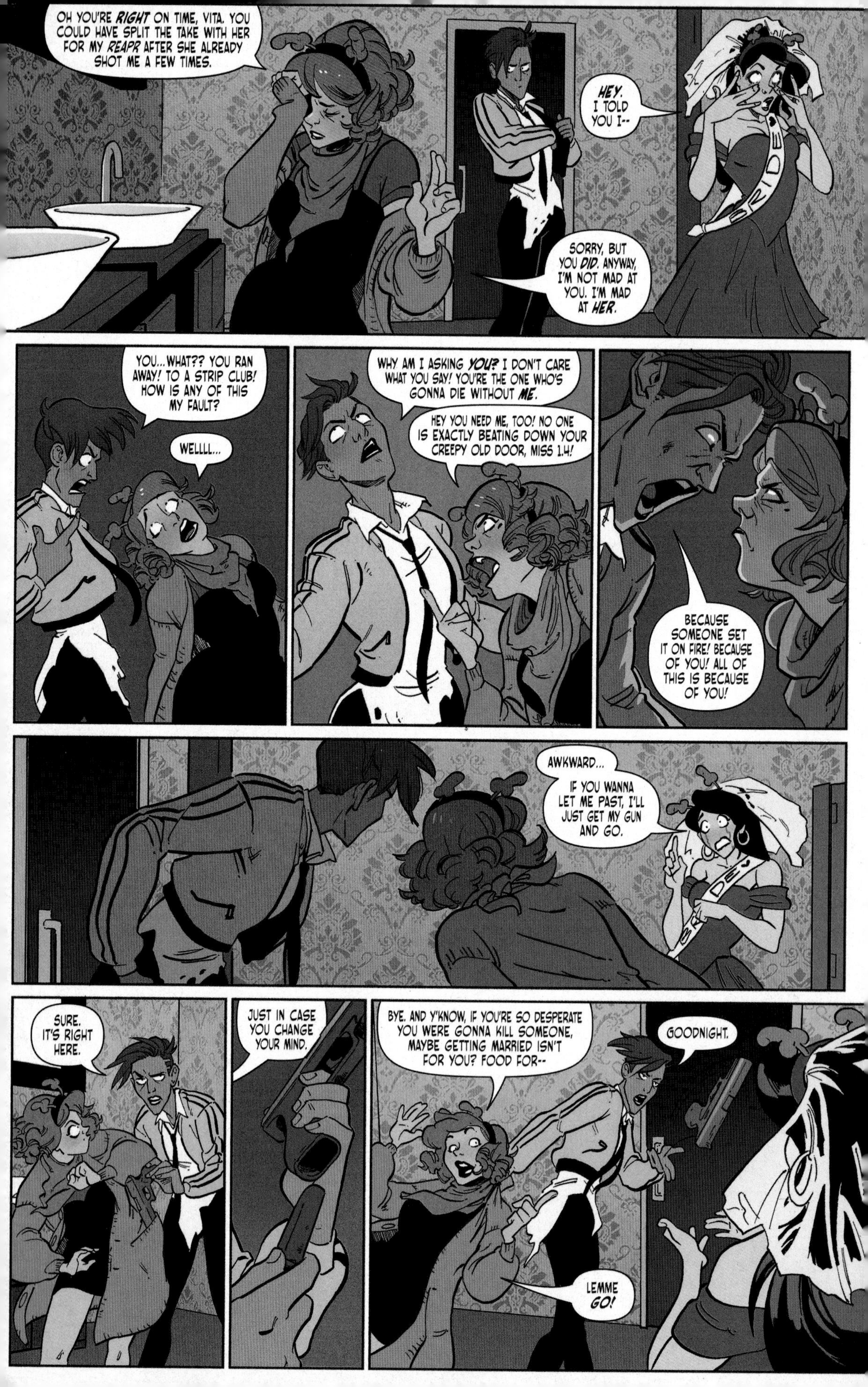
OH YOU'RE RIGHT ON TIME, VITA. YOU COULD HAVE SPLIT THE TAKE WITH HER FOR MY REAPR AFTER SHE ALREADY SHOT ME A FEW TIMES.
HEY. I TOLD YOU I--
SORRY, BUT YOU DID. ANYWAY, I'M NOT MAD AT YOU. I'M MAD AT HER.
BRIDE
YOU...WHAT?? YOU RAN AWAY! TO A STRIP CLUB! HOW IS ANY OF THIS MY FAULT?
WELLLL...
WHY AM I ASKING YOU? I DON'T CARE WHAT YOU SAY! YOU'RE THE ONE WHO'S GONNA DIE WITHOUT ME.
HEY YOU NEED ME, TOO! NO ONE IS EXACTLY BEATING DOWN YOUR CREEPY OLD DOOR, MISS 1.4!
BECAUSE SOMEONE SET IT ON FIRE! BECAUSE OF YOU! ALL OF THIS IS BECAUSE OF YOU!
AWKWARD...
IF YOU WANNA LET ME PAST, I'LL JUST GET MY GUN AND GO.
SURE. IT'S RIGHT HERE.
JUST IN CASE YOU CHANGE YOUR MIND.
BYE. AND Y'KNOW, IF YOU'RE SO DESPERATE YOU WERE GONNA KILL SOMEONE, MAYBE GETTING MARRIED ISN'T FOR YOU? FOOD FOR--
GOODNIGHT.
LEMME GO!

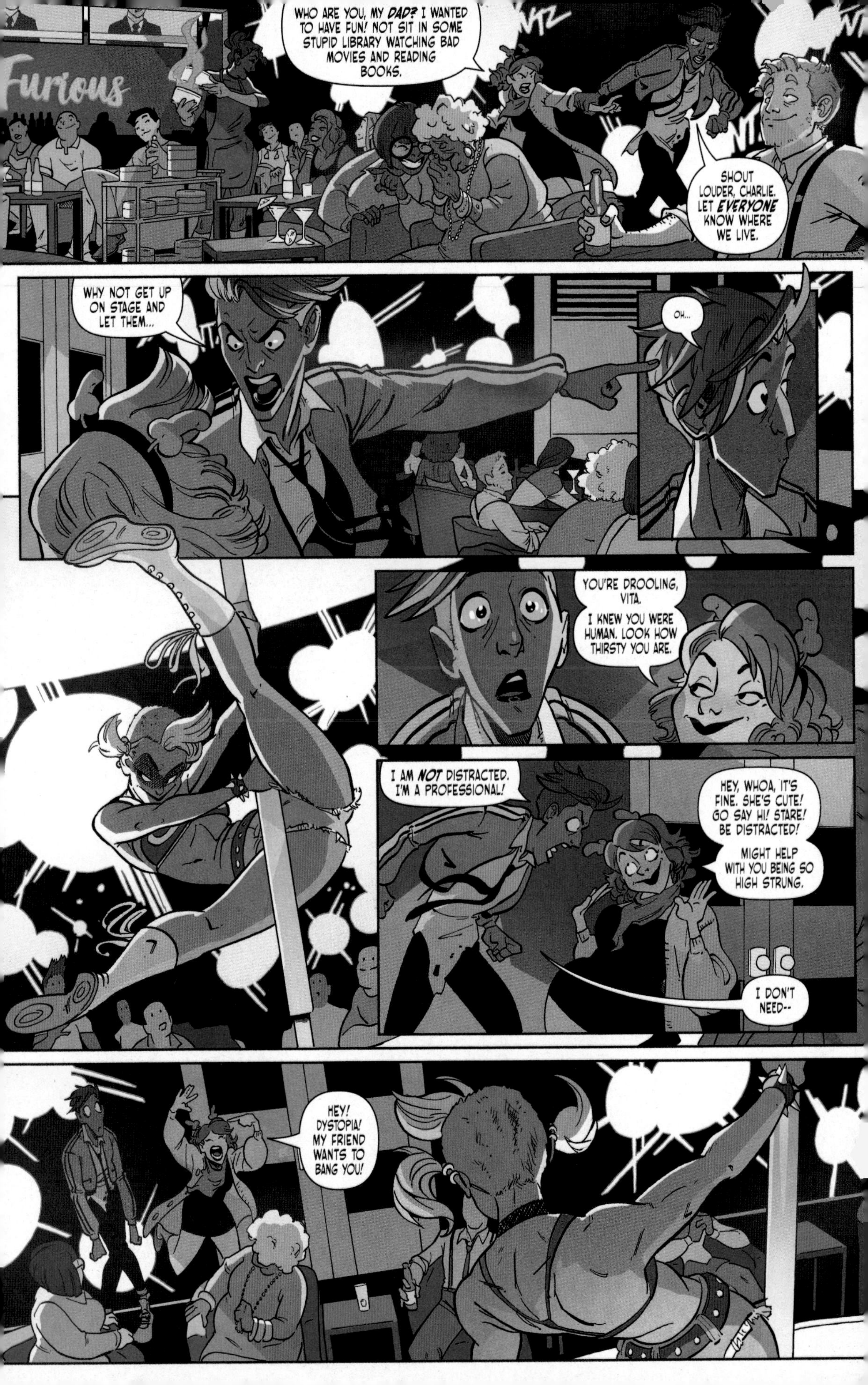

Furious
WHO ARE YOU, MY DAD? I WANTED TO HAVE FUN! NOT SIT IN SOME STUPID LIBRARY WATCHING BAD MOVIES AND READING BOOKS.
SHOUT LOUDER, CHARLIE. LET EVERYONE KNOW WHERE WE LIVE.
WHY NOT GET UP ON STAGE AND LET THEM...
OH...
YOU'RE DROOLING, VITA.
I KNEW YOU WERE HUMAN. LOOK HOW THIRSTY YOU ARE.
I AM NOT DISTRACTED. I'M A PROFESSIONAL!
HEY, WHOA, IT'S FINE. SHE'S CUTE! GO SAY HI! STARE! BE DISTRACTED!
MIGHT HELP WITH YOU BEING SO HIGH STRUNG.
I DON'T NEED--
HEY! DYSTOPIA! MY FRIEND WANTS TO BANG YOU!

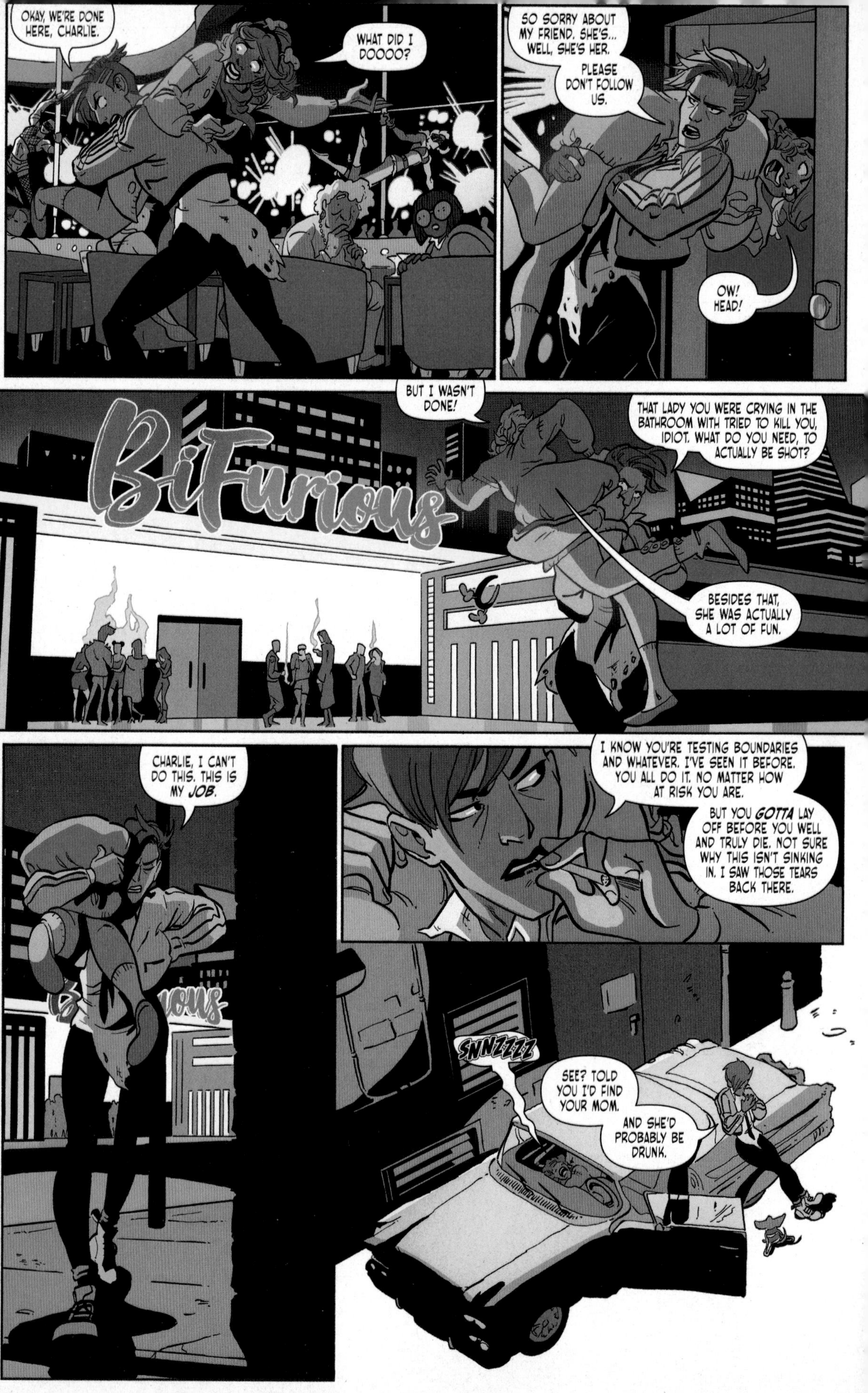
OKAY, WE'RE DONE HERE, CHARLIE.
WHAT DID I DOOOO?
SO SORRY ABOUT MY FRIEND. SHE'S... WELL, SHE'S HER.
PLEASE DON'T FOLLOW US.
OW! HEAD!
BUT I WASN'T DONE!
BiFurious
THAT LADY YOU WERE CRYING IN THE BATHROOM WITH TRIED TO KILL YOU, IDIOT. WHAT DO YOU NEED, TO ACTUALLY BE SHOT?
BESIDES THAT, SHE WAS ACTUALLY A LOT OF FUN.
CHARLIE, I CAN'T DO THIS. THIS IS MY *JOB*.
I KNOW YOU'RE TESTING BOUNDARIES AND WHATEVER. I'VE SEEN IT BEFORE. YOU ALL DO IT. NO MATTER HOW AT RISK YOU ARE.
BUT YOU *GOTTA* LAY OFF BEFORE YOU WELL AND TRULY DIE. NOT SURE WHY THIS ISN'T SINKING IN. I SAW THOSE TEARS BACK THERE.
SNNZZZZ
SEE? TOLD YOU I'D FIND YOUR MOM.
AND SHE'D PROBABLY BE DRUNK.

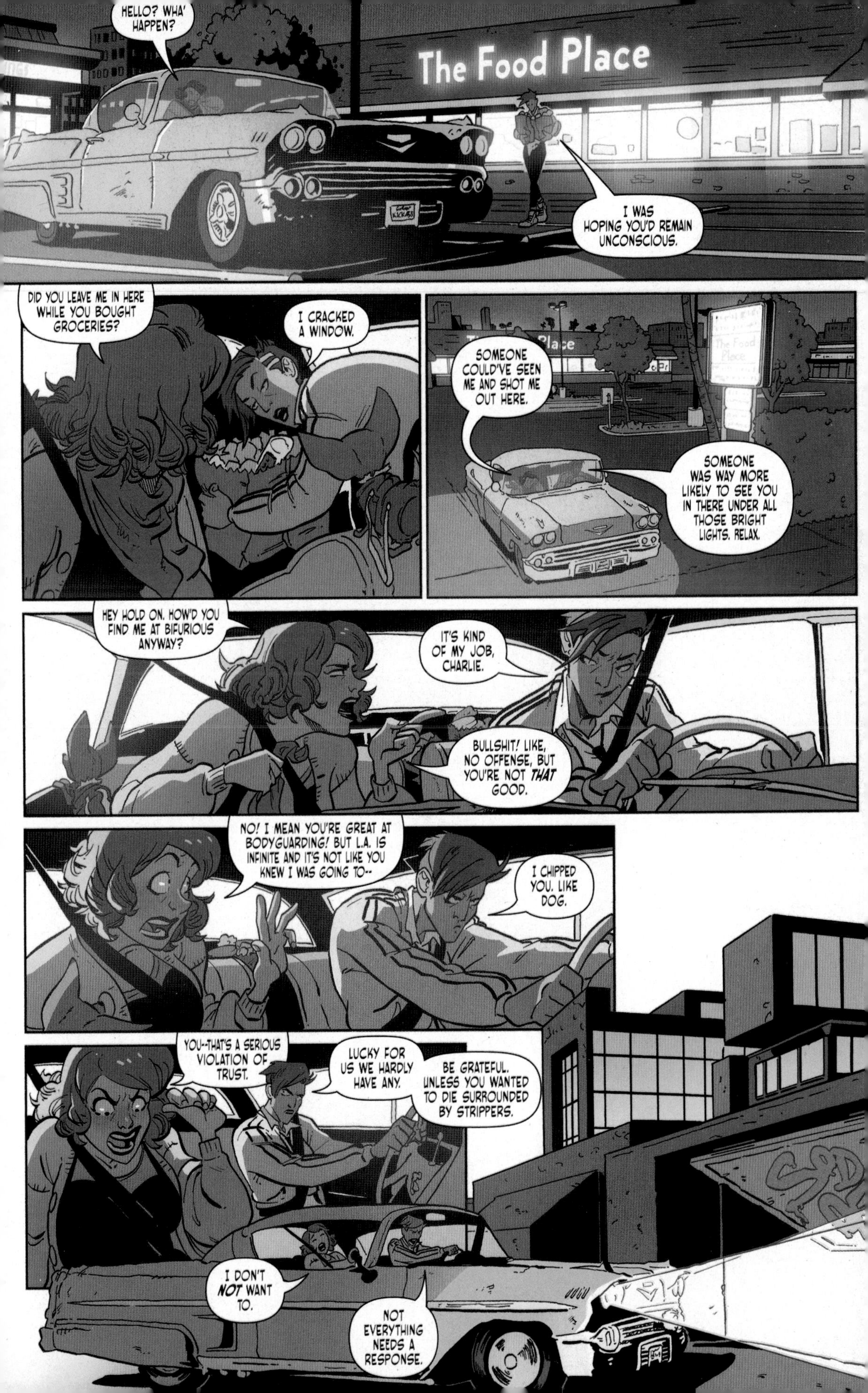
HELLO? WHA' HAPPEN?
The Food Place
I WAS HOPING YOU'D REMAIN UNCONSCIOUS.
DID YOU LEAVE ME IN HERE WHILE YOU BOUGHT GROCERIES?
I CRACKED A WINDOW.
SOMEONE COULD'VE SEEN ME AND SHOT ME OUT HERE.
SOMEONE WAS WAY MORE LIKELY TO SEE YOU IN THERE UNDER ALL THOSE BRIGHT LIGHTS. RELAX.
HEY HOLD ON. HOW'D YOU FIND ME AT BIFURIOUS ANYWAY?
IT'S KIND OF MY JOB, CHARLIE.
BULLSHIT! LIKE, NO OFFENSE, BUT YOU'RE NOT *THAT* GOOD.
NO! I MEAN YOU'RE GREAT AT BODYGUARDING! BUT L.A. IS INFINITE AND IT'S NOT LIKE YOU KNEW I WAS GOING TO--
I CHIPPED YOU. LIKE DOG.
YOU--THAT'S A SERIOUS VIOLATION OF TRUST.
LUCKY FOR US WE HARDLY HAVE ANY.
BE GRATEFUL. UNLESS YOU WANTED TO DIE SURROUNDED BY STRIPPERS.
I DON'T *NOT* WANT TO.
NOT EVERYTHING NEEDS A RESPONSE.

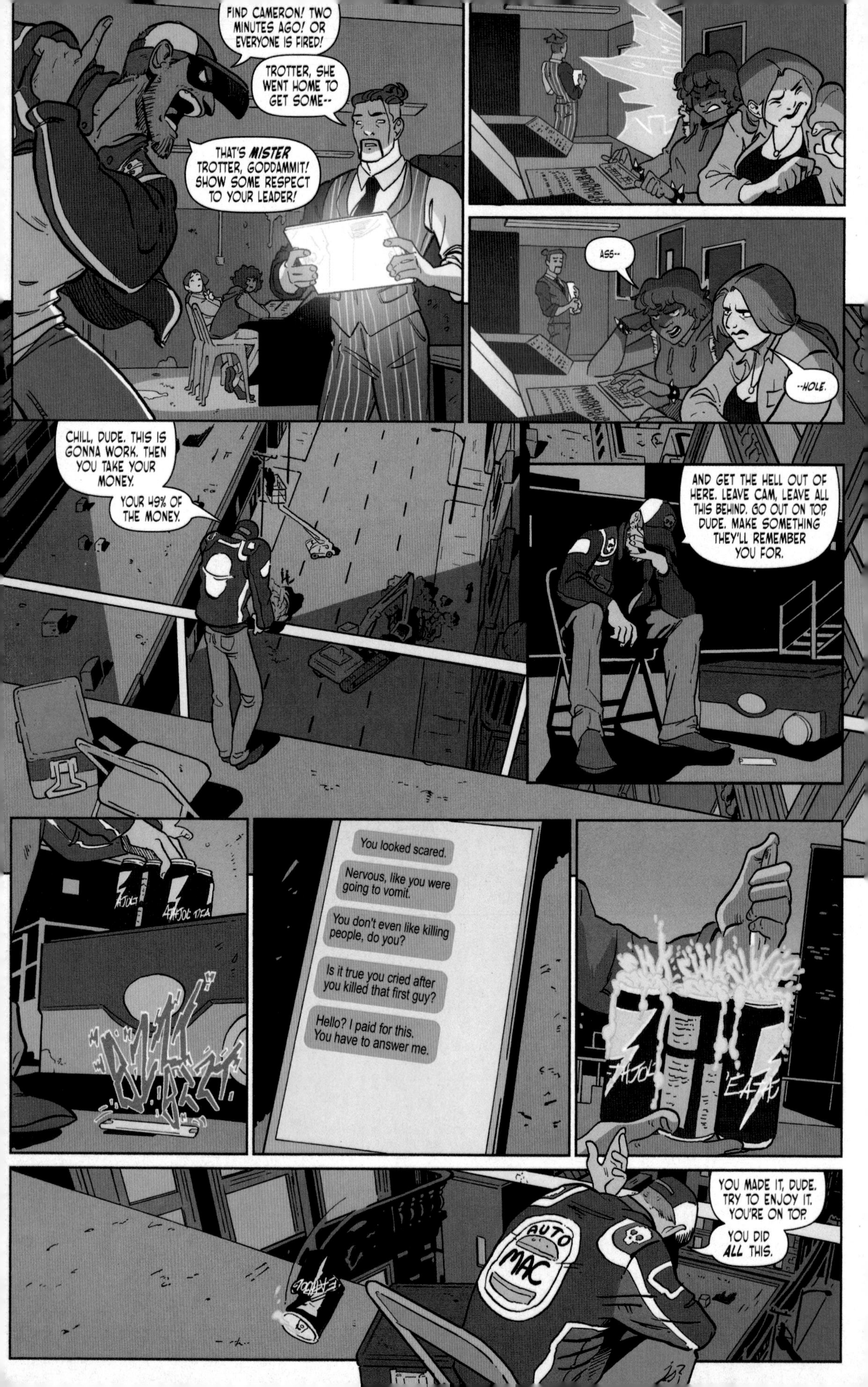
FIND CAMERON! TWO MINUTES AGO! OR EVERYONE IS FIRED!
TROTTER, SHE WENT HOME TO GET SOME--
THAT'S MISTER TROTTER, GODDAMMIT! SHOW SOME RESPECT TO YOUR LEADER!
ASS--
--HOLE.
CHILL, DUDE. THIS IS GONNA WORK. THEN YOU TAKE YOUR MONEY.
YOUR 49% OF THE MONEY.
AND GET THE HELL OUT OF HERE. LEAVE CAM, LEAVE ALL THIS BEHIND. GO OUT ON TOP, DUDE. MAKE SOMETHING THEY'LL REMEMBER YOU FOR.
You looked scared.
Nervous, like you were going to vomit.
You don't even like killing people, do you?
Is it true you cried after you killed that first guy?
Hello? I paid for this. You have to answer me.
YOU MADE IT, DUDE. TRY TO ENJOY IT. YOU'RE ON TOP.
YOU DID ALL THIS.
AUTO MAC

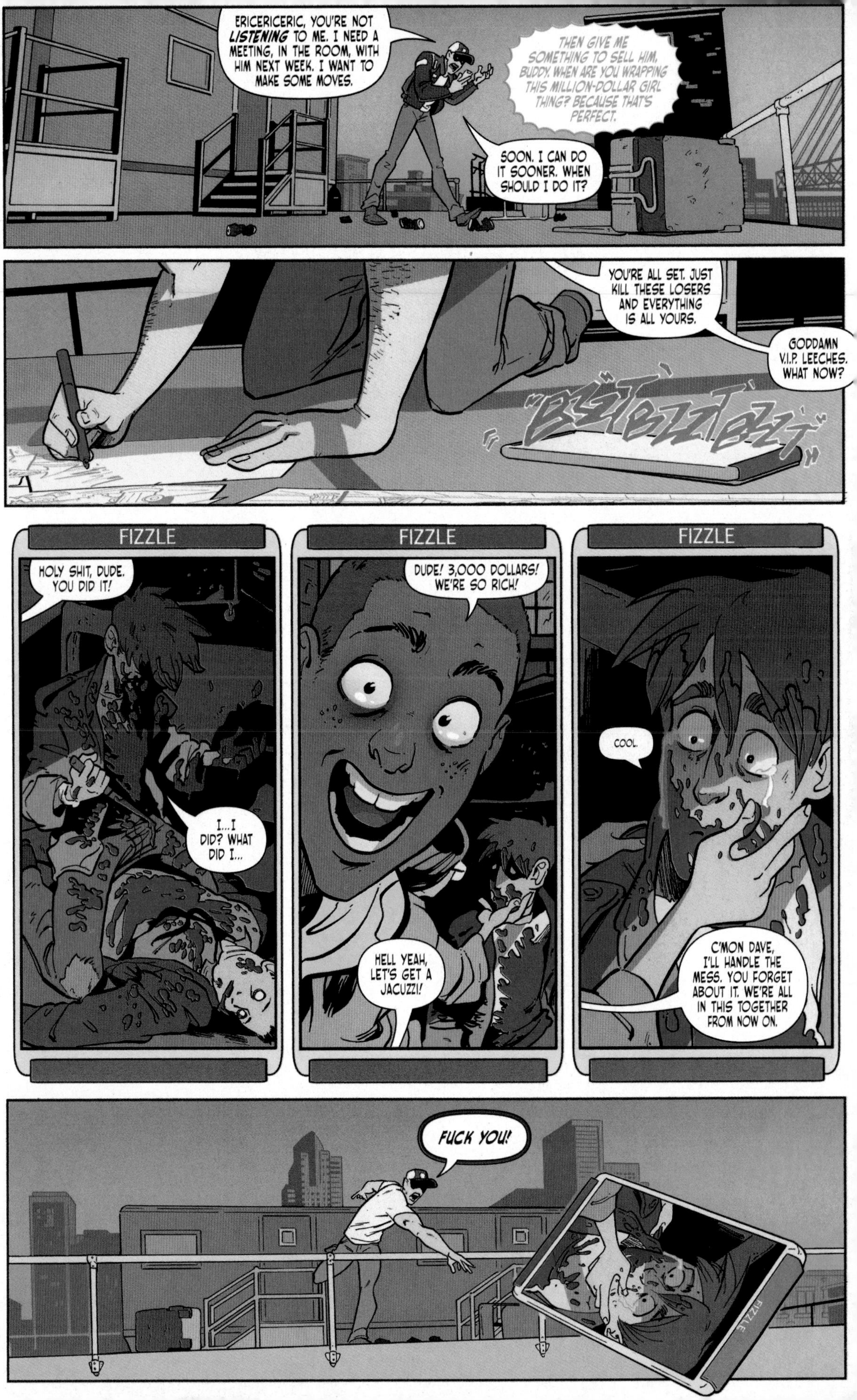
ERICERICERIC, YOU'RE NOT LISTENING TO ME. I NEED A MEETING, IN THE ROOM, WITH HIM NEXT WEEK. I WANT TO MAKE SOME MOVES.
THEN GIVE ME SOMETHING TO SELL HIM, BUDDY. WHEN ARE YOU WRAPPING THIS MILLION-DOLLAR GIRL THING? BECAUSE THAT'S PERFECT.
SOON. I CAN DO IT SOONER. WHEN SHOULD I DO IT?
YOU'RE ALL SET. JUST KILL THESE LOSERS AND EVERYTHING IS ALL YOURS.
GODDAMN V.I.P. LEECHES. WHAT NOW?
"BZZT BZZT BZZT"
FIZZLE
HOLY SHIT, DUDE. YOU DID IT!
I...I DID? WHAT DID I...
FIZZLE
DUDE! 3,000 DOLLARS! WE'RE SO RICH!
HELL YEAH, LET'S GET A JACUZZI!
FIZZLE
COOL.
C'MON DAVE, I'LL HANDLE THE MESS. YOU FORGET ABOUT IT. WE'RE ALL IN THIS TOGETHER FROM NOW ON.
FUCK YOU!
FIZZLE

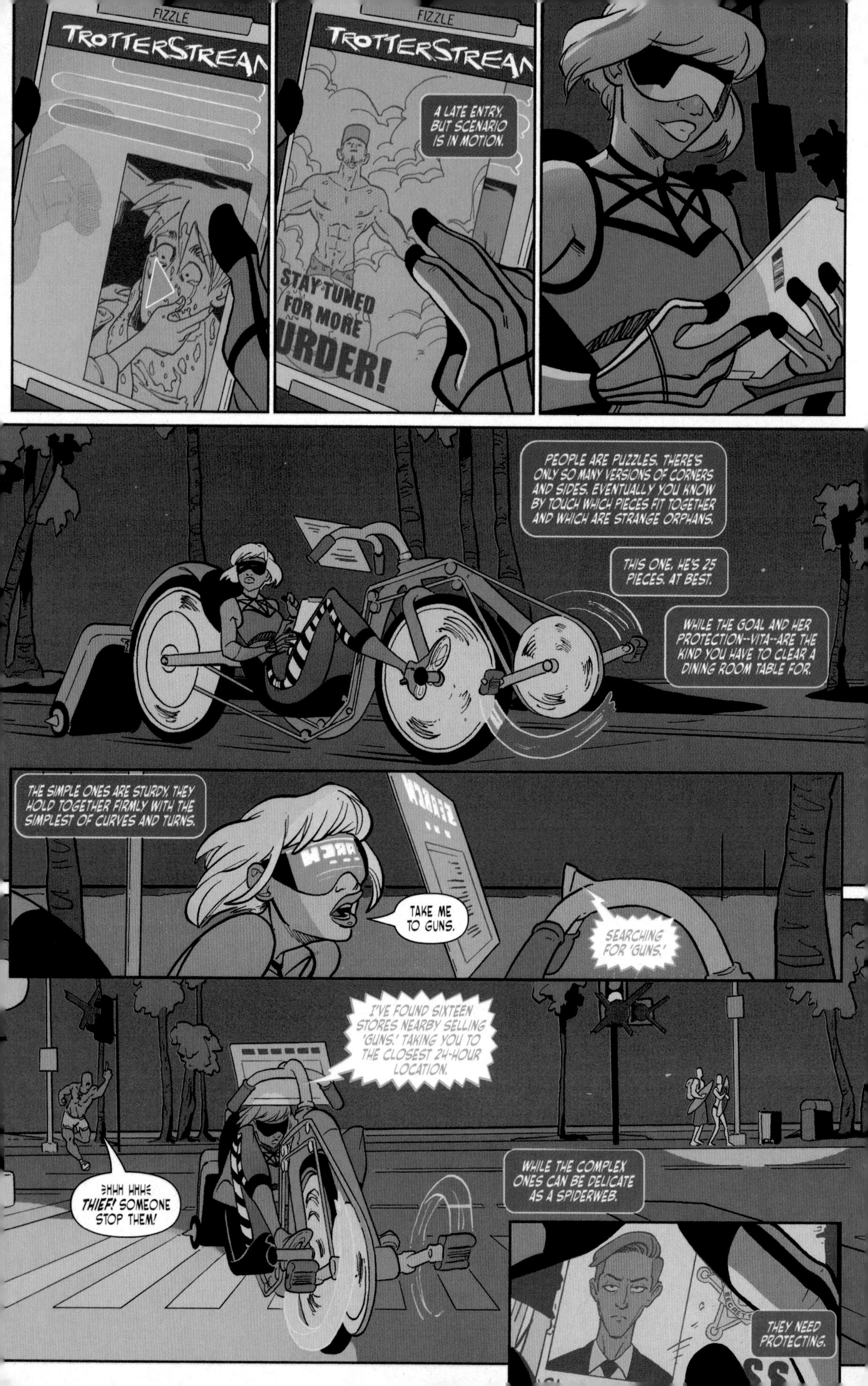
FIZZLE
TROTTERSTREAM
FIZZLE
TROTTERSTREAM
A LATE ENTRY, BUT SCENARIO IS IN MOTION.
STAY TUNED FOR MORE URDER!
PEOPLE ARE PUZZLES. THERE'S ONLY SO MANY VERSIONS OF CORNERS AND SIDES. EVENTUALLY YOU KNOW BY TOUCH WHICH PIECES FIT TOGETHER AND WHICH ARE STRANGE ORPHANS.
THIS ONE, HE'S 25 PIECES. AT BEST.
WHILE THE GOAL AND HER PROTECTION--VITA--ARE THE KIND YOU HAVE TO CLEAR A DINING ROOM TABLE FOR.
THE SIMPLE ONES ARE STURDY. THEY HOLD TOGETHER FIRMLY WITH THE SIMPLEST OF CURVES AND TURNS.
TAKE ME TO GUNS.
SEARCHING FOR 'GUNS.'
I'VE FOUND SIXTEEN STORES NEARBY SELLING 'GUNS,' TAKING YOU TO THE CLOSEST 24-HOUR LOCATION.
HHH HHH THIEF! SOMEONE STOP THEM!
WHILE THE COMPLEX ONES CAN BE DELICATE AS A SPIDERWEB.
THEY NEED PROTECTING.

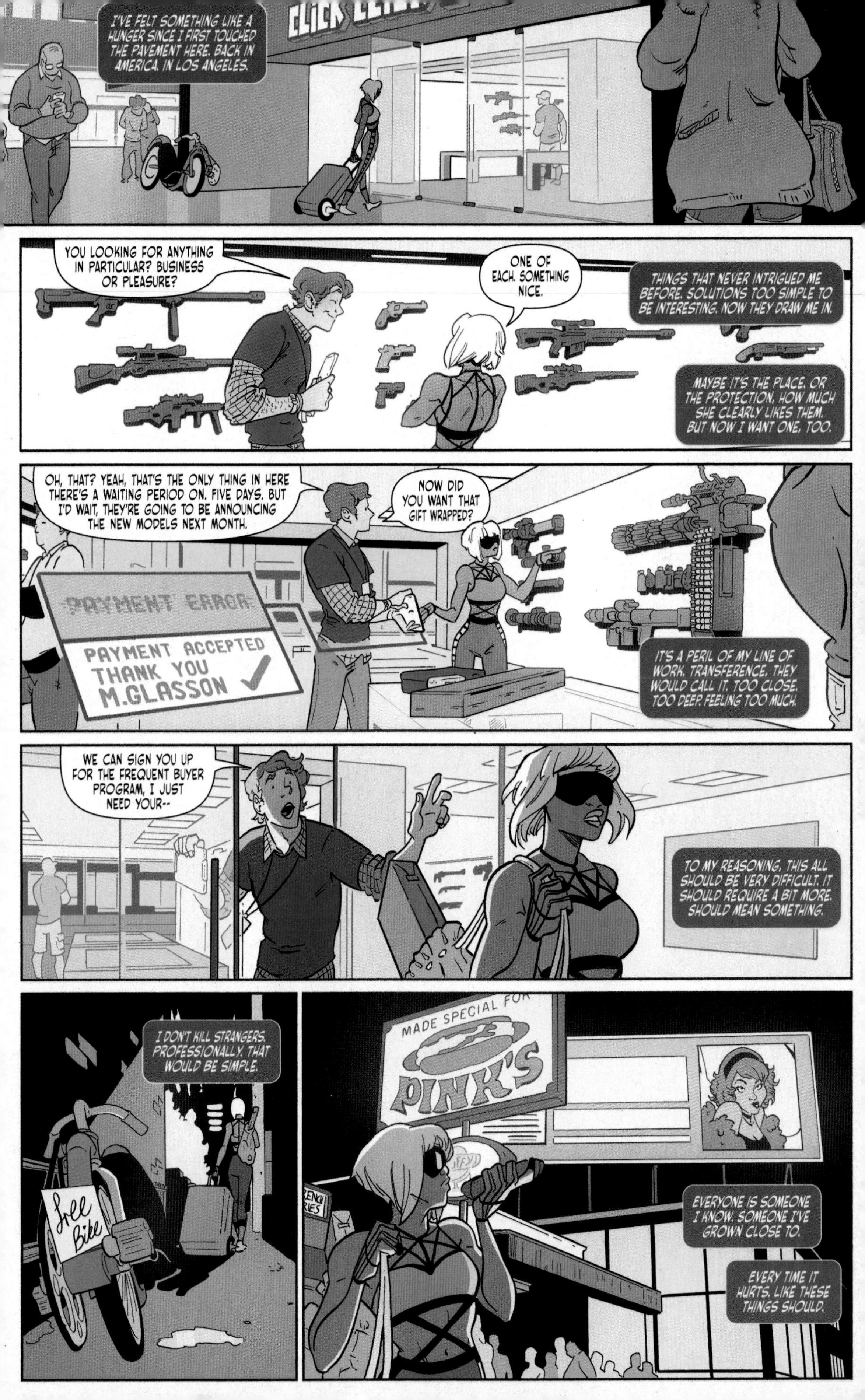
I'VE FELT SOMETHING LIKE A HUNGER SINCE I FIRST TOUCHED THE PAVEMENT HERE. BACK IN AMERICA. IN LOS ANGELES.
YOU LOOKING FOR ANYTHING IN PARTICULAR? BUSINESS OR PLEASURE?
ONE OF EACH. SOMETHING NICE.
THINGS THAT NEVER INTRIGUED ME BEFORE. SOLUTIONS TOO SIMPLE TO BE INTERESTING. NOW THEY DRAW ME IN.
MAYBE IT'S THE PLACE. OR THE PROTECTION, HOW MUCH SHE CLEARLY LIKES THEM. BUT NOW I WANT ONE, TOO.
OH, THAT? YEAH, THAT'S THE ONLY THING IN HERE THERE'S A WAITING PERIOD ON. FIVE DAYS. BUT I'D WAIT, THEY'RE GOING TO BE ANNOUNCING THE NEW MODELS NEXT MONTH.
NOW DID YOU WANT THAT GIFT WRAPPED?
PAYMENT ERROR
PAYMENT ACCEPTED THANK YOU M.GLASSON
IT'S A PERIL OF MY LINE OF WORK. TRANSFERENCE, THEY WOULD CALL IT. TOO CLOSE. TOO DEEP. FEELING TOO MUCH.
WE CAN SIGN YOU UP FOR THE FREQUENT BUYER PROGRAM, I JUST NEED YOUR--
TO MY REASONING, THIS ALL SHOULD BE VERY DIFFICULT. IT SHOULD REQUIRE A BIT MORE. SHOULD MEAN SOMETHING.
I DON'T KILL STRANGERS. PROFESSIONALLY. THAT WOULD BE SIMPLE.
Free Bike
MADE SPECIAL FOR
PINK'S
EVERYONE IS SOMEONE I KNOW. SOMEONE I'VE GROWN CLOSE TO.
EVERY TIME IT HURTS. LIKE THESE THINGS SHOULD.

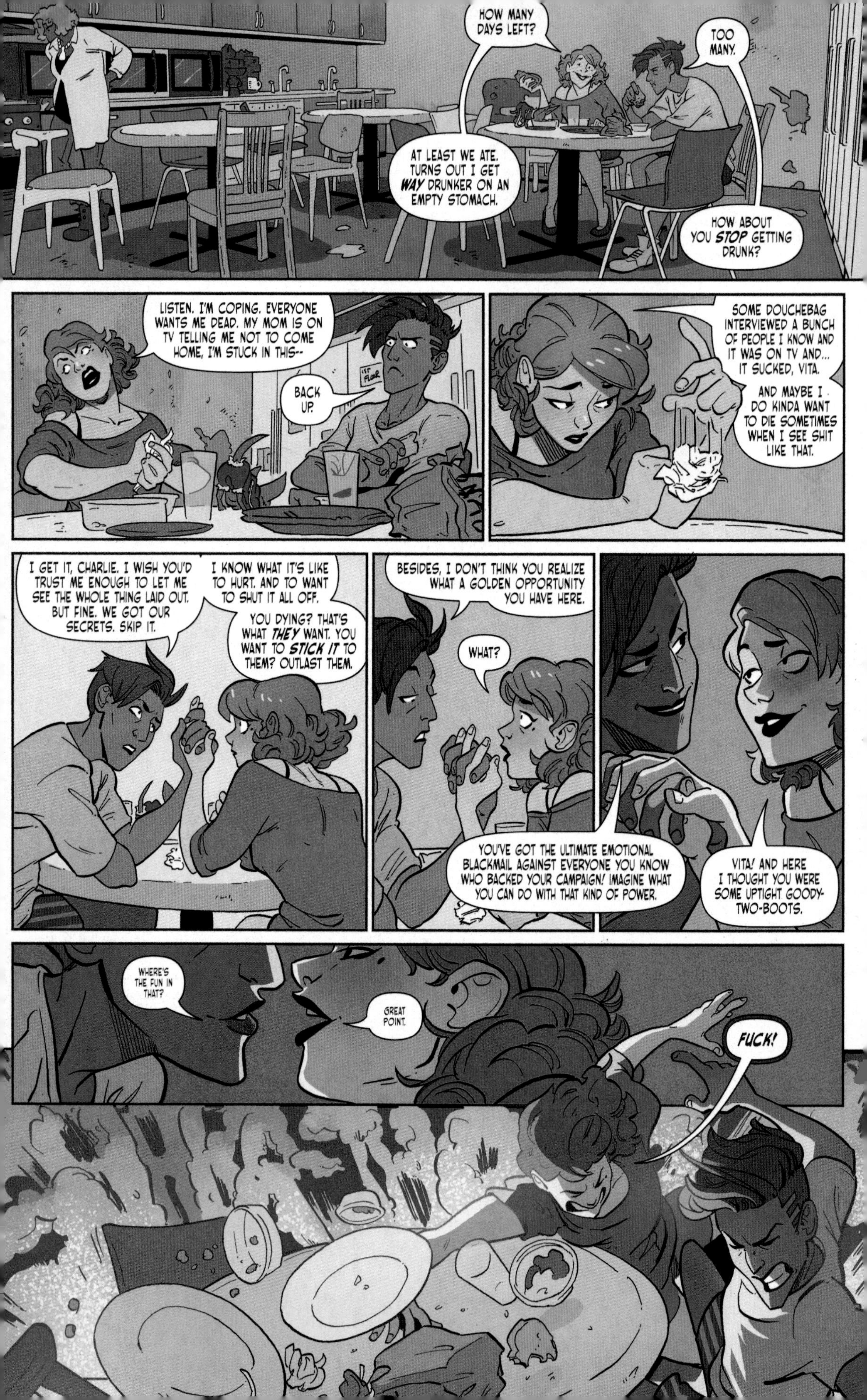
HOW MANY DAYS LEFT?
TOO MANY.
AT LEAST WE ATE. TURNS OUT I GET WAY DRUNKER ON AN EMPTY STOMACH.
HOW ABOUT YOU STOP GETTING DRUNK?
LISTEN. I'M COPING. EVERYONE WANTS ME DEAD. MY MOM IS ON TV TELLING ME NOT TO COME HOME, I'M STUCK IN THIS--
BACK UP.
1ST FLOOR
SOME DOUCHEBAG INTERVIEWED A BUNCH OF PEOPLE I KNOW AND IT WAS ON TV AND... IT SUCKED, VITA.
AND MAYBE I DO KINDA WANT TO DIE SOMETIMES WHEN I SEE SHIT LIKE THAT.
I GET IT, CHARLIE. I WISH YOU'D TRUST ME ENOUGH TO LET ME SEE THE WHOLE THING LAID OUT. BUT FINE. WE GOT OUR SECRETS. SKIP IT.
I KNOW WHAT IT'S LIKE TO HURT. AND TO WANT TO SHUT IT ALL OFF.
YOU DYING? THAT'S WHAT THEY WANT. YOU WANT TO STICK IT TO THEM? OUTLAST THEM.
BESIDES, I DON'T THINK YOU REALIZE WHAT A GOLDEN OPPORTUNITY YOU HAVE HERE.
WHAT?
YOU'VE GOT THE ULTIMATE EMOTIONAL BLACKMAIL AGAINST EVERYONE YOU KNOW WHO BACKED YOUR CAMPAIGN! IMAGINE WHAT YOU CAN DO WITH THAT KIND OF POWER.
VITA! AND HERE I THOUGHT YOU WERE SOME UPTIGHT GOODY-TWO-BOOTS.
WHERE'S THE FUN IN THAT?
GREAT POINT.
FUCK!

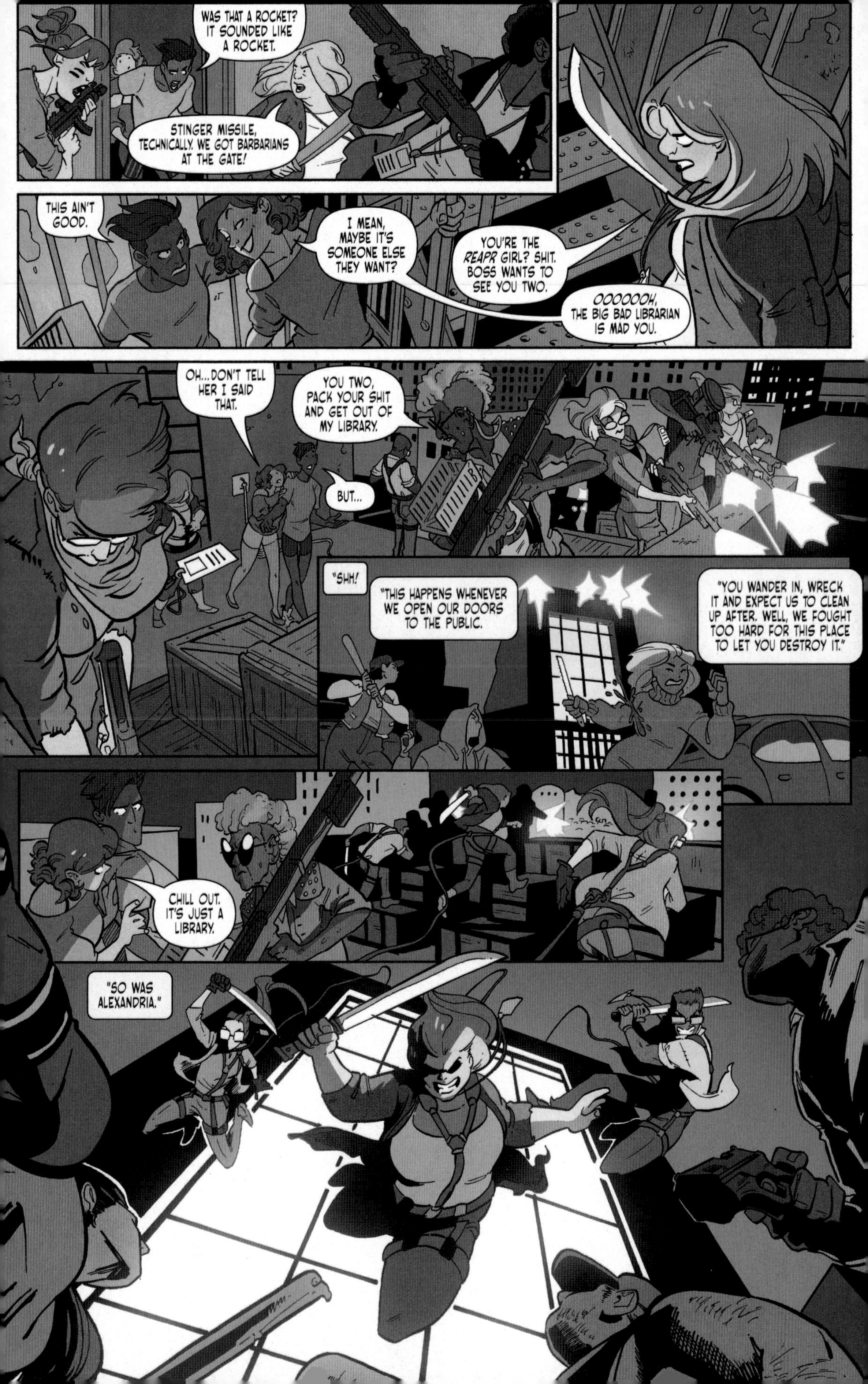
WAS THAT A ROCKET? IT SOUNDED LIKE A ROCKET.
STINGER MISSILE, TECHNICALLY. WE GOT BARBARIANS AT THE GATE!
THIS AIN'T GOOD.
I MEAN, MAYBE IT'S SOMEONE ELSE THEY WANT?
YOU'RE THE *REAPR* GIRL? SHIT. BOSS WANTS TO SEE YOU TWO.
OOOOOOH, THE BIG BAD LIBRARIAN IS MAD YOU.
OH...DON'T TELL HER I SAID THAT.
YOU TWO, PACK YOUR SHIT AND GET OUT OF MY LIBRARY.
BUT...
"SHH!
"THIS HAPPENS WHENEVER WE OPEN OUR DOORS TO THE PUBLIC.
"YOU WANDER IN, WRECK IT AND EXPECT US TO CLEAN UP AFTER. WELL, WE FOUGHT TOO HARD FOR THIS PLACE TO LET YOU DESTROY IT."
CHILL OUT. IT'S JUST A LIBRARY.
"SO WAS ALEXANDRIA."

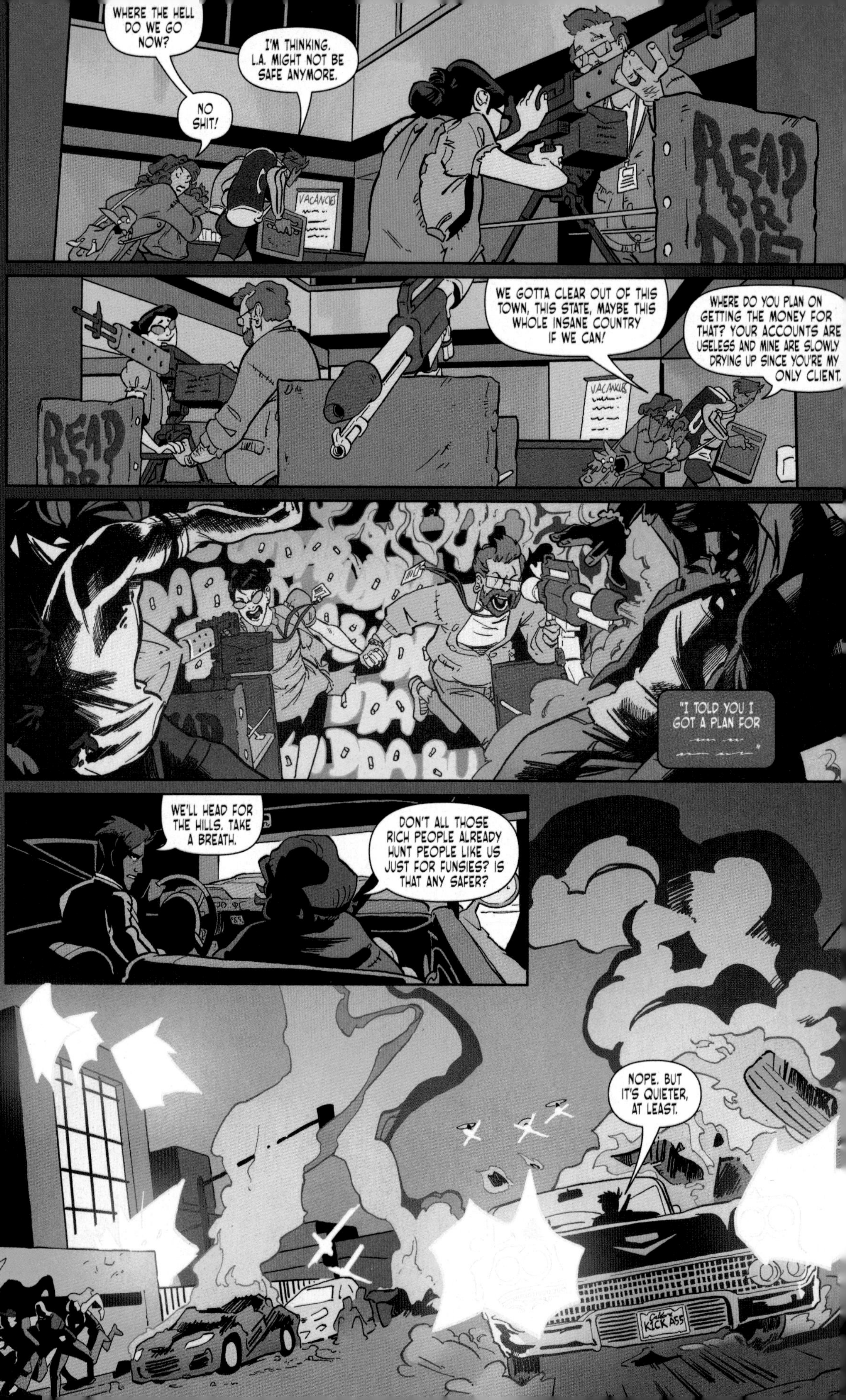
WHERE THE HELL DO WE GO NOW?
I'M THINKING. L.A. MIGHT NOT BE SAFE ANYMORE.
NO SHIT!
READ OR DIE
VACANCIES
READ
WE GOTTA CLEAR OUT OF THIS TOWN, THIS STATE, MAYBE THIS WHOLE INSANE COUNTRY IF WE CAN!
WHERE DO YOU PLAN ON GETTING THE MONEY FOR THAT? YOUR ACCOUNTS ARE USELESS AND MINE ARE SLOWLY DRYING UP SINCE YOU'RE MY ONLY CLIENT.
VACANCIES
"I TOLD YOU I GOT A PLAN FOR
"
WE'LL HEAD FOR THE HILLS. TAKE A BREATH.
DON'T ALL THOSE RICH PEOPLE ALREADY HUNT PEOPLE LIKE US JUST FOR FUNSIES? IS THAT ANY SAFER?
NOPE. BUT IT'S QUIETER, AT LEAST.
KICKASS

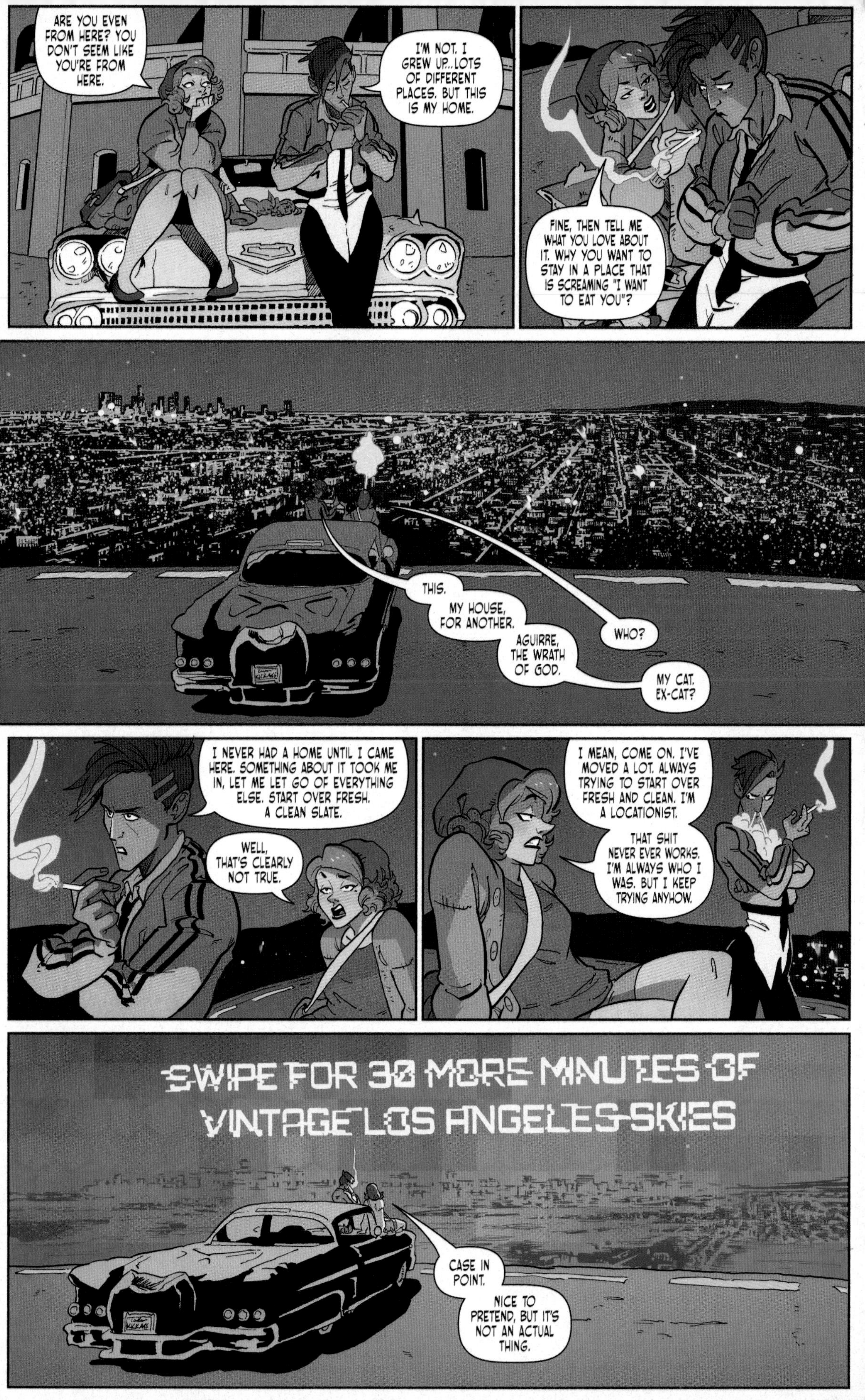
ARE YOU EVEN FROM HERE? YOU DON'T SEEM LIKE YOU'RE FROM HERE.
I'M NOT. I GREW UP...LOTS OF DIFFERENT PLACES. BUT THIS IS MY HOME.
FINE, THEN TELL ME WHAT YOU LOVE ABOUT IT. WHY YOU WANT TO STAY IN A PLACE THAT IS SCREAMING "I WANT TO EAT YOU"?
THIS.
MY HOUSE, FOR ANOTHER.
WHO?
AGUIRRE, THE WRATH OF GOD.
MY CAT. EX-CAT?
I NEVER HAD A HOME UNTIL I CAME HERE. SOMETHING ABOUT IT TOOK ME IN, LET ME LET GO OF EVERYTHING ELSE. START OVER FRESH. A CLEAN SLATE.
WELL, THAT'S CLEARLY NOT TRUE.
I MEAN, COME ON. I'VE MOVED A LOT. ALWAYS TRYING TO START OVER FRESH AND CLEAN. I'M A LOCATIONIST.
THAT SHIT NEVER EVER WORKS. I'M ALWAYS WHO I WAS. BUT I KEEP TRYING ANYHOW.
SWIPE FOR 30 MORE MINUTES OF VINTAGE LOS ANGELES SKIES
CASE IN POINT.
NICE TO PRETEND, BUT IT'S NOT AN ACTUAL THING.

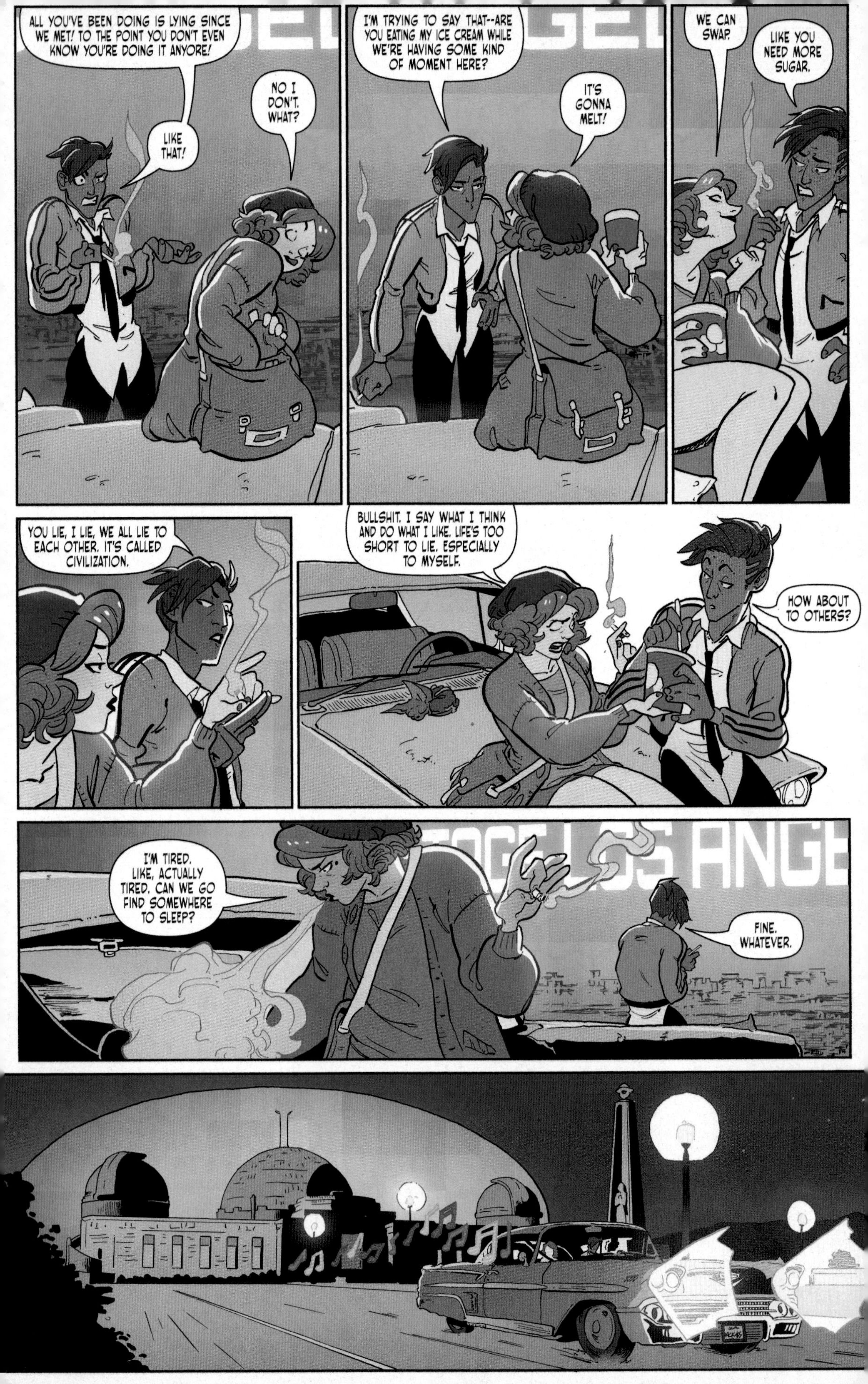
ALL YOU'VE BEEN DOING IS LYING SINCE WE MET! TO THE POINT YOU DON'T EVEN KNOW YOU'RE DOING IT ANYORE!
NO I DON'T. WHAT?
LIKE THAT!
I'M TRYING TO SAY THAT--ARE YOU EATING MY ICE CREAM WHILE WE'RE HAVING SOME KIND OF MOMENT HERE?
IT'S GONNA MELT!
WE CAN SWAP.
LIKE YOU NEED MORE SUGAR.
YOU LIE, I LIE, WE ALL LIE TO EACH OTHER. IT'S CALLED CIVILIZATION.
BULLSHIT. I SAY WHAT I THINK AND DO WHAT I LIKE. LIFE'S TOO SHORT TO LIE. ESPECIALLY TO MYSELF.
HOW ABOUT TO OTHERS?
I'M TIRED. LIKE, ACTUALLY TIRED. CAN WE GO FIND SOMEWHERE TO SLEEP?
FINE. WHATEVER.

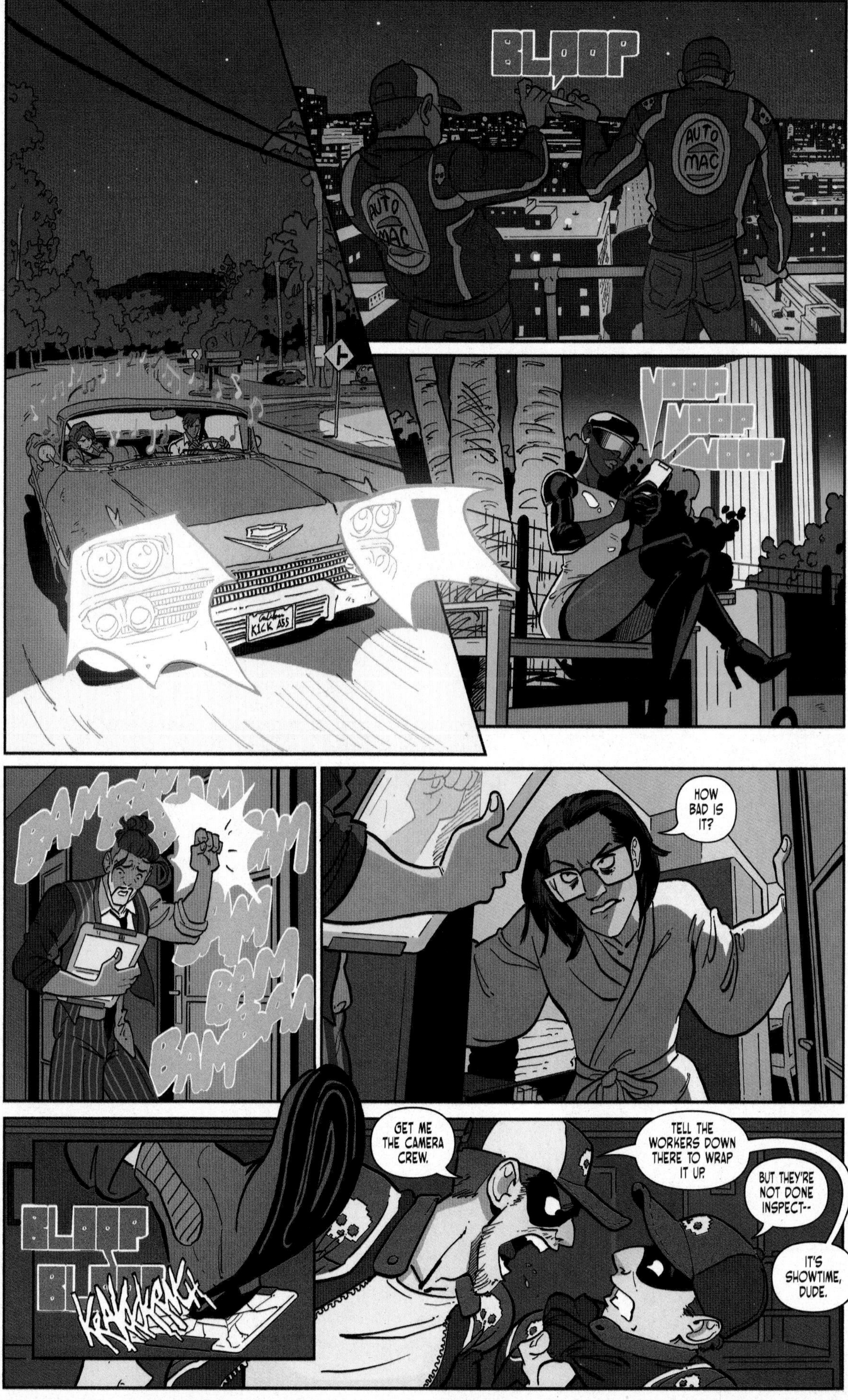
BLOOP
VOOP
VOOP
VOOP
HOW BAD IS IT?
GET ME THE CAMERA CREW.
TELL THE WORKERS DOWN THERE TO WRAP IT UP.
BUT THEY'RE NOT DONE INSPECT--
IT'S SHOWTIME, DUDE.
BLOOP

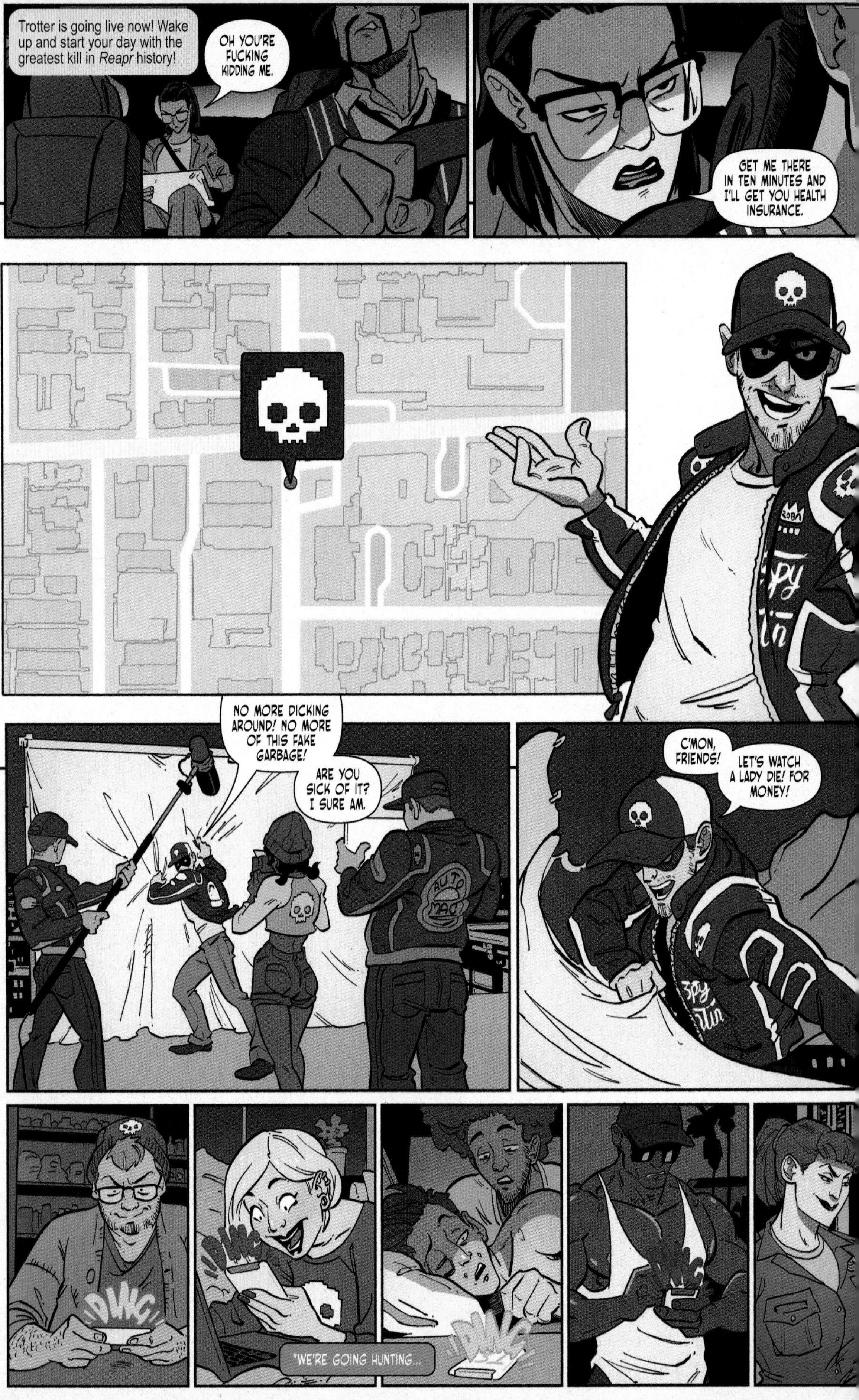
Trotter is going live now! Wake up and start your day with the greatest kill in *Reapr* history!
OH YOU'RE FUCKING KIDDING ME.
GET ME THERE IN TEN MINUTES AND I'LL GET YOU HEALTH INSURANCE.
NO MORE DICKING AROUND! NO MORE OF THIS FAKE GARBAGE!
ARE YOU SICK OF IT? I SURE AM.
C'MON, FRIENDS!
LET'S WATCH A LADY DIE! FOR MONEY!
DING
DING
DING
"WE'RE GOING HUNTING...

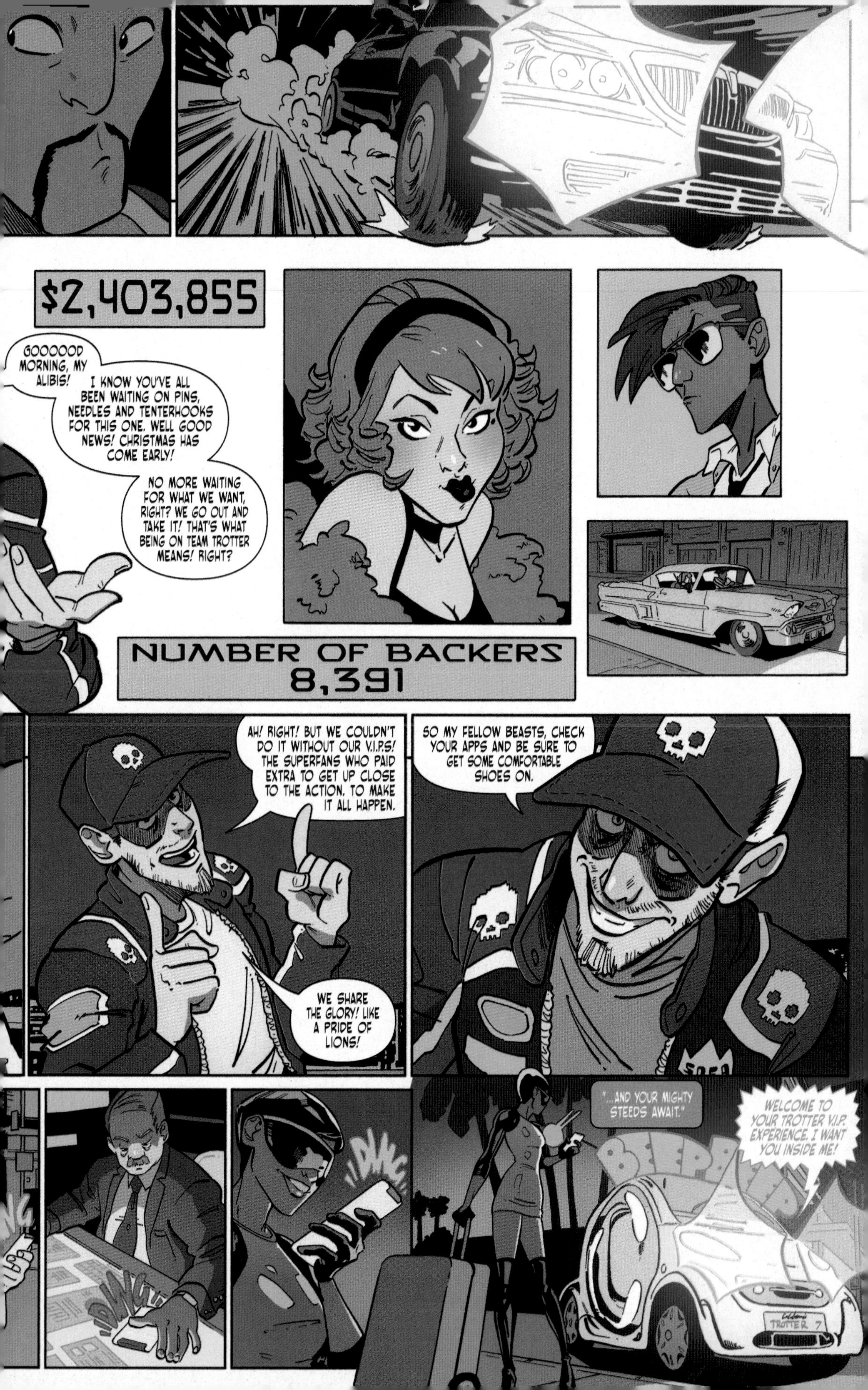
$2,403,855
GOOOOOD MORNING, MY ALIBIS!
I KNOW YOU'VE ALL BEEN WAITING ON PINS, NEEDLES AND TENTERHOOKS FOR THIS ONE. WELL GOOD NEWS! CHRISTMAS HAS COME EARLY!
NO MORE WAITING FOR WHAT WE WANT, RIGHT? WE GO OUT AND TAKE IT! THAT'S WHAT BEING ON TEAM TROTTER MEANS! RIGHT?
NUMBER OF BACKERS 8,391
AH! RIGHT! BUT WE COULDN'T DO IT WITHOUT OUR V.I.P.S! THE SUPERFANS WHO PAID EXTRA TO GET UP CLOSE TO THE ACTION. TO MAKE IT ALL HAPPEN.
WE SHARE THE GLORY! LIKE A PRIDE OF LIONS!
SO MY FELLOW BEASTS, CHECK YOUR APPS AND BE SURE TO GET SOME COMFORTABLE SHOES ON.
DING!
DING!
"...AND YOUR MIGHTY STEEDS AWAIT."
WELCOME TO YOUR TROTTER V.I.P. EXPERIENCE. I WANT YOU INSIDE ME!
TROTTER 7

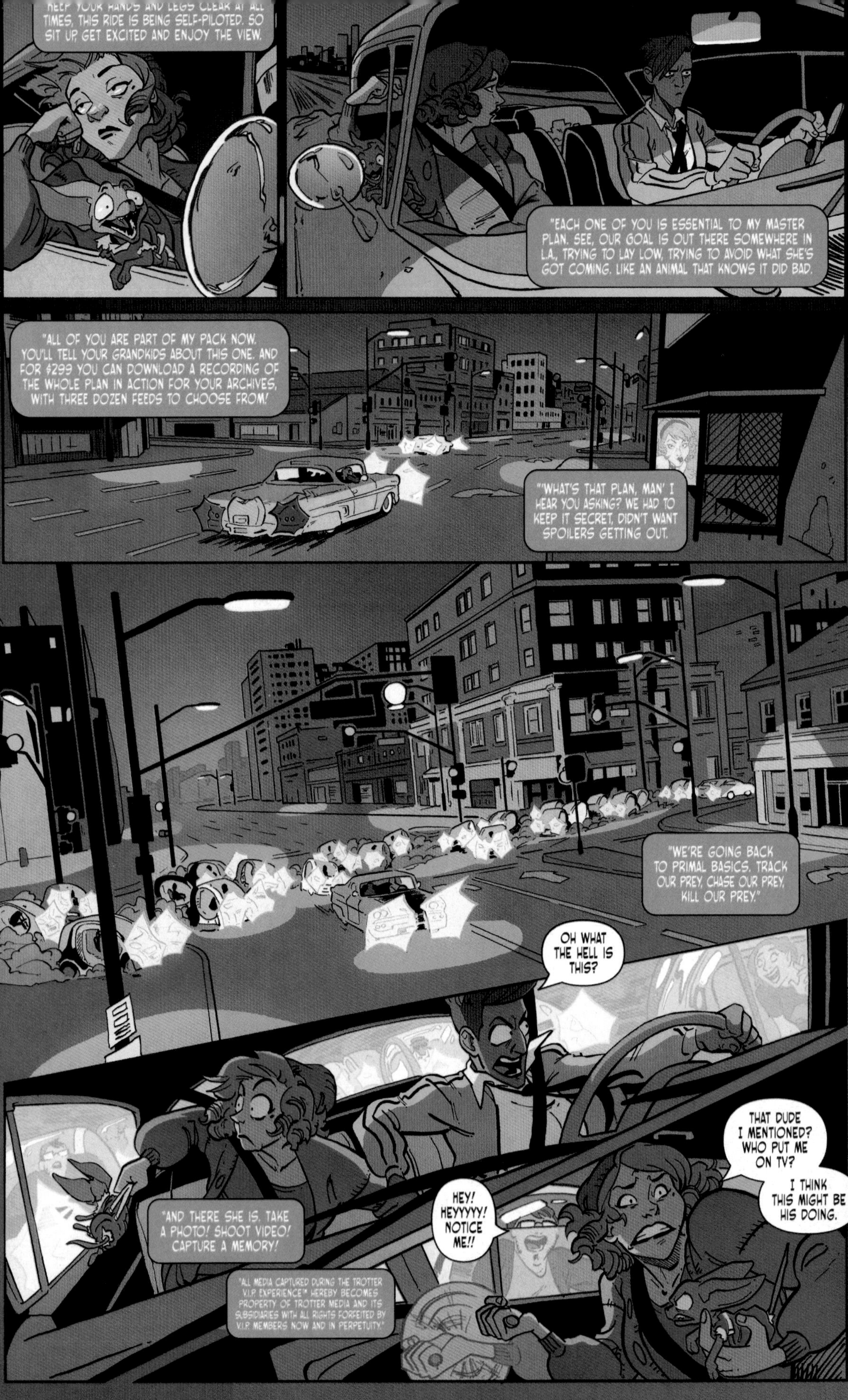
KEEP YOUR HANDS AND LEGS CLEAR AT ALL TIMES, THIS RIDE IS BEING SELF-PILOTED. SO SIT UP, GET EXCITED AND ENJOY THE VIEW.
"EACH ONE OF YOU IS ESSENTIAL TO MY MASTER PLAN. SEE, OUR GOAL IS OUT THERE SOMEWHERE IN L.A., TRYING TO LAY LOW, TRYING TO AVOID WHAT SHE'S GOT COMING. LIKE AN ANIMAL THAT KNOWS IT DID BAD.
"ALL OF YOU ARE PART OF MY PACK NOW. YOU'LL TELL YOUR GRANDKIDS ABOUT THIS ONE. AND FOR $299 YOU CAN DOWNLOAD A RECORDING OF THE WHOLE PLAN IN ACTION FOR YOUR ARCHIVES, WITH THREE DOZEN FEEDS TO CHOOSE FROM!
"'WHAT'S THAT PLAN, MAN' I HEAR YOU ASKING? WE HAD TO KEEP IT SECRET, DIDN'T WANT SPOILERS GETTING OUT.
"WE'RE GOING BACK TO PRIMAL BASICS. TRACK OUR PREY, CHASE OUR PREY, KILL OUR PREY."
OH WHAT THE HELL IS THIS?
"AND THERE SHE IS. TAKE A PHOTO! SHOOT VIDEO! CAPTURE A MEMORY!
"ALL MEDIA CAPTURED DURING THE TROTTER V.I.P. EXPERIENCE™ HEREBY BECOMES PROPERTY OF TROTTER MEDIA AND ITS SUBSIDIARIES WITH ALL RIGHTS FORFEITED BY V.I.P. MEMBERS NOW AND IN PERPETUITY."
HEY! HEYYYYY! NOTICE ME!!
THAT DUDE I MENTIONED? WHO PUT ME ON TV?
I THINK THIS MIGHT BE HIS DOING.

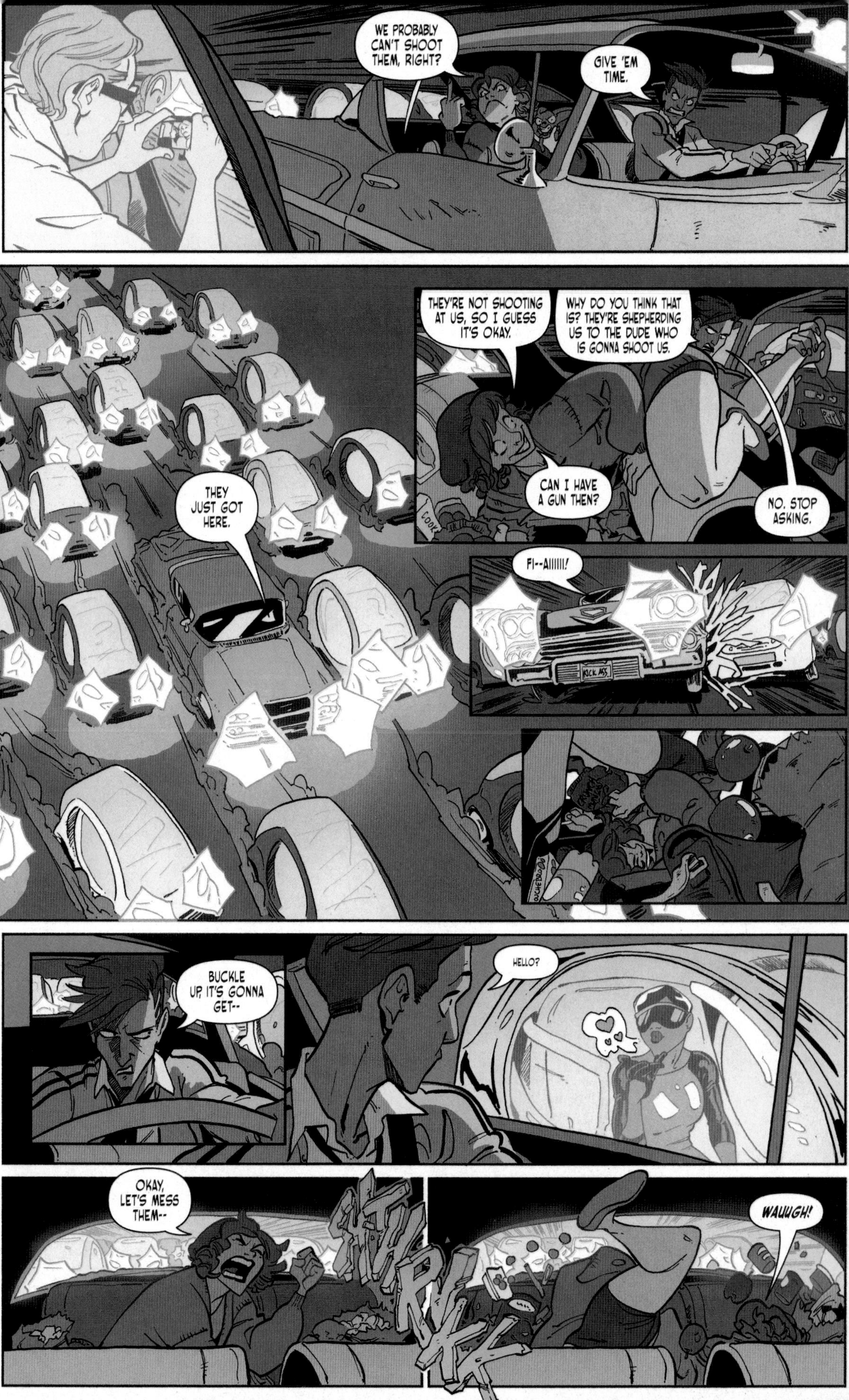
WE PROBABLY CAN'T SHOOT THEM, RIGHT?
GIVE 'EM TIME.
THEY'RE NOT SHOOTING AT US, SO I GUESS IT'S OKAY.
WHY DO YOU THINK THAT IS? THEY'RE SHEPHERDING US TO THE DUDE WHO IS GONNA SHOOT US.
CAN I HAVE A GUN THEN?
NO. STOP ASKING.
THEY JUST GOT HERE.
FI--AIIIIII!
KICK ASS
BUCKLE UP, IT'S GONNA GET--
HELLO?
OKAY, LET'S MESS THEM--
WAUUGH!

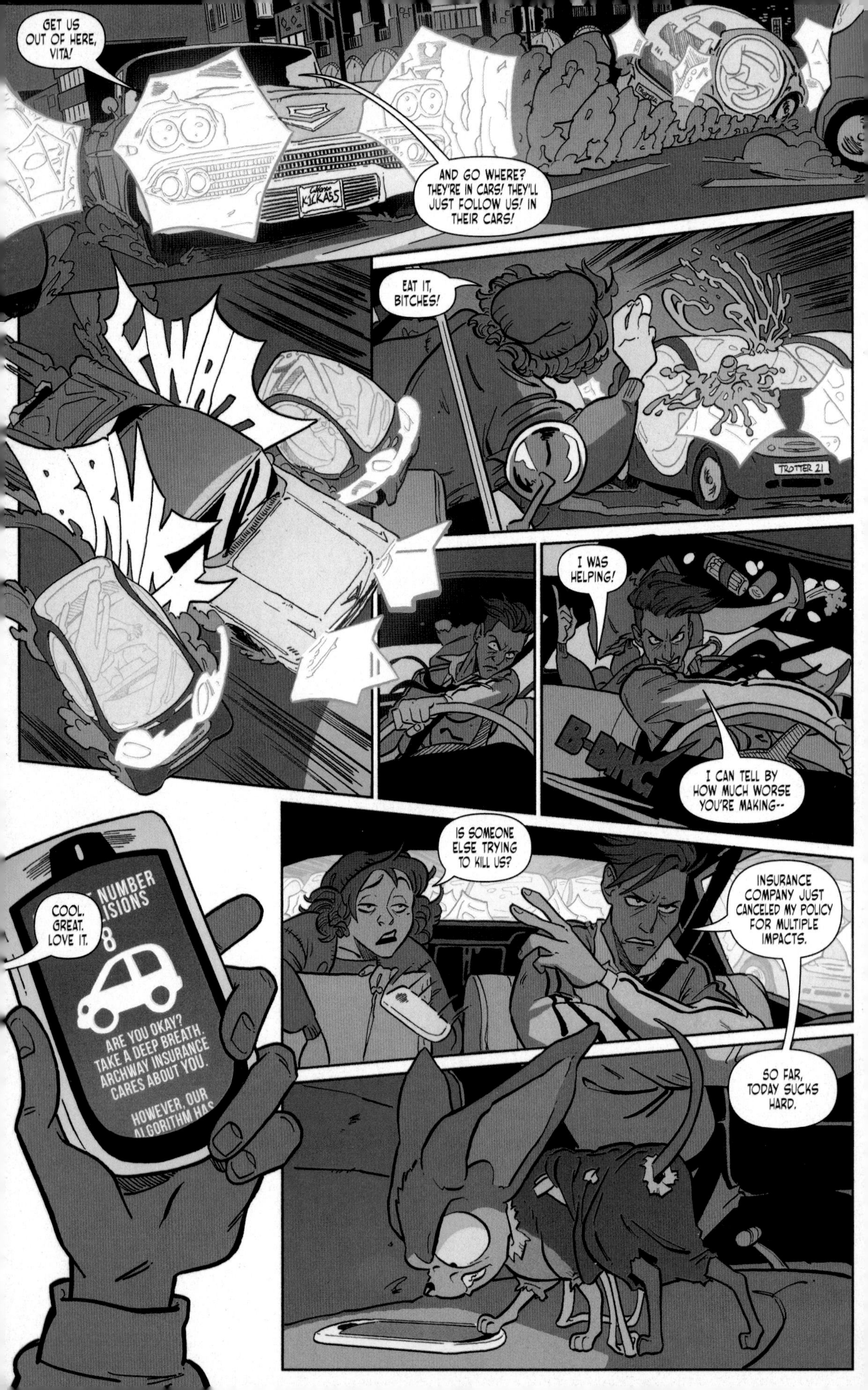
GET US OUT OF HERE, VITA!
KICKASS
AND GO WHERE? THEY'RE IN CARS! THEY'LL JUST FOLLOW US! IN THEIR CARS!
EAT IT, BITCHES!
TROTTER 21
I WAS HELPING!
I CAN TELL BY HOW MUCH WORSE YOU'RE MAKING--
IS SOMEONE ELSE TRYING TO KILL US?
INSURANCE COMPANY JUST CANCELED MY POLICY FOR MULTIPLE IMPACTS.
SO FAR, TODAY SUCKS HARD.
NUMBER
LISIONS
8
ARE YOU OKAY? TAKE A DEEP BREATH. ARCHWAY INSURANCE CARES ABOUT YOU.
HOWEVER, OUR
COOL. GREAT. LOVE IT.

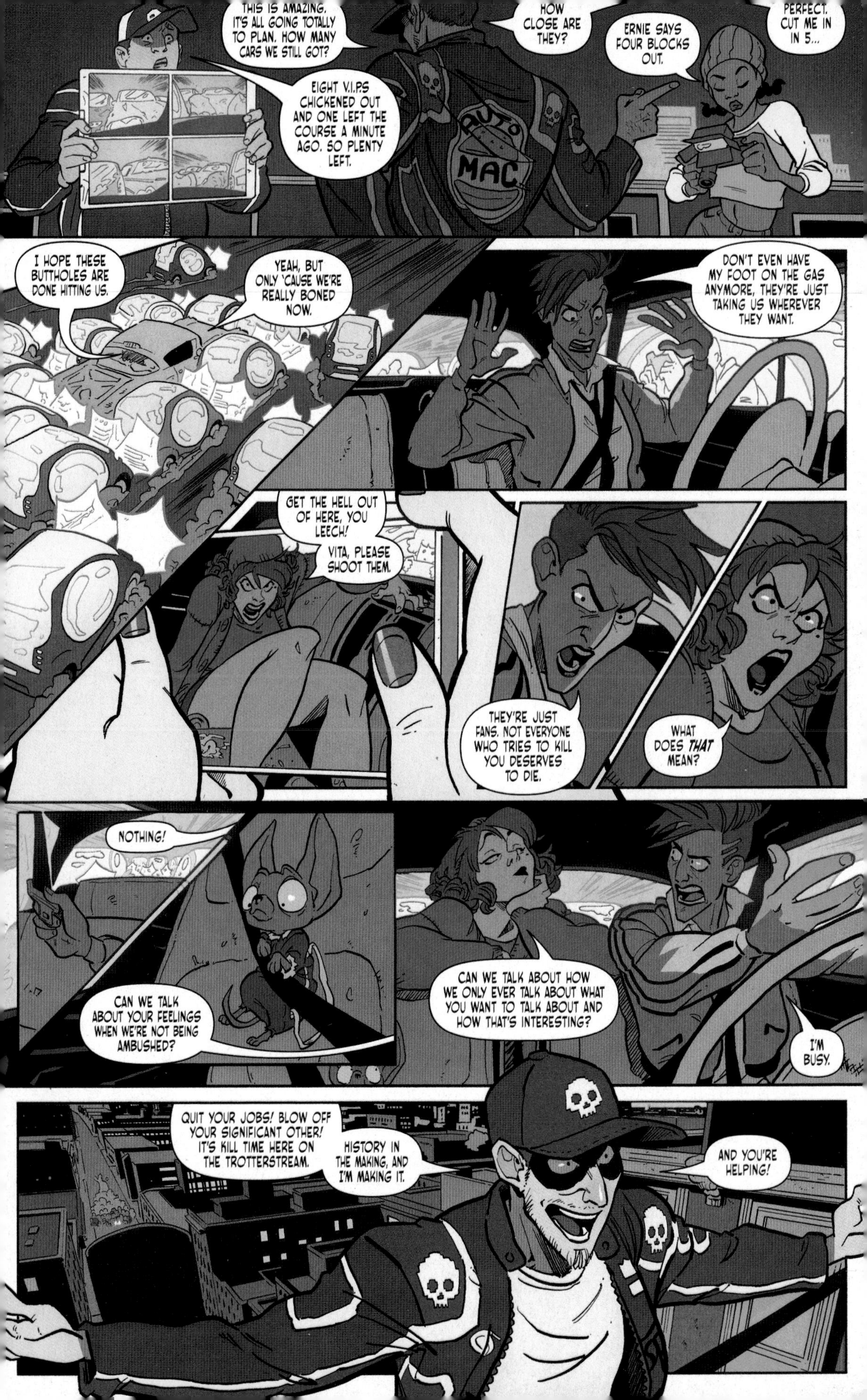
THIS IS AMAZING. IT'S ALL GOING TOTALLY TO PLAN. HOW MANY CARS WE STILL GOT?
EIGHT V.I.P.S CHICKENED OUT AND ONE LEFT THE COURSE A MINUTE AGO. SO PLENTY LEFT.
HOW CLOSE ARE THEY?
ERNIE SAYS FOUR BLOCKS OUT.
PERFECT. CUT ME IN IN 5...
AUTO MAC
I HOPE THESE BUTTHOLES ARE DONE HITTING US.
YEAH, BUT ONLY 'CAUSE WE'RE REALLY BONED NOW.
DON'T EVEN HAVE MY FOOT ON THE GAS ANYMORE, THEY'RE JUST TAKING US WHEREVER THEY WANT.
GET THE HELL OUT OF HERE, YOU LEECH!
VITA, PLEASE SHOOT THEM.
THEY'RE JUST FANS. NOT EVERYONE WHO TRIES TO KILL YOU DESERVES TO DIE.
WHAT DOES *THAT* MEAN?
NOTHING!
CAN WE TALK ABOUT YOUR FEELINGS WHEN WE'RE NOT BEING AMBUSHED?
CAN WE TALK ABOUT HOW WE ONLY EVER TALK ABOUT WHAT YOU WANT TO TALK ABOUT AND HOW THAT'S INTERESTING?
I'M BUSY.
QUIT YOUR JOBS! BLOW OFF YOUR SIGNIFICANT OTHER! IT'S KILL TIME HERE ON THE TROTTERSTREAM.
HISTORY IN THE MAKING, AND I'M MAKING IT.
AND YOU'RE HELPING!

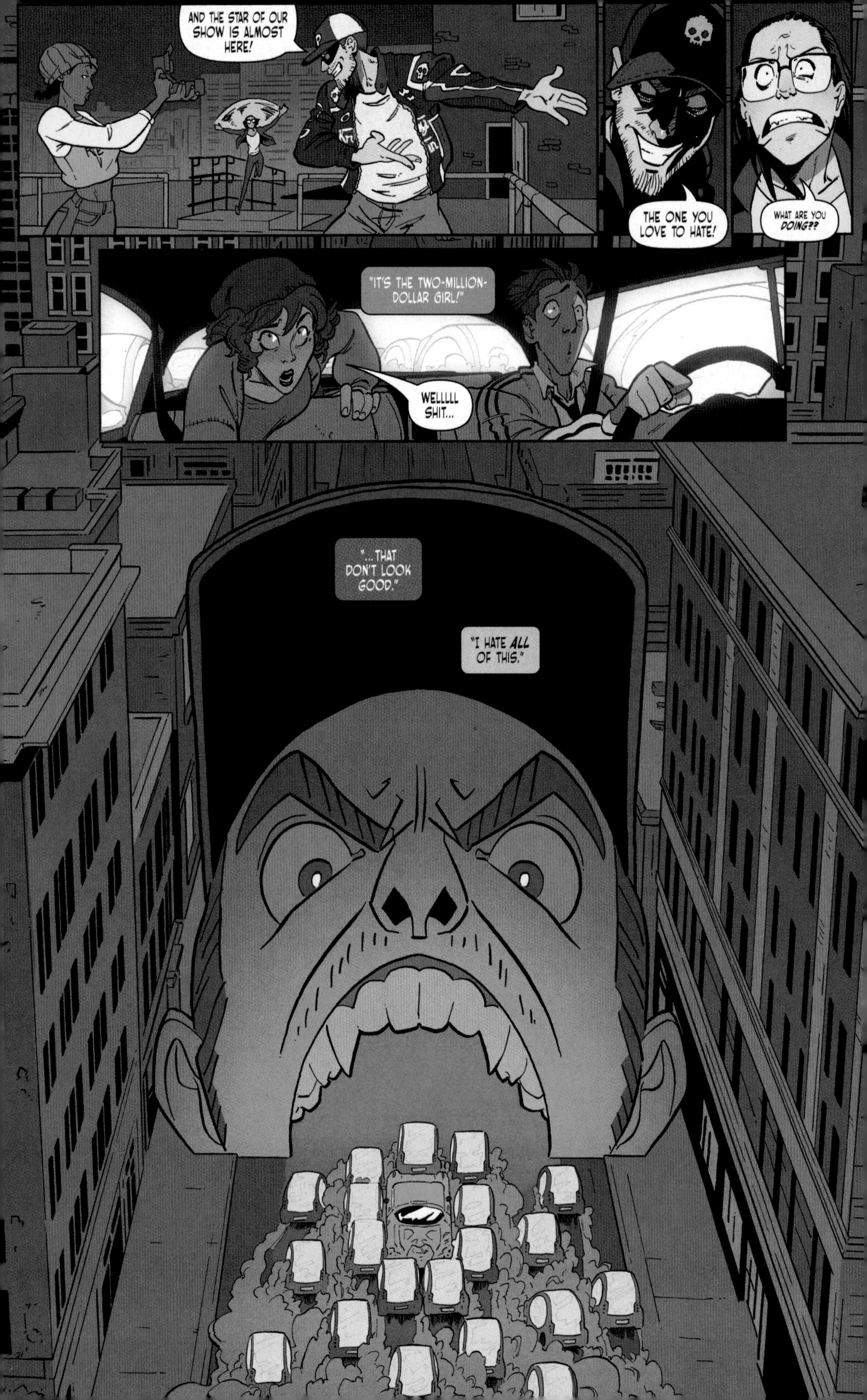
AND THE STAR OF OUR SHOW IS ALMOST HERE!
THE ONE YOU LOVE TO HATE!
WHAT ARE YOU DOING??
"IT'S THE TWO-MILLION-DOLLAR GIRL!"
WELLLLL SHIT...
"...THAT DON'T LOOK GOOD."
"I HATE ALL OF THIS."

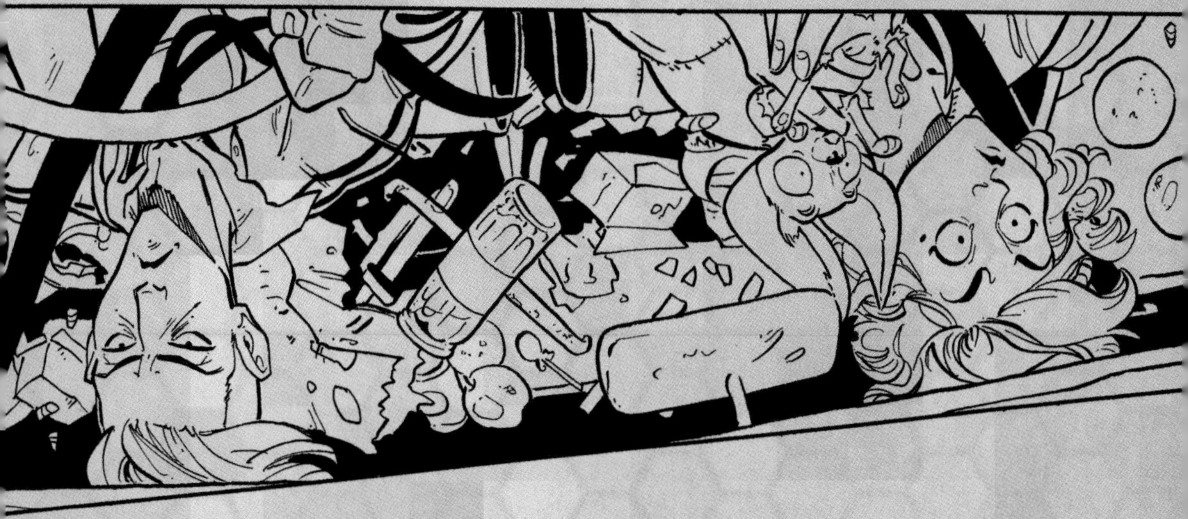

CHAPTER SIX

I CAN'T DIE IN L.A.

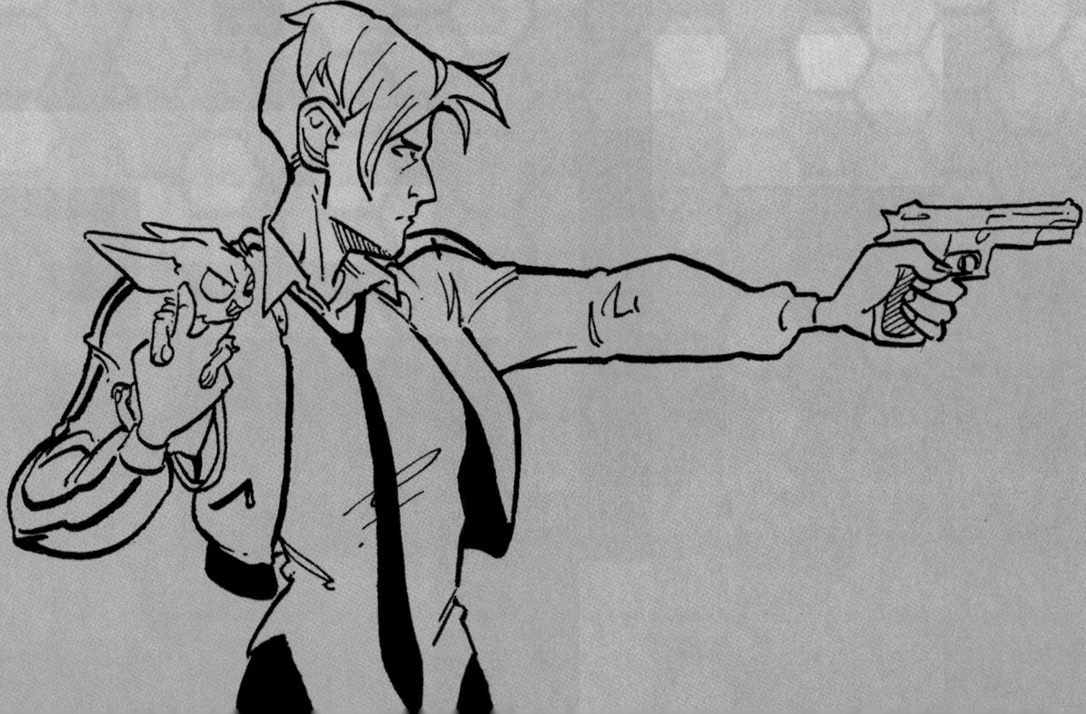

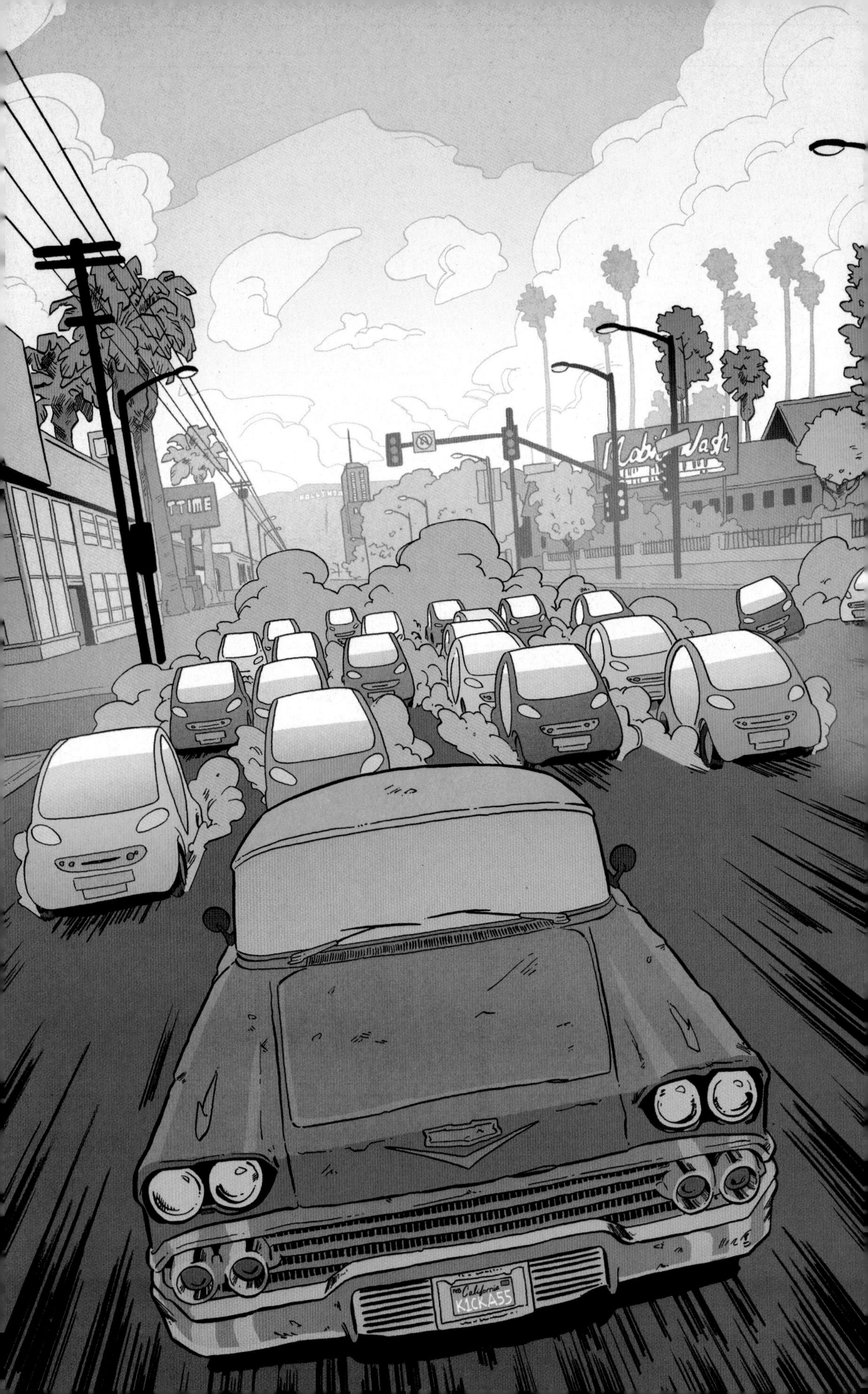
TTIME
California
K1CKA55

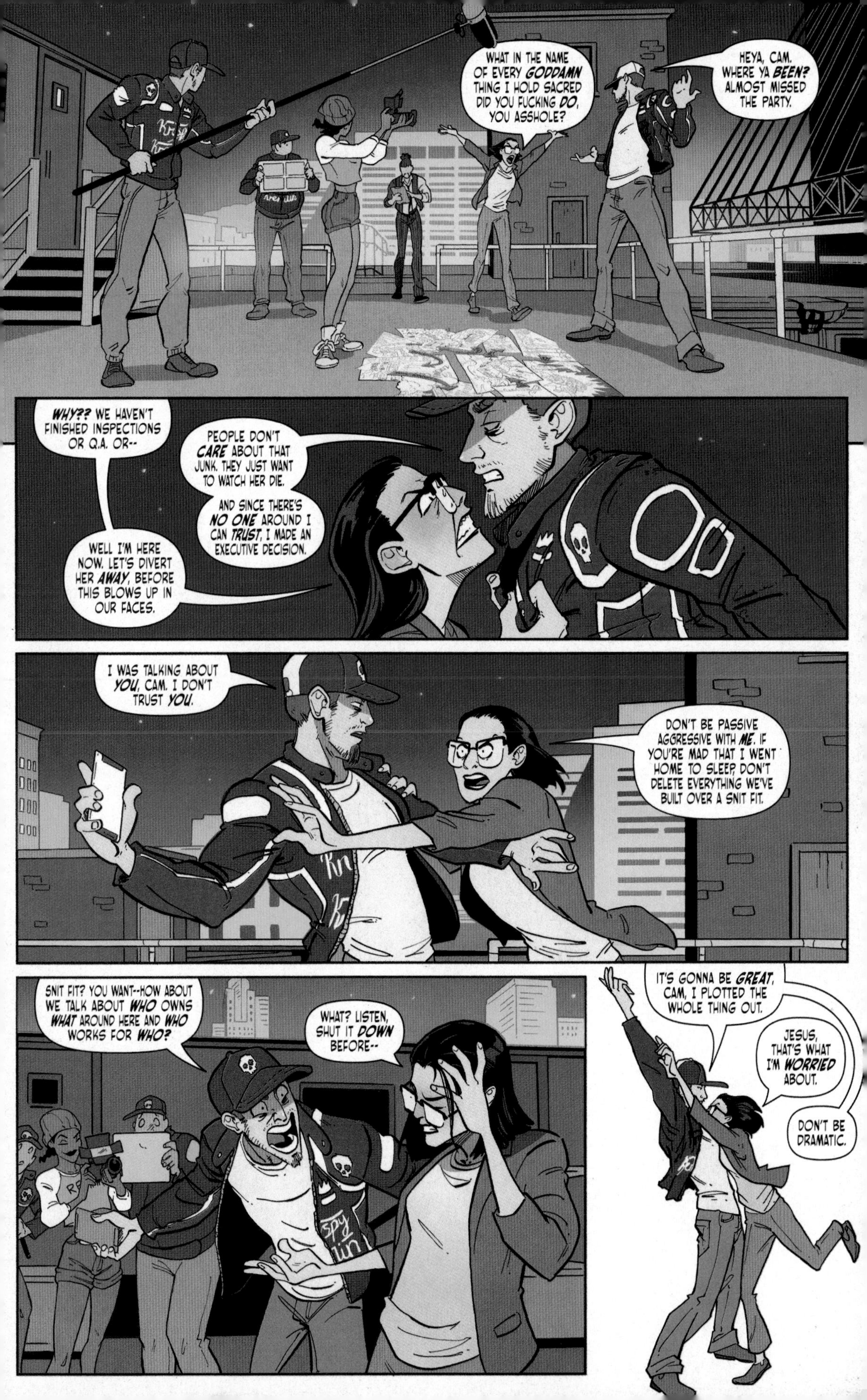
WHAT IN THE NAME OF EVERY GODDAMN THING I HOLD SACRED DID YOU FUCKING DO, YOU ASSHOLE?
HEYA, CAM. WHERE YA BEEN? ALMOST MISSED THE PARTY.
WHY?? WE HAVEN'T FINISHED INSPECTIONS OR Q.A. OR--
PEOPLE DON'T CARE ABOUT THAT JUNK. THEY JUST WANT TO WATCH HER DIE.
AND SINCE THERE'S NO ONE AROUND I CAN TRUST, I MADE AN EXECUTIVE DECISION.
WELL I'M HERE NOW. LET'S DIVERT HER AWAY, BEFORE THIS BLOWS UP IN OUR FACES.
I WAS TALKING ABOUT YOU, CAM. I DON'T TRUST YOU.
DON'T BE PASSIVE AGGRESSIVE WITH ME. IF YOU'RE MAD THAT I WENT HOME TO SLEEP, DON'T DELETE EVERYTHING WE'VE BUILT OVER A SNIT FIT.
SNIT FIT? YOU WANT--HOW ABOUT WE TALK ABOUT WHO OWNS WHAT AROUND HERE AND WHO WORKS FOR WHO?
WHAT? LISTEN, SHUT IT DOWN BEFORE--
IT'S GONNA BE GREAT, CAM, I PLOTTED THE WHOLE THING OUT.
JESUS, THAT'S WHAT I'M WORRIED ABOUT.
DON'T BE DRAMATIC.

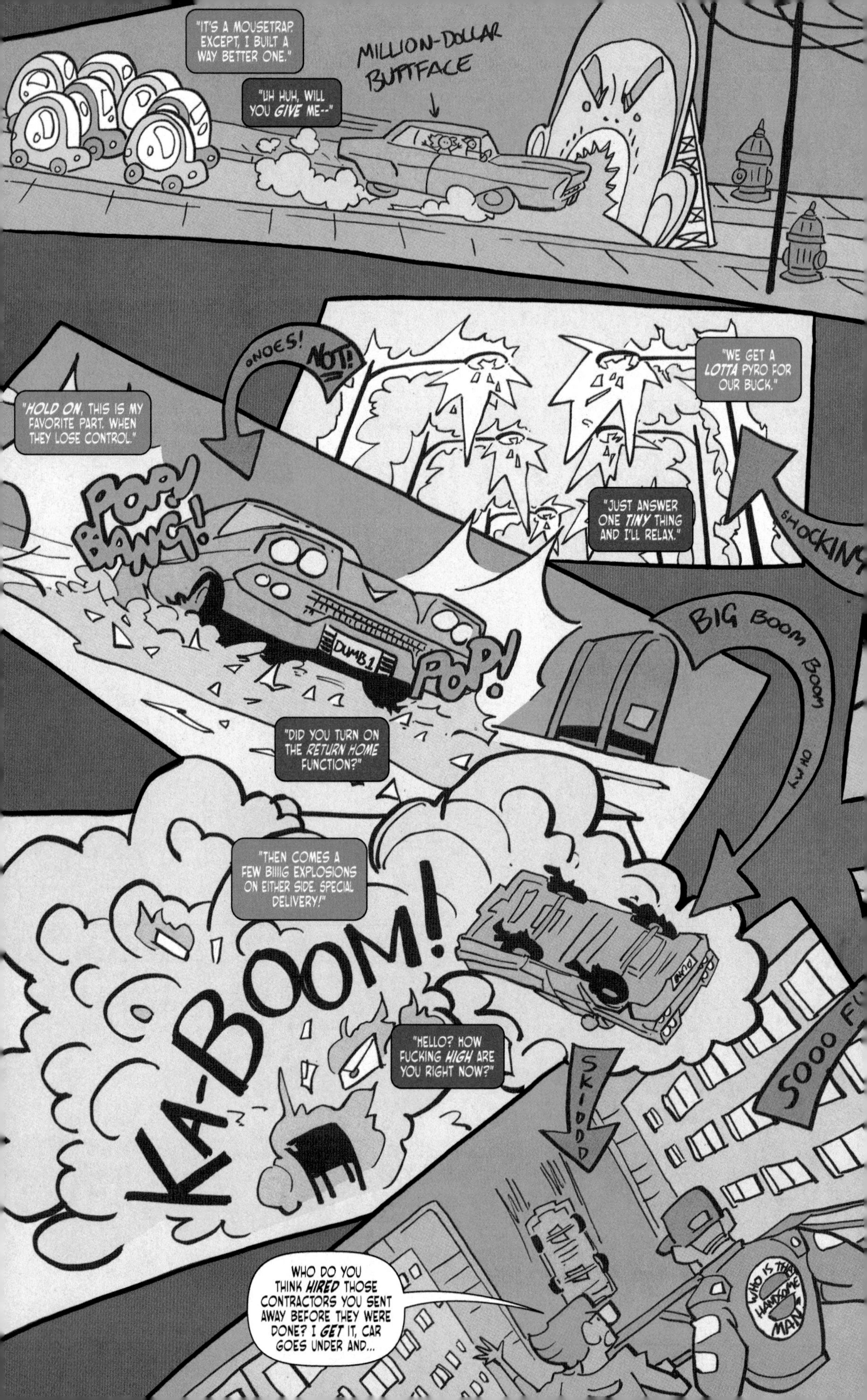
"IT'S A MOUSETRAP. EXCEPT, I BUILT A WAY BETTER ONE."
"UH HUH, WILL YOU *GIVE* ME--"
MILLION-DOLLAR BUTTFACE
"HOLD ON, THIS IS MY FAVORITE PART. WHEN THEY LOSE CONTROL."
GNOES! NOT!
"WE GET A *LOTTA* PYRO FOR OUR BUCK."
POP! BANG!
"JUST ANSWER ONE *TINY* THING AND I'LL RELAX."
DUMB 1
POP!
BIG BOOM BOOM OH MY
"DID YOU TURN ON THE *RETURN HOME* FUNCTION?"
"THEN COMES A FEW BIIIIG EXPLOSIONS ON EITHER SIDE. SPECIAL DELIVERY!"
KA-BOOM!
"HELLO? HOW FUCKING *HIGH* ARE YOU RIGHT NOW?"
SKIDDD
WHO DO YOU THINK *HIRED* THOSE CONTRACTORS YOU SENT AWAY BEFORE THEY WERE DONE? I *GET* IT, CAR GOES UNDER AND...
WHO IS THAT HANDSOME MAN

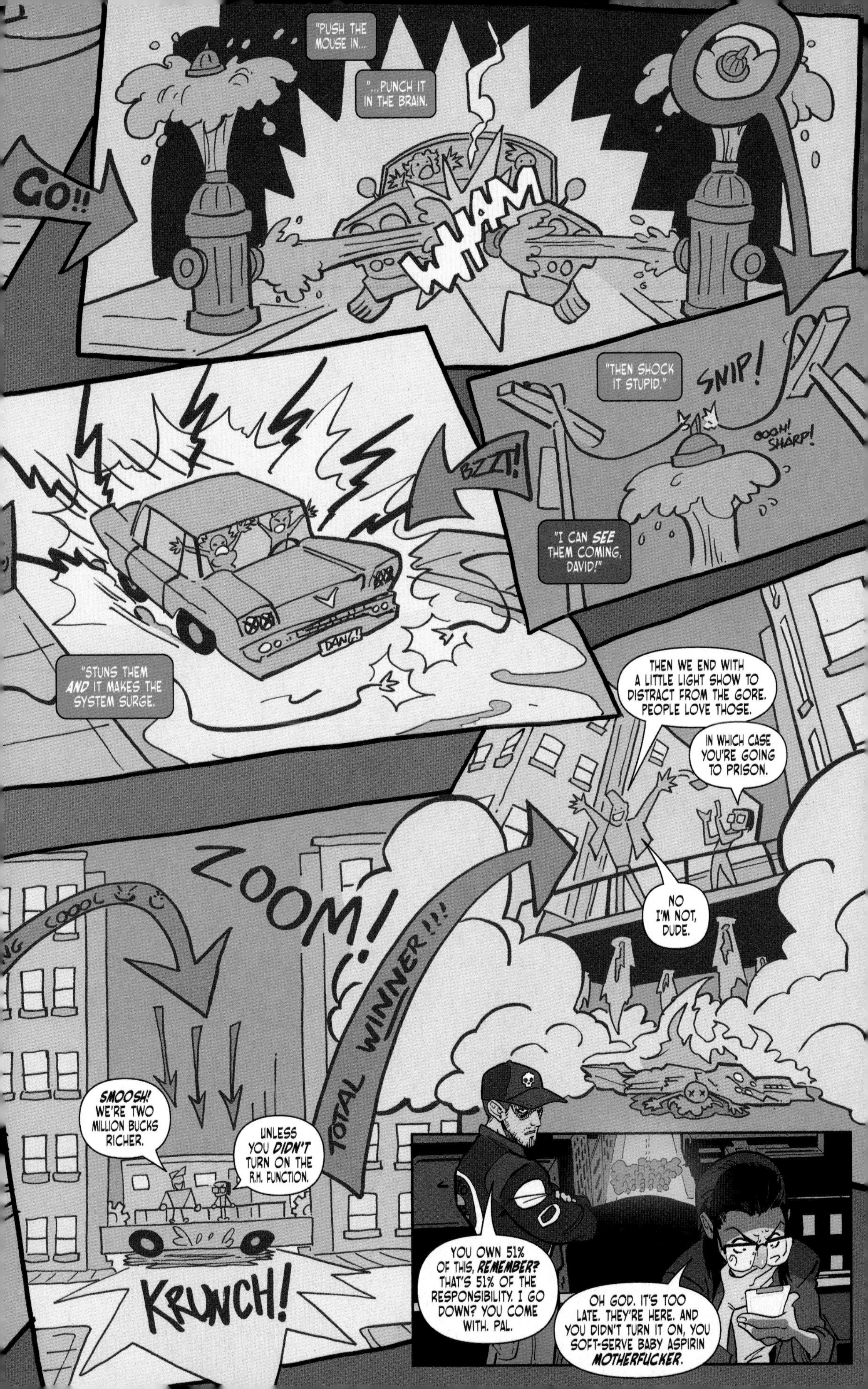
"PUSH THE MOUSE IN...
"...PUNCH IT IN THE BRAIN.
GO!!
WHAM
"THEN SHOCK IT STUPID."
SNIP!
OOOH! SHARP!
BZZT!
"I CAN SEE THEM COMING, DAVID!"
DANG!
"STUNS THEM AND IT MAKES THE SYSTEM SURGE.
THEN WE END WITH A LITTLE LIGHT SHOW TO DISTRACT FROM THE GORE. PEOPLE LOVE THOSE.
IN WHICH CASE YOU'RE GOING TO PRISON.
NO I'M NOT, DUDE.
ZOOM!
TOTAL WINNER!!!
SMOOSH! WE'RE TWO MILLION BUCKS RICHER.
UNLESS YOU DIDN'T TURN ON THE R.H. FUNCTION.
KRUNCH!
YOU OWN 51% OF THIS, REMEMBER? THAT'S 51% OF THE RESPONSIBILITY. I GO DOWN? YOU COME WITH. PAL.
OH GOD. IT'S TOO LATE. THEY'RE HERE. AND YOU DIDN'T TURN IT ON, YOU SOFT-SERVE BABY ASPIRIN MOTHERFUCKER.

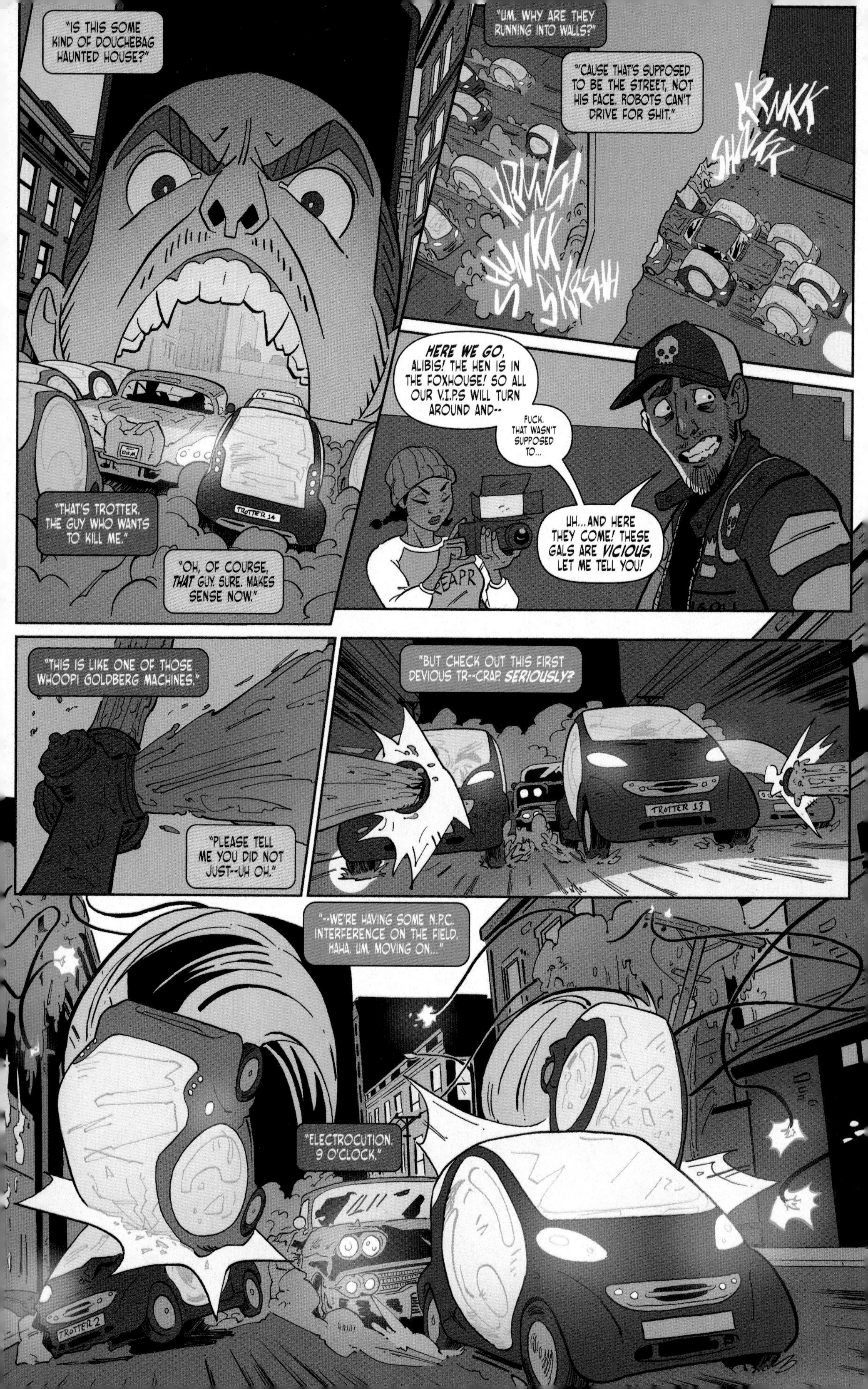
"IS THIS SOME KIND OF DOUCHEBAG HAUNTED HOUSE?"
"THAT'S TROTTER. THE GUY WHO WANTS TO KILL ME."
"OH, OF COURSE, THAT GUY. SURE. MAKES SENSE NOW."
"UM. WHY ARE THEY RUNNING INTO WALLS?"
"CAUSE THAT'S SUPPOSED TO BE THE STREET, NOT HIS FACE. ROBOTS CAN'T DRIVE FOR SHIT."
KRUNCH
SHUNKK
SKRSHH
KRNKK
SHUNKK
HERE WE GO, ALIBIS! THE HEN IS IN THE FOXHOUSE! SO ALL OUR V.I.P.S WILL TURN AROUND AND--
FUCK. THAT WASN'T SUPPOSED TO...
UH...AND HERE THEY COME! THESE GALS ARE VICIOUS, LET ME TELL YOU!
"THIS IS LIKE ONE OF THOSE WHOOPI GOLDBERG MACHINES."
"PLEASE TELL ME YOU DID NOT JUST--UH OH."
"BUT CHECK OUT THIS FIRST DEVIOUS TR--CRAP. SERIOUSLY?"
TROTTER 13
"--WE'RE HAVING SOME N.P.C. INTERFERENCE ON THE FIELD. HAHA. UM. MOVING ON..."
"ELECTROCUTION. 9 O'CLOCK."
TROTTER 2

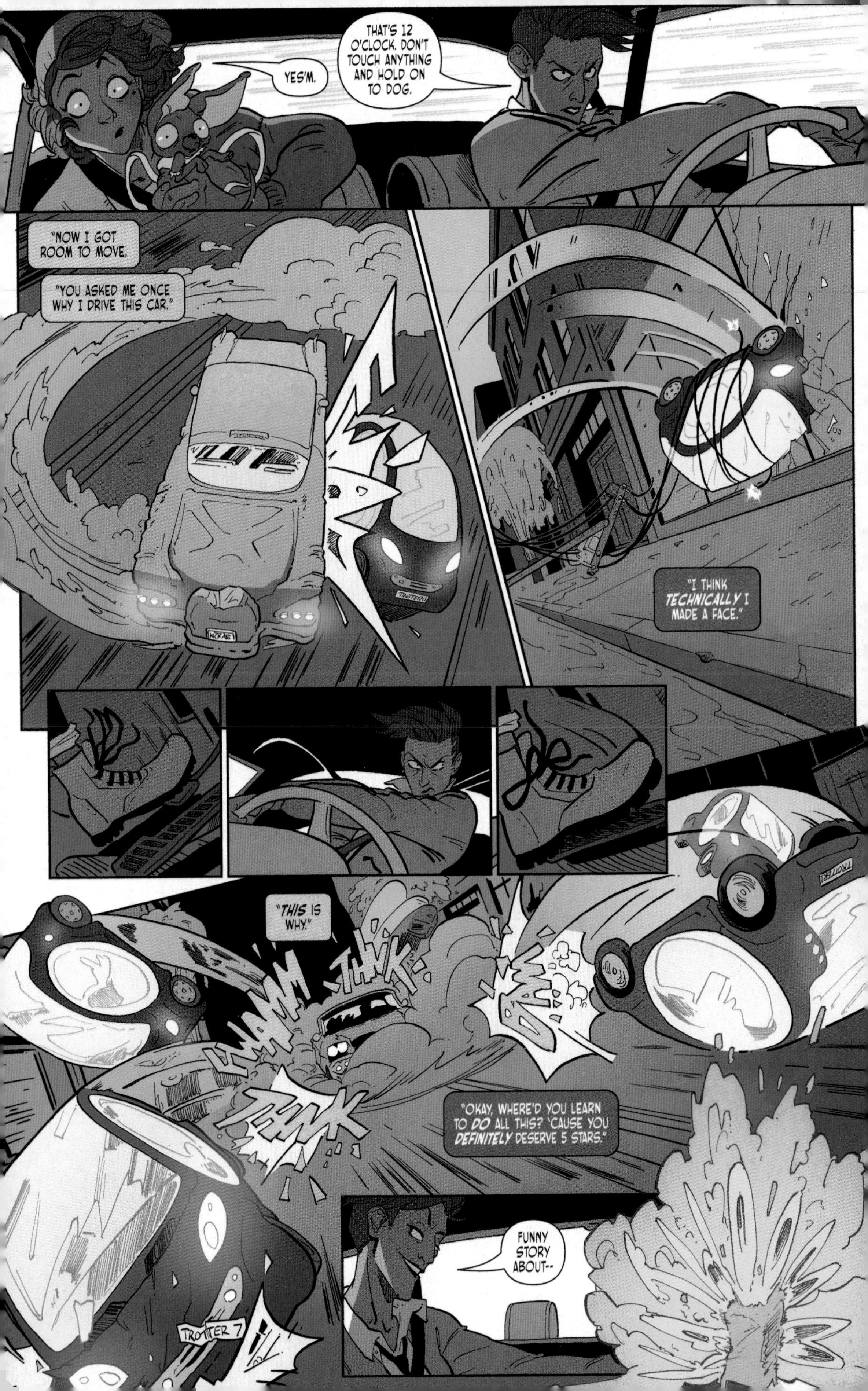

YES'M.
THAT'S 12 O'CLOCK. DON'T TOUCH ANYTHING AND HOLD ON TO DOG.
"NOW I GOT ROOM TO MOVE.
"YOU ASKED ME ONCE WHY I DRIVE THIS CAR."
"I THINK TECHNICALLY I MADE A FACE."
"THIS IS WHY."
WHAM
THNK
BAM
THNK
"OKAY, WHERE'D YOU LEARN TO DO ALL THIS? 'CAUSE YOU DEFINITELY DESERVE 5 STARS."
FUNNY STORY ABOUT--
TROTTER 7

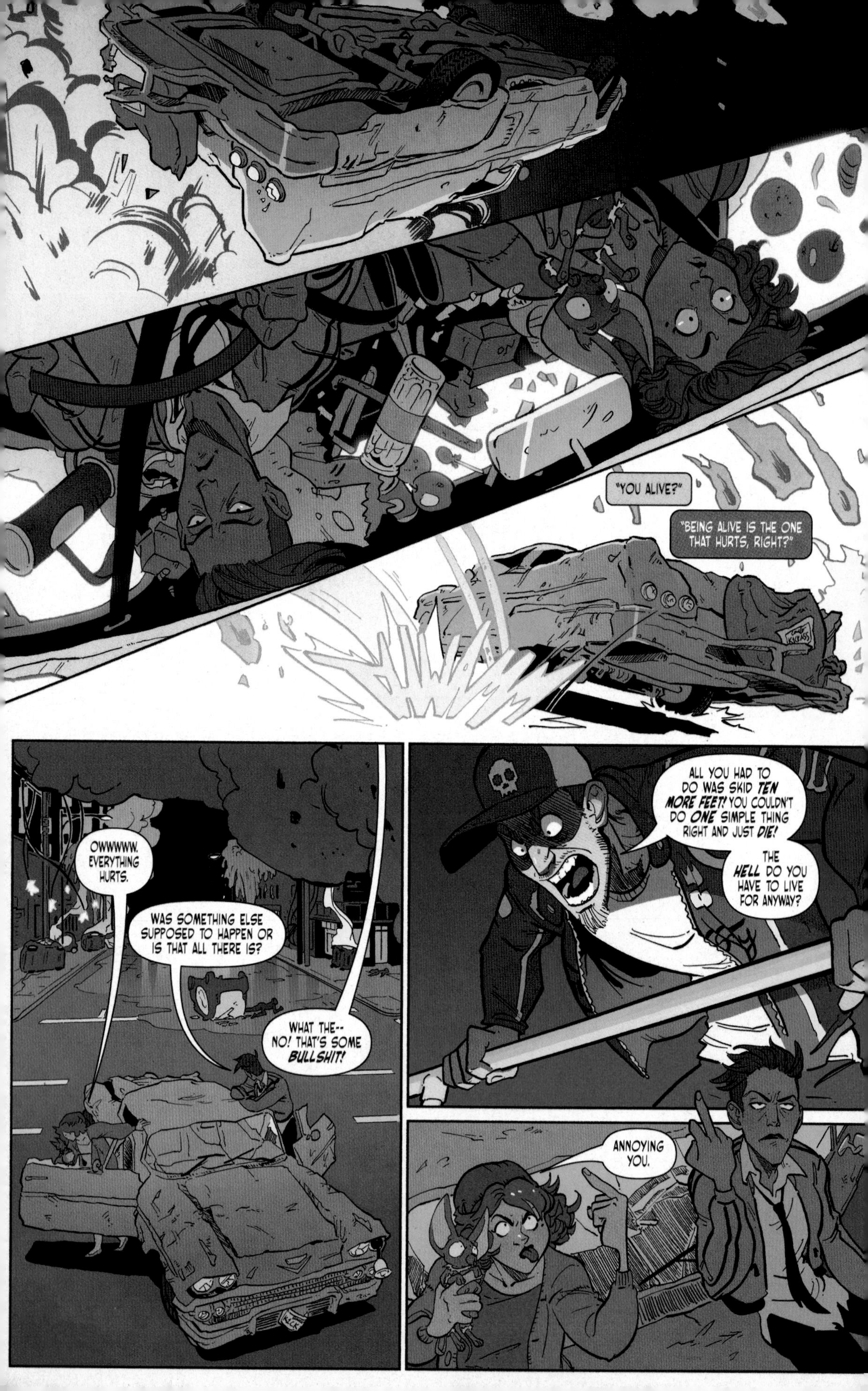
"YOU ALIVE?"
"BEING ALIVE IS THE ONE THAT HURTS, RIGHT?"
OWWWWW. EVERYTHING HURTS.
WAS SOMETHING ELSE SUPPOSED TO HAPPEN OR IS THAT ALL THERE IS?
WHAT THE-- NO! THAT'S SOME BULLSHIT!
ALL YOU HAD TO DO WAS SKID TEN MORE FEET! YOU COULDN'T DO ONE SIMPLE THING RIGHT AND JUST DIE!
THE HELL DO YOU HAVE TO LIVE FOR ANYWAY?
ANNOYING YOU.

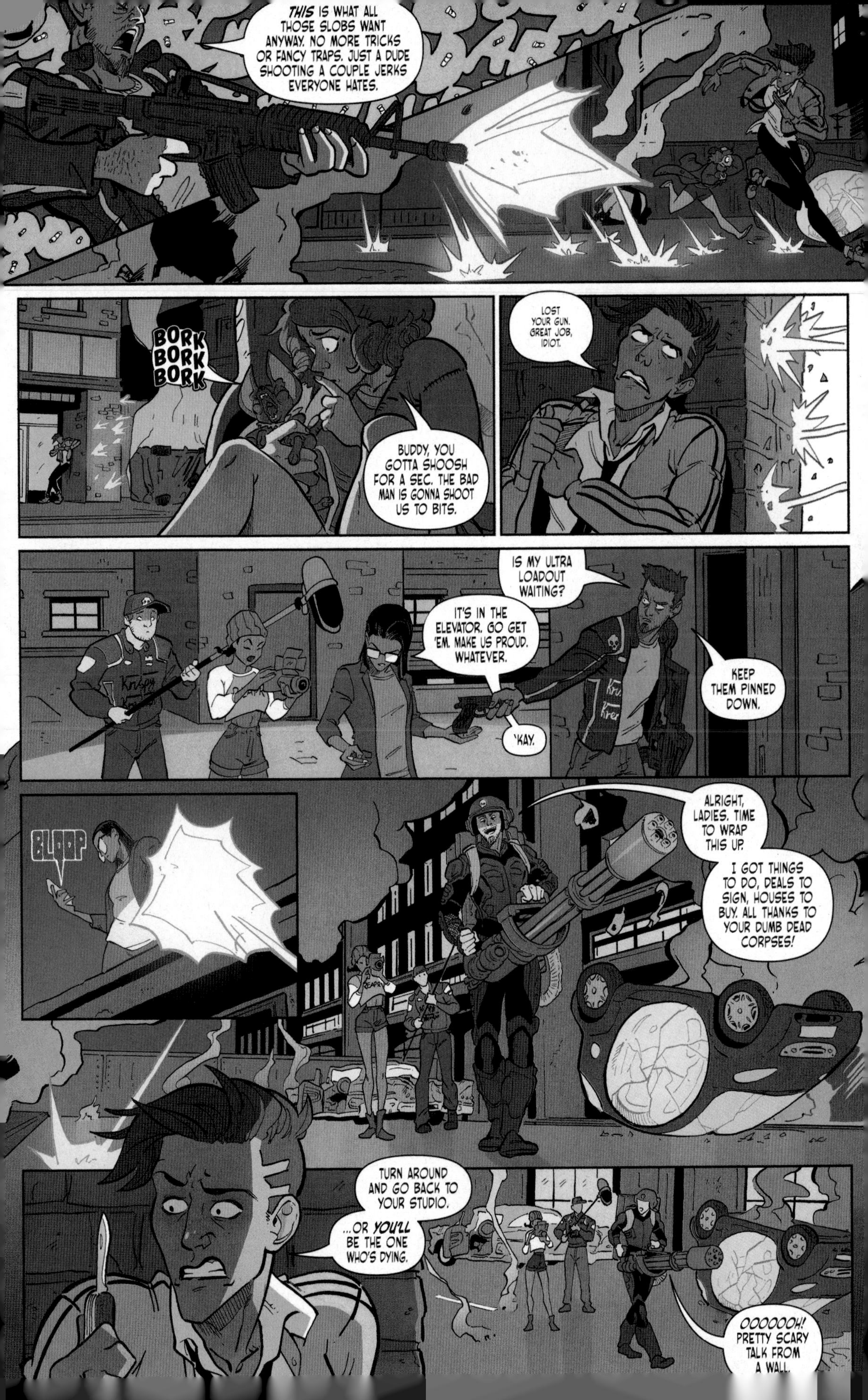
THIS IS WHAT ALL THOSE SLOBS WANT ANYWAY. NO MORE TRICKS OR FANCY TRAPS. JUST A DUDE SHOOTING A COUPLE JERKS EVERYONE HATES.
BORK BORK BORK
BUDDY, YOU GOTTA SHOOSH FOR A SEC. THE BAD MAN IS GONNA SHOOT US TO BITS.
LOST YOUR GUN. GREAT JOB, IDIOT.
IS MY ULTRA LOADOUT WAITING?
IT'S IN THE ELEVATOR. GO GET 'EM. MAKE US PROUD. WHATEVER.
KEEP THEM PINNED DOWN.
'KAY.
BLOOP
ALRIGHT, LADIES. TIME TO WRAP THIS UP.
I GOT THINGS TO DO, DEALS TO SIGN, HOUSES TO BUY. ALL THANKS TO YOUR DUMB DEAD CORPSES!
TURN AROUND AND GO BACK TO YOUR STUDIO.
...OR YOU'LL BE THE ONE WHO'S DYING.
OOOOOOH! PRETTY SCARY TALK FROM A WALL.

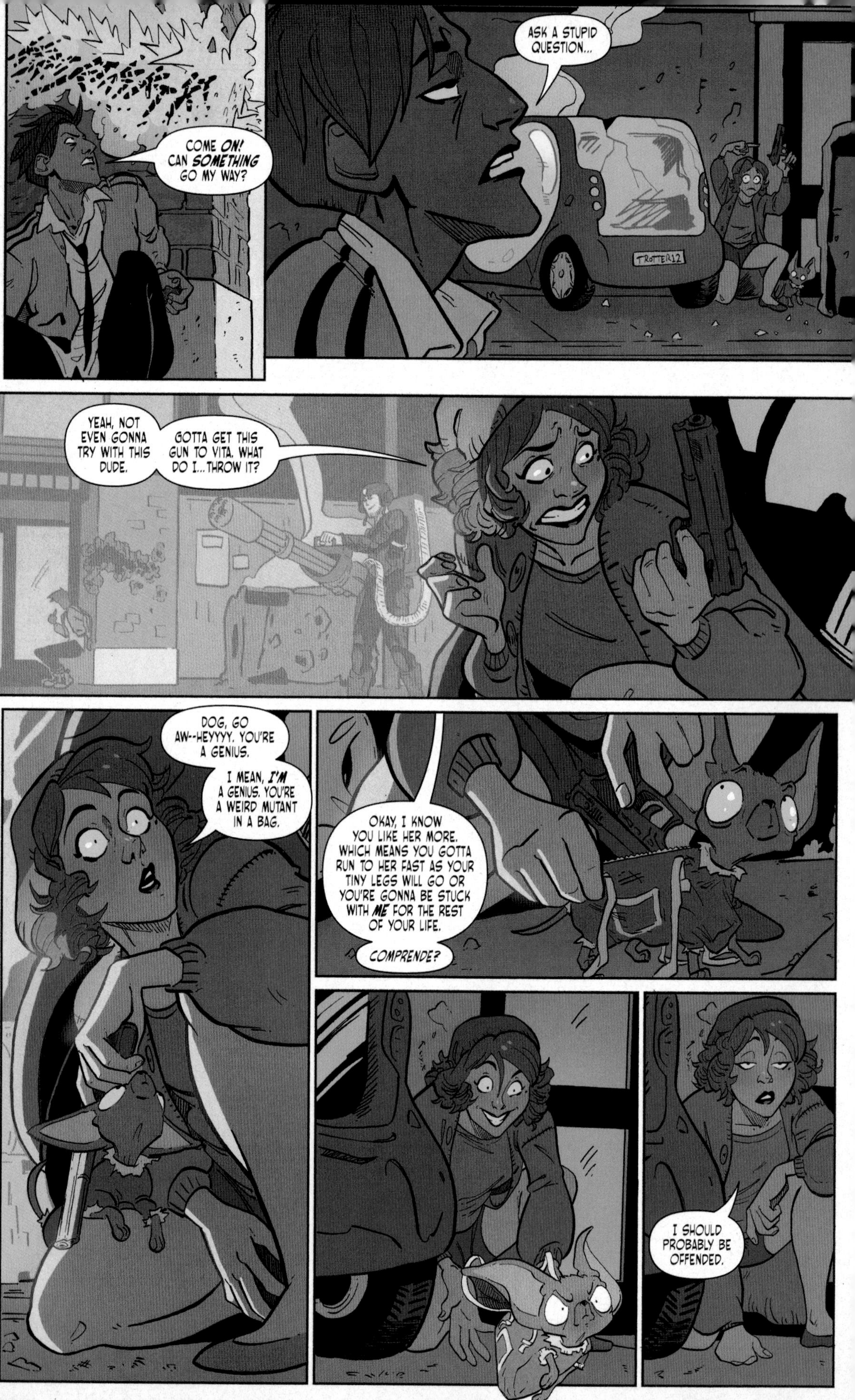
COME ON! CAN SOMETHING GO MY WAY?
ASK A STUPID QUESTION...
TROTTER12
YEAH, NOT EVEN GONNA TRY WITH THIS DUDE.
GOTTA GET THIS GUN TO VITA. WHAT DO I...THROW IT?
DOG, GO AW--HEYYYY. YOU'RE A GENIUS.
I MEAN, I'M A GENIUS. YOU'RE A WEIRD MUTANT IN A BAG.
OKAY, I KNOW YOU LIKE HER MORE. WHICH MEANS YOU GOTTA RUN TO HER FAST AS YOUR TINY LEGS WILL GO OR YOU'RE GONNA BE STUCK WITH ME FOR THE REST OF YOUR LIFE.
COMPRENDE?
I SHOULD PROBABLY BE OFFENDED.

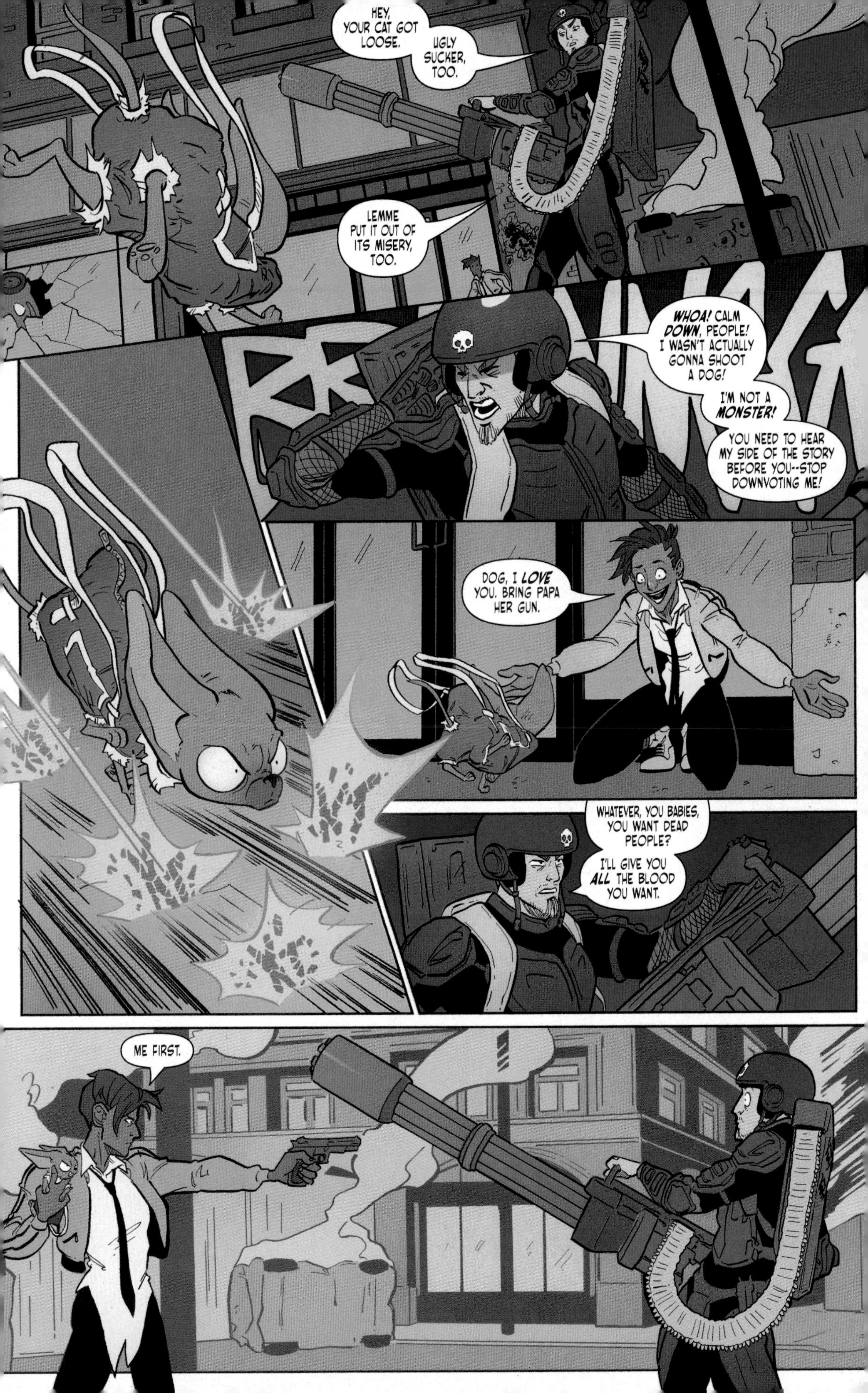
HEY, YOUR CAT GOT LOOSE.
UGLY SUCKER, TOO.
LEMME PUT IT OUT OF ITS MISERY, TOO.
WHOA! CALM DOWN, PEOPLE! I WASN'T ACTUALLY GONNA SHOOT A DOG!
I'M NOT A MONSTER!
YOU NEED TO HEAR MY SIDE OF THE STORY BEFORE YOU--STOP DOWNVOTING ME!
DOG, I LOVE YOU. BRING PAPA HER GUN.
WHATEVER, YOU BABIES, YOU WANT DEAD PEOPLE?
I'LL GIVE YOU ALL THE BLOOD YOU WANT.
ME FIRST.

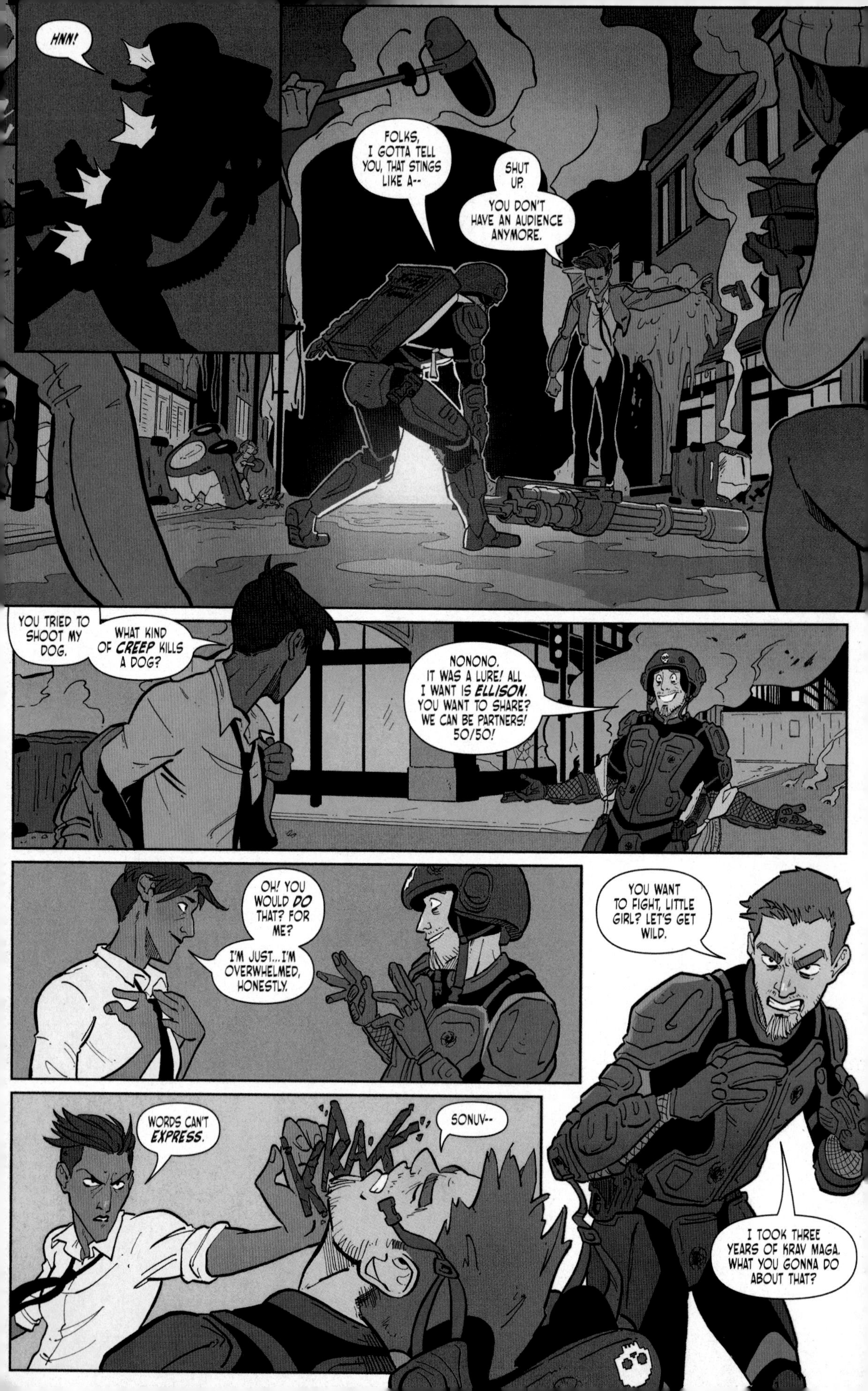
HNN!
FOLKS, I GOTTA TELL YOU, THAT STINGS LIKE A--
SHUT UP.
YOU DON'T HAVE AN AUDIENCE ANYMORE.
YOU TRIED TO SHOOT MY DOG.
WHAT KIND OF CREEP KILLS A DOG?
NONONO. IT WAS A LURE! ALL I WANT IS ELLISON. YOU WANT TO SHARE? WE CAN BE PARTNERS! 50/50!
OH! YOU WOULD DO THAT? FOR ME?
I'M JUST...I'M OVERWHELMED, HONESTLY.
YOU WANT TO FIGHT, LITTLE GIRL? LET'S GET WILD.
I TOOK THREE YEARS OF KRAV MAGA. WHAT YOU GONNA DO ABOUT THAT?
WORDS CAN'T EXPRESS.
KRAK
SONUV--

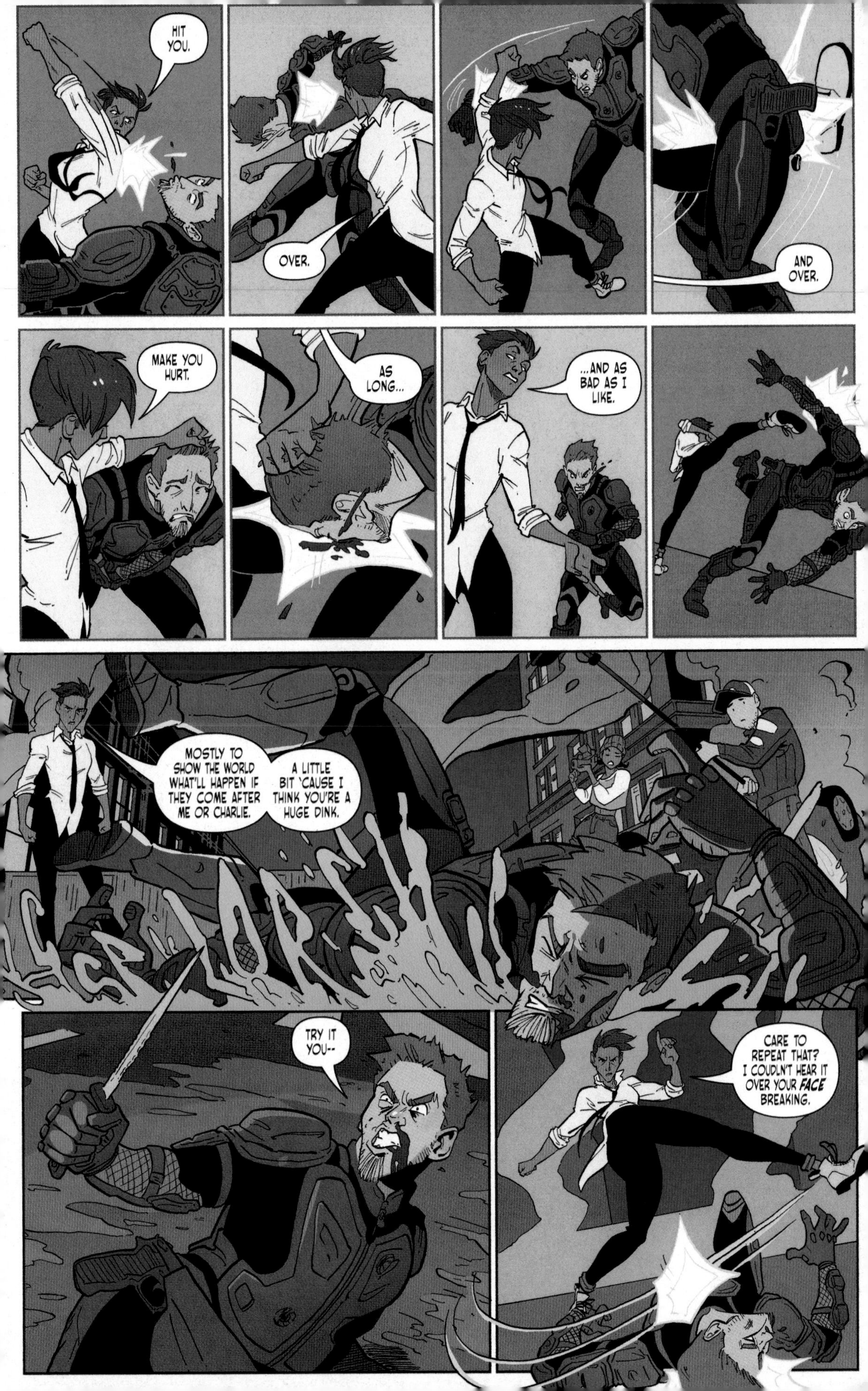
HIT YOU.
OVER.
AND OVER.
MAKE YOU HURT.
AS LONG...
...AND AS BAD AS I LIKE.
MOSTLY TO SHOW THE WORLD WHAT'LL HAPPEN IF THEY COME AFTER ME OR CHARLIE.
A LITTLE BIT 'CAUSE I THINK YOU'RE A HUGE DINK.
TRY IT YOU--
CARE TO REPEAT THAT? I COULDN'T HEAR IT OVER YOUR *FACE* BREAKING.

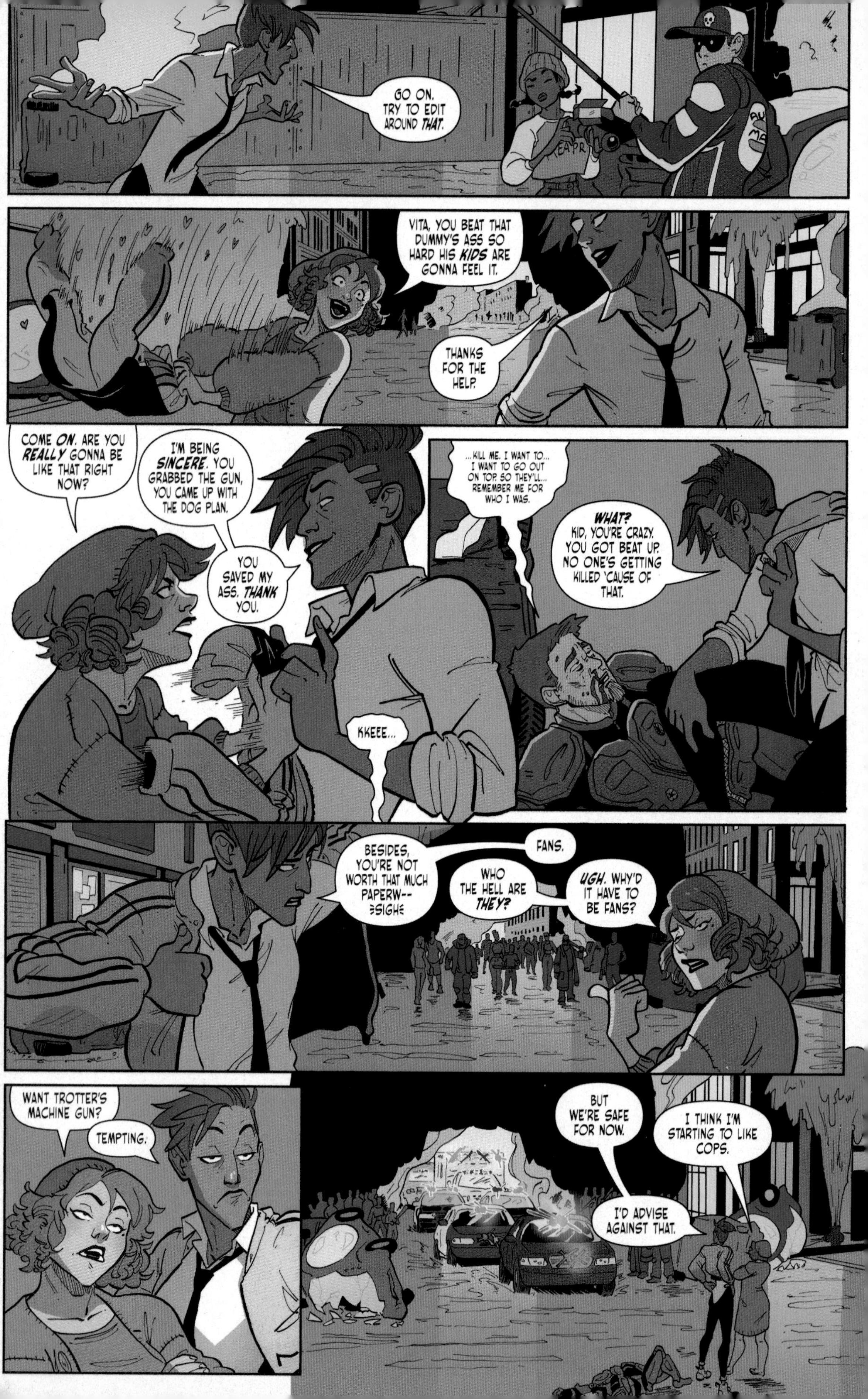
GO ON. TRY TO EDIT AROUND THAT.
VITA, YOU BEAT THAT DUMMY'S ASS SO HARD HIS KIDS ARE GONNA FEEL IT.
THANKS FOR THE HELP.
COME ON. ARE YOU REALLY GONNA BE LIKE THAT RIGHT NOW?
I'M BEING SINCERE. YOU GRABBED THE GUN, YOU CAME UP WITH THE DOG PLAN.
YOU SAVED MY ASS. THANK YOU.
KKEEE...
...KILL ME. I WANT TO... I WANT TO GO OUT ON TOP. SO THEY'LL... REMEMBER ME FOR WHO I WAS.
WHAT? KID, YOU'RE CRAZY. YOU GOT BEAT UP. NO ONE'S GETTING KILLED 'CAUSE OF THAT.
BESIDES, YOU'RE NOT WORTH THAT MUCH PAPERW-- ≋SIGH≋
FANS.
WHO THE HELL ARE THEY?
UGH. WHY'D IT HAVE TO BE FANS?
WANT TROTTER'S MACHINE GUN?
TEMPTING.
BUT WE'RE SAFE FOR NOW.
I THINK I'M STARTING TO LIKE COPS.
I'D ADVISE AGAINST THAT.

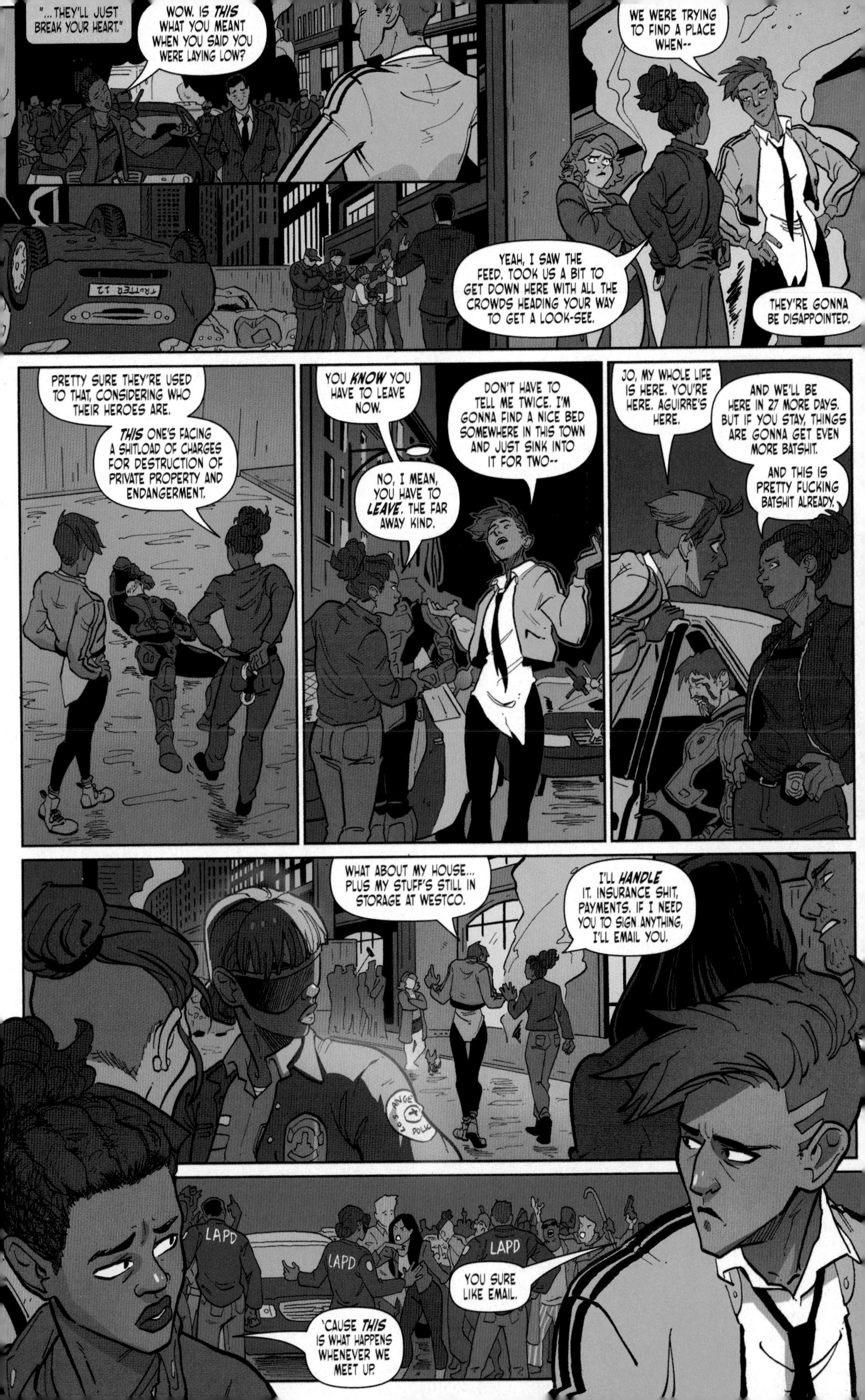
"...THEY'LL JUST BREAK YOUR HEART."
WOW. IS *THIS* WHAT YOU MEANT WHEN YOU SAID YOU WERE LAYING LOW?
WE WERE TRYING TO FIND A PLACE WHEN--
YEAH, I SAW THE FEED. TOOK US A BIT TO GET DOWN HERE WITH ALL THE CROWDS HEADING YOUR WAY TO GET A LOOK-SEE.
THEY'RE GONNA BE DISAPPOINTED.
TROTTER 12
PRETTY SURE THEY'RE USED TO THAT, CONSIDERING WHO THEIR HEROES ARE.
THIS ONE'S FACING A SHITLOAD OF CHARGES FOR DESTRUCTION OF PRIVATE PROPERTY AND ENDANGERMENT.
YOU *KNOW* YOU HAVE TO LEAVE NOW.
DON'T HAVE TO TELL ME TWICE. I'M GONNA FIND A NICE BED SOMEWHERE IN THIS TOWN AND JUST SINK INTO IT FOR TWO--
NO, I MEAN, YOU HAVE TO *LEAVE*. THE FAR AWAY KIND.
JO, MY WHOLE LIFE IS HERE. YOU'RE HERE. AGUIRRE'S HERE.
AND WE'LL BE HERE IN 27 MORE DAYS. BUT IF YOU STAY, THINGS ARE GONNA GET EVEN MORE BATSHIT.
AND THIS IS PRETTY FUCKING BATSHIT ALREADY.
WHAT ABOUT MY HOUSE... PLUS MY STUFF'S STILL IN STORAGE AT WESTCO.
I'LL *HANDLE* IT. INSURANCE SHIT, PAYMENTS. IF I NEED YOU TO SIGN ANYTHING, I'LL EMAIL YOU.
LAPD
LAPD
LAPD
YOU SURE LIKE EMAIL.
'CAUSE *THIS* IS WHAT HAPPENS WHENEVER WE MEET UP.

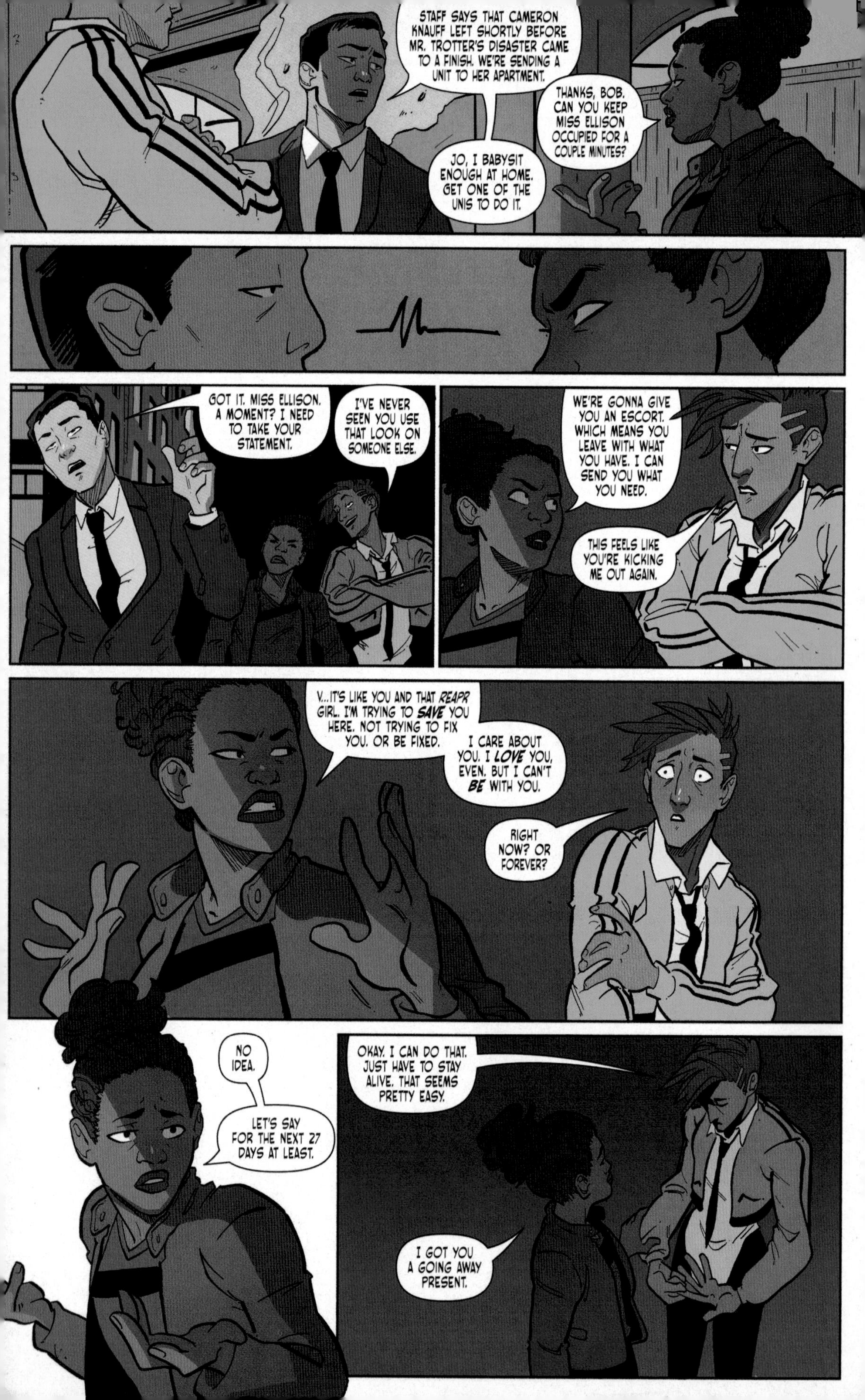
STAFF SAYS THAT CAMERON KNAUFF LEFT SHORTLY BEFORE MR. TROTTER'S DISASTER CAME TO A FINISH. WE'RE SENDING A UNIT TO HER APARTMENT.
THANKS, BOB. CAN YOU KEEP MISS ELLISON OCCUPIED FOR A COUPLE MINUTES?
JO, I BABYSIT ENOUGH AT HOME. GET ONE OF THE UNIS TO DO IT.
GOT IT. MISS ELLISON. A MOMENT? I NEED TO TAKE YOUR STATEMENT.
I'VE NEVER SEEN YOU USE THAT LOOK ON SOMEONE ELSE.
WE'RE GONNA GIVE YOU AN ESCORT. WHICH MEANS YOU LEAVE WITH WHAT YOU HAVE. I CAN SEND YOU WHAT YOU NEED.
THIS FEELS LIKE YOU'RE KICKING ME OUT AGAIN.
V...IT'S LIKE YOU AND THAT *REAPR* GIRL. I'M TRYING TO ***SAVE*** YOU HERE. NOT TRYING TO FIX YOU. OR BE FIXED.
I CARE ABOUT YOU. I ***LOVE*** YOU, EVEN. BUT I CAN'T ***BE*** WITH YOU.
RIGHT NOW? OR FOREVER?
NO IDEA.
LET'S SAY FOR THE NEXT 27 DAYS AT LEAST.
OKAY. I CAN DO THAT. JUST HAVE TO STAY ALIVE. THAT SEEMS PRETTY EASY.
I GOT YOU A GOING AWAY PRESENT.

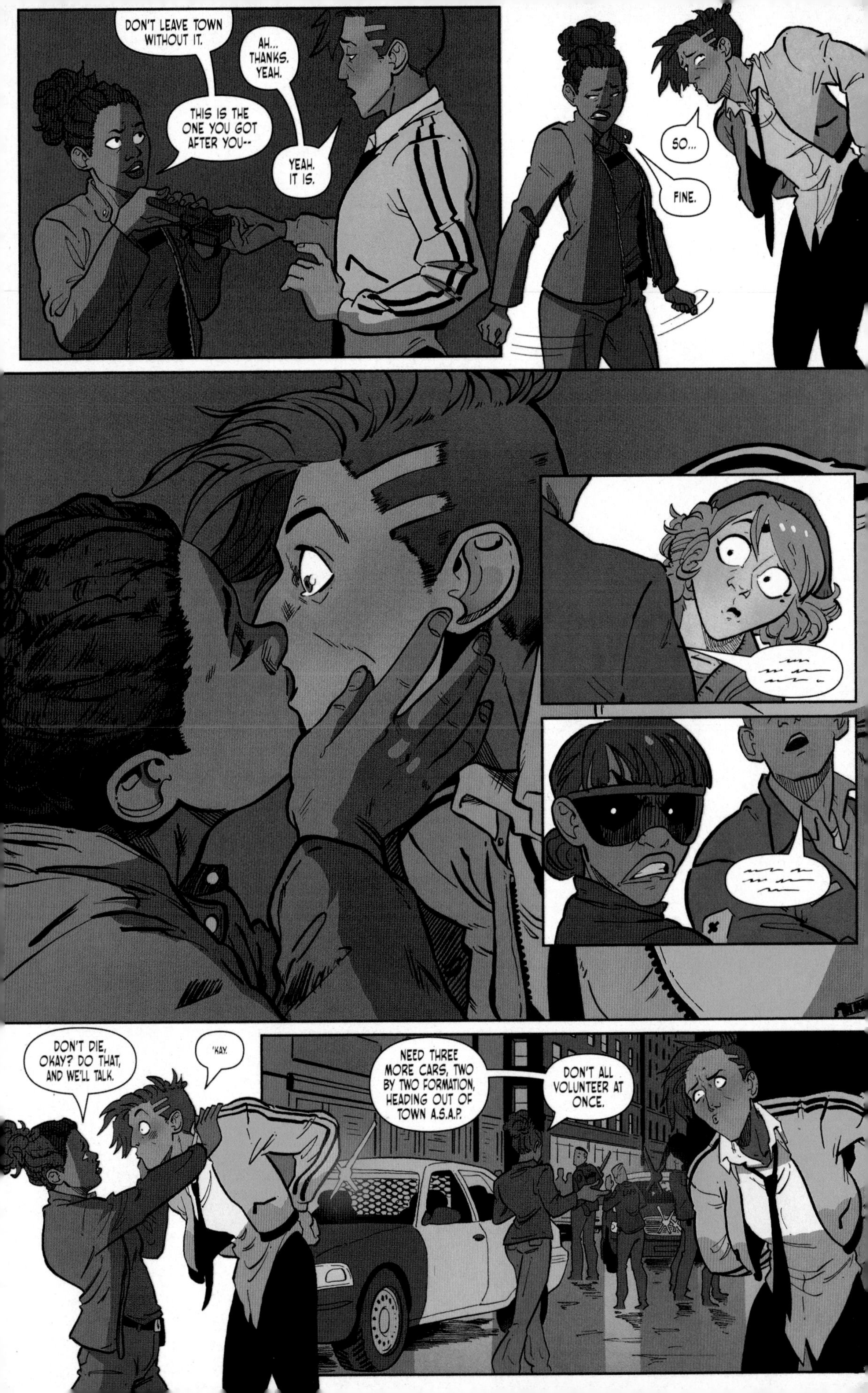
DON'T LEAVE TOWN WITHOUT IT.
AH... THANKS. YEAH.
THIS IS THE ONE YOU GOT AFTER YOU--
YEAH. IT IS.
SO...
FINE.
DON'T DIE, OKAY? DO THAT, AND WE'LL TALK.
'KAY.
NEED THREE MORE CARS, TWO BY TWO FORMATION, HEADING OUT OF TOWN A.S.A.P.
DON'T ALL VOLUNTEER AT ONCE.

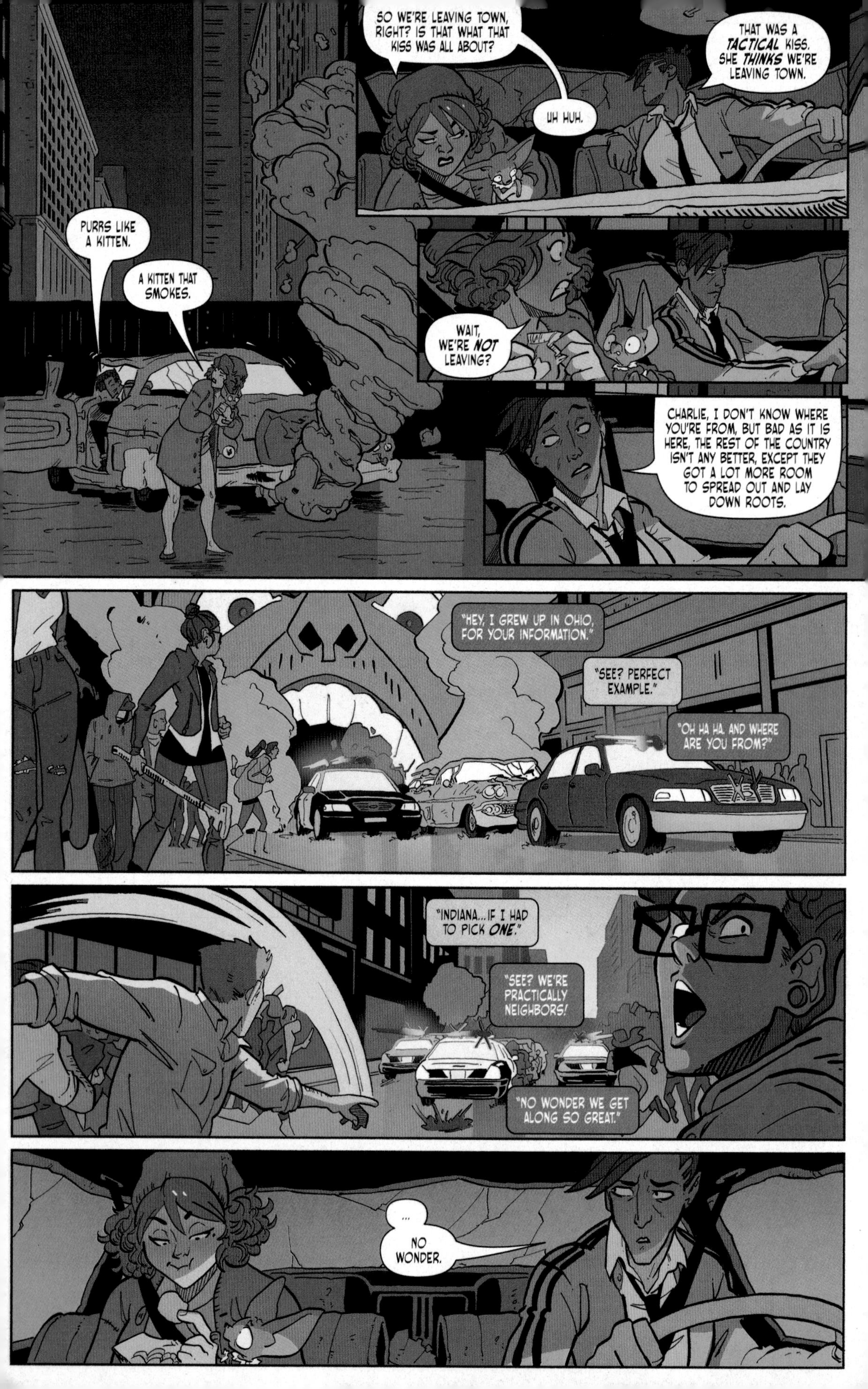
SO WE'RE LEAVING TOWN, RIGHT? IS THAT WHAT THAT KISS WAS ALL ABOUT?
UH HUH.
THAT WAS A TACTICAL KISS. SHE THINKS WE'RE LEAVING TOWN.
PURRS LIKE A KITTEN.
A KITTEN THAT SMOKES.
WAIT, WE'RE NOT LEAVING?
CHARLIE, I DON'T KNOW WHERE YOU'RE FROM, BUT BAD AS IT IS HERE, THE REST OF THE COUNTRY ISN'T ANY BETTER, EXCEPT THEY GOT A LOT MORE ROOM TO SPREAD OUT AND LAY DOWN ROOTS.
"HEY, I GREW UP IN OHIO, FOR YOUR INFORMATION."
"SEE? PERFECT EXAMPLE."
"OH HA HA. AND WHERE ARE YOU FROM?"
"INDIANA...IF I HAD TO PICK ONE."
"SEE? WE'RE PRACTICALLY NEIGHBORS!
"NO WONDER WE GET ALONG SO GREAT."
...
NO WONDER.

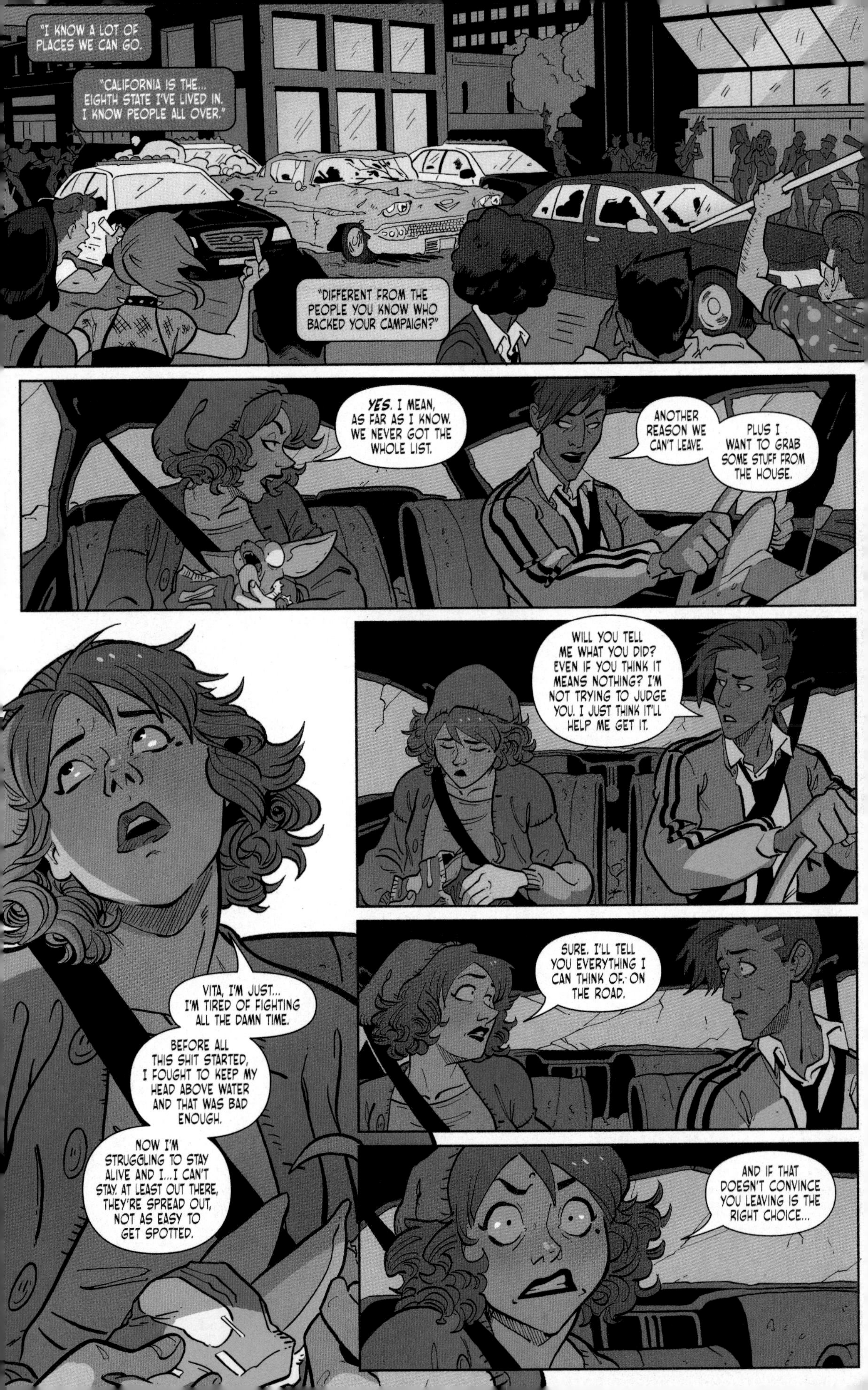
"I KNOW A LOT OF PLACES WE CAN GO.
"CALIFORNIA IS THE... EIGHTH STATE I'VE LIVED IN. I KNOW PEOPLE ALL OVER."
"DIFFERENT FROM THE PEOPLE YOU KNOW WHO BACKED YOUR CAMPAIGN?"
YES. I MEAN, AS FAR AS I KNOW. WE NEVER GOT THE WHOLE LIST.
ANOTHER REASON WE CAN'T LEAVE.
PLUS I WANT TO GRAB SOME STUFF FROM THE HOUSE.
VITA, I'M JUST... I'M TIRED OF FIGHTING ALL THE DAMN TIME.
BEFORE ALL THIS SHIT STARTED, I FOUGHT TO KEEP MY HEAD ABOVE WATER AND THAT WAS BAD ENOUGH.
NOW I'M STRUGGLING TO STAY ALIVE AND I...I CAN'T STAY. AT LEAST OUT THERE, THEY'RE SPREAD OUT, NOT AS EASY TO GET SPOTTED.
WILL YOU TELL ME WHAT YOU DID? EVEN IF YOU THINK IT MEANS NOTHING? I'M NOT TRYING TO JUDGE YOU. I JUST THINK IT'LL HELP ME GET IT.
SURE. I'LL TELL YOU EVERYTHING I CAN THINK OF. ON THE ROAD.
AND IF THAT DOESN'T CONVINCE YOU LEAVING IS THE RIGHT CHOICE...

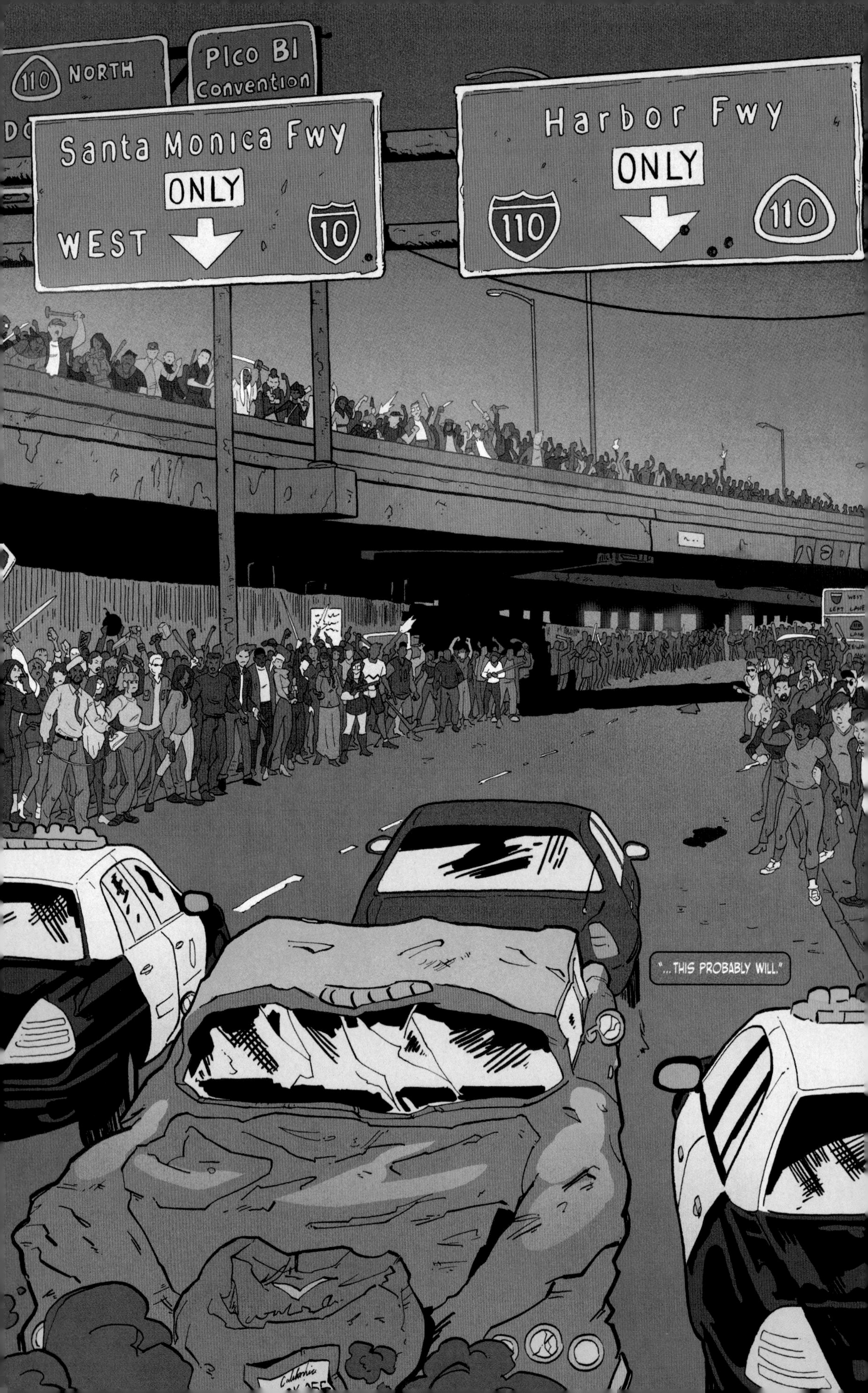
110 NORTH
Pico Bl
Convention
Santa Monica Fwy
ONLY
WEST
10
Harbor Fwy
ONLY
110
110
"...THIS PROBABLY WILL."

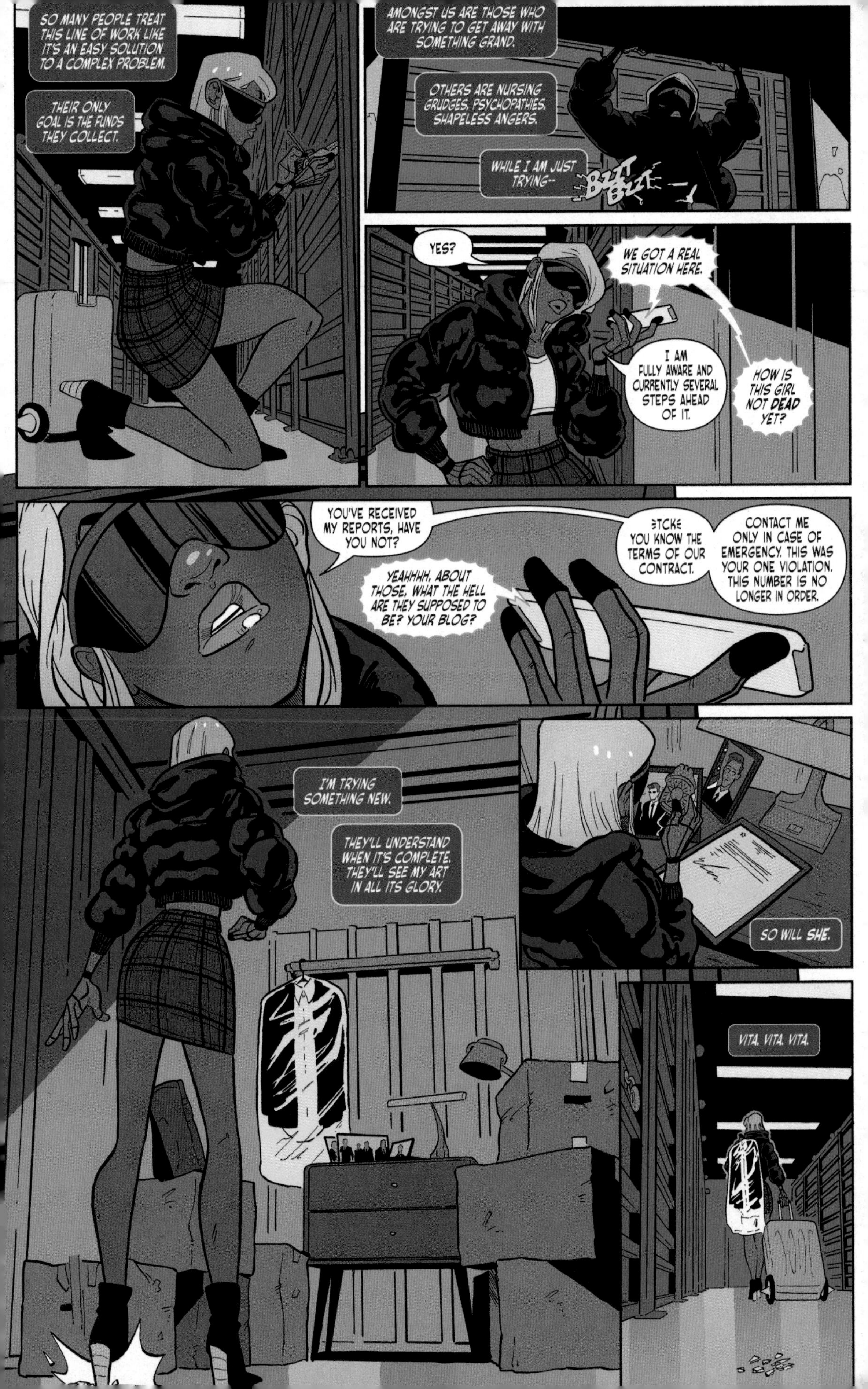
SO MANY PEOPLE TREAT THIS LINE OF WORK LIKE IT'S AN EASY SOLUTION TO A COMPLEX PROBLEM.
THEIR ONLY GOAL IS THE FUNDS THEY COLLECT.
AMONGST US ARE THOSE WHO ARE TRYING TO GET AWAY WITH SOMETHING GRAND.
OTHERS ARE NURSING GRUDGES, PSYCHOPATHIES, SHAPELESS ANGERS.
WHILE I AM JUST TRYING--
BZZT BZZT
YES?
WE GOT A REAL SITUATION HERE.
I AM FULLY AWARE AND CURRENTLY SEVERAL STEPS AHEAD OF IT.
HOW IS THIS GIRL NOT DEAD YET?
YOU'VE RECEIVED MY REPORTS, HAVE YOU NOT?
YEAHHHH, ABOUT THOSE, WHAT THE HELL ARE THEY SUPPOSED TO BE? YOUR BLOG?
TCK YOU KNOW THE TERMS OF OUR CONTRACT.
CONTACT ME ONLY IN CASE OF EMERGENCY. THIS WAS YOUR ONE VIOLATION. THIS NUMBER IS NO LONGER IN ORDER.
I'M TRYING SOMETHING NEW.
THEY'LL UNDERSTAND WHEN IT'S COMPLETE. THEY'LL SEE MY ART IN ALL ITS GLORY.
SO WILL SHE.
VITA. VITA. VITA.

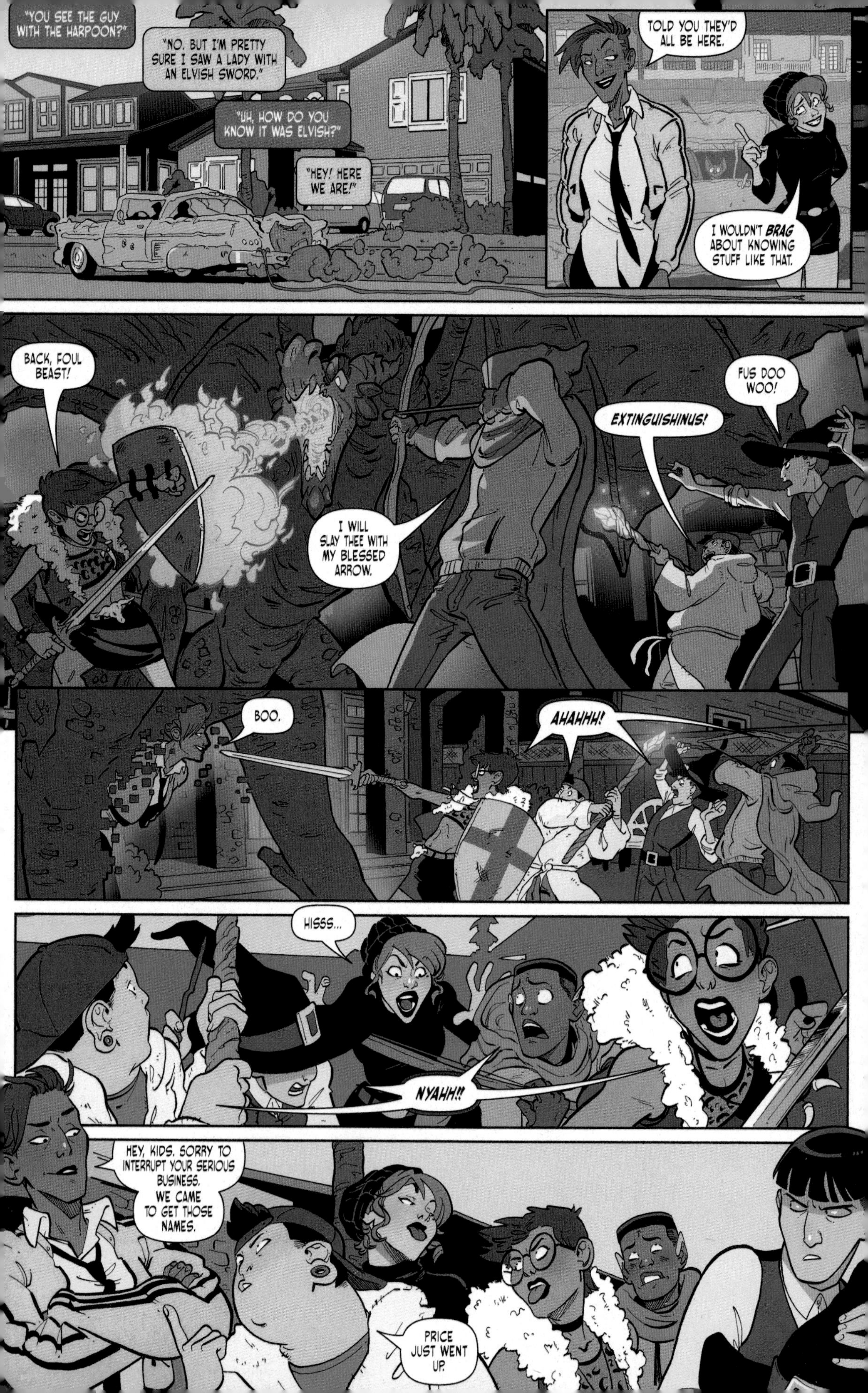

"YOU SEE THE GUY WITH THE HARPOON?"
"NO. BUT I'M PRETTY SURE I SAW A LADY WITH AN ELVISH SWORD."
"UH, HOW DO YOU KNOW IT WAS ELVISH?"
"HEY! HERE WE ARE!"
TOLD YOU THEY'D ALL BE HERE.
I WOULDN'T BRAG ABOUT KNOWING STUFF LIKE THAT.
BACK, FOUL BEAST!
I WILL SLAY THEE WITH MY BLESSED ARROW.
EXTINGUISHINUS!
FUS DOO WOO!
BOO.
AHAHHH!
HISSS...
NYAHH!!
HEY, KIDS. SORRY TO INTERRUPT YOUR SERIOUS BUSINESS. WE CAME TO GET THOSE NAMES.
PRICE JUST WENT UP.

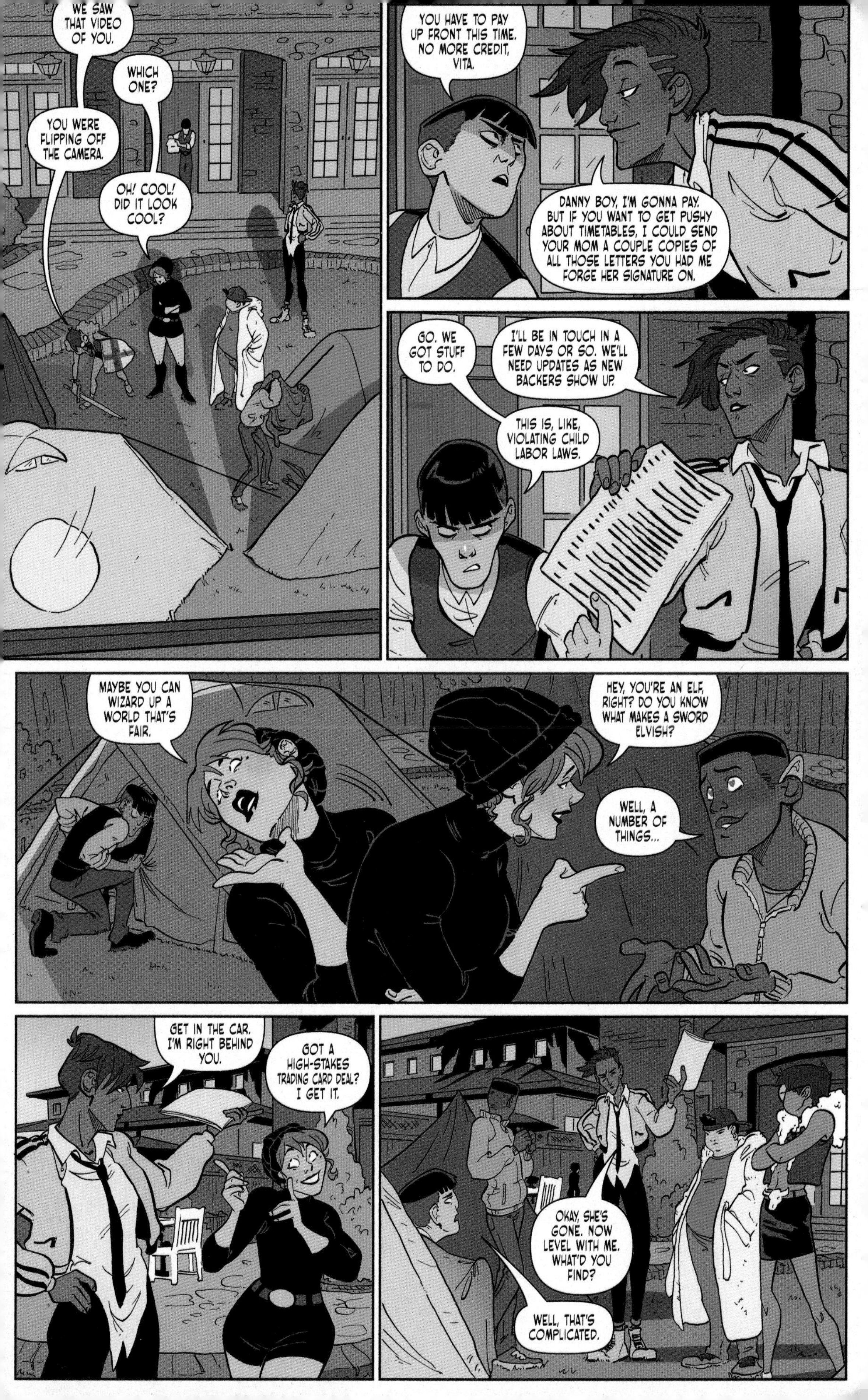
WE SAW THAT VIDEO OF YOU.
WHICH ONE?
YOU WERE FLIPPING OFF THE CAMERA.
OH! COOL! DID IT LOOK COOL?
YOU HAVE TO PAY UP FRONT THIS TIME. NO MORE CREDIT, VITA.
DANNY BOY, I'M GONNA PAY. BUT IF YOU WANT TO GET PUSHY ABOUT TIMETABLES, I COULD SEND YOUR MOM A COUPLE COPIES OF ALL THOSE LETTERS YOU HAD ME FORGE HER SIGNATURE ON.
GO. WE GOT STUFF TO DO.
I'LL BE IN TOUCH IN A FEW DAYS OR SO. WE'LL NEED UPDATES AS NEW BACKERS SHOW UP.
THIS IS, LIKE, VIOLATING CHILD LABOR LAWS.
MAYBE YOU CAN WIZARD UP A WORLD THAT'S FAIR.
HEY, YOU'RE AN ELF, RIGHT? DO YOU KNOW WHAT MAKES A SWORD ELVISH?
WELL, A NUMBER OF THINGS...
GET IN THE CAR. I'M RIGHT BEHIND YOU.
GOT A HIGH-STAKES TRADING CARD DEAL? I GET IT.
OKAY, SHE'S GONE. NOW LEVEL WITH ME. WHAT'D YOU FIND?
WELL, THAT'S COMPLICATED.

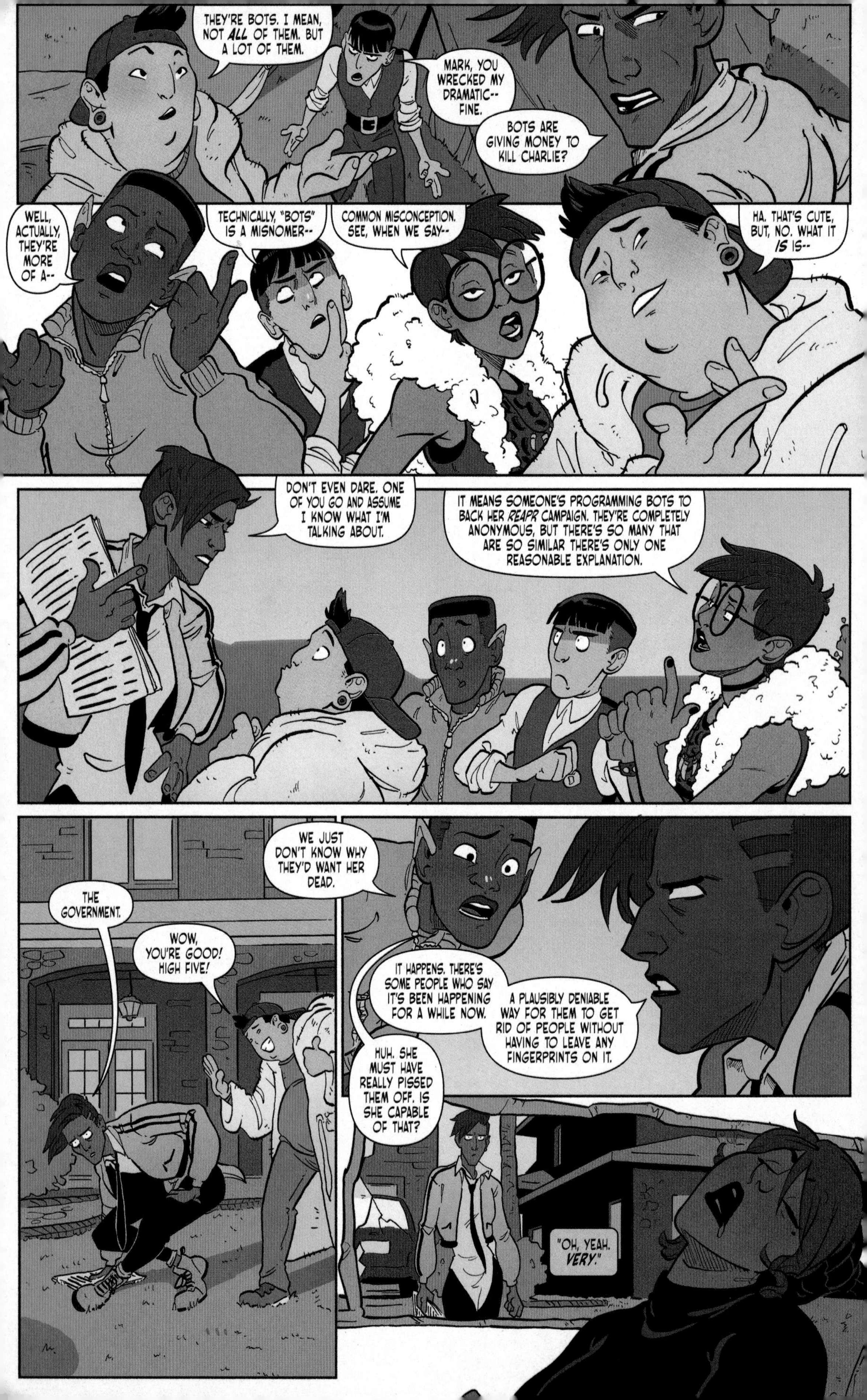
THEY'RE BOTS. I MEAN, NOT ALL OF THEM. BUT A LOT OF THEM.
MARK, YOU WRECKED MY DRAMATIC-- FINE.
BOTS ARE GIVING MONEY TO KILL CHARLIE?
WELL, ACTUALLY, THEY'RE MORE OF A--
TECHNICALLY, "BOTS" IS A MISNOMER--
COMMON MISCONCEPTION. SEE, WHEN WE SAY--
HA. THAT'S CUTE, BUT, NO. WHAT IT IS IS--
DON'T EVEN DARE. ONE OF YOU GO AND ASSUME I KNOW WHAT I'M TALKING ABOUT.
IT MEANS SOMEONE'S PROGRAMMING BOTS TO BACK HER REAPR CAMPAIGN. THEY'RE COMPLETELY ANONYMOUS, BUT THERE'S SO MANY THAT ARE SO SIMILAR THERE'S ONLY ONE REASONABLE EXPLANATION.
WE JUST DON'T KNOW WHY THEY'D WANT HER DEAD.
THE GOVERNMENT.
WOW, YOU'RE GOOD! HIGH FIVE!
IT HAPPENS. THERE'S SOME PEOPLE WHO SAY IT'S BEEN HAPPENING FOR A WHILE NOW.
A PLAUSIBLY DENIABLE WAY FOR THEM TO GET RID OF PEOPLE WITHOUT HAVING TO LEAVE ANY FINGERPRINTS ON IT.
HUH. SHE MUST HAVE REALLY PISSED THEM OFF. IS SHE CAPABLE OF THAT?
"OH, YEAH. VERY."

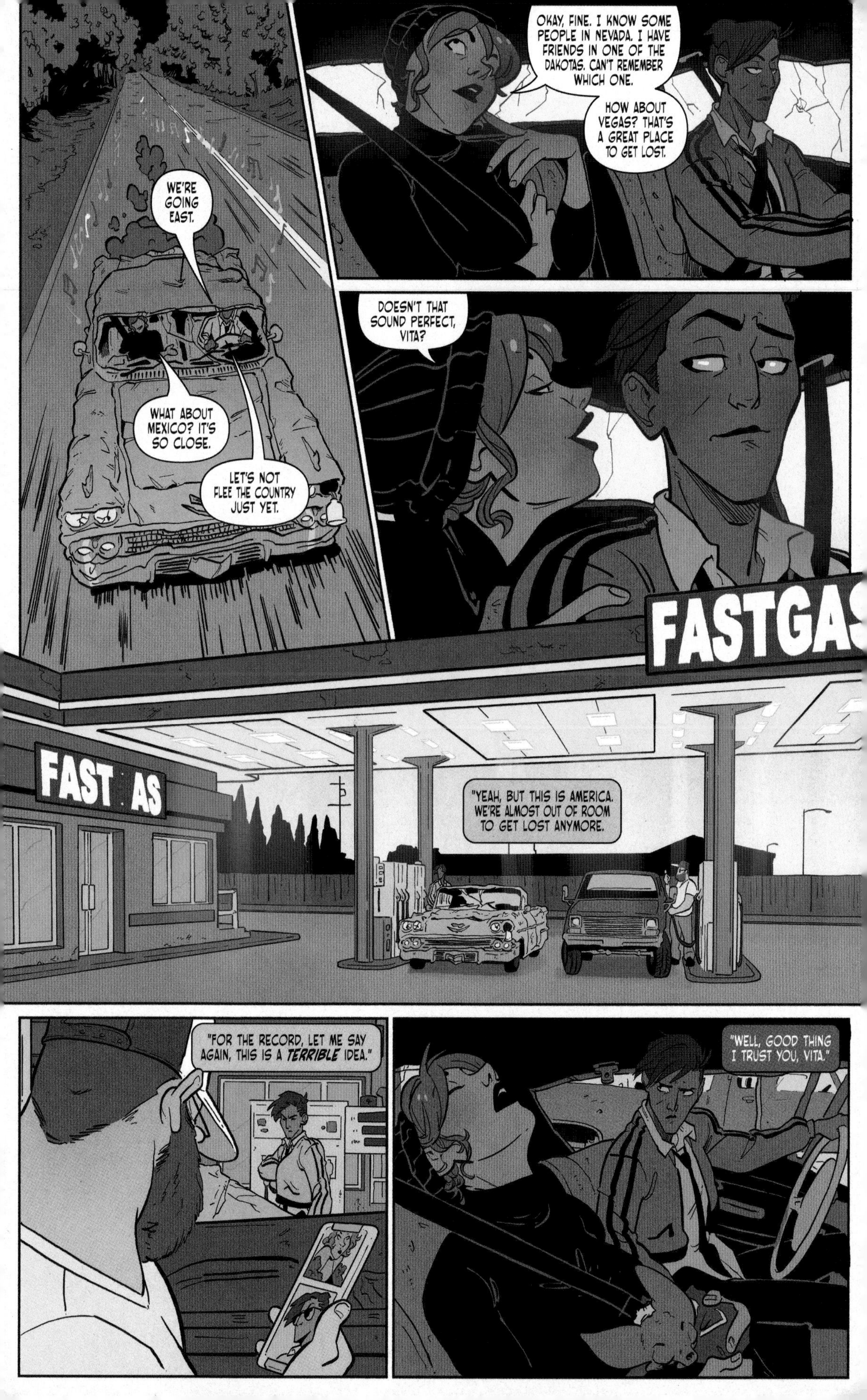

WE'RE GOING EAST.
WHAT ABOUT MEXICO? IT'S SO CLOSE.
LET'S NOT FLEE THE COUNTRY JUST YET.
OKAY, FINE. I KNOW SOME PEOPLE IN NEVADA. I HAVE FRIENDS IN ONE OF THE DAKOTAS. CAN'T REMEMBER WHICH ONE.
HOW ABOUT VEGAS? THAT'S A GREAT PLACE TO GET LOST.
DOESN'T THAT SOUND PERFECT, VITA?
FASTGAS
FAST AS
"YEAH, BUT THIS IS AMERICA. WE'RE ALMOST OUT OF ROOM TO GET LOST ANYMORE.
"FOR THE RECORD, LET ME SAY AGAIN, THIS IS A TERRIBLE IDEA."
"WELL, GOOD THING I TRUST YOU, VITA."

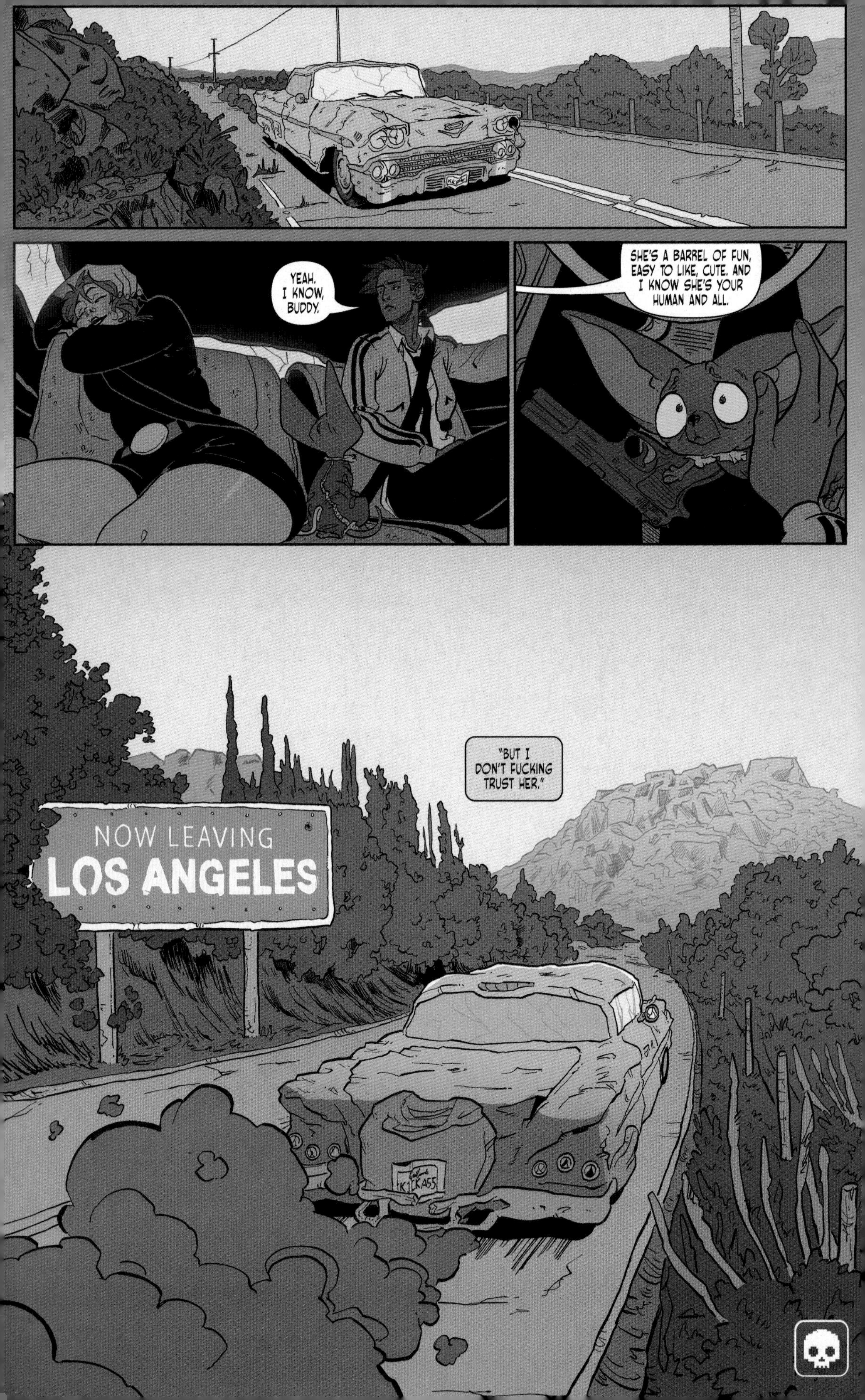

YEAH. I KNOW, BUDDY.
SHE'S A BARREL OF FUN, EASY TO LIKE, CUTE. AND I KNOW SHE'S YOUR HUMAN AND ALL.
"BUT I DON'T FUCKING TRUST HER."
NOW LEAVING
LOS ANGELES

RACHAEL STOTT #1 VARIANT COVER

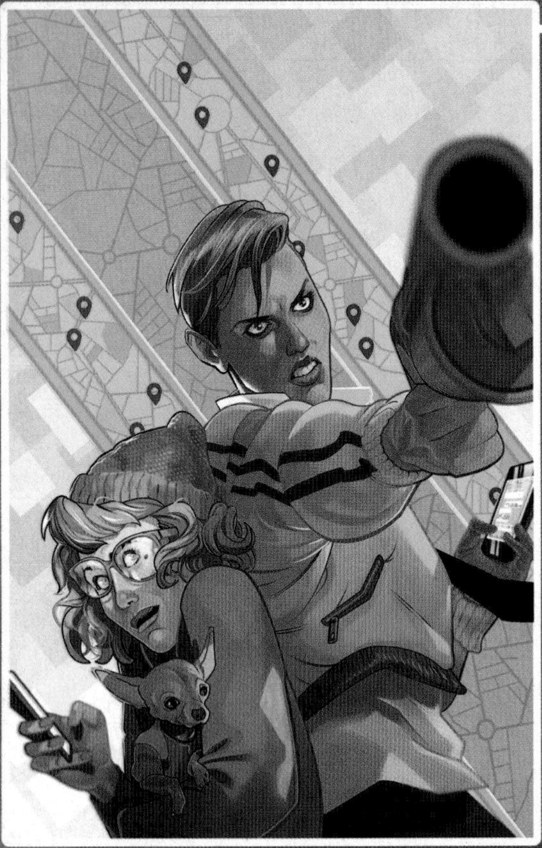

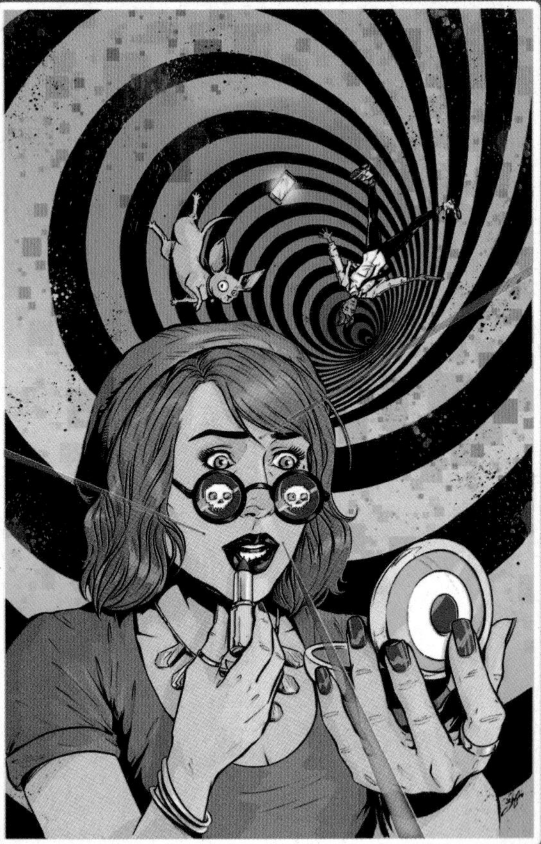

SKYLAR PATRIDGE #2 VARIANT COVER

ROSI KÄMPE #3 VARIANT COVER

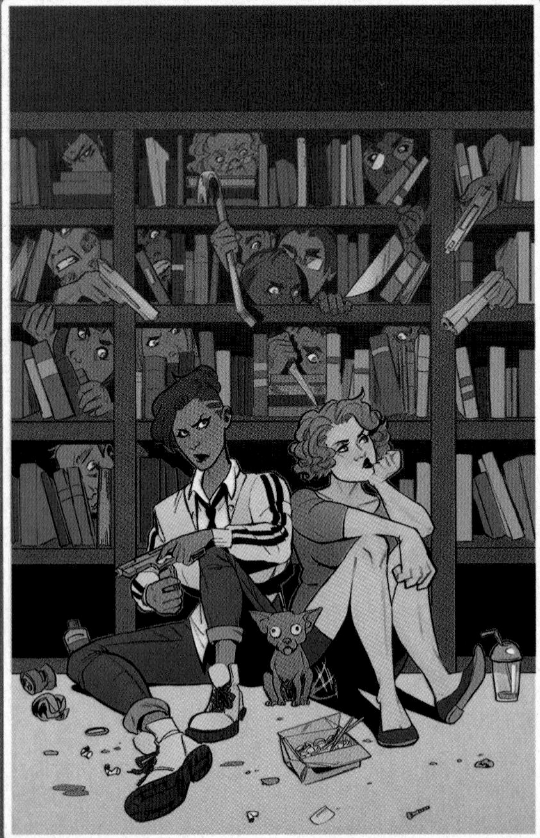

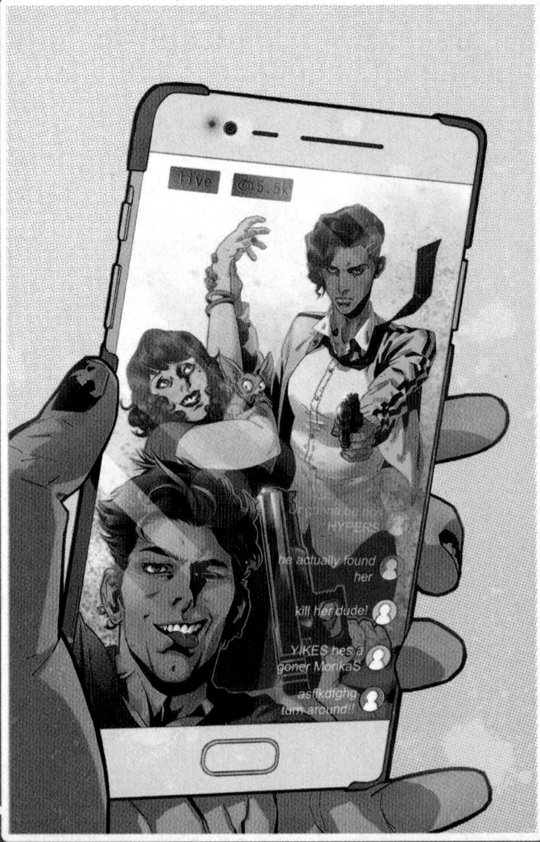
live
5.5k
HYPERS
he actually found her
kill her dude!
YIKES hes a goner MonkaS
asfkdfghg turn around!!

CLAIRE ROE #4 VARIANT COVER

PAULINA GANUCHEAU #5 VARIANT COVER

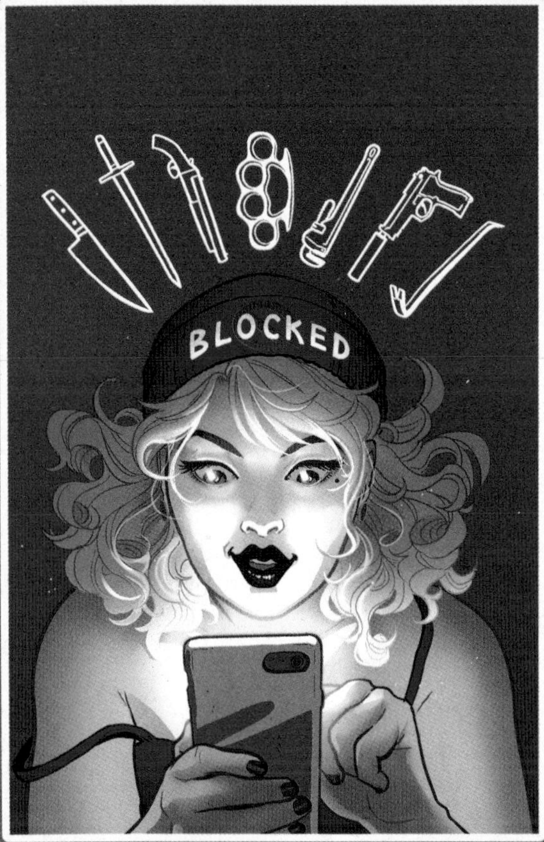
BLOCKED

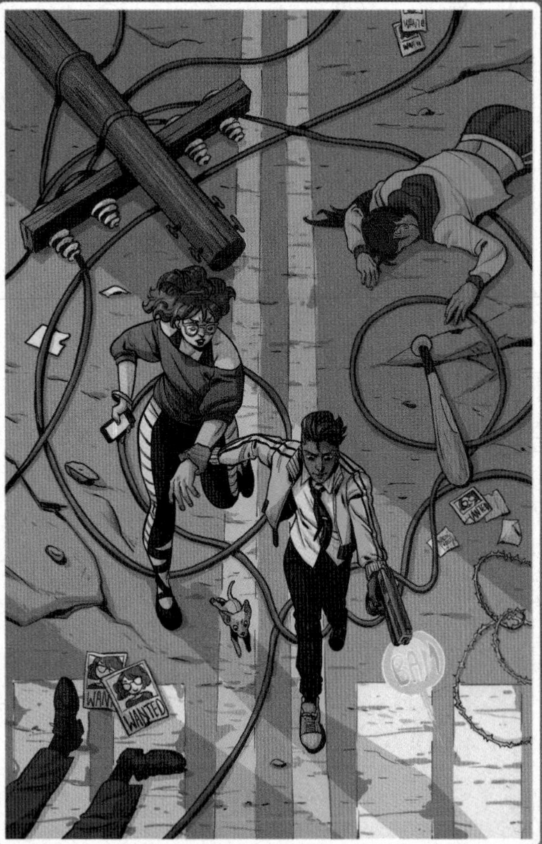
WANTED

NAOMI FRANQUIZ #6 VARIANT COVER

CAPE & COWL COMICS EXCLUSIVE COVER

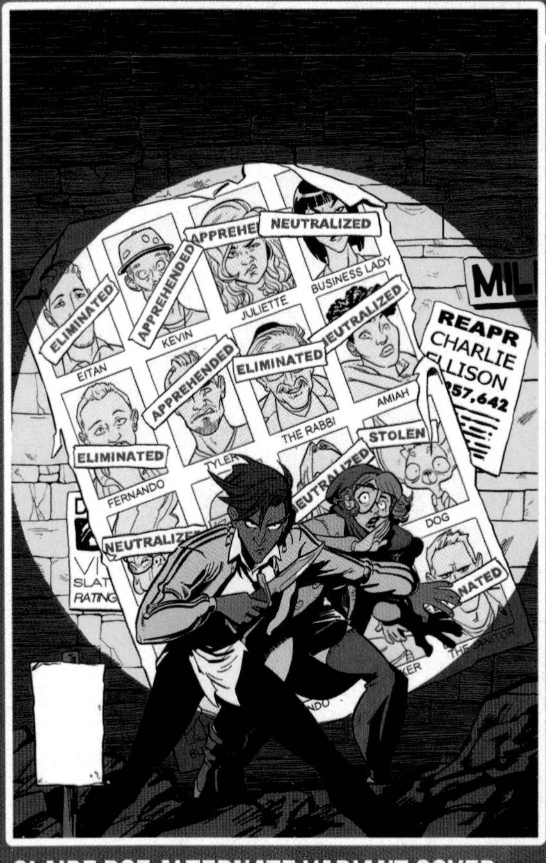
NEUTRALIZED
BUSINESS LADY
ELIMINATED
APPREHENDED
KEVIN
JULIETTE
EITAN
ELIMINATED
APPREHENDED
REAPR
CHARLIE
ELLISON
AMIAH
THE RABBI
STOLEN
ELIMINATED
FERNANDO
DOG
THE JANITOR

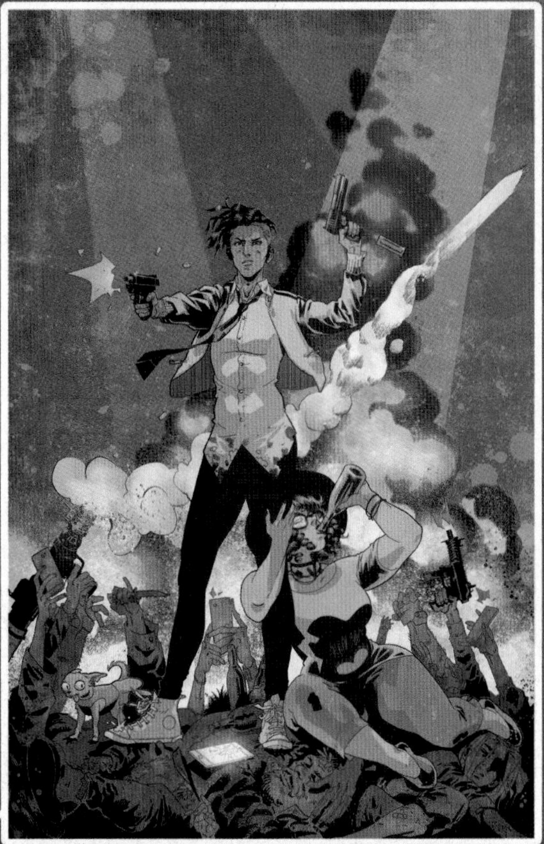

CLAIRE ROE ALTERNATE VARIANT COVER

VITA SLATTER
The 1.4 star bodyguard.

CHARLIE ELLISON
The million dollar girl.

MONDAY
Meetcute. Several assassination attempts.
Blow up a motorcycle. Steal a dog.

TUESDAY
Run for their lives. Threaten teenagers.
Accidentally terrorize a nightclub.

WEDNESDAY
Crowdfunding campaign to kill client hits
2 million dollars. Fill out paperwork.

THURSDAY
Picture each other dead.

FRIDAY
Save each others' lives.

CROWDED

THEY MIGHT END UP FRIENDS IF
THEY DON'T WIND UP DEAD.

AN IMAGE COMICS ONGOING   "CROWDED"   VITA SLATTER   CHARLIE ELLISON   DOG
PENCILS by RO STEIN   INKS by TED BRANDT   COLOURS by TRIONA FARRELL   LETTERS by CARDINAL RAE
SCRIPT by CHRISTOPHER SEBELA   EDITS by JULIETTE CAPRA   LOGO by DYLAN TODD